Claire,

Believe in

Trust

Book 1 of the

Believe Series

L. Chapman

Dedication

In memory of my Nan and Brother.

Forever in our hearts, Miss you.

Gracie Hutchinson

James William

You will lead a rich and successful life.

Amazon Fan Picked Debut Romance Author 2013

Table Of Contents:

Prologue

I love this time. *Our time*. John has the weekend off, which rarely happens. He normally ends up working on weekends or is called in. I'm only off for the weekend, then I leave for a three-day first aid course. I can't wait to refresh my memory and get stuck in, but at the same time, I don't want to have to rush away from John. He usually starts work late on Mondays. John should be arriving soon; he normally leaves around five on Fridays instead of staying later. I just finished showering and getting dressed. Well, when I say *dressed*, I mean putting on my sexy strapless red bra and panty set— the type he likes, nice and lacy. I put on a short, red halter neck dress over the top of my lingerie to give him a bit of work to do. I never wear things this short when I'm out. I don't have the guts to. These clothes are for John's eyes only.

John and I have been together for just over five years. It doesn't feel like it's been that long. I don't remember the last time we have actually been able to spent a full day together. We still have separate homes. With us working in different areas, it's easier for his travelling. That's something we might have to sort out soon, though. He stayed at his house last night. I haven't seen him for three days now.

"Hi, Megan," John bellows as he walks through the door, locking it behind him as he has done since our first date. Just to make sure no one disturbs us.

"I'm in the lounge," I call out, taking a deep breath, pushing down my dress once more, making sure there isn't a crease in sight. I am so excited. I stand still and wait for him to walk into the room.

"Now then, sexy." He pauses as he gives my ensemble the once-over. I can't do anything but blush. I don't know what it is about this man, but he has always made me blush in seconds.

He stands there checking me out in his normal dark blue T-shirt with the logo of the company he works for imprinted on it and jeans. His brown hair is short as it can be. I wish he would let it grow. It would give me more to grab ahold of during our intimate times. His eyes are a dark intriguing green.

"I love what you're wearing. Are you going to give me a twirl?" John enquires, winking at me.

I walk straight into his arms. "I don't twirl... unless you twirl me."

"Oh, sexy, I am going to twirl you so much, and you know it," he says as he places his lips to my neck.

Oh, he knows how to get me going.

Chapter 1

"Megan, I can't decide which dress to wear tonight. What do you think? The pink or the purple one?"

I walk into the room from the en-suite bathroom of the hotel that we are staying in for a few days wearing a soft cream dressing gown. The hotel's logo of two green twirls intertwining with the letters HH under them are elegantly embroidered on the left-hand lapel. Straightening her shoulder-length blonde hair, Jenny stands in front of the large mirror mounted above the electric fireplace wearing a matching dressing gown. As I walk past the oversized black corner sofa, I look over at the dresses that are hanging in front of the floor-to-ceiling windows, which provide me with a fantastic view of the city. It is like looking at a picture postcard. This part of the city, which is away from all the tourist traps, is the real city, and I have fallen in love with it. How can that happen to a country girl?

Everything about this suite and the hotel impresses me. This is the first hotel in the city I have actually stayed in; I have only ever come down for the day before. When I look at hotels like this, I can see why some people live in them. How they afford it is another question.

"Jenny, these dresses are the same, right?" I enquire as I stand in front of the two dresses, feeling them. They are both made out of some thin cotton material, perfect material for January.

Her green eyes sparkle as she walks towards me. "Yes, they are the same. You know me. If I like a dress, I get it in every colour I like."

Both dresses are strapless, straight up and down with a ripple section across the chests. Jenny always chooses amazing dresses, very pretty and elegant, never anything too long. She loves her legs. The dress is gorgeous, but not something I would wear, as it is too short for me since I am taller than her. Jenny will look stunning in either.

"Go with the purple one, Jenny. You look good in purple, especially that shade. I'm going to get changed."

I walk back into the en-suite bathroom and change into black leggings before slipping my feet into a pair of gold Grecian goddess sandals. I pull on the cream dress, though to me it feels more like a top. I like the way the rounded neckline is cut low, but not too low, and I like the way the material billows and floats. I apply some lip-gloss, a must have in my life. Some people love shoes; some love handbags, but I adore lip-gloss.

I run a brush through my long brown hair with its natural blonde highlights standing out. Unlike Jenny, whose hair has always been naturally curly, I don't have to straighten my hair. Mine is naturally straight, which can be a pain, as I love it with a little wave. Not much to ask for, I know.

I stand, looking at my reflection in the rectangular bathroom mirror to make sure I look all right before I leave the bathroom to rejoin Jenny. Jenny continues to stand in front of the mirror applying her makeup; she doesn't need it, as she has flawless fair skin. Nevertheless, she always wears it, a lot of it!

This could take some time, I think to myself as I walk over to the sofa and sit down.

"Jen, you look fab," I comment. I wish she realised she doesn't need to take so much time getting ready, well, putting her makeup on. She is naturally pretty.

"Thanks, Megan, you look fab, too. I love those shoes. They would work so well for my wedding." Jenny giggles, looking at her reflection in the mirror.

I chuckle. "Yeah, Jenny, they would." I lift my foot up and look at them. I love these sandals, and they are so comfortable and pretty and work with everything, unless it's raining. Which is most of the time in the UK.

Jenny is one of my closest friends; we first met at work four years ago. She was the extremely shy girl that didn't say much, but that quickly changed. She soon came out of her shell. She is now one of the most confident people I know. In addition, if truth be told, I do not know what I would do without her in my life. When Jenny left the company two years ago, we remained friends. We are like sisters, so close. Jenny has never been close to her sister, Sam, like she is with me.

2

Jenny's been with her fiancé, Rich, for longer than I have known her. We're in the city shopping for Jenny's big day. It's only six months away, as Jenny constantly reminds me. Daily. I can't wait for the wedding, and I still can't get over the fact that she asked me to be her Maid of Honour.

"Are you ready?" I ask, as I am getting bored of sitting and waiting. If she is going to take much longer, I'm going to bed.

"Done, let's go." Jenny spins around, showing me her outfit that she has finished off with a pair of black stilettos. Not surprised at all, always has to be heels.

I stand up and grab my sparkly black cardigan along with my sequined clutch from the back of the sofa. They match perfectly. I always say that life without a little sparkle is far too boring. With my clutch safe beneath my arm, I head for the door with Jenny following behind me.

Jenny decided that we should go out for a drink while we're here, though I would have preferred to stay in. Jenny looked at me with that look of hers that says *Please, you know you really want to*, so I decided I would go out with my friend and have a little fun, while I still could.

Rich is out with his best man, Luke. I still don't know what to make of Luke. I've only met him on a couple of occasions. He is famous and knows it. He comes across as very cocky, but you never know what he might be like in a different situation. Luke is about the same height as Rich. He is slim with dark blond hair and very dark green eyes.

We leave the hotel and head out into the night. Walking next to Jenny, I listen to my friend as she chats about all her plans once she and Rich are husband and wife. I hope her plans work out; she wants the fairy-tale wedding and marriage; like the ones you see in the movies. I hope she gets her happily ever after because I am not sure such things happen. Of course, I haven't told her that. I don't want to upset her.

This part of the city is a mixture of boutiques and wine bars, and Jenny quickly finds a place that she likes the look of. I gaze up at the establishment's name, and it intrigues me. I smile at Jenny as we head for the entrance. My eyes once again settle on the neon sign that reads *Bar 3000*.

We giggle as we walk towards the bar. It has six expensive floor-to-ceiling windows mounted in black modern frames, making the bar look both smart and classy, but looks can be deceiving. It seems quite empty from the outside, but that's fine by me, as we only popped in for a quick drink somewhere quiet. I'm still not feeling up to this.

As we open the double doors to the bar, I notice that the exterior design continues into the club. Everywhere is stylized black and red décor with huge flat screen televisions hanging on the walls. The main bar is centralized and runs in a complete circle, and I can see staff busy behind the gleaming counter and stools positioned the entire length of the bar.

It is busier than it looked from the outside, with mainly men sitting in small groups or in pairs. Most of the customers have their eyes on the screens. A football match is playing, and this would certainly account for the lack of women.

Although I am not looking for a man, I cast my eyes across the room, but none of the men warrant a second look. As we reach the bar, I notice a group of three men standing farther down the bar.

Chapter 2

One of the men does catch my eye. My gaze lingers, and I fear that he has caught me looking at him. His eyes sparkle as his amazing smile reaches his eyes. He has neatly trimmed short brown hair, but it is long enough to play with. *Where did that thought come from*, I think to myself as I let out a nervous giggle.

He is wearing a black shirt with the top two buttons undone. The shirt is tight, and I can tell that he works out. I can see that his arms and chest are well defined from here. He looks strong. He's also wearing dark-coloured jeans, but with his companions standing between him and me, I can't really see any more.

We are standing at the bar not too far from the three men, and I cannot keep my eyes off him. Once again, he catches me looking, so I quickly divert my eyes back to the bar.

I question Jenny on her drink order, knowing it will be the same as always, vodka and Coke. A barman, wearing a black T-shirt with the Bar 3000 logo embroidered on the chest, comes over. I order Jenny's drink followed by a Diet Coke for myself. Jenny just winks at me, knowing what I'm like when we are out. I never begin straight into drinking alcohol, always a Diet Coke first. No point in coming out if you're going to get drunk within the first hour. This time I have no intention on drinking.

From the corner of my eye, I see that the stranger who had caught my eye is heading in our direction. Once more, I find my gaze drawn towards him, and I am unable to take my eyes off him. He is absolutely breathtaking, and his blue eyes are almost mesmerizing. As he walks towards us, he rolls up his sleeves, showing off his tanned and well-defined forearms.

I look at Jenny, only half listening to what she is saying, all the while keeping an eye on him as he continues to head towards us. I can feel my heart beating faster with each step he takes, and finally, he stops right next to us. I have never felt like this. It can't be right.

Paying for our drinks, I turn my attention back to the barman.

"Good evening, ladies." He smiles.

I am so glad Jenny is here. She is more confident than I am, and her being here is very reassuring.

"Hi," Jenny replies, as she turns fully around to face him, moving closer to me and giving me a little nudge to say "Hi".

"How are you both this evening? My name's Mark." He looks straight towards me.

I look at him, unable to talk for a moment, and thankfully, Jenny speaks up, thus avoiding an awkward silence. "We're very well, thanks. I'm Jenny." Jenny is friendly as always, looking at him and smiling.

I finally find my voice and introduce myself. "I'm Megan. It's nice to meet you, Mark."

Jenny lets out a little giggle, one of those you did as a child when a boy was talking to you. I glance quickly towards Mark, noticing him smiling down at me. There is no question he is definitely taller than me.

"Megan, I'll be back in a minute. I need to ring Rich." Jenny moves closer towards me, wrapping one arm around me, giving me a little hug.

I smile, taking Jenny's drink for her. "Oh, okay, honey. Tell him I said hi," I bellow as Jenny walks off, blowing me a kiss.

I should have known that she was going to leave me alone with Mark. Jenny knows the type of man that I like, and by leaving us, she has given me a push in the right direction. I am not happy about this, but I know she is trying to help me. I never used to back away from males. I would chat and flirt a bit, but never make a move unless I really liked him. I now avoid all men, and Jenny knows I do.

"Now, that is better," Mark states, sounding so cheerful; he lets out a big smile and moves closer towards me.

"Why's that?" I ask, worried. My heart is beating so fast. Am I in danger? I look in the direction Jenny went in, but I can't see her. Why did she leave me? You never know what people are like. He could be a murderer for all I know.

With that incredible smile of his, he looks me straight in the eyes. "Megan, it was you that I noticed. You and your beautiful eyes." I can feel the flush of heat rise to my face. "Why has your boyfriend left you on your own on a night like this?"

I can't help but shake my head and laugh. "That's a terrible line, Mark. You're only trying to find out if I'm in a relationship." I sip my Diet Coke before continuing. "I'm single and pregnant, which I'm sure you have already noticed. That means I'm going to be single for a long time to come," I say as I place my hand over my small round belly. "So, where's your girlfriend on a night like this, or should I assume that you're just a player?" I can't believe I just said that, but Mark just smiles at my bluntness.

"I'm single, Megan, just like you are," he answers. I feel myself starting to blush again, so I glance down to the floor. "Yes, I noticed that you are pregnant, but I am still drawn to you. You're beautiful. I had to come and say hello." I take a sip of my drink, not looking at him. "Shall we go sit down? I heard once that standing for a long time is not very good for women who are expecting."

Why would he want to talk to me? I have heard of men hitting on pregnant women, but I never thought it would happen to me.

I smile as Mark picks up his drink and makes his way towards a table near one of the windows where the seats are front-to-back. I follow him like a lost sheep. Mark stands there, waiting for me to slide into the seat farthest from the window. He sits down opposite me, his eyes never leaving mine.

"I'd better let Jenny know where we are. I don't want her to worry." I laugh softly.

"Good idea," Mark agrees.

I take my mobile out of my bag and message her.

Jenny, how hot is this guy? I just don't know what to say to him. We're sitting near the window. Xx

"There, done. Why did you leave your friends to come talk to me?" I am so nervous I can feel my voice wobbling. I don't know what to expect. I wish Jenny had not left me.

Mark smiles, taking a sip of his drink before setting his glass down without taking his eyes off me. I look at his glass. What is the drinking? As I raise my eyes back up to look at him, his gaze is intense.

"They're all off to meet their partners soon. They're work colleagues rather than actual friends. I wanted to talk to you to find out more about you, Megan," Mark says reassuringly at me. "So, tell me about yourself. I already know you're beautiful with eyes that sparkle like diamonds and a smile that's magnetic." Is this one of his lines? I can't help but giggle.

I can't look at him; my face is on fire. My mobile vibrates on the table.

He is totally your type. Full on hottie and I knew that you'd never talk to him if I stayed with you. Xx

"I want to know all about you, Megan."

I can't believe how confident this man is. Who would hit on a pregnant woman? I just don't get it.

I struggle to think of what to say, finally settling on, "I have lived in Yorkshire my entire life."

Mark looks at me and leans forward in his seat. "If you live in Yorkshire, what brings you to London?"

I take a sip of my drink using the straw. "I'm down for a few days to help Jenny with her wedding shopping." I'm getting a little uncomfortable talking about myself, so I attempt to turn the tables. "Tell me about yourself."

Mark leans a little more towards me across the table, smiles an almost wicked smile, and as he does, he touches my leg with his foot. I can't believe he has just touched me. I jump, which gets a bit of a chuckle out of him.

"I'm twenty-five, grew up in London, but now live in the suburbs. I work here in the city. Anything else you'd like to know, Megan?" he questions while taking another sip of his drink, keeping his eyes on me.

When he says my name, it seems softer, almost seductive. I watch his lips form each letter, I can almost imagine how soft they would feel.

"So, I don't have to worry about Jenny then?"

Mark's words suddenly enter my train of thought. "Excuse me, worry about Jenny?"

"You said you were down here wedding shopping, so Jenny's taken, and I don't have to worry about her."

I smile shyly. "No, you don't have to worry about Jenny."

I don't get why he would be worried about Jenny, unless he has a thing for her. Oh, I can't be doing this stuff. He is probably another player at this rate.

"So, what have I missed?" Jenny asks, as she takes a seat next to me, sounding all excited. She is up to her little tricks, trying to set me up. Jenny has always been so supportive of me. She has come to every appointment for Bump since I found out I was expecting her. She does not want me to go through it all on my own. Now that's a sign of a true friend.

Mark smiles at Jenny, turns his head back to me, and then winks. He winks at me! What does that mean?

"I hear you're getting married, Jenny. When's the big day?" Mark questions.

"In six months," Jenny informs him. "July the twenty-eighth and I can't wait. I'm so happy. We found the dress today, so I can relax a bit now and enjoy London while we're here. Oh, Megan, I almost forgot. Rich and I are going to that place tomorrow. I'll come back as soon as we're done, though." I love how excited Jenny sounds when she is talking about her wedding, her big day. She has dreamt of this for years. I can't wait for her to finally have her day. I just hope it lives up to its expectations.

I watch from the corner of my eye as Mark slides his hand over the table, taking my mobile. I glance up at him questioningly as he picks it up, looks at the screen, and then begins to frown.

"Can you unlock your mobile, please?" Mark asks, smiling at me.

"Why?" I ask. I haven't known him long enough for him to read or use my mobile.

"I just wanted to add my number," Mark states while Jenny nudges me. I take my mobile from his hand, enter my pin, and place it onto *Add Contact*. I don't trust him that much not to look at what I have said to Jenny. At least if he is adding it to mine, then I am in control. I have nothing to hide, so I sit there watching him as he types something out before handing my mobile back to me.

I glance down at the screen. He's added his home, mobile, and work numbers. I peek up at him, saying nothing but giving him a gentle smile.

Jenny excuses herself, leaving me alone with Mark once more. I can't believe she keeps doing this to me.

"What are you doing tomorrow, Megan?" He looks at me as if there is a right answer and a wrong answer, but I just reply honestly.

"I'm not sure yet. I have plenty of things to do. I never find it difficult to keep busy." I take a deep, cleansing breath and sit straight in my chair. "Mark, I've had a lovely time, and it was so nice meeting you, but it's been a long day. I think it's time for me to say goodnight."

I stand up and grab my bag. Mark gets up and stands in front of me. We are so close I can smell his aftershave. He smells wonderful. If it is possible for a man to be beautiful, Mark is, and once again, I feel my heart race.

"After you," Mark says as he points his hand in the direction that Jenny has gone.

I walk towards the exit, just a step or two in front of him. In the background, a love song by a male singer I love begins playing.

I close my eyes. "Oh, I love this song," I say softly, a little more than a whisper.

"Dance with me, Megan." Mark takes my hand in his, pulling me to a stop.

"Here?" I look around the room, noticing no one else dancing yet. Mark turns towards me, and our eyes once again meet. His eyes make me stop. I love his eyes.

"Yes, Megan, here and now." His hand is bigger than mine.

I feel as if the rest of the bar and its patrons have melted away. The only ones left are the two of us. We walk towards the dance floor, holding each other's hand.

"Wonderful song to choose," I softly say into Mark's ear as he lifts my hand with our fingers clasped together, holding them to his chest.

His other arm is wrapped around my waist, my bump close to him. I don't know what to do. I want to run, but I am enjoying this. I feel so nervous.

We begin to dance. It's a hard song to dance to with someone you have only just met, but I want to stay close to him. I want him to hold me; I want to feel his body tight against mine. I don't know how I can be thinking like this about someone I have just met. I haven't even known him for an hour.

I find myself humming along to the song as we move.

As the song ends, Mark places his other hand around me. We stand toe-to-toe in an embrace, and I look into Mark's eyes. I feel his body press closer when he leans in and places a small butterfly kiss on my head.

"So, you like him?" I ask.

"Yes, but I'd deny it if asked by my friends. It would be no good for my street credit." We both laugh.

He knocks me out with the smile I am now privy to behold. He releases his hold on me, and my body feels the immediate emptiness of just the smallest distance.

We walk back towards the exit with Mark keeping my hand in his. I feel almost sadness at the thought of our parting. However, I will say my goodbyes and return to my hotel.

"It was very nice to meet you, Mark."

Mark smiles, revealing a hint of sorrow.

"It was wonderful meeting you, too, Megan." Mark squeezes my hand a little bit, but this is not goodbye for us. "I intend on seeing you again very soon."

I begin to feel anxiety well up in my stomach. I hope I see him again, and I know that the probability is not good. He's probably just a player, a very hot and sexy player.

"Goodnight, Mark." I start to walk away from him, and once again, he brings his lips to me. This time he kisses my hand. I turn to walk along the path down to where Jenny is waiting for me with a huge smile spread across her face.

"Goodnight, Megan," he calls after me, and I turn briefly to wave as he watches me walk away.

Chapter 3

The short walk to the hotel is nice and gives me time to think about what just happened. The sky is full of stars, the almost-full moon is so bright, and it's like looking at the bright end of a torch. The London night sky has surely never been so beautiful.

Jenny walks along in her own world talking about possible honeymoon destinations, I find myself only paying a little attention. If the last four years are anything to go by, then she'd choose Egypt, as she goes there every year. She isn't much for changing places she visits. As we get to the hotel, I feel my mobile vibrate. I retrieve it from my bag.

Hi Megan, I just wanted to check on you and Bump and make sure you got back to the hotel okay. X

Oh my, it's from Mark. How did he get my number? I never gave it to him. He must have been sneaky while he was adding his contact information. I decide not to reply yet. I will wait until I am on my own.

We head up in the lift to Jenny's room, number 280, which is very sentimental to her. This is the room where Rich proposed to her. As we stand there saying our goodnights, Rich appears. You can see how much Jenny loves him within seconds. Rich is six feet tall, which makes me feel so short when I stand near him. He has a slim build with an athletic body and dark green eyes that pierce through you. He has the kindest heart ever. He is wearing a black tracksuit, a sign he must have been out running again.

"Hey, Rich, been for a run?" I ask, trying to be polite.

Rich turns and faces me with sweat running down his face. "Yeah, five miles. It's the perfect evening for it."

"No Luke?" I question.

"No, he had to get some sleep. He has to be at work early, some kind of photo shoot. I made the most of the weather and went for a run.

”

"Busy Luke as always," I reply.

"Oh, we have booked paintballing for my bachelor party, so I am happy." Rich lets out a massive smile.

"I'm shattered, so I'm off to bed. Have a good time tomorrow, you two." I wish them both a good night and head off down the corridor to my own room. I slip my key into Room 289 and enter. Apart from a different view out the window, the room is identical to Jenny's. This is another one of the rooms Jenny has stayed in before. Rich does quite a lot of work down here.

I reach into my bag, pulling my mobile back out.

Hi Mark, yes we all got back to the hotel okay. Thank you for asking.

I use the en-suite bathroom to get ready for bed. After changing into my pink pajamas, I am more comfortable. I can feel sleep crowding in on me. I stagger back towards the bedroom. My feet are killing me. We travelled down yesterday and shopped all day today. The one good thing is we found the perfect dress. It will be sent up to our local bridal shop for Jenny to have her fitting.

The bed is king-sized with a canopy; the clean white linen is so pretty. As I climb onto the soft, crisp sheets, I feel like a princess out of some fairy tale. The bed really is something special, and I plump some pillows behind me. Once again, I pick up my mobile. Mark has replied. He must have done it while I was in the bathroom.

What is your favourite colour? Sorry, if you think that's a weird question. I like to know little random facts. X

I smile at the innocent sweetness of his question. I glance over at the clock. It's past midnight, but I answer Mark's message anyway.

Sorry for the delay in replying. I was busy getting ready for bed. Well, I like pink and purple. What's your favourite? I don't mind you asking questions. I have another one for you. How did you get my number?

I press *Send* and lie there checking my emails. As usual, most are junk, but a few need answering, which I will do tomorrow. Just as I place my mobile down, it goes off again, and once more, I find myself smiling.

Don't apologise, Megan. I thought you might have fallen asleep as it is so late. Sorry, I took it from your mobile. I couldn't leave it like that, and I needed to be able to see you again, talk to you. Mine's blue, the colour of your beautiful eyes. Can I see you tomorrow, well, today? X

Without thinking, I reply.

I can't see you tomorrow, sorry. I have work to do, and it's been such a long day that I need my sleep now. Goodnight, Mark, sleep tight.

I send the message and get comfortable beneath the sheets. Yawning, I place my mobile onto the small bedside table. I can't help but think about how his eyes looked earlier that evening, and his memorable smile.

I am jolted awake by the sound of my mobile. I don't even remember falling asleep. I pick up my mobile and see that it's five fifteen in the morning. I wonder who could be texting me at this time. Sitting up in the bed, I check my messages; there are five of them, all from Mark. Seeing the times that he sent them to me, I had slept through each one.

12.30 Goodnight, Megan, sleep well, I hope Bump lets you sleep. X

02.10: I can't sleep. I want to see you again, to find out more about you. I don't know why, but you have captured me, Megan. X

02.15: Sorry that last message made me sound like a stalker, sorry, I promise I'm not. I'm just confused by these feelings. X

03.20: Looking out my window at the night sky, everything is so peaceful. X

05.14: I'm amazed I got a little bit of sleep, think I will go and get these meetings over with and have a lazy day. X

Okay, he is crazy and does not sleep. A lazy day is not such a bad idea. Bump would enjoy a lazy day. It would do me some good, but I am spending today catching up with some work on the laptop. I fire off a quick text.

Good Morning, Mark (even though I plan on going back to sleep). Bump behaved herself and let me sleep. A lazy day sounds like a good idea. I think you need to get some sleep.

I climb out of bed and go to the bathroom. I hear my mobile go off as I am in there. I climb back into bed before picking it up. I smile when I see it's Mark.

Good morning, sunshine, I'm glad Bump's been good - it's a girl? I've had about an hour's sleep, but I'll be okay. You get some more sleep, Megan, and text when you wake up. X

I can't believe how sweet he is.

Yes, Bump is a little girl, and I can't wait to meet her, less than three months now. You need more sleep than an hour. I'll text you when I get up. Hope your meeting is a quick and easy one.

I set my alarm for ten o'clock, then roll onto my side, quickly falling back asleep.

******

I wake up just before the alarm goes off, which I've been doing since I hit about twenty weeks. It's just one of the many "joys" of being pregnant. I sit up, leaning back on the soft pillows. I reach to the side table for my mobile. I smile broadly; once again, there is a message from Mark.

Sorry if I woke you. I'm glad Bump's been behaving. Not long until the little lady will be here. I shouldn't be long in this meeting. I can't wait to see you again, hopefully soon. X

I respond to him right away.

You didn't wake me. I tend to be up before the alarm these days. Lazy days are meant to be lazy, means you can relax and catch up on sleep.

I place the mobile down and sit up on the side of the bed. I stretch my hands high above my head to wash the sleep from my system. I decide to shower and quickly vacate the warmth of the bed.

Chapter 4

After my shower, I slip on the bathrobe provided by the hotel. Back in the main suite, I open the ornate wardrobe and choose a T-shirt that I like and a pair of comfortable jeans. I disrobe and step into fresh underwear and then my clothes. As I am pulling down the T-shirt over my stomach, I hear a rapping at the door. Opening the door, expecting it to be Jenny or Rich, I am surprised to see the concierge. He offers up a professional smile.

"There is a delivery for you, Miss Megan."

I smile, taking the large, grey box from his hands. He wishes me a good morning. I return the sentiment before shutting the door. I place the box onto the coffee table, following the warning printed on it to keep it upright. Carefully I open the box, and the scent of fresh flowers reaches my nose. I reach inside and pull out a cut-glass vase with a dozen long-stemmed pink roses. Placing it onto the coffee table, I notice a small, white envelope nestled among the leaves. Written in perfect script is my name. I open the flap and remove a small white card.

Megan,

I hope you like roses. Will see you again very soon.

Mark.

How did he know where I was staying? This is a bit creepy. I place the box over by the waste-bin, leaving the card and the vase of flowers on the coffee table. I then hear my mobile trilling out an incoming message. I walk to the bed, pick it up, and smile. It is another text from Mark.

My meeting has finished early. I'm going to go and get some breakfast and head home. What are your plans? X

I reply immediately:

I'm up, relaxing with a cuppa. Thank you so much for the flowers. They are beautiful.

You are very welcome; they are as beautiful as you are. Okay, this might be a bit bold of me, but do you fancy having lunch with me today? X

Maybe, what are you thinking?

There's a little bistro near the bar from last night. X

What time?

12ish, then we can relax. X

I reply quickly before I can change my mind.

Sounds like a plan.

I wonder if I have done the right thing, agreeing to meet him for lunch. Will I be safe with him on my own? I need to stop worrying, live a little while I can. I like him, and, well, he seems nice. I need to just trust my heart and go for it. I text Jenny to see what she thinks.

Mark's asked me out for lunch. I've said yes. Don't know if I should go or not. Xx

Jenny's reply comes back five minutes later.

Go for it. Live a little. Xx

I decide not to change, but touch up my lip-gloss and apply some mascara. I put the lip-gloss and a few other essentials into my little black bag and spend the next half hour fretting over the lunch date.

I receive a text from Mark.

Can I come and collect you from the hotel? X

If you want to, Mark.

I don't want to seem like I don't want him to collect me, but I don't want to seem like I need to be looked after all the time. I will leave it up to him.

I do want to. Meet you in the lobby at 12. X

How did you know which hotel I was staying in?

It sounds a bit 'stalker-like,' but I rang all the hotels in the area until I found a Jenny and Megan staying in the same hotel. X

Oh, okay, determined man, I see. Thank you again for the flowers.

18

They're beautiful.

I slowly go down to the lobby of the hotel, not wanting to be late, but not wanting to seem too eager either. Mark is already standing there, wearing dark-coloured jeans and a tight white T-shirt. He looks amazing. I walk over to him, watching him watch me, as I get closer to him.

"Hi, Megan, you look gorgeous." I feel myself start to blush and butterflies start to appear in my stomach.

"You look good. The jeans and T-shirt look works for you." Mark winks at me.

"Thank you. Shall we head out?"

I nod, walking beside him out to a waiting taxi. Mark opens the rear passenger door, being a total gentleman, letting me get into the black taxi first.

Throughout the short taxi ride to the bistro, Mark tells me about his meeting, and it is nice to just sit and listen. I should really ask what he does, but I'm too nervous. I don't want to talk. I don't know how to act. It has been so long since I have been on a date, or even been out with a guy.

Arriving at the bistro, Mark takes the lead, holding his arm out for me to hold on to before linking my arm in his. Mark walks with me into the bistro and tells the headwaiter that he has a table booked for two. Giving the man his name, the waiter leads us to our table. It's a very upmarket establishment; I am surprised when the waiter pulls out a chair from the table for me to be seated first. I thank him. The waiter bows his head with professional courtesy. This all feels a little strange. I'm not accustomed to such places.

"Order anything you like, Megan," Mark says. Perhaps he has noticed my nervousness.

"Thank you."

I sit, looking at the menu as Mark tells me about the bistro's history, and I think he's beginning to realise just how shy a person I am.

The menu is full of posh meals; there are so many things I don't recognise. I decide to go for a Caesar salad to start, followed by pan-fried sea bass. Mark orders a tomato and herb salad, followed by steak tartare. Neither of us orders pudding. Mark explains that they ask you about them after the main course.

I keep my head down, looking at the table. I feel so open to attack that I can't look at him. I don't know what to do or to say.

"Megan, relax, please," Mark says as he moves his hand around the table and places it on top of mine, rubbing it gently.

"Sorry, I am just very shy." His hand on mine is nice.

"Don't be."

I raise my head, and my eyes meet his immediately. His big smile manages to relax me a bit.

"You look amazing, if I didn't already tell you."

"Thank you," I reply, feeling myself blush.

"Aw, you are so shy. It's cute. You look even more beautiful when you blush."

We sit here talking about plans for holidays this year. Mark informs me that he has just returned from America. He had been to Fairfield, Connecticut, for a work holiday. He was still able to go to his favourite donut shop, managing to get some donuts with chocolate icing and sprinkles.

"Beth introduced me to them. She is one of the ladies who works for the company, but she is based over there."

"Oh, that was nice of her," I state while wondering if they have a past. Were they a couple?

"These donuts are nothing like the ones you get here. They were amazing. I will have to get you some to try next time," Mark responds.

"I have never been to America. Actually, I have never been abroad. Those donuts sound nice, though."

"Are you a chocolate girl?"

I nod. Who is not a chocolate girl?

"You need to relax more." Mark pauses and looks at me. "I know that's the worst chat-up line. So, I know what to avoid," he says, raising his eyebrows.

I can't do anything but laugh.

"Well, that worked, so what would it be?"

"Did it hurt?" I question.

"Did what hurt?"

"When you fell from heaven?"

"That's a bad one." Mark laughs, trying to muffle it.

"It is. I don't get why people would use those kinds of lines, but they do make me laugh," he says just as our food arrives.

The smell of the food is wonderful and makes my mouth water instantly. I love food, but *I* hate being watched. It makes me feel so self-conscious, and definitely when it is a man watching me. It makes me feel so uncomfortable. I need to try, though.

After our delicious main course, Mark lets the waitress leave us to choose our puddings.

"Would you like a pudding, Megan?" Mark asks.

"No, thank you. I am too full," I state.

"Are you sure? The white chocolate Panna Cotta is to die for here," Mark tells me.

"I'm fine. Please have one for yourself," I say, waving him off.

Mark waves the waitress back over and orders Panna Cotta with two spoons. I just shake my head. I excuse myself to go to the bathroom. I just need time to step away from the situation. I'm feeling more comfortable, but I'm not sure at all what to say to him. I feel so unsure of myself.

As I slowly walk back to the table, Mark gets up to pull my chair out.

"Thank you."

"You're welcome. Would you like anything else to drink?" Mark asks and points to my glass.

"No, I'm okay with my water. Thank you." I look at my glass, noticing I still have over half left.

The waitress appears with pudding and places it onto the table between us.

"Please try a bit." Mark passes me a spoon.

"Okay, only a little bit, though." Our hands brush as I take the spoon from him.

I take a little bit and taste it. He was right; it is amazing, but I am too full to eat more. I'm definitely not a three-course meal kind of person.

"It's nice," I say, forcing down the mouthful.

"Please, have more if you want it," Mark states, pushing the dish towards me.

"I'm fine. Thank you." I place my hand out in front of me to stop him from pushing it farther towards me.

We finish our meal and leave the bistro. The journey back to the hotel is quiet. We don't seem to say much at all. Mark points out a few monuments of the area as we walk along.

Mark kindly takes me back to the hotel. We say our goodbyes in the lobby, and he gives me a hug before letting me go. I notice him standing there watching me until I am out of sight.

Thank you for coming to lunch with me. X

Thank you for inviting me.

Anytime. X

Mark and I spend the rest of the day chatting by texts, finding out little bits about each other. It is so weird how natural I feel talking to him and how open I can be. We arrange plans to meet tomorrow and spend a little time together. Jenny will be away with Rich again, so I am free to do whatever I want. I secretly can't wait for tomorrow to arrive.

Chapter 5

Morning, how are you? Are you awake? X

I reply to Mark's text.

Yes, I'm up, showered and dressed. I'm fine, thanks, and you?

It's just after nine. I have not been awake long. I put my mobile down and walk into the bathroom. I stand in front of the mirror and apply mascara and lip-gloss, not overdoing my makeup, as I prefer the natural look. I give my hair a good brush. After I've finished in the bathroom, I walk to the bedside table and slip a handful of silver bracelets over my wrist. I hear my mobile beep, letting me know I have another text.

Knock, Knock. X

Almost immediately, I hear a knock on the door. I make my way to the door as a smile lights up my face when I open it.

Mark smiles, handing me one pink rose. I take it and inhale the rose's intoxicating fragrance. Mark steps closer, cupping his hand to my cheek. "Beauty for a beauty," he whispers.

Mark is wearing a white T-shirt with a black open leather jacket, dark blue jeans, and that amazing smile of his.

"Good morning, beautiful."

"Morning, Mark," I reply softly. "Did the meeting go well?" I ask while moving to the side, allowing Mark to enter the room. He smiles at me. I move to the table and place the rose into the vase with the others.

"My meeting went well, just all the normal boring stuff. I hate having so many morning meetings booked, but you have to work to live these days. I found it hard to concentrate. I couldn't stop thinking about you!"

I offer up a small smile, enquiring him if he wants to sit down. He is standing so close to me that I am nervous at our proximity. He ignores my invite to sit, and again he caresses my cheek with his hand.

"What would you like to do today?" Mark asks. My heart is beating so fast that I'm surprised Mark cannot hear it. I can't believe how close we are. He smells fantastic. He is definitely wearing the same aftershave as the night we met. Somewhere deep inside, breaking through my inhibitions, is a desire to touch him. I just cannot bring myself to do it.

"I don't know. What would you like to do?"

Mark's eyes are full of intensity. His gaze holds me, and he almost growls. "This..."

Mark leans in and kisses me. His lips are so soft, yet there is a power in his kiss. However, I cannot return the intensity, not yet, not like this. He must notice my indecision as he slowly pulls back. I see the sadness hidden deep in his eyes, but then it is gone. He kisses me softly on my forehead, just above my left eyebrow. I feel a spark shoot through my head. I close my eyes, so wanting to trust this beautiful man with my broken feelings. As he pulls away, he smiles down at me. I meet his gaze and smile apologetically.

"I can take it slowly, Megan," Mark tells me. "How about we go and get some breakfast?"

"That sounds perfect. Thank you." He lets go of my hand after placing another brief kiss on my knuckles. He walks over to the door where the room service menus are located. I stand watching him.

"Right, what would you like to eat?" he asks, as he reads the menu out loud. As he reads, I go to the bedroom and retrieve my socks from the bed where I had laid them earlier. I attempt to pull them on, but it is not as easy as it was prior to Bump growing in my belly. Mark comes over to me, smiling, kneeling at my feet, and taking the socks from my hand to help me.

"I'm not an invalid, Mark. I'm capable of doing this myself," I say with a little sass and a smile. Mark gives me a look, shakes his head, and pulls the socks up over my toes, then ankles.

"What do you want to eat then, Megan?" he asks, passing me the menu.

"Well, I can't have what I fancy, due to this little one," I answer, placing my hand on my swollen stomach.

Mark smiles. "How about a bacon sandwich? That's what I'm having."

"Perfect."

Mark walks over to the room service phone and places our order with the hotel. I walk over to the sofa, taking a seat, and listening to him double checking they have the order correct, before turning on his heels and taking a seat next to me on the sofa.

"May I?" Mark asks as he moves his hand closer to my stomach.

As Mark caresses my bump, I nod, and a tear rolls down my cheek. He sees the emotions etched on my face, and with tenderness I had yearned so long for, he leans down and speaks to my swollen belly, talking directly to Bump.

"So, little one, do you know how blessed you are? Your mummy is stunning. She's sweet, and that means you will be, too."

I smile at Mark as Bump kicks his hand.

"Oh, hello, you're awake in there. Mummy's going to have some breakfast soon. I hope you're hungry."

Time flies by as I just sit here listening to Mark. I can't help but smile. There is a loud knock at the door, and Mark jumps to his feet so quickly that I'm surprised he didn't fall over.

I stand up and walk over to the wardrobe, slipping on my favourite cardigan. A lovely grey one with baby pink spots. I slip my feet into a pair of comfortable boots before returning to the sofa.

Mark comes and joins me, carrying a tray loaded with our breakfast.

"How do you take your tea?"

"Milk, no sugar. I'm sweet enough," I say while giggling.

"I agree with that." He winks at me.

Mark pours out the tea before handing me a small plate with a steaming hot bacon sandwich on it. I nibble it and smile as he devours his.

"Megan, are you all right? You look a little pale."

"I'm fine," I reply, looking down at the food, which now appears anything but appetizing. I have so many conflicting thoughts about this man.

"Okay, well, if you're done with breakfast, let's get going."

"Are you always so bossy?"

Mark looks at me with a cocky grin. "I'm not bossy. I'm just anxious to spend the day with you."

"Mark," I say nervously. "I like the idea of spending the day with you, relaxing and having fun as friends, but beyond that... we can't."

"Why not?" Mark moves closer to me and takes hold of my hand.

"I live four hours away, if not further. I'm pregnant with someone else's child. What can't you see? I'm not a fling, nor am I a weekend joke. So, if you don't mind, I think I'd like to cancel for the day. I really do appreciate the dance and the flirty texts, but for my sake, I really would like for you to leave." Again, tears well up in my eyes. Mark is quiet, but not for long.

"I get your point, but I'm not leaving. Megan, let's give today a chance, okay? I am not looking for a fling either, and I certainly do not see you as a weekend joke. Yeah, maybe once I was a bit of a player, but I want something more than a one-night stand. I want something meaningful."

I'm silent, not even able to look at him. I try to pull my hand away from his, but he holds on tightly. He is not hurting me, but he will not let go.

"Megan, please spend the day with me, as friends. Let's just see what happens." He looks sincere. I stand up and walk to the bathroom, not turning to see what Mark is doing. I close the door and sit in the bathroom, thinking. Could I? I mean, what could it hurt to spend an afternoon with a friend? Oh, I know what it could hurt. It could hurt *me*! But Mark seems to be kind, not out to hurt me. I would love to have an afternoon with no pressure, no expectations, and forget past hurts. That settles it. Just once I am not going to do what my head says, but listen to my very terrified heart. I stand up, straighten my hair, and grab my lip-gloss from the sink. I walk out into the sitting room. I need to be spontaneous for once in my life.

"Okay, let me get my bag."

Mark just smiles. He does not say a word; his silence speaks volumes. It shows he understands my concerns. I gather some personal effects and put them into a bag. It is a different one to the one I had last night because I am such a freak for bags. I have dozens of them at home. I slip a grey scarf around my neck and grab my room key.

Mark takes my hand. "Are you going to be warm enough?"

I smile at his thoughtfulness and point towards the door where I had hung my jacket the night before.

"This one?" he asks, taking a black jacket down from the hook. There are a couple of coats hanging with it. I take the jacket.

"Thank you, Mark."

Mark holds the jacket for me. I look at him questioningly, and he offers up a playful smirk.

"What? Even friends can be gentlemanly."

I slip my arms into the sleeves of the jacket, thanking him once again. Mark opens the door for me, but stops me on the threshold and turns to look directly at me.

"Just promise me one thing today, Megan. Don't be putting yourself down. Please don't think that I'd rather be off with someone else. I want to be with you today, and there is nowhere else I'd rather be, okay?"

"Okay, I promise I'll try."

As we exit the hotel, Mark slips his hand into mine, and every hair on the back of my neck stands up. Why is he having such an electrical effect on me? Being around him is like nothing I have ever experienced before.

Mark leads me along the pavement to a parked silver car. Although I know nothing about cars, I can tell from just looking at it that it is some kind of expensive foreign car. Perhaps a Mercedes, maybe a Lexus, I am not sure, and when Mark opens the passenger door for me, I can smell the rich leather interior. The car is spotless as I get inside. When Mark slips behind the steering wheel and starts the engine, it purrs to life. Classical music comes on over the stereo. I have never been a fan of classical music, but I find this piece to be beautiful.

Mark drives through the city, and I am quickly lost as one street merges into another. After a while, I realise that we are heading out of the city, leaving behind the urban sprawl and moving into the richer suburbs. Eventually, Mark pulls off the road and up to a pair of large black metal gates. He buzzes his window down and enters a code into a small silver box mounted on a post. The gates begin to swing inward, and I look beyond the opening gates at the largest house I have ever seen.

"Where are we?" I ask.

"This is my house. I just need to grab some things."

Mark parks his car in a large circular shingled driveway near the front door. I see that there is also a black Range Rover and a red Mini parked nearby.

"I'll only be ten minutes or so," he says as he switches off the engine. "Come on in. This won't take long."

I look at Mark, then back at the house. "Are any of your family in there?" I put a hand protectively on my swollen belly while jumbled thoughts play to get a foothold in my mind. I'm not sure that I want his family to see me while I'm pregnant. I don't want them judging me without knowing my story.

"No one is here but my personal assistant. He's doing some work for me. I don't live with my family. Even if I did, it wouldn't matter." He places his hand over mine. I smile, but my nerves are in my throat. As I begin to climb out of the car, Mark races around the car, telling me to wait. As he opens the car door wider and offers me his hand, I take it, letting him help me out of the car. I close the door behind me, glancing at the other cars. Mark follows my gaze and tells me that the Mini belongs to his assistant.

"The Range Rover's mine. Don't worry, Megan. No one else is here. I only moved in six months ago after I saw this place and fell in love with it."

I can't help but look at how grand this house is.

"It's only a house, Megan. Come on," he tells me, as he leads me up a set of steps to the front door. There are planters filled with

28

overflowing flowers on either side of the steps. They are so pretty I can't help but wonder if he has a gardener to do all this work. Mark opens the door and ushers me inside first.

The foyer is minimalist, with only a few small pictures on the walls, and the black, central spiral staircase is obviously the main focal point of the entry hall.

"I just need to do some stuff in my home office. You're welcome to join me, or you can just have a look around. It's up to you," Mark tells me as he shuts the door behind us.

I turn and face him. "I'll just wait here."

I watch Mark go through an archway, obviously heading for his office. I walk around the foyer, noticing pictures that appear to be of Mark's family. I hear his voice as I walk through the archway that he had gone through. I walk down the neat hallway to an open door where I can see Mark talking to another man. The man is a little bit taller than Mark and dressed in a smart pinstriped suit.

Mark notices me and smiles. "Megan, I'd like you to meet my assistant, Connor." Connor is an attractive man with short blond hair.

"Nice to meet you, Connor," I say.

Connor walks around a black leather sofa.

"Good morning, Miss. Nice to meet you. Is there anything I can get you?"

Did he just call me Miss? That is a new one on me. I smile and say, "I'm fine, thank you."

Mark walks around Connor, taking my hand. He walks along with me to a room he told me was his office. It has a desk, a computer, and three chairs. It has French doors behind what would be Mark's chair. Mark lets go of my hand and sits down in the chair, looking for something in his drawers. I walk around behind his chair, and I can see what he meant about the view. It is amazing. The garden is pretty. There is a built-in barbeque and a black garden arch with built-up flowerbeds at either side.

I suddenly feel a hand on my shoulder. "I'm ready to go when you are, Megan."

I turn around to face Mark. "I see what you meant about the view. It is breathtaking."

Mark and I walk out of the office together and then head out of his house.

"Where are we going now?" I ask.

"Into the city, just to get something. We can pick up a film to watch later if you'd like." Standing at the side of the car, I nod and smile.

"That sounds great."

Chapter 6

During the drive back into the city, we talk non-stop about what movies we like and find out that we enjoy the same kind. I cannot stop looking over at Mark. He looks so amazing. Mark glances over at me, and I get butterflies in my stomach. We drive to the shopping plaza. Mark keeps a tight hold on my hand. I am sure friends do not normally hold hands. We choose three different films—a comedy, a chick flick, and a horror. Mark asks if I need some snacks, but before I can answer, he heads out to pick some up. Then, he leaves me looking at clothes so he can pick something up he needed at the printers. I meet Mark outside the printers, and he smiles. "One last shop, then we can go back or get some lunch, if you would like."

I walk alongside Mark. We stop outside a jewellery shop. "I will be back in a minute."

"Okay, I'll stand right here." I look at the jewellery in the window. Oh my god, I would need a mortgage to shop here. Why are we here?

"All right, Megan, would you like to go for some lunch?" Mark asks when he returns, slipping his hand into mine. "Come on, then."

We walk to a restaurant, which is very close. It looks very much like the bar where we met. The same corporation must own it, because the name is Restaurant 3000. The décor is the same as the bar. As we walk farther into the restaurant, a small woman walks over to show us to our seats.

She has blonde wavy hair, blue eyes, and she is in a uniform. Mark lets go of my hand and walks with the server. She flirts openly with him, stroking his arm. I walk slowly behind them. I cannot believe how jealous I feel. I feel out of place, like the proverbial third wheel on a date. Nevertheless, he is not mine, and she very well could have a claim to him. Mark and I sit opposite each other.

"What would you like to drink?"

I raise my head up and look at Mark. I have no expression, but look straight into his eyes. I feel empty and prefer to go back to the hotel. I answer quietly, "Lemonade, if they have it."

Mark smiles at me, "Of course, they do. What do you fancy to eat?"

I pick up the menu and hide behind it. As I read it, a tear rolls down my cheek. I select the cheapest thing on the menu.

"Chicken wrapped in bacon with rice, please."

Mark waves the server over and orders for us. The server continues flirting with Mark and giggling at him. Unable to sit there any longer, I make my excuses and head for the restaurant's restroom.

I sit in the bathroom, crying. Why, oh why, am I crying? We are just friends. I straighten myself out, telling myself not to be so silly.

I walk back to the table just as the food is arriving. It is not the blonde server this time. I sit down.

"Megan, are you okay?"

"I'm fine. Lunch looks good, thank you."

Mark smiles at me, but there is a hint of concern in his eyes. We sit in peace and quiet, eating our lunch. Once lunch is over, he takes my hand.

"Megan, please smile. Something is bothering you. I can see it's written all over your face."

He kisses my hand.

Once again, tears well up in my eyes, "Look, Mark. I really can't do this. I can't play games, nor can I handle being compared to the other women in your life."

Mark looks at me, puzzled.

"What? What games? What women? Megan, what are you talking about?"

I lower my head as tears again begin to fall.

"The waitress, it's obvious you two..."

Mark shakes his head. "No, no, no. I don't know where you got that idea. *Her*? No, Megan, I told you we could begin as friends, but I'd like to be more than just friends."

Mark waves the server over and pays for lunch, refusing to let me pay. He helps me stand, and we walk hand-in-hand to the car. The journey back to the hotel seems long. We are quiet, but it is a tender silence. Mark holds my hand, kissing my fingertips and the back of my hand often.

After arriving at the hotel, I feel relieved to just sit on the sofa and take off my shoes. I put the snacks onto the coffee table with the films while Mark is talking quietly on his mobile. I sit, trying to listen to what he is saying, but I cannot make out a word. I settle back on the sofa, pulling my legs beneath me and getting comfortable.

Mark walks over to join me.

"Right, I'm all yours. I have something for you."

Mark places his hand into a bag and pulls out small cream-coloured teddy bear with a pink bow on its head.

"Oh, Mark, thank you." He places a kiss on my hand. "It's for Bump. Your gift is still in the bag."

Mark hands me the bag and tells me to open it. I reach into the bag, and I find a small black box with the name of the jewellery store Mark stopped at during our afternoon walk. I open the box slowly and find it contains an exquisitely crafted silver charm bracelet. Attached at intervals are several charms, each different to the rest. I look back to Mark's face and directly into his eyes. Do I see nervousness? On the other hand, maybe it is fear.

"Mark, this is so beautiful. I don't know what to say." Mark removes the bracelet from the box.

"Here, let me." Mark takes my hand, lifting it towards him and loops the delicate chain around my wrist. He lifts each charm and explains its meaning.

"A pram for Bump, a heart because you make mine beat more than I knew it could, number 23 for the day we met, and a key to my heart. We can add to it, Megan, as our relationship grows."

My eyes had been flooded with tears from the moment he opened the box. Mark looks at me with such a look of confusion.

"Mark, as I said, this is beautiful. I've never seen anything like it, but there is no possible way I can accept this."

"Megan, beautiful girl, I bought you a gift. I ask for nothing in return. It is for yesterday, today, and hopefully, tomorrow. I will not listen to any refusals, or excuses, from my heart to yours."

"Thank you, Mark, but..."

Mark looks at me with a smile of warning. I lean over to kiss his cheek, but he turns his head, and our lips meet. He cups his palm to my cheek as the kiss deepens. It is so perfect, this kiss. It's soft, yet full of so much meaning. I do not fight it. Slowly we pull away, lost in each other's eyes. Has time stopped? Mark brings us back to reality.

"So, which film first?" He grins.

"How about we watch the comedy?" I smile back.

"Perfect." Mark immediately gets up and places the film into the machine. He walks back to the sofa and tells me to relax.

"I am relaxed," I sass back. Mark sits and lifts his arm. With his other hand, he pats his chest.

"Come. Sit close and put your feet up. I'll be your pillow. You will keep me close and happy."

I do as I'm told. We sit in silence, watching the film. I must have fallen asleep at some point, as when I awaken, Mark's jacket is covering both of us.

"Nice nap, beautiful?" Mark asks with a huge smile.

"I can't believe I fell asleep."

"It's okay. You only missed the last five minutes of the film. You must have needed it."

I sit up, leaving the jacket to fall away. "Sorry, I guess that's one of the many joys of pregnancy. My body is always changing. I don't know what I need from one moment to the next."

Standing up and walking around Mark, I go over to the bathroom. Just as I am about to walk in, Mark asks if he can get me a drink.

"Please, you know what I like."

I finish in the bathroom and walk back into the other room. Mark places drinks onto the table. As I smile and place my hand on his shoulder, he turns around and hugs me. I cannot stop smiling. I sit down on the sofa.

"I have lemonade, Diet Coke, and tea. All for you, Megan."

I smile. "You forgot water."

"I will get you some."

I place my hand out in front of him just as he begins to stand up and touch his stomach. "I'm joking, Mark. Sit down." I cannot believe how hard his stomach feels. He sits back down.

"What're you like, Megan?" Mark says playfully.

"I'm lovely." I start giggling.

"You are indeed."

"Let's watch another film. The chick flick?" I suggest, trying to hide the redness of my face from the comment he just made.

"That's fine with me."

"Are you sure?"

Mark gets up and places the film into the player.

"I just want to be with you, Megan, plain and simple."

I grab some snacks and wait for Mark to sit down. I push the footstool under our feet and throw the jacket back over us. Mark turns towards the bed and pulls the duvet from it. He discards his

jacket, and we snuggle down beneath the duvet. I rest my head on his shoulder, and the film begins.

Chapter 7

Mark rises from the sofa and walks to the television, taking the film out of the machine while I wander off to the bathroom again. I need a little time to myself to think. I really like him. I feel safe around him, but this is all moving too fast. This is just not possible. I feel like a lifetime of hurt dissolves just looking into his eyes. It amazes me that all the insecurities I have ever felt vanish when he touches me. I walk back into the sitting room to find Mark sitting on the sofa, looking at his mobile.

"Your mobile went off while you were in there," he informs me.

"Thank you." I smile.

I walk around Mark, sit down next to him, and pick up my mobile.

"It's Jenny, telling me about her day." I tilt the mobile so he too can see the text.

Hey beautiful, have had a fantastic day with Rich. We managed to sort so much out. How are you and Bump? Did you do anything special today with Mark? Xx

I smile, look at Mark who smiles at me, and reply to Jenny's question.

Hey Hun, I'm so glad you got lots sorted. We are both well. Mark has been here since around ten. I've had an 'eye-opening' day. Xx

Mark smiles again, but this time it is a different smile. He shifts his body and turns towards me. With his index finger, he makes small circles on my knee. I look into his eyes and suddenly start feeling nervous.

"May I ask you something?" He takes my hand with both of his.

"Of course, you may. Anything, Mark," I answer, but I am afraid of what he will ask, and if I am able to trust him enough to answer him. It always boils down to trust.

"Where is Bump's dad? You don't have to answer if it's too difficult to talk about, only if you want to, and only if it feels right."

I smile. Can I trust him with this? I don't want him feeling sorry for me. I pause, take a deep breath, and look down at our hands.

"He lives near me, the next town over." I pause again, taking a deeper breath. "I caught him cheating on me with another woman. I found out he was married. He also has three children." I can't quite believe I told him all this information and so willingly.

Mark moves his hands from mine and puts one beneath my chin, ensuring I make eye contact with him. "Thank you for telling me. Are you okay?"

I can see the sorrow in Mark's eyes. "I'm fine. I'm over him," I state emphatically, hoping Mark can tell I want to move on from my ex and all the troubles associated with that chapter of my life.

Mark smiles, and it is not his normal cheeky one. "Does he not want Bump?"

"He doesn't know about her. I found out a month after I last saw him. He wouldn't answer my messages, and he's since changed jobs. I don't want to break up his family. It would not be fair for his children. He has made his choice. I will never get back with him anyway. I want someone I can trust, someone who wants me for me and no other."

Mark kisses my hand. "He's not a real man because no real man would do that."

"I'm okay, and I'm going to make sure he can't hurt Bump."

"He doesn't deserve either of you."

"Thank you, I know we'll be okay. I'm going to do everything I can for her."

Mark pulls me close to him, wrapping his arms around me.

"She'll be fine, especially with you as her mum. Thank you for telling me." I feel a huge weight lift from my chest.

As I sit in Mark's arms, I listen to his heartbeat.

"Shall we get something to eat? It's getting late. You need to eat." Mark lets go of me. It's nice that he is thinking of me, or possibly himself. We all know men love their food. I'm not really hungry, but

Bump needs me to eat.

"Sounds like a good idea. What do you fancy?"

"It's up to you. We can go out for something to eat, order room service, or get take-away. I'm okay with whatever you like."

Mark smiles his usual cheeky smile, the smile that makes me melt. "How about we eat here? We can have take-away or room service. I don't mind."

"Sounds like a good idea, baby. How about take-away?" *Did I just hear him right? Did he just call me baby?* I must be hearing things.

"Are there any take-outs you don't like?" I enquire.

"I'll eat anything, baby." Mark kisses my hand, and I realise he did it again. I'm not hearing things. He called me baby.

"Chinese it is then."

Mark uses his mobile to locate a Chinese restaurant and brings up a menu, and then he passes the mobile to me so that I can choose what I like. I choose something simple, playing it safe, as I am conscious at all times that I have a precious life growing inside me, and I have read that certain foods can be potentially dangerous to an unborn child.

"Chicken fried rice," I inform Mark. "That shouldn't have anything I'm not allowed."

Mark smiles and places his palm against my bump and asks my unborn child if she's hungry, which makes me smile. I love the way he considers Bump, making me feel like the pregnancy is not an issue for him.

"I'm going to have duck and pineapple in sweet and sour sauce. Shall I call for it?"

Mark rings the order in, and he informs me he is going to go and collect it as it's just down the street. It would be quicker than waiting on a delivery.

He leaves me, giving me more time to think. I have never been a person who believes in love at first sight. I have been hurt too many times. I'm only twenty-four, and I've have had my heart broken twice. I was never one of those girls who had boyfriends at school. I kept to myself.

I tidy up a bit and put the last film into the machine, ready for when Mark returns. I sit back down on the sofa and check my messages. I know what Jenny's like, and she's forever texting me.

OMG, he's so into you. Have you kissed him? Xx

I can't do anything but laugh. Trust her to want all the juicy details.

Yeah, I've kissed him. Are we still hitting the shops tomorrow? Xx

I hear a knock on the door. I walk over to the door to see Mark. He is back already with the food. That was very quick. I smile and move to the side, letting him back in. He places the food onto the counter and quickly dishes it out onto plates. I stand near the table, watching him. He seems like such a happy man. I sit back down on the sofa, making sure I am comfortable as he told me to do. I don't often do as I'm told; I'm usually the one in control. Mark comes over with the food, sits down next to me, and starts the film.

Whose bright idea was it to leave the horror movie until this time of the night? I'm not a person who gets easily scared, but this one is a scary film. I find myself grabbing the cushion from next to me to hide behind. Mark takes hold of my plate, puts it onto the coffee table, and pulls me closer to him. I can hear him tittering at me.

"Hey! Be nice. It's a scary film," I protest.

"I know it is, baby. I'll keep you safe." There it is again. *Baby*. We are friends. I am not his baby.

I sit there in his arms, watching the film and feeling safe, the safest I have ever felt with a man. I know nothing will happen between us. I know it will just be a couple of days, and that's it. I don't want this time together to end. Part of me wants to tell him to leave, but the other part wants me to ask him to stay, to stay with me.

"Mark, would you like to stay the night? It's almost midnight. I don't want you crashing your car driving home."

I can't believe I just said that. I'm not usually so forward.

"I will if you want me to. I'll sleep on the sofa."

"You're not sleeping on the sofa. I'm sure we can be adults and share the bed. No groping me, though."

Mark's cheeky smile reappears. "I'll try my best not to grope you."

He winks.

I have to laugh. I get up and head over to the drawers to get my pyjamas.

"I'm going to get changed for bed."

Mark gets up from the sofa and walks over to me.

"Sleep in this." He takes off his T-shirt and passes it to me. He has an amazing body with a tanned six-pack. I want to touch him, to caress his toned abdomen, but I keep my hands to myself.

"Okay," I reply. His suggestion caught me off guard, and I don't know what else to say.

I turn back to the chest-of-drawers and find a matching set of underwear, white lace French knickers and a bra. Mark's T-shirt is very long, so it should look okay. I make my way to the bathroom. I have a quick wash and then get dressed for bed. I brush my teeth and then my hair, making sure I look okay, even though I'm only going to bed. I pull on his T-shirt, then a dressing gown. I walk back into the other room to see Mark sitting on the sofa with the folder from his house on his knees.

I walk up behind him. "Hey, you're busy working again." Mark jumps and covers the folder with his hands.

"Something like that. Nice robe." He winks with his cheeky smile.

"What are you hiding, Mark?"

"Nothing at all, Megan," he replies.

"Are you sure?"

Mark moves his hand to reveal a beautiful drawing of me.

"Just something I enjoy doing when I have the time."

"It's beautiful. Is art your career?"

I stand there, looking at this amazing picture with such intricate detail. It's like looking at a photograph of me.

"No, I'm an entrepreneur. I own Reed Enterprises."

"Wow, you're a big-wig then?" I might have to look up this company. I choose to change the conversation, as I feel uncomfortable talking about such things.

"So, what do you want to do? I'm thinking of going to bed and relaxing."

"I'm happy to do anything you want, baby. Snuggling in bed sounds like a great idea to me," Mark says.

"Well, it is past midnight, so I think bed is the best idea." Mark gets up and turns off the television. He takes the duvet off me and places it onto the bed. While he does this, I switch on the bedside lamp. I put my mobile on charge after remembering to set the alarm for eight o'clock.

I remove the dressing gown and climb into bed, trying not to look and see what he is doing. I just hope he's not watching me. The thought of that makes me blush. Mark climbs into bed on the other side. I snuggle down in the bed and face him. I smile at him, and he places his hand on my bump.

"Night, Bump. Goodnight, Megan." Mark leans over and kisses me on the cheek.

"Night, Mark." How sweet he is. He considered Bump.

I snuggle farther down in the bed and suddenly realise that Mark is naked. I can see his manhood, and to curb any further thoughts, I roll away from him onto my side. I am surprised when Mark snuggles in close behind me, my back pressed against his chest and his arm over me. I am sure I did not say I would snuggle, yet I feel safe. I still can't believe he has on no underwear.

Chapter 8

It's seven fifteen in the morning, and I can't remember the last time I slept for so long or as comfortably. I can feel Mark's breath on my neck. His arm is still around me, with his hand resting just above my bump. I wonder what time Mark has to be at work. I hear Mark's mobile go off again. That is the third time since I woke up. I move slowly onto my back, and Mark moves over.

He looks so peaceful in his slumber, almost angelic. I could lie here and watch him sleep all day if I had my way.

"Mark, wake up. Your mobile keeps going off."

He groans, "Morning, beautiful, what's the time?"

"Morning, it's seven twenty."

Mark reaches over to his mobile and checks his messages. I slide out of bed, grab the dressing gown, and slip my arms through the sleeves before heading to the bathroom. I return to the bed about five minutes later. I slide back in, keeping the dressing gown on. Mark is sitting up in bed, studiously looking at his mobile.

"Is everything okay?"

"Sorry, yeah, everything's fine. Just another busy day."

"Don't apologize if you need to get a move on and go to work," I state.

"I will. I just want to cuddle with you first." Mark smiles, putting down his mobile. He slides his arm around me, pulling me closer. I smile, moving to him. "So, what are your plans for today, Megan?"

"Jenny and I are off shopping."

"For the wedding?" he asks, and I nod my head.

"Don't you need to get going, Mark?"

I don't want to appear to be pushing him away, but he's needed at work by the sounds of it.

"I do. Is it okay if I use the shower?" Mark smiles and kisses me on the forehead.

"Of course."

He jumps out of bed and walks across the room to the bathroom without covering anything. I shield my face after having a sly look. Wow, what a bum. He is so fit.

"You don't have to hide, Megan. Have a good look." Mark laughs, going into the bathroom. I feel my face turning red. My mobile goes off, and as I expected, it's Jenny messaging me yet again.

Morning, meet me downstairs at about nine and we'll get some breakfast. Hope you are well. I need the gossip. Xx

Morning Jenny, that sounds perfect to me. I am starving. X

Mark walks back into the room, wearing a towel around his waist. What is it with men looking so sexy when they are wet? He sits on the side of the bed and pulls on his jeans, and I realise I'm still wearing his T-shirt. I slide off the dressing gown. Being in the bed, I don't feel so exposed.

"Do you want this?" I pull his T-shirt over my head. Mark keeps his eyes on me as I remove it. His face lights up while that cheeky smile appears.

"Wow, Megan."

I feel myself turning redder.

"Get dressed, Mark. You better get your cute bum to work," I say as I throw his top at him.

"Megan, did you check me out?" he asks playfully.

"Of course, I did." I cover my face with the sheets. I can't believe I took my top off in front of him and admitted to checking him out.

"Do you want to have breakfast before I leave?" he asks.

"I'm meeting Jenny for breakfast."

"Okay, sexy, I'll get something at work," Mark replies, winking at me.

"You best do. You need to eat." Mark climbs onto the bed and crawls towards me. He plants his lips on mine, and I let his tongue slide into my mouth. Our tongues dance within each other's mouths.

Mark leaves, giving me time to get ready to see Jenny. I opt for jeans and a cream jumper. I have fifteen minutes until I meet her, and I head down to the lobby, find a seat and decide to look up Reed Enterprises on my mobile. I need to know more about the man who spent the night in my bed.

Reed Enterprises

Reed Enterprises was created by Mark Oliver Reed, the youngest son of Andrew Oliver Reed and Heather Elizabeth Reed (nee Glenn). Mark's siblings are Amelia and Craig Oliver Reed. The family resides in the plush suburbs of London.

Mark Reed created Reed Enterprises at the age of twenty after graduating university, where he obtained a degree in Business & Business Finance.

Reed Enterprises is a rapidly growing concern, which currently has a wide network of business interests beneath its corporate umbrella.

The young and enthusiastic entrepreneur is always on the lookout for his next deal, though. He is taking time out later this year to concentrate on charity work.

I look up from my mobile to see Jenny. I'm so happy to see her, and I thrust my mobile at her. "Jenny, please read this." I sit there while Jenny reads.

"Is that the Mark from the bar? The one you spent the day with?" Jenny asks while smiling at me.

"Yes, it is."

We walk to the café next door, order our food, and sit down. While we wait for our breakfasts to be made, we spend time gossiping about Mark and what happened yesterday. I find out all about what Jenny and Rich did yesterday. Our food arrives, and we start to eat. I hear my mobile go off.

Hey Megan, how was breakfast? Is Jenny all right? X

"It's Mark. He's asking if you're okay."

We are so close and tell each other everything. I can trust her with everything because she's like the sister I never had. She seems to like Mark. Why do I still have these doubts? I know I need to protect myself. I need to think of Bump, and then there's the fact that we live at other ends of the country. In the real world, this wouldn't work, no matter how much I want it to.

Jenny and I leave the café and spend a full day shopping. We find everything we need. We are having lunch with Rich, and I plan to leave Jenny and him after lunch so that they can have some time together.

After a very nice lunch, I say my farewells and head back towards the hotel. As I walk, I can't help myself, so I check my mobile to see if Mark has texted me. I see several alerts and smile when I see that he has indeed been texting me. It feels good to be wanted.

10:10: *Megan, it does not matter to me what I do in my life. I like you. Okay? X*

11:30: *Megan, are you ignoring me or just busy? X*

12:50: *Where are you? I need to talk to you. X*

13:34: *Please meet me. X*

It's two in the afternoon, and my wandering the congested streets of the capital has left me lost. I have no idea where the hotel is, and I stop and look around and realise where I am. Whether I knew on a subconscious level, or it's just a coincidence I know not, but I am outside Mark's workplace. I notice his car parked nearby, and I start to worry. The last thing I want is for Mark to see me. Right now I just need to think, to clarify my thoughts and feelings. We are meant to be just friends, but I know I have feelings for him—that I like him. The thought of being hurt again is a constant reminder of why I am reticent to get involved romantically.

"Hello, Miss, how are you? Are you here to see Mr. Reed?" a voice asks from behind me. I slowly turn around to see it's Connor. He looks all business in a black suit, white shirt, lilac tie, and polished shoes.

"Hi, Connor, and please call me Megan. I... ah, I'm okay, thanks. How are you?" I ask, avoiding what he wants to know.

"Great, thanks for asking. I think you should come and see Mr.

Reed. He's worried about you."

"That's okay, Connor. Really, I'll just send him a quick text."

"Okay, Miss, I better be going," Connor says, and I absentmindedly wish him a good day as he disappears into the building.

I send Mark a text.

I'm fine. Why do you want to meet?

I start walking slowly down the street. I can see why he has chosen this part of the city to have his headquarters. The view is spectacular. It's not built up like the rest of the city. It is quiet. There are so many little benches around a waterfall and a nice little grassy area farther ahead. Overall, it's a very tranquil place to sit during your lunch break. My mobile goes off, and I see Mark has replied.

Megan, anywhere just to talk. Please. x

I'm near your workplace right now.

Wait for me please. X

I sit down on one of the benches near the waterfall and wait. I soon see Mark walking towards me. He's wearing what he left the hotel in earlier this morning, and he looks sexy as all hell.

"Oh, God, baby." Mark sits down next to me.

"Hello, Mark," He looks so relieved and yet so worried.

"Okay, let's get this over with...yes, I'm loaded. I can afford anything I want, and I suppose it would be easy to use my wealth to get any woman I want. From the moment I saw you walk into that bar, I knew I wanted you. I understand we live hundreds of miles apart and that you're pregnant. It's not an ideal situation by any means, but I want to at least try. Please?"

I do not say anything. I place my head down, and I can't look at him. I feel my eyes start to well up with tears that slowly roll down my cheek. Mark tries to place his arm around me and bring our bodies in. I will not let him move me. He sits, rubbing my back and asking me to talk to him, to let him in, begging with me.

"Oh, Megan, please, talk to me. Baby, I need you. I should have told you to start with who I was, that I own a large company. I never

47

meant to hurt you. Please, I'll finish work now, and we can go do what you want."

I take a deep breath, "No, finish work. I'll be okay. Yes, you should have told me, but it will not work. The distance, the fact you're needed here, I'm needed there."

"Come in, please. Wait inside for me. I want us to talk. It's getting cold out here. I am not letting you go back to the hotel alone." Mark places his hand on mine.

"Okay," I state. I have no energy to argue with him.

Mark grabs ahold of my hand and picks up my bags and escorts me into the building. Neither of us says a word; I can't even look at him. We take the lift to the seventh floor, stepping out into a large lounge and then walking through it to his office. Inside, his office is exactly the same layout to the one at home. It has an equally as good view from the window.

"Relax, baby," Mark says, placing my bags onto the floor beside the sofa. I don't look at him. "Make yourself at home." I do as he says and sit myself down on the sofa. Letting Mark get on with his work, I realise I don't want to be here. I don't want to talk to him. I reach into my bag and get a book out, sitting there reading. "I did not publish that book if that helps," Mark adds. I laugh, not looking up at him.

"No, she is a self-published amazing author. Great friend, great story, too."

"I didn't know you had a passion for reading, Megan," Mark says. I look up to see him, sitting on the corner of his desk and looking at me.

"There is a lot of stuff you don't know yet. I love to read. It is one of my many passions," I tell him before letting my eyes drop back down to the book. I feel slightly uncomfortable. I bring my legs up onto the sofa and curl up. Gazing up at Mark, he is typing on his laptop, looking busy. I want to leave, but I know he is not going to let me.

Next thing I know, I see Mark is not at his desk. He is standing at the door, talking to a female because I can hear her voice. I look down and see his jacket covers me. I must have fallen asleep. It was nice of him to cover me. Mark walks back into the room with a folder and places it onto the clear desk, smiling at me.

"I did it again. Fell asleep. Sorry," I admit as Mark sits on the edge of the sofa.

"It's okay. I have finished all the work I need to do. We can go back to the hotel now." Mark places a kiss onto my forehead. I don't move.

Mark drives up the gravel driveway to his house. He said he needed to drop something off here. Refusing to take me back to the hotel, he is so determined that we talk. I still cannot believe the size of this house and its fantastic view. I would hate to clean it, though. Questioning Mark on the way here, needing to break the silence, I found out his house has eight bedrooms all with an en-suite bathroom, two additional bathrooms, two studies—one on each floor—and a large open plan room containing the lounge, kitchen and dinner area. Mark wanted to cook for me, no way of doing that at the hotel. It is somewhat sweet. I am feeling funny, and I do need to eat something.

We head into the house. I sit on a barstool in Mark's kitchen on one side of the light wooden island while he is on the other. I watch him take off his jacket, leaving just his white tight shirt on. The same T-shirt I wore the night before.

"What would you like to eat, Megan?" Mark asks.

"Anything, just no eggs or cheese. I am not allergic to anything to my knowledge," I state.

"Right, no eggs or cheese, so my special dish is out the window until after the baby is here. Pasta it is then. I do a lovely pasta dish with tomatoes."

I smile. The thought of food right now is making me feel sick.

"Perfect, anything I can do?" I cannot believe what he just said. That means he intends to see me after Bump is here.

"Yes, sit there and carry on looking beautiful."

"I am not beautiful, Mark, but thank you."

Mark carries on going around the kitchen, getting the ingredients he needs for the meal, stretching and bending to get the things, and showing off his fantastic body. I cannot believe how lucky I am. He is not phased one bit by the distance or my pregnancy. The smell of the food permeates the room with heavenly aromas. He places the cutlery, plates, and glasses onto the dining room table, yet another large table. I know it must be for the size of his family. It must seat at least ten people. Mark continues to refuse my help.

We sit at the table and begin eating Mark's wonderful cooking. He has made it a bit spicy, but totally mouth-watering. "It is amazing, Mark. Who taught you how to cook?" I question him.

"My nanny, Annabella, from when I was a child. With my parents being busy at work, she brought us all up. She taught me to do everything, to be independent. She is my role model. I go and see her every week. She is retired now. You should come with me tomorrow. I would love for you to meet her and for her to meet you. She will absolutely adore you."

"She sounds amazing, Mark, a lovely role model for you," I state.

"She is lovely. She told us that as long as you believe in yourself, you can do anything in life. I believed in myself and had her as a huge support and look where I am. Please, come and meet her tomorrow at whatever time suits you." I sit there, looking at my half-eaten pasta.

I take a deep breath. "Mark, why do you want me to meet her? I am a nobody."

Mark takes hold of my hand. "Look at me, Megan." I do as he asks. "Don't say that. You're a loving and caring person. I want you to be happy. I intend to make you happy. Either you accept it or not."

"I will come with you if you want me to. I am happy that she helped you believe in yourself. I might never have met you otherwise. It will be nice to find out all about the troublesome little boy you were." I give Mark a cheeky wink.

"Fate brought us together. I was an angel, never trouble. Okay, maybe I was trouble, sometimes. Thank you, baby. What time is best for you?"

"I have plans with Jenny till around two, depending on how much talking we do. After that, I'm free."

"So, I will come get you from your hotel at say, three, giving you time if you are running late."

Mark lets me help him load the dishwasher. It is the least I can do after our lovely meal. I yet again turn down dessert, even though I have a very sweet tooth. I have to keep away from sugary treats; otherwise, I will end up being a beached whale.

Mark goes off and gets some things he needs. I stand at the French doors in the lounge looking at the incredible view; this shows the other side of the house to what the view in his study is. There is nothing much in the garden at this side, just what appears to be a rosebush in the middle. Behind the garden, you can see the picturesque hills. Mark appears back in the doorway with a grey overnight bag; he's wearing black jeans and a black T-shirt with a black jacket in his hand.

"Hey, are you ready to go back to the hotel, beautiful?"

"Are you talking to me? I'm not beautiful. I am just me. Yeah, I'm ready."

"You are beautiful," Mark firmly says as he moves closer, placing a little kiss on my cheek.

He continues to be a gentleman, holding the door open for me. The stars illuminate the drive back to the hotel. The moon is so big and bright in the night sky. I can't believe it is eight at night. Time has gone by so fast. Mark takes me up to my hotel room, leaving his overnight bag in the car.

"Thank you for dinner. It was lovely," I stand on my tiptoes and place a kiss on Mark's cheek.

"You are very welcome again. When do you go home?"

"In two days. We leave at six pm."

"Can you stay any longer?" Mark takes my hand, walks me over to the sofa, and we sit down.

"I wish I could, but I have a midwife's appointment at lunchtime the next day."

"Okay, what are you going to do with yourself for the rest of the night?"

"No idea. Have you got work to do?"

"No, why?"

"You can come stay for a bit then if you want. You don't have to."

Mark smiles, kisses me on the cheek, and walks out of the hotel room, without saying a word to me. I take off my shoes. Oh, I have wanted to do that all day. I hear the door open, and it is Mark with his overnight bag. He places his bag on the side with my things. Taking out his folder, he places it onto the sofa.

Hi hun, how are you? Are we still up for in the morning? Have you heard from Mark? Xx

Hi Jenny, I am okay. Yeah, we are up for the morning. We had dinner together. Mark cooked, and I'm back at the hotel now with him. Xx

The rest of the night I spend in Mark's arms, watching him do some work and drawing. I cannot believe how talented he is. Time is going by too fast; it will soon be time for me to leave London and leave Mark. At least, I have two days with him. I get to meet Annabella tomorrow. I wonder if she will like me. Mark is asleep next to me on the sofa. His breathing so settled. I sit there watching him.

"Mark, you fell asleep."

"Mmmm…" He opens one eye, looking at me.

"Come on, sleepy. It's bedtime."

"It's your job to fall asleep, not mine," he says cheekily.

***

It's only six in the morning. I don't know why I am awake so early, and I am not tired. I have no plans of waking Mark up this early. He is in the same attire as last night, and I am wearing his black T-shirt. I could get used to this. I watch Mark's bare chest rise and fall. I pull the cover over him; I do not want him getting cold, even though I could watch his naked chest all night. Sitting up in bed, I check my messages.

Hi hun, can we cancel today? I have a sickness bug. Xx

Hi Jenny, of course. Get well soon. Let me know if you want or need anything. Xx

Thank you. Can you go with Luke, collect the rings and suits? I do not trust him on his own. Xx

Sure. Message me the details and get some rest. Xx

I do not know Luke very well. I know he is one of those actors who loves himself more than he loves others, and thinks he is the best at everything he does. I have enjoyed some of his films, but not because of him. He just happened to be in them. I might find out more about him today while we are out. I would prefer the day with Mark, but if I get going, I can spend more time with Mark.

Hi, Luke. It's Megan. Let me know what time and where you want to meet. X

"Morning, beautiful."

"Morning, did I wake you?" I place my mobile on the side, turning and facing Mark who is sliding himself up in the bed so he is sitting up.

"No, you didn't, baby. How long have you been awake?"

"Over an hour."

"You should have wakened me."

"You looked so peaceful asleep. No point in us both being awake at silly times."

"True, so you're off shopping with Jenny today?"

"No, off with Luke. Jenny has a sickness bug, so Luke and I are off to collect the things."

"Oh, you have never mentioned Luke."

"Have I not? Luke is Rich's best man. You will have heard of Luke, Luke Galloway. Yes, *the Luke Galloway*, the actor."

"Oh, wow! I loved his last film. You will have fun. Should I be worried, though?"

"Did you? I cannot remember it. No, Luke and I only met at the engagement party. He seems weird to me."

"Good." Mark leans forward, placing his lips onto mine, "Mmmm... perfect lips you have, Megan."

"So do you, Mark. What time do you need to be at work?" I cannot let things get too far away. I am not going to sleep with him while I am pregnant. I know you can, but I do not want his first memories of us together having 'little lady' in the middle.

"How about breakfast in bed, Megan?" Mark suggests.

"I think I can do that."

Shopping with Luke could be fun. Luke is the same age as me, just famous and makes sure everyone knows it. He has been acting for the last five years. I think he can sing, too, from what Jenny has said about him. Mark treated me this morning to breakfast at a café, then kindly dropped me off where I am meeting Luke. As always, Luke is late, just as Jenny warned me he would be.

"Hi, sexy, you're blossoming well." Luke pulls me close in a tight hug.

"Hi, Luke," I reply in a pissed-off manner.

"Right, do you have the list of what to do, sexy?"

"Yeah, shall we get on with it?"

"Indeed, sexy." If he calls me "sexy" one more time, I will scream. Luke is cute, but he does not do anything for me. The next three hours we collect all the things on the list. Luke is actually so sweet, helping people, people who don't know who he is. He must call women "sexy" all the time, because he has not stopped all day.

"That's us done, Luke."

"Brilliant, sexy, finished with plenty of time to get to my business lunch date. Thanks for a good day. You definitely made shopping easier."

"Have a good lunch date, Luke. I'll see you before the wedding."

"I hope we do. I can't wait to meet the little lady," Luke replies.

"Bye, Luke."

"Bye, sexy." Luke pulls me in close, giving me another hug and placing a little kiss onto my cheek.

Now, that everything is sorted for Jenny, and it is only lunchtime. With Luke having plans, it saves the do-we-go-out-for-lunch decision. I think I am too nervous to eat. I can't wait to see Mark, but I don't know if Annabella will like me. I am just a normal person; there's nothing special about me. I choose not to let Mark know I have finished early and head back to the hotel to pick out what to wear. I am thinking hair down, leggings, ballet shoes, and a float top. Mark said I had to be me, not posh, so this will do. I change and settle down onto the sofa. There is just over an hour until Mark is coming for me, so I'll relax here.

Hi, Megan, have you finished shopping? X

Hi, Mark, yeah we finished just after 12. I am at the hotel, changed and ready to go.

You should have said. I could have finished early. X

I know, Mark, but you need to do some work. The hotel door is open. Just let yourself in.

I will do, Megan. X

"Hey, baby."

"You were quick. Did you get your work sorted?"

"I was in the car in the parking lot. Yeah, it's all sorted for now. You look very pretty, Megan."

"Thanks, will it do?"

"Of course. Let's go." Mark takes hold of my hand and places a little butterfly kiss onto my lips. Perfect, his lips are so soft.

"Let's go." I grab my jacket and bag off to the side. The journey to Annabella's is in the same direction as Mark's house. Annabella's house is small with plenty of grass. It has a little white fence surrounding the garden with a garage to the side where Mark parks.

"Are you ready?"

"Yeah, let's do this before I change my mind." Mark gets out, opens the car door, and takes my hand. We walk towards the house. There is a hanging basket full of flowers at either side of the door. He opens the door, and we walk straight in. A little black Labrador comes running towards us.

"Hey, Jessie, awww... you are getting so big!" Mark goes down onto his knees. "You like that? You like your belly being rubbed? Awww, shall we go find Mummy?" Jessie seems to love Mark, licking him like crazy, so cute to see. Mark takes hold of my hand. "This way, I forgot to warn you about Jessie."

"It's okay. She is cute." The house is just like a normal house, no oversized stairs and some pretty pictures on the walls. We walk into the lounge. It has two dark-brown three-seater sofas and a television in the corner with a dog bed in front of the big window. There is an open fireplace with wood burning in it. I can see the fire is about to go out.

"Hi, Annabella, how are you?"

"Mark, you are here! I have been looking forward to seeing you and finally meeting Megan. I am okay."

"Annabella, this is Megan."

Chapter 9

Annabella is an older woman. She is sitting in a high-backed brown chair in the lounge. She has white hair, which looks newly permed, and she has bright blue eyes.

"Hello, Megan, it's very nice to meet you. Mark has told me a lot about you. Please take a seat," she says as she points at the sofa that matches the chair she is sitting in. Smiling at me, she looks like a kind person, but as I have learned in my life, looks can be very deserving and deceiving.

"It is lovely to finally meet you as well, Annabella. Thank you for inviting me." I can feel my heart beating so fast. I am far from being a confident person. When I first meet someone, I am very shy. It takes me time to relax and manage to talk. I take a seat on the sofa. Annabella reminds me of a sweet old grandma. Mark never told me she was from America. She has the accent that gives it away. She must visit home multiple times a year to keep her accent. Mark is sitting on the floor, playing with Jessie. It is so nice seeing him happy and relaxed.

"Are you having a nice time here? Would you like anything to drink?" Annabella asks.

"It has been lovely. I've met Mark, which has been nice. No thank you, I don't care for anything to drink." She is so sweet. I have a feeling this is going to turn out like a game of twenty questions.

"Mark told me you are expecting your first child, a girl. What a big blessing!" she exclaims while her eyes look down to my bump.

"Yes, I am. I can't wait. I hear you used to look after Mark." I do wonder what he has told her about me. I decide to turn the questions to her. I don't feel comfortable talking about where Bump's father is with her.

"No telling stories about me, Annabella," Mark adds with a cheeky smile on his face.

"Oh, I want to know all these stories, though." I wink at Mark.

"Give me a minute. I have some pictures you can look through," Annabella says, rising from her chair.

"That would be great." I smile, looking at Mark, who is tickling Jessie's belly.

"Oh, Megan, look what you have done." Mark rolls his eyes playfully.

"Well, I need to see if you have always been cute." I wink at him again.

"I am not cute now, never was."

"Oh, you are cute, Mark," I say teasingly. I can't believe I just openly said that out loud.

"Here they are." Annabella walks back into the room slowly, holding not one, but three photo albums.

"A lot of photos you have there, Annabella. I hope there are a couple of good stories to go with them."

"I'm out of here. I'm not listening to this. I'll go walk Jessie." Mark stands up, kisses me on the forehead, and disappears out the door with Jessie.

"I looked after Mark from a baby. He was three months old when I first met him. He had a good set of lungs on him, could scream for hours. Craig was two, and Mia hadn't even been conceived."

"He was cute as a baby. I must admit I have a soft side for all children. I love babies. You must have had your hands full with all three of them."

"I am used to having a lot of children around me. I have four children of my own. Three of them live in the USA, in Etowah, North Carolina. One is in England, no idea where. She doesn't want anything to do with me because she thinks I love the children I have cared for more than I love my own. She does not understand that I came here and worked to have money to look after them. When I retired, Mark was kind enough to buy me Jessie and this place. He said it was the least he could do for me after everything I had done for him. He knew how much I had wanted a puppy. I always have." I see a tear roll down Annabella's cheek. I would love to know more about her family, but I don't want to upset her anymore.

"I have noticed he is very generous. He has spoken very highly of you," I inform her.

"Megan, I have never known him to be like this about anyone. I have never met any of his past girlfriends or heard of any of them. He came and saw me straight after he met you at the bar."

I cannot believe he's been talking about me. What has he been referring to me as... his *girlfriend*?

"I am just worried, with the distance and a baby on the way that he isn't going to want me. I do have feelings for him, though." As I just admitted this to her, she is making me feel comfortable enough to be a bit open with her, and she must think I'm strange.

"How would you like to hear a couple of stories about Mark while you look at the pictures?" Annabella asks. I think she can hear the worry in my voice.

"I would like that very much." I give her a little smile.

"Have you ever noticed the little scar on the bottom of Mark's right leg?" she enquires.

"I haven't." Does she know he has stayed with me? I wonder what she must think of me.

"Mark was riding his bike down at the park they had in their garden growing up, just beside the little lake. There is a picture of it somewhere. He slid on the mud and went sliding down the grass into the lake, slit his leg open, and got soaked. He came inside, but I had not noticed he had cut his leg. Six stitches later at the nearest emergency room, he was back home on his bike. He didn't cry at all. He was very brave." Annabella smiles while looking proud of him.

"What a soldier he was," I add.

"Oh, this one time, Mark came home from school all excited to tell me what he had learned. They had been to a farm on a trip. He was so happy that he couldn't wait to tell me the animals he had seen, like goats, chickens, horses, all the normal farm animals. He also saw a pig and a cow... 'a pink cow,' so he said."

"He must have been so excited."

"He went on about it for days. He drew pictures and everything," she says, and I can't help but smile.

The next half hour seems to fly by so quickly. Annabella tells me even more stories about Mark, him running around the garden, naked, and fighting with his brother over who gets the bread crusts. I have so many things I can use now. Annabella is so nice and so easy to talk to. I can see why Mark likes her so much.

"Megan, remember one thing." Annabella takes hold of my hand, looking directly at me. "Everything happens for a reason. You must believe in it and trust that it will work out."

"Thank you, Annabella. I think Mark has gotten lost."

"Mark normally takes Jessie for a run when he is here. I can't go as far with her as he can."

"We're back." Mark comes into the room with Jessie who flops down in front of the fire.

"Did you have a nice time with Jessie?" I enquire, looking directly into his eyes.

"We had a fantastic time! We best be off, Annabella. I need to pop by the office," he says, taking out his mobile from his pocket.

"It was great to meet you, Megan," Annabella says, smiling at me.

"And you, too. Thank you, Annabella. I hope to see you again."

We say our goodbyes and head off to the car. On our way, Mark points out a greenhouse at the side of the building, a simple little brick building with multiple glass windows. Only the frame is not glass. I can see flowers growing inside it.

"I remember spending numerous hours in there when I was younger. I would go in there to escape."

"Aww, escape from what?" I ask.

"I shall tell you at some point. I want to get you back where it is warm." I get into the car, not asking any questions. Maybe I shouldn't ask questions yet.

"Don't you be planning on using any of what Annabella said against me, Megan!"

I giggle. "Would I do such a thing?"

Chapter 10

I can't believe I am going home today. I didn't want to come down to London with Jenny, and I had tried to get out of it, but now I am so pleased that I did. These few days have been amazing. I have not only had some fun shopping with Jenny and getting the last few things for the wedding, but I met Mark. How amazing is he? I cannot quite believe I am having feelings like this, feelings I have never had before. I slowly climb out of bed, trying not to wake Mark, who is lying on his side, facing me with one of his hands under his cheek. I slowly walk along the room into the en-suite bathroom getting myself changed for the day. I will be travelling for a few hours, so I choose to wear simple blue jeans and a cream jumper with comfortable shoes. Mark has offered to take Jenny, Rich, and me to the train station. I creep back into the main room to see Mark sitting up in bed watching me with his bare chest showing.

"Are you sneaking around?" Mark enquires with a sleepy smile on his face.

"Sorry, I didn't want to wake you. You looked so peaceful." I return the smile.

"I'm still taking you to the station," he says in a stern tone. "If you still want to go home," he adds in his normal tone.

"I need to. I have appointments." I look down at the floor. He feels like I do. He doesn't want me to go. I can't look him in the eye.

"I am going to miss you, baby." Mark tips his head down so he can see my eyes. I don't want to go. I do not want to leave Mark. Nevertheless, it is just a little holiday romance. Something to tell the girls about. They will want all the juicy details that never happened. I am not breaking my rules just for a one-night stand. I can't sleep with him, not when I have such feelings, and then have to walk away from him. From us.

The journey home will be roughly four hours, from leaving the hotel here to getting home. I will be happy to sit and read on the train back. Maybe I can even listen to my music and keep my mind busy by falling in love with a new book boyfriend. At least you can't get hurt by that one.

"Megan, let's have breakfast. Let me take you to the train station. I am not ready to say bye, even though it is only for a short time," Mark states as he walks along the room in his black, tight boxers. He takes hold of my hand.

I nod and look right into his eyes. Mark leans forward, placing a kiss onto my forehead before heading into the bathroom. I walk over to the drawers and place my things together in a pile preparing to leave. I just want to get away before he kisses me. I want him to kiss me, a real kiss. I want him to tell me he does not want me to go without him, and I want him to come with me.

I suddenly feel his arms wrap around me, pulling me back against his naked chest. I freeze to the spot, unable to move, unable to breath. I don't want him to let go of me.

"Hey, baby, don't rush. You have plenty of time," he whispers into my ear as he places a little kiss onto my shoulder, so soft, gentle, and oh-so-perfect. I wish he did not do that. I so want to turn around and place my lips on his. I am not going to, though, or should I?

"You mentioned breakfast. Are you cooking, or am I?" I ask, changing the conversation.

"I'll cook, baby. It's my home, my job. You go and relax." Mark had me to stay at his place last night, and he had Connor to collect my stuff from the hotel. He stated that he had work to do and needed to be at home, but wanted me with him. I agreed to spend the night. Mark's bed is bigger than the one in the hotel, so I was willing to stay.

We spent the night in his office; I sat and read while Mark worked. Well, that's what he thought I was doing. I spent most of the time watching him. Watching every movement he made. He was in such a cheeky mood. He had me shopping online for a gift for Connor. Connor has been working for him for five years next month, and he wanted to get him something special.

In the end, we agreed on a nice silver watch. He ordered it with the engraving *Connor, thank you for the past five years. M.* A very simple, but meaningful message. He is giving Connor the week off so he can have some time to relax and be alone. Connor had been talking about wanting to take his daughter to a nice holiday resort off the East Coast.

It will do them both some good. I don't know much about him. I know he works for Mark and has a daughter, but no mention of a partner or a ring. Yes, I did check if he had a ring.

I slide out of Mark's hands, head into the kitchen, and hear his footsteps behind me. Every hair on the back of my neck stands up on end. Oh my, do not come any closer. I go around the counters and stand in the lounge part of his open plan kitchen.

"So, what are you going to cook me?" I question, keeping the distance between us.

"As you can't have some things, how about toast, sausage, and bacon? Maybe some beans?"

"No beans for me, but perfect otherwise. Thank you. Can I have a glass of water?" I ask as I sit down on the barstool near the kitchen.

"Anything for you, baby." He smiles, spinning around and reaching over to get a glass. What a view! He is still only in his tight boxers, and his bum looks amazing.

I spend the next half hour watching Mark walk around the kitchen doing breakfast, being a right little chef. I can't do anything but smile at him, seeing him so happy and so relaxed. Always smiling, Mark does not seem to stress about anything.

I reach down into my jeans pocket and pull out my mobile.

Morning Megan, what is the plan for today? Xx

Hi Jenny, I am at Mark's. He said he will take us to the station. I'll message you with the time in a bit. Xx

Sitting on the bar style chair on the other side of the kitchen island, Mark turns around with two plates of food. "Are you ready to eat?"

"I am. I'm starving," I say, sitting up straight in the chair.

"Shall we go sit outside in the sun and eat?" Mark asks as he walks to the French doors and opens them.

I stand up, taking hold of my glass of water and follow him out into the garden. There is a small glass-topped round table with two matching chairs. Mark places the food onto the table.

"Give me a minute. I'll get you a cushion. Don't sit down," Mark states as he jogs into the house. Wow! What a beautiful view Mark has to look at in his backyard.

"Here you go," Mark says as he places a cushion onto the seat.

I take a seat. "This looks amazing."

The next couple of hours seem to fly. I finish packing my belongings and how I would do it. Connor's style of packing is not mine. Mark takes a shower and does the washing up. It is so nice to see he is a tidy person and doesn't just expect someone to pick up after him.

We get into Mark's people carrier. I am sure I have not seen this car before, but it is outside when we leave. Mark places my bags into the boot as we head off to the hotel to collect Jenny and Rich. As we pull up at the front of the hotel, they are standing there waiting with their bags.

"Stay there, Megan. I'll get their bags," Mark states as he gets out of the car.

The journey to the station is so quiet that no one really says anything, and Mark points out places Rich should visit when he is next down on business. As we arrive at the station, Rich jumps out to get our bags.

"Megan, I have your stuff," Rich says as I stand at the side of the car.

Mark walks around, gently pushing me against the car. "I don't want to say goodbye. I know I have to for now, but not forever. I will text you." He leans down, placing his lips onto mine.

I finally get the kiss I have wanted all day. I feel a tear roll down my cheek as his lips remain on mine, his hand sliding behind my head, pulling me closer, and his tongue invading my very soul.

"Megan, please, don't cry," Mark begs as he takes his lips off mine, pushing my hair from my face.

"You best stay here," I tell him while looking down at the ground.

"I will do, or I'm not going to let you go. Ever." He places a little kiss onto my forehead, tightly squeezing my hand before letting go. I slowly walk away from the car to Jenny. I don't turn around. I can't turn around. I don't want to leave.

Chapter 11

It has been a week since I left Mark, but it feels so much longer than that. I feel like I have lost a part of me. He texts me all the time checking that I am okay. He calls every night after work, and we chat for hours. I miss him; I do not feel right without him around me. I want to feel his arms wrapped around me and holding me tight.

Tonight I do not have my normal phone call with Mark because he is at a charity event that he has organised. Mark told me that the event would have a lot of press coverage, so I should keep an eye out in the papers. He is a very busy man. I am surprised he has time to talk to me every night. I cannot help but think he is not getting much work done. I am proud of him, though, because he works hard. He is not a selfish person at all.

I don't know if I should feel like this. It's so weird without him here. He is miles away from me. I have not seen him in a week; I have not spent time around him. How has this man gotten under my skin so quickly and deeply? I just don't understand. The feelings I had for him while I was there are the same. I find myself checking my mobile so much, hoping it's him every time I hear it chime.

The event tonight is a charity auction, and there will be many expensive items up for bidding. Mark told me that he had hired a top DJ for after the auction. The DJ is being nice and doing it free of charge. He is the most wanted man in the world of DJ's, so Mark had been very lucky to get him. He has worked for many big companies and featured on multiple top ten songs. People who are attending the event paid a lot of money for an invite to the auction and dinner. Mark is very excited about the whole thing, and I am so proud of all that he has accomplished.

Mark plans on coming up next weekend to see me, but I don't know if I want him to. I know I have feelings for him, but I have had too much heartache in my life. I am snapped out of my thoughts by my mobile beeping, and I see that Mark has messaged me.

Hi baby, how's your night going? I just got here. The event is very busy. I am missing you, though. I wish you were here with me. Hugs and kisses for you and Bump. Xx

Hi Mark, I watched a film. Now going to have a long relaxing bath. Have a fun night.

I am shocked to hear from him this late. I am sure he said the event started at half past six. It is seven now. I get up off the sofa, feeling a twinge in my stomach. "Ouch," I mumble as I sit back down and wait for the pain to subside. Maybe this is one of the Braxton-Hicks. It can't be. It is excessively early to be feeling these kinds of things. On the other hand, can it be? I choose not to check the Internet, as it could be anything. I am six months now. It could be wind. I am just so happy I had a holiday to use up before I go on maternity leave because I don't think I could work now. I seem to have grown a lot and quickly. I had already chosen to go on leave at seven and a half months. I didn't want to push myself too far. I have been lucky that the new holiday allowance just started, so I have a full year's holiday leave to use and then the year on maternity leave that I plan to take. I cannot leave Bump as a baby. I still do not get how some people can leave their children from six weeks old.

I lie there with my hand on Bump. I know she and I are going to be okay because I am never going to let anyone hurt her. She is my world, and she is not even here yet. John is not going to hurt her like he hurt me. Jenny will help me if I ever need assistance. She will do anything for me, as I will for her. She is the only person I have told all my secrets.

I reach for my baby names book to look through the names. Some names are so common these days, and I know many people who have used most of them. Every page is full of names, but not many jump out at me. The ones I do like just don't seem right now. I think this is going to be the hardest task I ever have to do. I know people say as soon as you see the baby, you will know for sure.

Putting the book down, I slowly get back up and head over to place a film in. There is nothing better than curling up with a blanket and watching a chick flick. It will help pass the time I would normally be busy talking to Mark. We can all wish that our lives would turn out like a romantic, chick flick, fairy-tale story. Who knows? Mark might be my Prince Charming. I start to giggle as I think that.

The film finishes, and I stand up, turn everything off, lock up, and head upstairs for a long soak in the bathtub. I tend to relax while lying in the bath. Reaching the top of the stairs, I walk into the bathroom, placing the plug into the bath, letting the water start to run, and pouring a little bit of bubble bath in. The fragrance hits me. It's sweet lavender flowers and will relax me. I leave the water running, go over to my room, and grab my pyjamas and dressing gown. Walking back into the bathroom, I lay my mobile on the side with music playing from it. I climb slowly and carefully into the bath for a long, relaxing soak.

I don't know how long I have been in the bath, but I must get out. The water has gone cold, and I am all wrinkly like a shrimp. Slowly I get out of the bath, dry myself off, and dress in my warm nightwear. I walk over to my room. I am too awake now to sleep. I am going to curl up on my bed and read for a bit, just a couple of chapters and I should be asleep. Lying in bed, all warm, I can see the time. Remembering Mark's schedule for the event, I know roughly what he should be doing and where they will be. I just hope it goes really well. He told me it's the first event his sister, Mia, will be attending. She sounds like such a nice girl. She is still in college trying to further her education. She wants to own a business like Mark, or have Mark own it, but have her own fashion range. Mark says she is talented at drawing, and her designs are used in art shows. I did have a look at some of them. She is gifted, and her designs are simple and elegant, nothing that makes you wonder what she was on when she did them. She seems like someone I might get along with, and I wonder if I will ever meet his family. I am not sure I want to. I don't think having Bump will go down so well with them. His parents seem very posh.

Chapter 12

I can't believe it's three a.m. already. That "I'll just finish this chapter and then I'll go to sleep" idea is a bad one. I always end up finishing the book. I should know that by now. I read so many books. My wish list is so big. I will get to them all at some point. There is always a new book coming out that I want to read, so I get that one instead.

I sit up in the bed, looking over at my mobile. I notice I have a message.

Hi Megan, the party is all over. Going to bed now, baby. I'll ring you in the morning. X

Hope you had a good night. Talk to you tomorrow. Night Mark.

Night baby, sleep well. X

I can't help but smile; he always makes me smile real genuine smiles. I cannot remember ever smiling so much before I met Mark. The way he says "baby" makes me smile and makes butterflies start to flutter in my tummy. I need my sleep, as I have an appointment with the midwife tomorrow. It's just a checkup, so nothing really to worry about, but after the twinges I felt earlier, I am very happy to see the doctor.

I hate my alarm. It cannot be seven a.m. yet. Looking over at my alarm that is still going off, I realise it is time to get up. I must have fallen asleep without realising it, as I still have my mobile in my hand. I check it to see if Jenny has messaged me.

Morning babe, let me know how your appointment goes. Luv ya. Xx

Morning Jenny, will do. Have a good day at work. Luv ya too. Xx

I like the fact Jenny now works the same shifts every week. It's not like the old days where we never saw each other.

I am lucky. I have been on a two-week training course for work then gone on holiday, which leads me straight into my maternity leave. I don't plan to go back to work for a year. It is going to be hard financially to be off for the full year, but I want to spend as much time as I can with Bump.

Ha-ha, work is work. It's no fun now that I don't work with you. Xx

Oh, ha-ha have fun anyway, hun. Xx

I get up slowly from the bed. As my pregnancy has progressed, I am moving much slower. I take a quick shower, and once I dry myself off, I get dressed. I choose a pair of black leggings and my emerald top, and I manage to slip on a pair of black dolly shoes. I put my hair up into my favourite butterfly clip, and I apply mascara and lip-gloss. Gazing out the window, I notice that it is going to be a very sunny day so I find my sunglasses. I am so happy that it is a gorgeous day because I love the sun, and it always lifts my spirits.

I decide to set off early for my appointment. I'm not allowed to eat anything before my appointment, so I choose not to hang around the house where temptation lingers. I take a bottle of water from the fridge and grab my bag before leaving the house and locking up as I go.

I get into my car. It was a treat to me for when Bump gets here. It is a sensible five-door family car with plenty of room for the pram when I need it. I tried the pram in the car when I bought it, making sure there is plenty of room for it. I chose not to go for an oversized pram. I don't like the look of them or the one where the top is a car seat. I cannot see how that can be comfortable for the baby. I chose a lightweight, compact contemporary pram and pushchair. That way I can use it longer with her, and there will be no need to buy a new one. It can also face you when it is in pushchair mode. I am so excited to try it out once I have Bump here with me. They had it in so many pretty colours, but I went for the sensible black version of it. I bought a pink mobile for the pram, and Jenny got a pink star for the top of the cover. Jenny is spoiling her already, and she has three months to wait. It also came with a matching car seat. I have had it in the boot of my car for weeks now.

The drive to the doctor's office takes about twenty minutes. The surgery is in the next town over, and I enjoy the scenery as I drive along, the fields of greens and yellows and the cows and sheep. I love the countryside, and I think about Jenny and her horse. She loves to ride, and she is forever trying to get me to take it up. I don't mind helping her out with her horse, Topaz. He's a magnificent Irish Hunter, and he towers over me whenever I help Jenny groom him. I think she once told me he stands well over fifteen hands.

I hope to get Bump into horse riding, well, pony trekking at a young age. Then, she has the experience if she decides to do it later on.

******

Morning Mark, I'm at the doctor's now. I will message you when I'm out. Xx

I still can't believe how I have fallen into a natural routine of messaging and talking to him. It is like I have known him for years. In fact, it has only been two weeks now. I have been thinking of going down and seeing him again, but I don't know if I want to on my own. Mark and I are just friends. I have that spark though when I talk to him, think about him, and talk about him. It is just so weird, but it feels so right.

I walk into the doctor's office after finally finding a parking space. A huge reception desk sits in the cream area as you walk in. Then you have to sit in the green area and later go to the room down a different colour corridor. It is a great idea, and so easy to find your way around the building. They have many children's toys in the green area to keep the kids entertained while waiting for the nurse to call your name.

"Good morning, Miss. Can I take your name and date of birth," the blonde haired receptionist asks.

"Morning, I'm Megan Madden, sixth of May, eighty-nine," I reply.

"That's great. Your appointment is with Midwife Lee. Please go and have a seat over there, and I'll call you when she's ready for you."

"Thank you."

I walk over to the green area and have a seat near the window. They have loads of magazines on the table, so I pick one up, and it has the top thirty baby names in it. I sit there reading them, and still not one of them jumps out at me.

"Miss Madden, room three on the green corridor," the receptionist says over the public address system.

I place the magazine back down and head to the room. Knocking on the door, I enter.

"Megan, how are you doing today?" Midwife Lee asks me.

Midwife Lee is such a bubbly natured woman; she has brown hair that is always up in a bun. She has been looking after me since I found out I was expecting Bump.

"I'm very well, thanks. How are you?" I reply.

"Great, Megan. How is this little lady doing?"

"She's fine. I did have a really bad, painful twinge last night."

"Where was the twinge?"

"Just along here." I indicate the area with an index finger.

"Sounds like a Braxton-Hicks. Let's get your observations done first, Megan."

The next fifteen minutes whip by as she takes my blood pressure, pulse, and draws several small vials of my blood. The most important thing is that I get to hear Bump's heartbeat again. It's so strong that it sounds like a train. It is so amazing hearing her. I just cannot wait to meet her.

"Megan, everything is fine. She is growing well. Not long until she is here. Book an appointment for three weeks."

"Thank you," I reply before walking out of the room.

******

While getting into my car, I check my mobile. Mark has messaged me.

I'm awake baby. Let me know when you are out and I will call you. Xx

I fire back a response.

I'm out.

I place my bag and jacket onto the passenger seat and turn on the radio just as my mobile starts to ring.

"Hi, baby."

"Hi, how are you?" I reply.

"I'm still sleepy, but I need to get up. I have a pile of paperwork waiting for me. How did it go?"

"Everything is fine."

"I miss you, Megan. There are some pictures posted on the Internet of the function last night, but I haven't had the time to look yet. I need a shower before anything else, and then I'll get the professional shots uploaded."

"Sounds like you have a busy day planned. I'm going to head into town and get some shopping done and then I'll head home."

"Sounds like you are going to be busy as well. I'll let you get on. Let me know when you are home, baby."

"Will do. Bye."

"Bye, baby."

I love how he says that. He melts me. I miss the sound of his voice already, and it has only been seconds.

Chapter 13

I do not like food shopping during the day; it is so busy. It must be school break, as there are many children about. Luckily, I just need the basics, so it will not take me long to get my shopping complete. I park my car and head inside the shop, collecting a trolley on my way. I walk through the automatic double doors and head straight into the lift up to the clothing and film area.

Looking around, I pick up a couple of new films that I want to see. Heading to the clothing next, of course, I look at the baby section. I find a cream dress with a little butterfly design on it.

Heading back down, I collect the few grocery bits that I need, milk and some fruit, and look around to see if anything else jumps out at me to eat. Since I have hit the six months' pregnancy mark, I have not actually wanted to eat anything, so the looking around might spark something.

"Megan." I turn around to see Jenny walking towards me.

"Hey, I thought you were at work," I say.

"Yeah, I am, but I had to come and collect a couple of things for work. How did it go?"

"Very well, everything is fine."

"Oh, that is fantastic. I best get on. I'll text you later."

"Bye, hun."

"Bye, Megan," she says as she hugs me. "Bye, Bump. Take care of Mummy." She rubs my belly.

I watch Jenny walk down towards the checkout. I decide to follow her down as well since nothing is jumping out at me. On the way down, I collect some more roast chicken crisps for Bump. I have such a craving for them. I have a lot in the cupboard at home, but if that is all I am really going to fancy, I may as well have some more in the house.

I head through the self-serve checkouts, saving some time by doing it myself. I head back out to my car, get inside, and place the shopping bag onto the floor of the passenger seat.

******

The drive home is quiet. With everyone at work now, there is less traffic to get through. Placing my shopping away, I decide to go and have a look at the photos Mark told me about.

Home from shopping. Just going to look at the photos.

Enjoy baby. Xx

Sitting down on the sofa, I place my laptop onto my knee while turning it on. I press *Play* on my music system and log onto the Internet, searching for the event pictures from last night.

I agree with what Mark had said. The colour theme looks good and very stylish. The tables are elegant and tidy, even though the cutlery is set for a posh dinner. There are balloons and nametags written in beautiful calligraphy, all with the same black and white colour theme, and dark purple little crystals scattered on the tables.

I continue looking through the photos. Many famous people attended, wearing pretty dresses, shoes, and accessories. They all look so fantastic. There are women showing off their handsome men and their to-die-for figures with not a hair out of place. I do wonder how many of the pictures have been airbrushed. You can't always look that good.

I notice a picture of a woman, and I am sure I have seen her somewhere before. But where? She is not famous. Maybe she just reminds me of someone I know.

Finally, I see the pictures of Mark. He looks so smart in his suit. Looking through all the photos, I can tell he has had his photo taken with most of the guests. I guess he would have to. He takes a good photograph, though. I love the white background with black and silver stars they have used for some of the photos.

The official photos are up, baby. Xx

Thank you Mark, I'll go have a look on the site. Xx

I close the search down and type in the website address to see the official photos. I surf the site while reading the information that has just been added to it.

Thank you so much to all who attended the Hope Event. We are happy to announce we raised over 3 million pounds last night for the Bright Hope Foundation.

We auctioned off several items that were kindly donated by so many people. Thank you to all the fantastic bands and singers who tirelessly spared their time for the event.

Oh, wow! I cannot believe how much money they raised last night. I am glad they were able to raise the money to support this foundation. Mark has placed a lot of time and effort into planning the event. Scrolling down the page, I see more pictures of the venue. Even the outside of the venue looks amazing.

I click on *Gallery* to see loads of pictures, professionally done. I can tell the previous ones are amateur photographers. These are full-on airbrushed pictures.

There is that woman again, and I know now she is from the restaurant Mark took me to. She is the server who upset me. Under the photo, it reads *Miss Karen Walker*. I remember the name Karen from the restaurant. She has her blonde, wavy hair down with plenty of makeup around her blue eyes, which creates a very smoky look to them. I continue looking through the photos and find a few more of Karen with Mark, their positioning questionable. I decide to have a look on a search engine to see if I can find more about her. So many pages come up about her. One catches my eye the most.

Is Karen Walker going to be the future Mrs. Reed?

Karen Walker has been spotted hanging around Mark Reed, the owner of Reed Enterprises.

Karen Walker has been seen holding hands with Mr. Reed on many occasions.

My eyes start watering. I cannot believe he is seeing her. The article was two days before I met him. There are pictures of him kissing her. I am astonished. My world is crumbling around me. I am losing the man I thought I could be with forever. Taking a deep breath, I look at the most recent article that has been posted only hours ago.

Is Mark Reed still seeing Karen Walker?

Unable to see through the tears, I place the laptop down onto the floor and lie down and cry my eyes out. Why? I knew it was too good to be true. I knew I should have never seen him again after the bar. I knew it. I knew it. I always say I prefer to take things slowly. I did and look what happened. He is already taken. *Why?*

Chapter 14

I look up to see it is now dark. I must have fallen asleep crying. I hear my mobile going off.

Sitting up, I look at it to see it's Mark. I press *Ignore*. I do not want to hear from him. Not now, not ever.

Did you like the pictures? Xx

Are you okay, Megan? Xx

Megan? Please answer me. Xx

Hi hun, are you okay? Mark rang me at work to check if you are okay. I'll be over after work. Xx

Megan? You are really worrying me. Xx

I place my mobile back down. I can't read any more messages. There are twenty-seven texts, all except one from him, and eighteen missed calls. Has he not gotten the picture?

I leave it a little bit before choosing to reply to them. I don't want Jenny worried.

Mark, I am fine. Leave me alone.

I am fine, Jenny. Mark is seeing someone. I am heartbroken. Xx

I leave my mobile there, go upstairs, and run myself a bath to get away from it all. Jenny has a key, so she will just let herself in. I climb into the bath full of bubbles, and lie there thinking. Why did he not say he was seeing her? Why did he hide it? Why did he take me for a meal where she would be? Are all men the same?

"Megannnnn!" I hear Jenny bellow in the house.

"Jenny, I am in the bath," I answer in a calm way.

"Okay, honey, I'll make us a cuppa."

I slowly climb out of the bath, dry myself, and slip into my pink polka dot pyjamas. While walking along the landing, I shrug into my white dressing gown. Before descending the staircase to join Jenny, I see she is sitting in the kitchen on the black barstools at the breakfast bar with two cups of tea.

"Jenny, why?" I question.

"Hun, I don't know why he has done it. What did you find out?"

"He told me to check the photos from the Hope Event from last night. There were pictures of that woman I told you about at the restaurant, the blonde one. I searched her name and found articles about him possibly seeing her, along with pictures of them kissing."

I grab my mobile and log on to the event photos, showing her the pictures. They both stand side-by-side, her hand on his bum, him giggling at her, staring at her from afar. I look even further through the photos this time and find one of him giving her a kiss on the cheek. Why? Why did he ask me to look at them? Was this his way of telling me nothing is going to happen?

"Oh, no!" Jenny exclaims.

"I don't know what to do, Jenny."

"Have you spoken to him?" Jenny enquires.

"No, I don't want to. I don't know what to say to him."

"Let's have an early time, face mask, DVD, ice cream. Forget about him," Jenny suggests.

I just nod, unable to speak for the tears rolling down my face. I numbly walk through to the lounge and take a seat onto the sofa while Jenny moves around and gets the stuff together. I do not know what I would do without Jenny in my life.

Megan, what's going on? Xx

Talk to me. Xx

Megan, what has happened? Xx

"Right, which film?" Jenny asks.

"Whichever you want," I answer, holding back the tears.

The rest of the night Jenny spends with me, trying to keep me laughing. We do face masks and paint each other's fingernails. We just have a girlie night. I end up having to turn off my mobile, as Mark is not giving up. Jenny stands up and leaves the room just after her mobile goes off. It is Rich. Sitting there being quiet, all I can hear is Jenny's raised voice.

"No, listen to me. You hurt my friend. You lied!"

Oh, no, it is Mark she is talking to. Isn't it? I suddenly jump from the sofa, heading through to the kitchen and waving my hand to get Jenny's attention. She stops and looks at me.

"Leave her alone!" she states before hanging up.

"Was that Mark?" I question.

"Yes, sorry."

"It's okay. It's late. I am going to bed," I tell her, not wanting to talk about him.

"I'll be up soon."

"You don't have to stay. Rich needs to see you."

"Are you sure you will be okay if I leave?"

"Yes, Jenny. Go see Rich. I'll text you tomorrow." I want to be alone. I want to be able to cry.

Jenny says her goodbyes and leaves, shutting off everything and locking up. I head up the stairs and climb into bed. I have to check my messages to see if there are any from family or friends.

Yet, another thirteen messages from Mark, all asking if I am okay and why I am not talking. There's even a voicemail, too. I have to listen to it.

Megan, baby, I don't know what I have done wrong. Please, talk to me. I can't imagine my life without you.

I send him one last message, hoping that he will leave me alone.

Goodnight.

Once I curl up in bed, tears come back in full force. I am so happy Jenny left me. I am so hurt. I am never going to be happy. I will never have my happily ever after.

Chapter 15

I slowly open my eyes and look around. The sun is blaring through my windows. I grab the duvet to cover my face. My head is banging from all the crying. I can't take anything for it, though. I lie under the covers with my hand on Bump. I think to myself, *No one is going to hurt us*. I mean it.

Hearing my mobile go off, I reach out for it and pull it from under the cover.

Hi Megan, how are you? Do you want me to come over? Xx

Hi Jenny, I'll be fine. You spend the day with Rich. Xx

I check through the rest of my messages, mostly notifications and emails, only a couple from Mark, though.

Goodnight princess, sweet dreams. I'll ring you tomorrow. Xx

I suddenly can no longer see through the tears coming down. I should have followed my gut instincts and cut all ties with him when I left. I should have known something was going on with him and that woman from the restaurant.

I decide to get up, have a hot shower, and start today without Mark. I don't need a man. I don't need to be happy. I have Bump, and that is all I need. Just as I am about to get into the shower, I hear a knock on the door. I slowly walk down the stairs to answer it.

Opening the door, there he is. Mark. I stand there with the door open, unable to move, just looking at him.

"Megan." He waits for an answer. "Megan, are you okay?"

I take a deep breath. I can do this. "Mark, why are you here?"

"I needed to see you, to see what happened," Mark states with worry in his voice.

"You mean to check I was not going to go to the press about you kissing me while being with that Karen woman?" I reply, making sure he knows I am annoyed with him.

"Who is Karen?"

"Karen Walker, the lady from the restaurant, and your event."

"That's nothing," He brushes it off as if he truly meant it.

"Nothing?" I scream at him.

"Yes, nothing. Come on. Let me in. We can sit and talk."

I storm away from the door and into the lounge, sitting down on the single seat on the other side of the room. I do not want him near me. Mark sits on the edge of the sofa as close to me as he can get.

"Megan, Karen and I do have history."

"And..." I sit there with my hands on my hips.

"And." Taking a deep breath, he says, "We did sleep together years ago. I gave her the job because I couldn't be with her. There is no spark. I felt bad."

"Why was she at the event?"

"She asked before I met you if she could come with me."

"You never thought to tell me about it?" I ask.

"No," he retorts.

"When did you two split up?"

"Years ago, way before I met you. We just met up every so often for adult time," he whispers while hanging his head.

"What?"

"Years ago before we met in the pub," he tells me again.

Tears pour from my eyes. Why is this happening to me?

Suddenly, I feel Mark's arm around me. "Shh, I should have told you."

"When did you last sleep with her?" I question because I need to know.

"The night before we met," Mark replies.

I take a deep breath. "Mark, just go. I don't want to see you. You need to go and find yourself a lovely woman."

"No, Megan, I want you. I have since the first time I saw you."

I remain quiet, not saying a word.

"Please come away with me. We can talk. Spend time together. Jenny and Rich can come, too," he says in a panicked voice. "My grandma left me this cabin. It's not far from here."

I sit there not able to look at him while I play with the ring Jenny gave me as a Maid of Honour gift.

"Megan, please," he pleads with me.

Chapter 16

"Ouch!" I yell, grabbing ahold of my stomach.

"Megan, what's wrong? Is it the baby?"

"Go!" I reply in a stern voice.

"Megan, no, what's wrong?"

"Nothing." Ouch, this pain is worse than the one before.

"Megan."

"Please, leave me. I need to relax, not get stressed." I take a deep breath.

"Lie on the sofa, Megan, please."

I do as he asks me just to save arguing.

"Goodbye, Mark. I will be fine now." I can't believe how hurt I feel. We are not even a real couple.

Mark stands up, walking out of the room and saying nothing. Next minute I hear him talking.

"Listen. You need to get to Megan's. Something is wrong. It's the baby." Mark leaves the room. I can hear his voice, and he is talking to someone. No idea who or why.

Mark walks back into the room, going onto his knees at the side of the sofa.

"Who were you on the mobile to?"

"Jenny. She is on her way."

"I don't need anyone; it is just a Braxton-Hicks." The pain is slowly easing. Why do I feel safe with Mark here? I slowly sit up to go get a drink.

"Where do you think you're going?"

"To get a drink," I state.

"I'll get it for you. What would you like?"

"Water, please. Glasses are in the third cupboard along from the sink on the right."

"The water is in the tap." Mark starts laughing. "I'm sure I'll manage, baby."

I remain there, listening to the clinking of the glass, water running, and hearing the switch on the kettle go. Mark reappears, kneeling down beside the sofa. "Here you go."

Slowly sitting up, I take a little sip. Thankfully, the pain in my stomach has subsided. I hear Jenny entering the house.

"Megan, are you all right?" she asks.

"I'm fine. It was nothing," I tell her.

Rich then walks into the room and heads straight to Mark, grabbing his shirt collar, pulling him up and shoving him against the nearest wall.

"You idiot. Why did you do that to her?" Rich screams. Mark stands there not saying a thing.

"Let him go, Rich!" I yell. Rich lets go of Mark's shirt, standing right in front of him with no space between them.

"I hope you got what I meant," Rich says in an angry voice before walking away from Mark, and then he storms into the kitchen.

"Jenny, you stay here. I am off to talk to Rich," I state, leaving Mark with her. I follow Rich into the kitchen, walk towards him, and place my hand on his arm. "Rich, what happened back there? I can look after myself."

"I know you can, but I can't have him hurt you," Rich turns around, taking my hand.

"I'm fine. Take Jenny home. Have a nice day together."

"No." Rich leans towards me and places a kiss onto my lips. I pull straight away.

"Why did you do that?" I question in an angry voice.

"Sorry." Rich runs past me.

Did that just happen? Why would he kiss me? I have only known him through Jenny. I have never spent any time alone with him.

"Jenny, I'll meet you at the car," Rich says in a calm manner.

Jenny walks in behind me. "What happened? Has he calmed down?"

I just stand there, not moving.

"Megan," Jenny says in a raised voice.

"Maybe, I don't know. You need to go and talk to him," I say in a shaky voice.

"Are you sure you will be okay?" she asks with concern in her voice.

"Yeah, Mark is leaving now."

"Mark's been telling me about the cabin. I think you and he should go."

"What?"

"Mark explained everything to me. You like him. Now, go and spend time with him."

"I don't want to," I say, standing my ground.

"Megan, you only live once, even if it is just a couple of days away from here."

"Rich kissed me," I said.

"What?" Jenny exclaimed.

"Yeah, exactly. All I was doing was telling him not to do that!"

Jenny stands there in stunned silence.

"Jenny, you need to go talk to him. I don't have any interest in him."

"I know, Megan. I'll text you later."

L Chapman

Chapter 17

I watch Jenny leave the room, with her head down, storming out the front door and running up to the car. I don't know what to do. Jenny needs me. I walk out of the kitchen into the lounge to see Mark sitting on the edge of the sofa, looking down at the floor.

"You can leave now," I tell him.

"Megan, I am not leaving. I'm staying. We need to talk."

I continue to stand there. "Go on then."

"Please, sit down, baby."

I sit down on the sofa next to him, needing to rest. I just want to be held. I am so close to tears.

"Megan, I met Karen at a friend's birthday party. We got drunk and ended up in bed. She continued to call me all the time. She would come around a lot. We got along well and would have a laugh, but I had no feelings for her. Yes, I have slept with her a lot. She was just a fuck buddy. That's all she ever was. I told her I had no feelings for her at all and just wanted to remain friends. I felt so bad about it that I gave her a job, so she could look after herself. I promised her that we would remain friends."

"Okay," I say, taking a deep breath.

"Now, baby, please let me take you away to the cabin."

"No, I don't want you to be around me. Just go to your stupid cabin!" I yell.

"Baby," Mark says calmly.

"Are you not listening to me?"

Mark looks directly at me.

"Get out!" I shout.

I cover my face as the tears start to fall. Why did he not tell me about her? I have so many questions to ask, but I cannot ask him. I don't want to know the answers. I just can't. I feel Mark move closer to me, his arms wrapping around me, pulling me closer to him.

"Shh…Shh… it's okay. I am not going anywhere." He smells like he normally does; he is wearing the same aftershave. He looks tired. I don't think he slept last night, yet he has managed to have a shave at some point.

I feel so safe in his arms. His comforting words work. Why though? Why? His voice is so calming.

"Why didn't you fight Rich off?" I ask while trying to calm myself down.

"I deserve to be hurt. I hurt you."

"Why did you not tell me she was going to be there, knowing I was going to see the event photos?"

"I didn't think. I didn't notice how bad they look."

"Yeah, her hand is on your backside in most of the photos," I say sarcastically.

"I know. I should have thought, Megan."

"I need time. I need to get dressed. Please, feel free to leave."

"I am not going," Mark informs me.

"I'm scared. I don't want to get hurt again. Please, leave," I beg.

"I'll tell you everything," he says with a note of promise in his voice.

"Okay, I'll be back," I state, standing up and walking upstairs. I need to know everything.

It seems like it is John all over again, He cheated, lied, and hurt me. I have only just moved on from it all. He made me feel so used and worthless. No real man would ever do that if he truly had feelings for the other person. I was just a sex toy to John, never anything else. I don't think I would have ever become anything else to him. I deserve better. I thought Mark was better, but maybe I was wrong.

I need to get dressed; I look like a mess. I feel like a mess. I decide against a shower because I don't want him alone down there. Going into the bathroom, I give myself a quick freshening up. After placing on some black leggings and a grey jumper, I throw a brush through my hair. It is best I do not wear any makeup. I don't want it running down my face. It would be a pointless waste of my time. I run downstairs to see that Mark has not moved.

"Drink?" I question.

Mark looks up at me and nods. I spin on my toe and head into the kitchen. Walking in, I flick the switch on the kettle, head over to the fridge, and grab a plastic carton of milk. Walking back to the kettle, I suddenly go dizzy. Maybe I should have eaten earlier.

Chapter 18

Opening my eyes, I look around. I am lying on a bed. Gloves and aprons are at the right of me, and there is a curtain all around me. Why am I here? I know it is the hospital. I know I felt dizzy.

"Megan, you're awake," Mark states as he walks through the end curtain.

"Why am I here?" I question.

"You collapsed."

"Is Bump okay?" I ask, placing my hand on my belly.

"The doctors say so. They are going to do a scan to check, though."

"Thank you," I say to Mark, keeping my hand on Bump. She must be okay. I can't lose her. She is my world. She is the only person who can't hurt me.

"What for? Causing you to collapse?"

"Don't blame yourself. I hadn't eaten." A tear rolls down my face; he is partly to blame. If he hadn't lied or upset me, I would have eaten. I want Mark to go away and never come back, but I don't want to be alone.

"I'll go find the doctor," Mark says.

"Can you get me a drink, please?" I ask him.

Mark walks closer to the bed, planting a little butterfly kiss onto my head. "I'll see what I can do."

More tears go rolling down my face. Why?

I lie there, listening to the sounds and rubbing Bump. With tears rolling down my face, I need everyone to hurry up. I need to know that Bump is okay. It is nice that Mark has stayed with me. He really does care about me. I feel safe with him. Did I overreact to the issue with Karen?

"Miss Madden, nice to see you're awake. I'm Dr. Smith."

"Please call me Megan."

Dr. Smith has blond hair that looks bleached and warm hazel eyes.

"How are you feeling?" he questions.

Blushing, I tell him, "Silly."

"Why?"

"I should have eaten, and then I wouldn't be here."

"Very true, and the past couple of days' stress has not helped you either."

"Sorry, men just cause stress normally."

The doctor stands there tittering. "My wife says the same thing. Now, that you are awake, I want to scan the baby and check that all is okay. Nurse Ward will be here soon with the machine."

"Thank you."

"Your boyfriend has just gone to the café to get you a drink."

"He is just a friend," I quickly say.

"He's been very worried about you."

"Really?" I question.

"Yes, Megan."

The curtain opens and in comes Mark and a nurse with the scanning machine. "Hi, Miss Madden."

"Hi, please call me Megan." Mark places the snacks onto the chair behind my head.

"You know what's going to happen, Megan?" Dr. Smith questions.

"I do. This is going to be cold. Very cold," I joke.

"Do you want Mark to leave?" Dr. Smith questions.

"He can stay if he wants."

"I'll stay. I'm not going anywhere," Mark states.

I smile, letting him take hold of my hand. Nurse Ward slides my jumper up, revealing Bump. I feel my eyes start filling up. What if something has happened to Bump? Mark's grip gets tighter.

Dr. Smith places a little gel onto my belly. It is so cold. I can feel my heart beating through my chest, and I begin to think, *What if something has happened to her?* I look away, facing Mark's stomach.

"There she is. All looks fine," Dr. Smith says, and I suddenly turn to face the monitor while tears roll down my checks.

"Are you sure?" Mark asks.

"Yes, all looks fine. I'm still keeping you overnight, though, Megan, to keep an eye on you."

"Wow, it's so amazing," Mark states.

"Is this the first scan you have seen, Mark?" Nurse Ward questions.

"Yes, it is," he answers.

I lie there and look at the monitor, glued to how she looks. She is fine. Dr. Smith points out everything on the scan to Mark, who continues to hold onto my hand. His grip has loosened a little bit.

"You will be transferred to a room shortly, Megan. Please press the bell if you need anything," Nurse Ward informs me.

"Thank you." I turn to face Mark, who is standing in amazement. "Are you okay, Mark?" I ask him.

"Yes, just amazed. Oh, I got you drinks and some food."

"Thank you. You can go whenever you want. Thank you for staying."

"Megan, I am not leaving. We will work through this. Here." Mark passes me a bag with a bottle of water, a sandwich, and some roast chicken crisps. He knows me well. I am so happy to have normal food. I know how bad hospital meals can be, and it is nice to have semi-healthy food. I smile, finally having something to eat. I start to immediately feel better. Food was the key. Mark takes a seat in the chair, keeping an eye on me.

"Megan, we are ready to transfer you to the other ward. Please, relax. Get away for a few days," Dr. Smith informs me.

"I will relax."

"We will go to the cabin, Megan," Mark says.

"We'll see," I state in a firm voice.

******

I am so happy it is morning, and I can finally go home. Hospitals are not my idea of fun. With too much noise and flicking lights all night long, I have not had much sleep. I just want to go home and sleep the day away. Mark stayed the night in the chair. He didn't want to leave me at all. He was very nice and informed Jenny I was in hospital. She has not messaged me, though. That is the first thing I am going to do when I get out of here.

Chapter 19

Hi Jenny, are you okay? Xx

Are you out of hospital? Xx

Yes, I am just. What is wrong? Xx

I am just tired, hunny. Rich and I spent all night arguing. Xx

It's all my fault. I am sorry, hun. Xx

NO, it is not your fault. Rich did it all himself. All is fine now. Xx

Are you sure? Xx

I am very sure. I love him. Xx

I will stop worrying now. Xx

Are you going to the cabin with Mark? Will do you a world of good. Xx

I am thinking about it. Xx

GO live a little before Bump comes. Xx

I think I am going to live some more. I will ring you in a bit. Xx

Something is not right. I need to talk to Jenny and find out really what is going on. That was not much of an answer. On the plus side, Mark has been fantastic. I can't fault him. He has been here when I needed him. I do need to keep my guard up, though. I think I am going to go to the cabin, even for a full day. It will be nice to get away.

"Baby, are you okay?" Mark asks.

"Yeah, I am fine, just thinking."

"Penny for your thoughts?" he bargains.

"My thoughts are not worth a penny."

"I bet they are."

"Tell me about the cabin."

I sit there in the passenger side of the car, letting Mark drive us back to my house. Mark continues to tell me about the cabin. His grandma gave it to him as a getaway place. It's only twelve miles away from where I live. Sounds perfect to me.

"I'll go."

"You will?" Mark questions.

"Yes, you said you wanted to take me away to the cabin for a while. I will go, but only if you listen to me. When I say I want to come home, you take me home."

"Deal."

"Right, I'll get my things ready. I need to call Jenny. When do you want to leave?"

"Whenever you're ready. We can go tonight or tomorrow."

"Okay, let's try for this afternoon then."

Pulling up into the driveway of my house, I head to the door, letting Mark open it as he still has my keys from locking up when I was rushed to the hospital. I bend down, picking up the post and taking it into the kitchen. I leave my mobile on the side with the charge on. I grab the hands-free home phone and ring Jenny. "Hi, Jenny, how are you?"

"I am okay, Megan."

"Be honest. You don't sound okay."

"It's Rich. He wants a break."

"What?"

"He says he is all confused and wants a break. He has gone away for a few days."

"Aww, I'll come and stay with you."

"No, I need to be alone. I need to get on with my life without him."

"Are you sure?"

"Yes, Megan, I love you. I don't blame you. He has been off for a while. He needs to get his head straight. Are you going away with

Mark?"

"I love you, too, hun. Yeah, I am. You are more than welcome to come with us."

"I'll pass."

"I am just a call away."

"I'm off to work now. See ya."

"Bye, hun."

I walk up the stairs to my room, so I can pack a few things for the trip. I grab my little suitcase from the wardrobe and collect clothes, toiletries, and shoes. All sorted.

Chapter 20

I can't remember half of the journey to the cabin because I must have dozed off. I remember many roads, which had fields on both sides, and a lot of farm animals and crops. In the background of the fields, there were hills covered with trees. They looked spectacular. The roads were quiet due to it being a weekday.

"We are here. Just up this drive," Mark states.

"Okay." I can't help but smile.

Mark is loads more awake and chatty now that he has had that little sleep. He was only out for about three hours, but it has done him a world of good. He has made sure we have everything. We popped to the shops on the way out of town, picking up all the basics: milk, bread, sugar, and, of course, plenty of roast chicken crisps. He knows how to keep Bump happy.

The driveway is gravel, very up and down, with either side of the drive full of trees, and looking so pretty with leaves on them. They look so tall. My imagination is going to start running wild if we are close to these trees. How many horror films have I seen where the killer hides in the woods?

Wow! Is that the cabin? It is a stunning, wooden building. There is a little picket fence going around what must be the cabin's grounds with a small patch of grass in front of it. We park to the side of the cabin.

"So, this is my hideaway."

"It's pretty," I say with complete honesty.

"It is lovely. I can't wait to show you around," Mark says proudly.

"Me either."

Mark is always a gentleman, opening the car door for me and offering his hand out for me to use to get out of the car if I wish. I decline it as always. Getting out of the car, I walk to get my things out of the back of the car.

"No, let's go inside. I will show you around then I will come and get the bags. You need to relax, remember?"

I just shake my head and walk towards the picket fence. I stop once I reach the fence and look around to see there are no trees on the other side of the building either, only a lot of dirt paths. I wonder if that means there are more cabins around or some interesting walks. Mark passes me the key to the cabin, and I walk towards the door, over the grass that looks freshly cut. Even the door is wooden. The building looks like trees cut in half, placed sideways and then on top of each other. There are three rosebushes to the side of the door, two pink and one white. They look so pretty.

"For you." Mark bends down, picking up a couple roses and handing them to me.

"Thank you."

I open the door. It looks like the inside of all the trees. It has amazing décor with a natural look while using an open floor plan. There are sofas to one side of the room and a fireplace with some logs to the side of it. It must be a real fire. On the other side of the room, there is a kitchen, all units wooden, and the appliances are all silver. There is a dining room table to the side with a huge amount of spare space in the middle of the room. I walk farther inside, noting there are steps at the back of the room, and they look like they are half trees as well.

"Are they safe?" I question, pointing at the steps.

"Yes, they are. You can't tell as yet, but they are all attached to each other and to the wall and frame. Don't worry."

I walk over towards them to see that he is right. I slowly stand on them, unsure if they are safe. I climb the stairs the quickest I have ever done in my life. I cannot believe it. The décor up here is the same, but with all wooden doors hiding the different rooms. I stand there, counting six different doors.

"What are behind all the doors?" I ask.

"Bedrooms, they all have en-suites."

"Wow! That's amazing. Huge house parties here then." I giggle. I check out all the rooms. The décor continues. There are different pictures on the walls, different coloured bedding, and huge windows that highlight the astonishing view of the hills, or they could be mountains in the background. I see what could be a hot tub near the picket fence section at the back. From each window, I see bits that I could not tell you what they are, but I will find out.

Mark leaves me looking around and goes to bring in our bags. I stay upstairs, knowing I will need to unpack before I head back downstairs. I still cannot believe I have been convinced into coming here alone with Mark. I trust him. I should be safe, but as a precaution, I am going to keep my mobile on me at all times.

Hi Jenny, we are here. It is amazing. How are you?

Mark appears with my suitcase. "Which room would you like to stay in?"

"Any of them will be perfect," I reply.

"How about this one?" Mark suggests.

"Can do, the view is magnificent from this one."

Mark smiles, places my bag onto the bed, and leaves me to unpack.

Chapter 21

I didn't hear back from Jenny last night. I am going to ring her before I go downstairs. Mark and I slept in different rooms last night. I did not want to be alone, but he did say goodnight to me on the landing and went to a different room. I have no choice but to sleep alone. I did not sleep very well, different bed, different place, alone with Mark. Bump was active most of the night, kicking me. I love her kicking; it reassures me that she is safe. It is nine in the morning, and I cannot hear Mark moving around. I am going to sneak downstairs to talk to Jenny, and I do not want to wake him.

Sitting on the black sofa in the open plan room, I ring Jenny. "Morning, Jenny."

"Morning, sorry I didn't answer last night. Rich was here when I came home."

"And, what happened?"

"Well, let's say I got my weekly exercise lesson."

"Ha-ha, you two are sorted then?" I can't believe how quickly they get over their argument. No one would get over things that quickly, or would they? They must truly be in love.

"Oh, indeed. We are holiday hunting tonight. Well, honeymoon shopping."

"Make sure it's somewhere hot," I tell her.

"Oh, I intend to. So, tell me about the cabin," Jenny enquires.

We spend the next half hour talking about the cabin, Mark, and Rich, while having a giggle as we always do and singing away when a good song comes on at Jenny's side. I have not played any music in here. I don't want Mark waking up.

Suddenly, I hear a noise. Upon turning around, I see Mark. He is standing there in black boxers, tight around his manhood. I can't do anything but look down at it. "You made me jump out of my skin," I state with embarrassment. He looks delicious. His bare chest shows his slight six-pack that's not too overworked. I notice a mark on his side, but I cannot quite see what it is.

"Sorry, I didn't want to disturb you."

"It's okay."

Jenny and I say our goodbyes. I turn around to see Mark in the kitchen, still in the same attire. I wander over to the kitchen to join him.

"I'm cooking breakfast. Please, have a seat."

"What are we having?"

"I'll cook breakfast without eggs for you, and I will do toast. I want to take you out for a nice, relaxing walk today and show you around here. If you are not up for it, though, we can go in the car or relax here."

"I can walk."

The smell of breakfast fills the room. It smells so nice. I do not remember anything I ate yesterday. I was so relieved that Bump was okay that I could have eaten anything, and it would not have bothered me. I love food, though. I am a food person. I can't stop smiling, watching Mark buzz around the kitchen, getting plates and glasses, while still keeping an eye on the food on the grill. It is so nice to see him cooking it as healthy as he can.

"Can I help you out, Mark?" I enquire.

"No, just relax and look pretty."

I shake my head, laying my head down. Why does he say that? I am not pretty. I am normal. I live in the real world where people are a normal size. I never consider myself as pretty. Too many years of put-downs. I can't wait to have breakfast. I am so hungry. The wait is killing me.

Mark places our breakfast and drinks onto the table. Oh my, it is so lovely. He is such a good cook. We sit there chatting, talking about the times he comes here. He only comes here to escape the stress. I am the only person he has ever had to stay here. Connor comes over to work with him or brings paperwork over for him to sign.

"Mark?" He looks up at me, smiling. "What is that on your side?"

"Oh, this," he says, turning around and lifting his arm so I can see.

"It's a Chinese tattoo. It means believe. I got it last week."

"It is pretty. Did it hurt?"

"No, it didn't hurt. I'm made of tough stuff." Mark winks. "Annabella told me when I finally believed things would get better, it would happen. So, I did, and you came into my life. I then got this tattoo."

"Wow, Annabella is one amazing lady. I am so honoured that you let me meet her."

Mark sits there, talking about Annabella and how she asks about me all the time. She has been buying Bump little booties. I am so lucky to have met her. The things she said have affected me and helped me tremendously, and I know she wants Mark to be happy. I want Mark to be happy.

"There are great places to climb, walk, and see around here. It is pure heaven to me," he proudly declares.

"It looks like heaven," I say, agreeing.

"Shall we head out?"

Mark runs upstairs and appears five minutes later in dark jeans and a tight, black T-shirt. Grabbing my jacket, we head out the door, walking side-by-side down one of the dirt paths. The sun is shining with no wind at all. I can see the sun shining through the trees as we leisurely walk down one of the paths surrounded by trees. It's such an amazing view, somewhere you would only see on the television. I love it. As we get to the end of the path, Mark changes directions and I follow him. We head upwards, climbing over a few rocks to a small amount of water with a waterfall falling from the rocks above us.

"This is my favourite place. There is an incredible place to sit up there, where you can watch everything that is going on around you." Mark points over towards some high rocks.

I follow Mark up some more steps onto the spot where he pointed. Taking a seat on the rocks, I can see why he said this is his favourite place because you can see the top of the waterfall and the colours of it as it falls.

He points out everything around. "Over there are some fields with different animals that graze. It's wonderful to watch the baby animals once they are born."

It is amazing watching everything around me. I am in my element, and this is my kind of place, so relaxing. We spend the rest of the day there. I wonder why Mark brought a picnic up here. He told me that once Bump is here, he is going to bring me back and take me around the waterfall. There is a path under the falls to walk. He did not want me to risk sliding in my current condition. How thoughtful.

We seem to spend hours just sitting up here, listening to the waterfall, and looking around. Talking, he finally tells me everything that happened with Karen. She did the fake pregnancy line on him to try to get him to stay with her. That is why there are so many pictures of them together. He did the honourable thing and went along, believing she was telling the truth and fully supporting her. He found out the truth when she went drinking with some friends and drunk texted him, telling him she was not pregnant. It was all a lie. She then thanked him for the new car. As he talks, I feel myself get more and more annoyed over this woman. I don't get why he would still be "friends" with her. I know he said it is to keep the peace, so she doesn't spread rumours about him to the press. She had threatened to do that when he told her about me. I just hope I *never* meet that woman again, or I do not know what I will do.

I lie there on the rocks, listening to Mark tell me about the last time he was here. He slept on this rock under the stars and relayed to me that it is such a pretty sight at night. He stated that he would let me experience it once Bump is here.

"I want you to be safe, and I want Bump to be safe," Mark says, taking hold of my hand.

"Thank you," I say as he leans over, placing a little kiss onto my forehead.

"Come on. Let's go back to the cabin. We can cuddle the night away," Mark says, standing up.

Chapter 22

I can't believe it's been over two and a half months since I escaped to the cabin with Mark. Time has flown by so quickly. We seem to spend more time together than we ever did. He comes up every weekend and stays with me, and we chill out at home or go out for the day. He has helped me sort out the nursery for Bump. He has been very supportive. I do know for sure that I have fallen in love with him. I want to be with him once Bump is here. Things are going to be so different. I want us to be a couple. There has been no physical contact since we first met, only kisses shared between us. I have fallen asleep on him a couple of times, although we have not slept in the same bed. He must have some feelings for me, since he comes to see me.

Jenny and Rich are all happy, nearly ready for their wedding. I personally cannot wait. I can't wait to show off the dress. Okay, I am not a girlie girl, but I love this dress. Only three and a half months till the wedding. They still have not decided where to spend their honeymoon. They have just moved into a new place. Their housewarming party is tomorrow, which Mark is going to be attending. Since he is coming up now on Saturdays, they are being different and having it on Sunday.

I am spending today baking some cupcakes for tomorrow. Jenny loves my cupcakes with different coloured buttercream icing on top. I do not mind doing them for her. I want her to have a good night, and it is just a few friends chilling. I might even make some brownies, too. I am just going to see how the day goes. I have a few hours until Mark is due to arrive for the weekend.

Time flies when you are having fun. I have finished all the cupcakes and brownies. I need to ice the cupcakes, but they are still too warm.

Mark is here now. His car has just pulled up onto the driveway. I am so excited to see him. He is in dark blue jeans and a tight, white T-shirt as normal and carrying his bag and briefcase. He lets himself in the front door, as I have told him to do.

"Hi, baby," Mark bellows as he walks through the kitchen door.

"Hi, Mark, how are you?"

"Perfect now. What have you been busy doing?"

"I've been baking for Jenny's housewarming tomorrow."

"You best be taking it easy. Bump needs you to rest. Only two weeks now."

"I know. Knowing my luck, it will be a lot longer than that."

Mark makes himself comfortable, unpacking his bag and treating my home as his own. I use the time he is busy to ice the cupcakes. Some have cream-coloured icing, some pink, and others blue. They will go down like a treat. I cut the brownies and box up everything. I'm ready for tomorrow.

"Right, I am getting takeaway tonight. What do you fancy, baby?"

"Pizza," I reply.

"Pizza it is. Pizza and a film," he cheerfully agrees.

"That is perfect, Mark."

******

Last night went too fast. The weekend always does. We watched a couple of films. Mark decided that we should spend a little time out shopping today because he needs to get a gift for Connor, as it is his birthday coming up.

Time to party. We managed to get Connor a present, a nice silver chain that matches his watch with some other little things that he had stated he wanted. I found a nice float black top to go over some leggings. Mark has gone for dark jeans and a white top with a black jacket over it. He looks very sexy in it. I love his eyes. They are so perfect. He has those sexy come-to-bed eyes.

Mark states, as always, that he is driving so we do not argue or have to choose which car we are taking. Mark kindly takes all the cupcakes, brownies, and everything else Jenny asked me to bring down to the car. This gives me time to make sure my hair is okay and lip-gloss is on. Perfect.

"Megan, you look amazing. Hi, Mark." Jenny bounces at the door, wearing yet another stunning dress, a red one, low cut as always, a very Jenny dress.

"Hi, Jenny, you look stunning. Where would you like these cupcakes?" Mark questions.

"On the kitchen side would be great," Jenny answers.

"Come in, Megan. Come join the fun. Well, there are only Rich, Luke, and Alison here. We are waiting on three more."

I follow Jenny, while watching Mark in the kitchen with Rich; they get along so well now. They chat all the time. It is nice to see them both happy.

"Alison is just telling us about her new business idea," Jenny states as I take a seat in the lounge.

"Oh, really." I pretend to be interested. Alison works with Jenny. She thinks she is a know-it-all.

"Yes, Megan, I am going to start designing garden waterfalls," she says.

I sit there, listening to her tell me all about her big plans of taking over the world. Luke kindly tells her about Mark. Alison soon makes an excuse to leave us to talk to Mark. That is somewhat evil of Luke, but I should have known.

"Hey, how are you doing, sexy?" Luke enquires.

"I'm fine, Luke," I reply.

"You are looking amazing. Not long now."

"Two weeks, but who knows, it could be four weeks," I reply.

"Megan, you and I need to have some time chatting, getting to know each other. How about we meet up some time and have a lazy day?" Luke suggests.

"Okay, let's do it."

"I'll text you when I am free." Luke smiles.

Jenny is playing the right little hostess by bringing food around and topping off everyone's drinks. She looks so happy. This is what Jenny likes to do. She likes hosting. She likes to be the centre of attention. I think tonight is the first time in months I have seen her smile a real smile. I think she must be relieved that she and Rich are back together. Her dream house is now finished. They bought a little cottage and made it their own. It has taken months, but it looks good.

We sit there, playing all different party games, most of which I have not played in years. Some I have to sit out, thanks to Bump, but I am happy to avoid them. I have lost count of how many photos I have taken. We have laughed all night long. A few more friends arrive, but do not seem to stay as long, as they all have work tomorrow.

"Jenny, I am going to have to say goodnight. I'm so tired, and Mark goes back tomorrow. He needs sleep," I say to Jenny as we stand in her kitchen.

"I understand, Megan. Go home. Thank you so much," Jenny says, giving me a hug.

$$******$$

Last night was a blast as always. We played party games and ate cupcakes all night. What else do you need to have a great party? The only bad side is Mark is going home now. I do not want him to go. Mondays suck. I want him around me all the time. I want him to touch me and tell me how he feels. I don't want to make the first move, just in case it's one-way.

"Right, baby, that's me all ready to go now. I will let you know when I get to work. Be good and relax." He always says that through sparkling eyes.

"I am always good. Drive safely."

Mark walks over, giving me a hug. *Please do not let go of me, please.* However, as always, he does. I stand at the door, watching him drive away. I feel my eyes well up.

Chapter 23

Ouch. Seriously Bump needs to stop kicking because it really hurts, much more than normal. Mercifully, it passes and I get a glass of water. I sit on the sofa, finishing the book I started the night before. I have read it before, but the next installment in the series is out next week. Nothing better than a re-read of a fantastic book.

OUCH! Could this be labour? Really, these are painful. I sit there, trying to carry on reading, but the pains are not subsiding. Grabbing my mobile, I time the pains. Six minutes. Maybe I should go to the hospital.

Standing up slowly, I take my mobile and book and drop them into my bag that I packed after my last visit to the hospital. Grabbing the house phone, I ring for a taxi. Ten minutes to wait, I carry the bag on my shoulder and open the door. I head outside, grabbing the baby seat from my car and locking the door behind me before heading for the street corner.

I want Jenny, but she is at work all day. I want Mark, but he has gone home, and my mum does not get back until tomorrow. I do not want to do this on my own. Why, oh why, am I alone? I am so happy when I see the taxi.

"Hospital, please," I say as I get into the taxi.

"Okay, love," the taxi driver replies in a gruff, yet friendly voice.

I sit in the back of the taxi and take several deep, calming breaths as I grab my mobile and text Jenny.

Hi, can you leave work early today? Xx

Hi hun, sorry I can't. We're short staffed. Why? Xx

I'm in labour. Well 99% sure I am. Xx

I'll try and get free. Ring Mark. Xx

Can't. He has important meetings all day. Xx

I know if I ring Mark, he will turn around and come be with me, but he has been busy sorting the details out for this meeting for weeks. I know it is a huge deal to him.

Finally, the taxi arrives at the hospital. The driver surprises me by running off immediately and fetching a wheelchair. He kindly helps me into the chair, pushing me through the main doors and rushing over to the main desk.

"She's having a baby," he states.

I look up at him in amazement. I didn't think anyone would care enough to do this. Soon, I'm dashing down the hospital corridors at high speed and into the lift that takes me to the maternity unit.

"I'm Megan Madden," I manage to say to the nurse at the reception desk, growling through another contraction through clenched teeth. The pain is like nothing I have ever experienced.

"Hello, Megan. I'm Kath, and I'll be your midwife today. Let's get you into a room pronto, shall we?" She smiles at me as she moves to take hold of the wheelchair handles from Trevor, the taxi driver.

"Thank you," I reply before grunting as another painful contraction reaches its crescendo. "And thank you, Trevor. I'm sorry about my water breaking in your taxi." I look at him, dying with shame.

"Don't you be worrying about something like that. You have enough to think about," he says, smiling kindly at me.

"Good luck," he says as Kath starts to wheel me towards the labour ward.

"Are you alone, Megan?" She looks at me, realizing that Trevor is just the poor cabbie who has a terrible mess to clean up.

"Do you need us to call anyone for you?" She looks at me again. "Looks like it."

After arriving in a private room, I slowly change into a nightie. Sitting on the edge of the bed, I feel another contraction beginning to tighten as the pain builds again. My labour is progressing, the spacing between contractions coming more regular now. The midwife has just left me to change while she reads my birth plan. As far as I am concerned, all Kath needs to know about my birth plan is the following: if I scream in pain, GET ME PAIN RELIEF. I just want her to administer those drugs. I would like to say that I want a natural, painkiller-free birth, but who am I kidding? If this pain gets any worse, I'll be crying out for any drug available.

"Megan, can you pop onto the bed so that I can examine you? I just need to feel your abdomen, listen to the baby, then do a quick vaginal examination." She smiles at me as she starts washing her hands in the sink by the door. I do as she asks and lie down on the bed as she approaches my right side. She begins to feel my abdomen, palpating first the size of the baby, the position, and then she steps back, smiling.

"Your baby's head is engaged low in your pelvis," she says, popping on her latex gloves.

"I'm going to wash the area down there and see how far along you are," Kath tells me. It looks like a ceremony as she prepares me, and then she gently performs an internal examination.

"Well... you're already eight centimeters." She smiles up at me as she stands straight and steps back from the bed.

"Looks like the baby is coming," she says as she snaps the gloves off and steps onto the metal pedal bin and discards them.

"Eight!! Eight... Already?" I question in complete shock.

"Well, that explains..." "All that pain you've had," she says, her face softening in sympathy as she nods. "The way you are progressing, the baby could be here before any pain relief I give you begins to take effect, I'm afraid." She shakes her head before she notices the look of utter horror on my face.

"Don't worry, my darling. Women have been having babies without any pain medication for centuries." She nudges my leg playfully.

"However," she says as she pulls out a plastic mouthpiece from a cupboard at the side of the bed, "You can have this." She gestures and attaches it to a tube leading to a black cylinder at the other side of me.

"Did you go to antenatal classes?" I nod. It's the gas and air thing they talked to us about.

"Now, do you know how to use this?" I shake my head.

"Well, take it between your teeth and suck in as soon as you feel the contraction starting to build. You won't need to use it when the contraction wears off." She giggles with a wink. I start to feel another pain coming, and she gestures for me to use it.

"That's it. Breathe like how they taught you in the classes." She nods. "That's it," she encourages me.

"Good girl. That will take the edge off you." Kath continues to talk me through the pains that grip me and course through my body. I have to say, it does help a little. I try to regain my breathing, feeling a little stronger with each breath.

"I'm just going to call the other midwife to let her know you're nearly fully dilated and let the doctor know that the baby is on the way." She smiles, patting me on the shoulder. She walks over to the phone and picks it up and starts speaking into it.

"Right, do you think you need any other pain relief?" "No, I'm okay for now, I think," I reply as I concentrate on my breathing exercises.

I'm going to try to control the pain for as long as I can. Well, it's too late now, even if I wanted it. Jenny came to a couple of birthing classes with me. She sent Mark to one once with me, too. It was the most uncomfortable thing I have ever done, breathing like an idiot and pulling these stupid faces in a room full of people. He was great at it, though. Kath leaves me alone, but not before showing me the call button should I need anything before she returns. She also places the gas mask near my left hand and shows me how to self-administer. I just keep thinking of my breathing. Knowing the labour will be over soon, and I'll be meeting Bump fills me with excitement. My baby will be here with me. Lying still, I give in and have a little suck on the gas and air while I try to breathe through another contraction. They are getting closer and lasting longer. During each one, the mixture of gas and air actually makes me feel nauseous. I knew it could do that to you. Kath returns sooner than expected, and she is smiling.

The phone in the labour room rings, and Kath answers it before covering the mouthpiece with her hand. "There's a Mark Reed outside?" she says with a questioning look.

"Says he is here to see you."

"What? Mark's here," I say between breaths.

121

"Yes." She pulls a funny smiley face. The poor woman must think that's my baby's daddy.

"Show him in," I reply as soon as another contraction subsides. I can only nod as another contraction starts. The next thing I know the door to my room opens.

"Baby, why didn't you call me?" Mark rushes over to me, full of concern.

"You… have… meetings… today," I say through yet another contraction.

"You're more important to me than any meeting. You know this." He takes my hand, looking worried. "Thanks." I smile a little between the pains.

"Megan, seriously, you know how I feel." I don't say anything and try hard to concentrate on my breathing. I anticipate the pain coming as I start to squeeze his hand. Mark takes my hand while Kath prepares to examine me again. I look up at him, and he smiles reassuringly at me. Having him here with me is such a comfort.

"I'm just going to check and see how far we are now," Kath says, approaching the bottom of the bed. As she does, another midwife enters the room and introduces herself.

"You're fully dilated, Megan. Push when the urge takes you." She grins proudly at me. I look at Mark and smile, but I'm starting to feel scared and excited at the same time, knowing the moment is finally here. I'm so glad he's here, and I'm not on my own. I know this won't be fun for him, especially me squeezing his poor hand white, which is what I am doing right now. The pain finally starts to subside, thankfully.

"You don't have to stay, Mark," I say, suddenly remembering I don't want him looking down there, seeing me so messy and vulnerable.

"I'm staying. I'm never leaving you or Bump." He smiles lovingly at me. The pains increase, and I barely have any reprieve from them before I'm crippled with another. The other midwife checks the machine in the corner in case it's needed for my baby. An overwhelming urge grips me, and I bear down.

"The baby is coming…" they announce in unison, looking up at Mark and me. I nod yes, as the contraction continues to build… Okay, let's do this… I hear Kath and the other midwife talking about when and how to push, and when they say to do it… The pain. God help me. I can't take it… I feel like I am being ripped in two. It starts in my back and creeps around to my belly… Oh God, I can't do this…

"Push… Push… Push." I hear Kathy tell me.

"That's it, Megan… good girl. You're doing brilliantly." I can do this. Short pants of breath are taking the little strength I have. All I can hear is Kath encouraging me. I push down when she tells me… Oh God, the pain. I'm going to be meeting my baby. This pain will be worth it. I don't feel the pain anymore because it's welcomed. It means I can push and work with it. Mark keeps a tight hold of my hand, and he strokes my back reassuringly through the now sweat-soaked nightie. I am dripping in sweat as I follow Kath's instructions and concentrate on pushing when told to. Mark brushes my wet hair from my face with his fingers, and despite the pain, I manage to offer up a smile to him. He places a damp cloth onto my forehead.

"Arghhhh!" I scream, as I push my chin into my chest and PUSH with all my might. "Arghhhh…" With each push, I can feel Bump progress. It burns, and Kath's voice breaks through my concentration. "I can see lots of hair now," she says as her hands work quickly, and my baby's head is delivered. I am stunned when the pain subsides before another contraction builds, and everything seems to happen in a blur. As horrendous as it had been, the pain is instantly gone.

Suddenly, I hear the most beautiful sound in the world... My baby's cry!

"She's here," Kath says as she delivers my baby straight onto my belly... my little girl. I hold her against my breast, and she begins to cry, and it is the sweetest sound I have ever heard. She is here. She is no longer a Bump, but a baby. She is real, and she is mine. A river of tears flows down my face. I don't even register Mark's kiss as he pecks me on top of my head. All I can focus on right at this moment is the miracle in my arms.

"I'm so proud of you, Megan. Welcome to the world, little one," Mark whispers.

"Megan, I love you."

"I love you, too," I reply as I start to tear up.

"I have loved you since the first time I saw you." Kath clamps the cord and looks at Mark.

"Would you like to cut the cord, Mark?" she asks. Mark looks at me, and I nod my head, letting him cut the cord. It is so surreal. All the pain has gone, and I don't care that I look a mess. I have my beautiful baby and Mark, and that is all I need.

"You're incredible, Megan," Mark tells me. "Thank you. Thank you for coming and staying," I say while looking deep into his eyes.

"I love you. Here." Mark passes me a little black velvet box. I slowly open it to see another charm. This one is a heart. Etched into it are the words *I Love You*.

"Thank you," I say, wiping a tear from my eye.

"It's traditional to give the mum of a newborn a present." "Again, thank you. It's a lovely sentiment," I say, smiling at him. This is the moment I want to remember forever. My beautiful baby and my amazing man. Both with me. No question about it. I finally have my Prince Charming.

"Have you thought of any names?" Kath enquires.

"Lucy."

"A beautiful name for such a beautiful baby," Kath says.

"Lucy Paige Madden," I declare with a huge smile on my tear-streaked face.

"Perfect. I love it," Mark says. "She is as perfect as her mum." Mark leans down, placing a butterfly kiss onto my head.

Kath comes back later, but I can't say how long it has been. I have not noticed anything. I have been in my own world, my special world. Kath takes Lucy from me to weigh and measure her, which I have been expecting. I want to know how much she weighs. I change into fresh bedclothes. Mark pops out at the same time to ring Connor. Soon, I am back in bed with my freshly cleaned and clothed baby, and I mouth her name silently as I look down at her face. Everything is perfect.

Mark's POV

I cannot believe what I have just witnessed, the woman I love giving birth to the most amazing baby ever. She is so cute. Her hair is so fine. You can see little strands of brown hair and bright blue eyes. She is perfect. I never knew a baby would make me feel like this. She has tiny little hands and tiny toes.

Kath says she weighs 6 lbs. 3 ozs and is 26 in. long. I just cannot stop looking at her. She is perfect. I can't believe Megan let me cut her cord. I feel so honoured.

Megan was so wonderful and determined. I love that woman with all my heart.

Walking back into the room, I see Megan sitting on the bed with Lucy swaddled in a baby-grow and blanket in her arms. Both mother and child look perfect.

"Are you okay, Mark?" she asks me.

"Yes, just looking at how amazing you are."

Megan does that cute thing again, where she looks away as I talk to her.

"Do you want to hold her?" Megan questions me.

"Are you sure?"

"Yes." She smiles at me in a reassuring manner.

Megan passes Lucy to me. I sit down in the chair next to the bed and just look at her. Although I know she is too young to know what she is doing and that it is just instinctive, Lucy's left hand closes on one of my fingers for the briefest of moments. I realise right then that this is what I want most. I want Megan and Lucy. I want this for a life, the two of them... forever.

Veiled – L. Chapman

Believe Series book 2

Dedication

Mum – You have always believed in me and pushed me to do everything
you know I can do. I owe everything to you.

I love you.

You will lead a rich and successful life.

Table of Contents

Prologue

I can't believe it is only a month away from my big day. I score a line through today's date on the personalised calendar I received from my friend, Megan. She designed the keepsake in my wedding colour scheme of white, black, and pink and personalized it with pictures of Rich and me. It is a "me" gift that Megan knew I would love. It is something only she would buy since she loves giving people personalised keepsakes. She knows me so well. The calendar is used solely for the wedding, and it has all my appointments written on it.

I only have fifteen days off from my full-time job as a nurse before the wedding. Due to the fact I'm organised, every one of those days has plans. I just can't wait. I'm finally going to have the fairy-tale wedding I have always wanted. I have dreamed of this special day since I was a child. When I was little, I received a book for my dream wedding, and I used to cut out little pictures of items that I wanted and wished for. We are getting married in a big old-fashioned church followed by a reception in a castle. A real castle. A big do, like what I have always imagined. It's supposed to be our day, and I want us to be the center of attention. I think Rich would be happy just getting married in a registry office with two strangers as witnesses. He is only going along with the big wedding for my sake. As soon as I began working as a paper girl at thirteen, I started saving for my dream day. Even though it is considered tradition, I didn't want to rely on my parents to pay for everything. I want it to be perfect with my own personal touch since I plan to marry only one time.

My mum and dad met when they were eighteen and have been together for twenty-nine years. They have three children, Samantha, my older pain in the arse sister, Martin, my baby brother, and me. Martin passed away three days after he turned six. He accidentally ran out in front of a car to get his ball. Just thinking of him makes me tear up. My only brother killed because of a ball.

Thankfully, the doctors say he died straight away so he wasn't aware of what was happening. But I'm aware. I remember it all too well and now wish we had not been there. It was my fault; I wanted to play at the park that day. If I had not asked to go, he would never have been there. He would still be alive. I saw everything, but wish I hadn't. I remember the car— the colour, make, model. Everything about that day. It was like watching a film when everything happens in slow motion. Mum ran after Martin to stop him, but she couldn't get there in time. Understandably, she's never gotten over losing him. She was diagnosed with severe depression and admitted to the hospital after his death. Martin was a very bright lad with a heart of gold. He loved football, and he wanted to be a science teacher when he grew up. I wish he could be here to help me on my big day and to be one of Rich's ushers.

My older sister is the complete opposite of me. Samantha has a very kind heart, but she can be a pain at times. She will help you do anything as long as it's done her way and convenient for her. The only feature we share is eye colour that changes to a darker colour when we get angry. Samantha has shoulder-length brown hair while I have blonde hair. Even with only two years separating us, she looks nothing like me. If one more person tells me we look alike, I will cry. We are two different people.

Chapter One
31 Days to Go

I am so glad that I don't have to work today. After the past five days, I look forward to resting and spending some time ordering the rest of the gems for the tables. I have chosen little pink and black scattering gems to add just the right amount of sparkle to the crisp, white linen tablecloths at the reception. Earlier, I ordered a nice baby pink cloth runner to go down the middle of each table to contrast all the other accessories, which are bright pink. For the centerpiece on each adult table, I have bought glass bowls to fill with water and star-shaped candles. The children's tables will display bowls with fairy lights rather than candles for safety reasons. I fell in love with these decorations within minutes of seeing them featured in other wedding pictures.

Tonight, I am making a lovely meal for my fiancé Rich and me. I wanted to plan an intimate candlelight dinner for us before the stresses of the wedding hit. I am cooking all of Rich's favourite foods, steak with mushrooms, chips and onion rings, with cheesecake for dessert. I don't really like cheesecake, so he can have the entire thing for himself. I made sure to place a couple of bottles of his favourite beer in the fridge earlier for when he gets home from work. I don't like beer, and he doesn't like wine. I love to cook. It makes me happy, but I can't bake. That's where Megan comes in useful.

Megan has gone away to London for a few days with her boyfriend Mark. She is due back early tomorrow morning or late tonight, depending on what they planned to do today. They have gone to attend the christening of the son of one of Mark's closest friends. That was yesterday. It's the first time Megan will have met any of his colleagues. She wanted to make a good impression, so I spent hours dress shopping with her before we found an amazing red halter neck maxi dress with little butterflies all over it. Megan looked gorgeous in it when she tried it on. We picked out a tie in the same shade of red for Mark so they would look like a real couple. I can't wait to see some pictures from the event. I was hoping she would have sent a few last night, but I bet she got busy.

She is due to meet Mark's family on her next visit. I know she is worried they will not like her. Megan has such a great personality; I don't understand why she thinks they will dislike her. I believe she is more afraid of his family not accepting Lucy, her daughter. She met Mark's sister, Mia, a few weeks ago when she came here for a visit. Mia agrees with me that Mark has been really good for Megan. He has looked after her as much as he can. He makes her happy, but I can tell she is worried that he is going to leave her one day. At that thought, my mobile signals an incoming text from her.

Hi Jenny, I will do some when I get back. Miss ya. XX

I can't help but laugh. I knew she would do it for me. She is such a gem. I want to find the perfect thank you gift for her for the wedding. It needs to be something extraordinary like her, more than just the necklace all my other bridesmaids will receive. Megan is special and I want her to know what she really means to me. I really don't think I could make it through some days without her.

I grab my laptop from under the coffee table and log on to the Internet. I take my pen and little purple notepad that contains the amounts of everything I need for the wedding. The other week Mia sent me a link for gemstones. I plan to order them from the website. They will arrive within twenty-four hours of placing the order, which means I can pack them into my box as soon as I receive them. Yes, I'm an organised freak regarding all wedding plans. I have several clear plastic boxes labelled and filled with everything needed for each venue. I think Megan might be rubbing off on me.

I order the gems and then go into my search engine and type "maid of honour thank you gifts". Let's see what ideas pop up. I can't pick just one because there are so many different choices. I know she will not be expecting anything and will probably tell me off for wasting money on her. I settle on a gift box to place lots of different gifts inside. That will be special to her because she loves keepsakes. I order a key charm and a personalised pink, circle pendant engraved with the wedding date and her name. It looks perfect. As I continue searching, I order a wine glass and a black photo frame with little pink butterflies adorning the corners. Of course, all these items receive personalised touches. I'll add her necklace to the box as well, and I may find even more items before the wedding.

That's all done, so now I just have to purchase the survival kits for my bridal party. The survival kit is a black cotton bag embellished with gems that spell out their title in the wedding. It will contain everything each girl might need before or after the ceremony— over twenty different items, including the necklace, tissues, and boob tape. The kit will also come fully stocked with condoms to prevent any "accidents" from occurring, even though I think it would be something special if a little baby were conceived on my wedding night. I even impressed myself and made some little nametags to tie to each bag.

Lucy is a bridesmaid for me, too. I have ordered her a baby gown that reads *Lucy is the Best Little Bridesmaid Ever*. I can't wait to see her in it. I know she will not wear her little bridesmaid dress all day. The dress is white with a little pink band around the middle that ties into bow at the back. She will look adorable in it.

I glance towards the clock. I need to begin preparing dinner before my loving hubby-to-be gets home. It will not take me long, though, since most of it's pre-made and just needs to cook, but I do need to make the cheesecake.

Chapter Two

I finish preparing dinner, shower, and paint my nails a red colour all before Rich returns from work. For the first time in ages, I even manage to shave everywhere without cutting myself. My biggest fear is just before the wedding I'm going to cut my legs while shaving. I have thought of waxing, but I don't think I can cope with the pain. I know people say that pain is just part of looking beautiful, but I'm not so sure about that one.

I made a speech prior to booking the wedding date that there would be no sex the week before we get married. I want our wedding night to be special. Now, I think I will be struggling with this decision. I plan to make sure I get plenty before our wedding week begins. I am wearing Rich's favourite little black halter dress that barely covers my bum and shows just enough of my cheeks to drive him wild. He loves it. I have been a little bit naughty. Okay, very naughty. I am not wearing underwear and have added my black stilettos. Perfect. My hair is down, exactly the way he likes it, and I'm not wearing any makeup. This is how my baby likes to see me.

"Honey, I'm home!" Rich yells as he comes through the door, looking all hot and sweaty from his run. He always goes for a three to five mile run after work. He is a fitness freak sometimes, so I would love for him to take a day off from running once in a while.

"Hi," I say, leaning against the doorway in a suggestive manner, my arm above my head in the full-on come-and-get-me pose.

"Oh, wow. Are you trying to kill me, Jen?" He winks.

"Never." I giggle, hoping I am killing him. I plan to make that man work his arse off after dinner.

"Quick shower and I am all yours, baby girl," he says, placing a little peck on my lips before smacking my bum and running up the stairs.

Rich began calling me baby girl the second time we saw each other. I can't help but blush when he says it, even after all this time together. I sit myself on a barstool in the kitchen and wait for him. He is only gone for five minutes because he takes quick showers when I am not with him. If I didn't have a nice meal planned, I would join him. I might take him for another one later.

"I'm back, baby girl," Rich announces as he walks into the kitchen wearing only black trousers. His bare chest is on full display and his perfect back is sparkling from water trickling down it. His hair is also wet. He looks so fuckable. Food first. *We need to eat first*, I try to convince myself.

"Are you ready for something to eat?" I question.

"Yes, always." He pauses. "Food later. You now." He places his lips straight on mine. While tilting my head back, his tongue slides straight into my mouth, and his hand gently pulls my hair. I let out a little moan. He is an amazing kisser.

He releases me. "Upstairs now, baby girl," he growls.

"Oh, really?" I tease, placing my hands on my hips and pushing my chest out farther while trying to keep a straight face.

"Yes, or I am going to take you here on the breakfast bar." He winks.

"Well, it does need christening." I giggle.

"That's it." Rich slips his arms around me, lifting me up onto the wooden breakfast bar situated in the middle of the kitchen. This is where I'm going to regret not closing the blinds. I just hope no one walks past or comes to the door. They will catch us right in the middle. Just the thought of being caught makes me blush.

"Oh, no knickers," Rich says, sliding his hand up my inner thigh, slowly making the hairs on the back of my neck stand up on end.

I lean, arching my back more. Oh, he is such a tease. He kisses his way down my thigh, calf, and ankle. Oh, man. He stands straight, walking in between my legs and pulling me up. Our eyes lock, and I feel his hand reach around my neck, untying my dress. His arms slip down my sides, grabbing hold of the bottom of the dress and pushing it over my head.

"You're perfect, Jen," he says, placing his lips back on mine. His hands travel to my breasts, and his fingers find my nipples, squeezing them gently. Mmm. His lips leave mine, moving straight onto my neck and trailing little kisses down to my breasts.

"Baby girl, I am going to make you scream tonight," he says before he moves to the other nipple.

I can't talk. I just lean farther back, pushing my chest more into his mouth. His hand moves around to support my back, and I feel his fingertips walking up and down my spine. His lips leave my nipples, going down my body to my navel, his tongue flicking over my belly bar. He knows how much I love his tongue travelling all over me, exploring me. His hand continues to explore, reaching my pussy, his finger slowly rubbing over my clit. His tongue leaves my navel going straight to my pussy, planting a little kiss on the top. His finger stops rubbing my clit, and he slowly slides it inside, only one, making sure I am ready for him.

"You're so wet, baby," he whispers, but all I can manage is a moan.

He slowly pulls out his finger, only to insert four at once. Oh. This time he moves faster; his fingers slide in and out, over and over again, while his tongue licks my clit. I begin to feel myself building.

"You're going to come soon, baby. Not yet," he states, removing his fingers from me.

"That's... not... fair," I reply while trying to catch my breath.

"How would you like it?" he asks as I slowly sit myself up to look at him. He has dropped his trousers and stands before me with his cock in his hand. I lean to take hold of it. This is not like Rich. Where is all the fun foreplay? Is he afraid someone might see us? He's wanted a lot of quickies recently; I can't even remember the last time he let me give him a blowjob. "Not yet," he says, pushing me back down. "Fast or slow?"

143

"Fast," I answer.

He slowly slides the tip of his cock into me, teasing me. Sometimes, I forget how big he is. He continues at a gentle pace, picking up speed as my body adjusts to him. Oh, man. He pulls me farther off the bar and starts pumping faster and faster. One hand is squeezing my bum, the other playing with my nipples. He knows exactly what I like. Oh, baby.

"I'm going to come," he announces between breaths.

I am so close. I hope he can hold on.

"Arghhhh!" he yells.

He slowly slides himself out before placing his tongue on my clit, sucking me, his fingers sliding back inside me.

"Ohhh, yeah, arghhhhh."

Rich stands beside me and picks me up with my legs hanging over his arms. "Bed, baby girl," he whispers into my ear as he carries me up the stairs. I reach out, pushing our bedroom door open. He gently lays me down onto the bed before climbing in beside me.

I turn to face him. "Jen, sleep time, baby," he says, placing a little kiss on my head before turning around.

That's not normal. Rich never does that. He always wants to cuddle first and then sleep, if not round two before sleep. Why is tonight different? What about the lovely meal I made? He never turns down food; he loves to eat everything. It just doesn't make any sense at all. What is wrong with my baby boy?

I try to talk to him, but he ignores my questions. I lie there confused and wait for him to fall asleep. He curls up into a little ball on the other side of the bed, looking so cute and peaceful. I just want to curl up behind him, but something's not right. I climb out of bed and make my way to the shower with tears rolling from my eyes. I have so many unanswered questions.

Chapter Three
30 Days to Go

The next morning, I awake to find Rich already gone. He didn't wake me up. *He always wakes me before leaving for work.* His morning routine consists of placing a kiss on my forehead and neck before making my brew, then chatting with me while he gets changed for work. This has always been great for me, lying in bed watching him, his body so toned. Something is not right. He wouldn't let me touch him last night at all. He always lets me take my time feeling him, stroking him, sucking him. Last night was so different. He made me feel like a blow-up toy, not a person.

I am not going to let it get to me, though. Tonight is my hen do. Unfortunately, I have some two-hour training at work before I party with my girlies. I hope the training will either take my mind off things or help me sleep.

*****

I know it is more of a tradition to have a hen party the week of the wedding, but I wanted to have it early so that I would have plenty of time to get over the hangover I am anticipating. Megan's only orders were that I needed to be ready to leave by six and dressed to party. That is not much to go on, so I choose to wear a white, thick backless halter neck dress. The bottom of the dress is a dark blue flowing skirt that is very short, of course. *Nothing but short skirts for me.* It has a lovely sequined waistband. I love my legs, and this dress shows them off perfectly. Megan always tells me that she would pay millions for my legs, but she has amazing legs herself. She just doesn't believe me.

I can't wait to see what Megan has planned. Lucy is staying with Megan's mum for the night, so we will have no interruptions, only fun. This is our first girls' night with no ties in ages. I plan to leave my hair down and finish off my outfit with some black strappy heels that lace up the ankle.

"Perfect," I say to myself as I stand in front of the full-length mirror, turning around to make sure everything is in place. I head downstairs to the front room just as Megan appears at the door. It must have been fate that she showed up at the same time, and as always, early.

"Hey, honey, you look beautiful," I state, smiling at her while moving her hair off her bare shoulders.

"Thank you, but how amazing do *you* look? You look like you're going to go on the pull." She winks.

"Well, only thirty days till I am not allowed to pull." I giggle.

"Right. Get your keys. It's time to have some fun," Megan informs me. She is bossy as always, but I love her for it.

I grab my bag and coat and watch Megan walk to the door. I am happy to see she has her legs out. *Mark is so good for her.* She is wearing a purple strappy dress with a thin ribbon under her amazing chest and a little bow at the side which links to the top of the ruffle section down the front. Megan has curled her hair tonight. It has angelic curls in it, and she looks so gorgeous to have given birth only three months ago.

I follow Megan, locking the door as we go. The front of this house has so many trees that it is impossible to see anything before reaching the gate. I can see Megan standing by the bench under the massive tree with a cheeky smile across her face. Once I get closer to her, I notice a pink stretched limo.

"OMG! I love it!" I squeal, waving my hands in front of my eyes. *I must not cry.*

"I knew you would love it, Jenny." Megan winks.

I snap a few pictures with my mobile to tease Rich, even though I am convinced he will be at a strip club if I know Luke at all.

"Look in the limo, Jenny," Megan orders.

I walk over to the back doors, opening one to see all my closest friends sitting there with glasses full of champagne. Black seats, carpeted floor, and a glittered disco ball hanging from the middle of the roof decorate the interior of the limo. A mini fridge with a glass front houses bottles of our favourite drinks. Oh, I could spend all day in here.

"Yeahhhhh!" they all shout.

"OMG! Could tonight get any better?" I turn to face Megan.

"*I don't know*. We will have to wait and see," she says before turning around so I can't read her face. She is up to something, I know it. I don't mind. It's *my* party, and I can't wait to get it started.

"Come on, everyone. Get out of the car for a group photo," Megan says.

I stand by the limo, giving all my guests hugs. They look dressed to impress. Tonight is going to be amazing. The driver gets out of the limo and walks towards Megan. He is wearing a black suit and hat. He passes something to her before taking her mobile, and she instantly begins to chuckle. I wonder what he said, and what they have planned.

"Everyone in a line beside the limo," Megan says. She opens the gift bag she has been holding while the rest of us form a line. "A hen party is not a hen party without sashes and stuff." Megan winks, going down the line, giving everyone a sash that reads *Jenny's Hen Party* along with a name that describes them.

I am dreading what mine says.

"Here is yours, Jenny," Megan says as she passes me a pink sash with little diamonds along both sides. It reads *My Hen Party* on the front; on the back, *Last Night of Freedom- Kiss Me Quickly*.

I can't believe she has had that printed on mine. *Oh, hang on*. I do believe it. Megan just stands there laughing at me.

"Thanks, Megan," I say, placing the sash around me.

"For you, a crown with an attached veil and a shot glass on a chain." Megan passes them to me.

"Thanks. You plan on getting me drunk?" I question.

"Not really, I just bought every hen party thing I could find."

Megan continues giving out the sashes. I follow her, laughing at everyone's name because it fits them so well. I do wonder what Megan's says.

"Megan, where is your sash?" I question.

147

"Here," she says, pulling out one that reads *Angel Missing Her Halo* on the front and *It's Around Her Waist* printed on the back.

I can't do anything but laugh. Every time Megan says she is an "angel," I always say she has lost her halo, and it's around her waist as a belt. That is the most fitting sash she could get.

The limo is so large that it accommodates us all. We drink champagne all the way to the club. It's the first time I have ever been in this club. They have private rooms, and Megan rented one for the night for my hen do. Walking through the club door, I immediately notice why she chose this place. It reminds me a lot of Bar 3000, and the colour theme is very stylish with hues of black and red. Clubs are normally pitch black with flashing lights, so no one really knows what colour the rooms are.

Megan walks ahead to our room. The door reads *Jenny's Hen Do... Only Sexy Men Allowed.* I can't believe she would have such a thing printed for the door.

"In you go, Jenny," Megan says, opening the door. Oh, wow! *It is amazing.* The same colour theme carries into the room. It's not all dark in here, yet. Straight in front is a picture of Rich and me and lots of pink and black cock-shaped balloons scattered around. Umm... I can't help but laugh.

Walking farther into the room, I see someone in a chair. I can tell the person has long red, wavy hair. *I wonder who it is.*

"Now!" all the party shouts.

The person in the chair slowly turns around.

"Michele!" I shout.

Michele is Rich's sister; she is like a big sister to me. She has such an amazing personality. Michele lives and works in America as a photographer and loves sending me naughty pictures of men.

I run over to Michele. "Hi," I say, jumping up and down.

"Jen, I've missed you," she replies.

"What are you doing here? How? Why? When did you get here?" I ask in a confused manner.

Michele takes my hand and walks over to the bar before sitting on one of the stools. The ladies follow and begin ordering a round of drinks.

"Your sash fits you perfectly," I state.

It reads *Flirty Minx* and couldn't be truer for Michele.

"Right, Jen. Megan invited me. I wanted to be here, and it's your last party before you marry that brother of mine," she replies.

"You kept it a secret," I point out.

"Yes, I have been here four days. Rich knows. I have been staying at Megan's. She didn't go away with Mark. She told you that story to hide the fact I was here."

"What? You two are crazy," I state.

"We just love you. We wanted to surprise you."

"Thank you, ladies. I love you both so much," I say, grabbing Megan and pulling her close.

Michele orders us our normal drinks, white wine, red wine, and Coke, before getting up and heading to the other side of the room, leaving me with Megan at the bar. Everyone else has scattered around the room, talking and having fun. As always, Michele looks great. She is wearing a little red dress with a lace back. Her red hair covers her back, and her flawless, smoky eye makeup makes her green eyes stand out more. I have always been jealous of her; she has the perfect body to match all her other unblemished features.

Even though she lives in America, Michele has been there for me since I began seeing Rich. She lives in Boston with her very sexy husband, Oliver. He loves to tease about the name of the street on which they live, Intercourse Lane. It is so fitting for them. They have a five-year-old daughter, Aria, whom they adore. She looks just like Michele. We chat weekly, so I am able to keep up with their family life.

The lights on the main dance floor suddenly change from flashing party lights to spotlights.

"What's happening, Megan?" I question.

"I don't know. Come over here," she says, taking my hand and walking me over to a seat before motioning me to sit down. I don't know what's going on. *What have they done?*

The lights come back on with the music. Everyone has moved closer to where I have been seated in the middle of the room. Michele walks out of the small back room behind the bar holding something. As she gets closer, I can tell it is a cake.

"What have you got there, Michele?" I ask.

"No party is a party without cake."

Yeah, cake. I love cake. She places it on my knee. It is a white square cake with a black picture silhouette of a woman in a wedding dress, and it reads *The Future Mr. & Mrs.* Pink ribbon adorns the edges. It fits perfectly with my wedding theme.

"I love it! Thank you," I reply, smiling.

"It's a chocolate cake," Michele points out.

"I love it even more now." I giggle. "Can we cut it?" I ask.

"You stay here. I'll go cut it."

The girlies drag me from the chair, and we head to the dance floor. We dance, drink, and giggle with cock-shaped naughty toys floating all around us. I should have known the girlies would do this to me. When we are together, we often joke who loves cock the most. Thankfully, not many people hear our crazy conversations.

"Excuse me!" a male voice shouts, causing me to turn around.

Chapter Four

I see a tall man wearing an Army uniform standing in front of me. I immediately face the girls, who all have wide smiles plastered across their faces. I should have known they would do this to me. I stated I didn't want a stripper when they asked me what I wanted to do for my hen do. They gave me lots of different options—weekend away, spa day, amusement park, activity day, night out. I thought a night out would suit everyone. I loved all the possibilities, but I wasn't really keen on the amusement park, though.

"Are you the bride-to-be?" he asks as he walks towards me.

With the amount of stuff I am wearing, it is a huge giveaway that I am the bride. Got to love the girls for doing it, but I have nowhere to hide now.

"Yes," I state, feeling myself start to burn up.

He winks at me before pointing over to the DJ. The music changes, and he starts to dance. I cover my face to hide my embarrassment. *No, they can't be doing this to me.* Is he really a stripper? *Oh, please someone tell me I am dreaming.* I feel his hand grab ahold of my wrist, pulling it away from my face. The girls are cheering in the background, one of them wolf whistling.

"Come with me," he says, placing his arm around my waist and forcing me to walk over to a chair that someone must have placed in the center of the dance floor. I gladly sit down.

The man bends down, whispering into my ear, "Relax. I will be finished soon. Enjoy it. I know you're embarrassed." He strokes my face with the back of his hand as he takes a few steps away from me.

I can't relax. I know what is going to happen. I do wonder if he is going to go all the way. Oh, please don't. I don't want to see that. *Or do I?* Oh my, I need to stop thinking. He stands there, turning around in a circle on the spot and shaking his arse in front of me. He slowly undoes each button as he shakes his arse, slowly sliding his shirt down each arm till his chest is totally exposed. Oh wow! Now that's what I call a perfectly toned six pack. His natural tan makes his abs stand out even more. He slowly rubs his hand up and down his six pack, drawing attention to his muscles. He takes small steps towards me thrusting himself at me with every move. As he reaches me, he places one leg on either side of mine and grabs my hand while he rubs it up and down his naked chest. *Oh, help me*. It feels so good, but it's so wrong. It is like we are the only two people in the room. I am quickly brought back to reality when one of the girls lets out a high-pitched squeal.

He steps back from me and begins thrusting and gyrating his hips to the hypnotic beat, while slapping his arse. *Please leave on your pants. Please*. The girls shout, "Off, off, off!" I must be as red as a tomato now. He takes a step towards me, then another, then another till he is right in front of me again. He slowly turns around and bends down, placing his bum in the air.

"Slap it," one of the girls says.

I lift my hand to slap it; instead, I tap it gently. "Harder!" they yell. I do as they say and slap it harder. I feel guilty, but it feels so good to touch him. He stands up, rubs his bum, and laughs. Again, the ladies begin to shout for him to take off his clothes. He stands with his face towards me and pulls the front of his trousers. I can't believe it. He loses his trousers in one swift movement. *Please no more*. He continues shaking his arse in front of my face while grabbing some oil nearby and rubbing it on his chest. *Oh my!*

He walks towards me, pulls me up from my seat, and places my hand on his chest. Nothing better than rubbing oil all over a man, especially when he's nearly naked. I walk around him, rubbing it on his back and sliding my hand towards his bum. He quickly turns to me.

"So, special lady, are you ready?"

I shout, "No!"

"I'll be quick," he says, grabbing ahold of either side of his tight black underwear. "Three."

"Don't. Please don't," I beg.

"Two," he replies.

Oh man, he is counting down.

"One." As he says it, he rips the underpants straight off and throws them at me. I can't help but look. *Wow!* He is hung like a donkey. *It must be fake.* That's massive, much bigger than Rich's. *Oh, stop it, Jenny.* I cover my face, feeling myself burn up even more. The girls are cheering.

I walk over to the chair to sit back down. He leaves with his hand covering his bits, only letting the girls see his bare arse as he bends down and slaps it one last time.

The music stops, turning back into something normal. I uncover my face to see he has left. Could it have been a dream? Well, a nightmare.

"Oh my, he was amazing. Did you see how big his cock was?" Michele questions.

"That really did just happen," I state.

"Yes, his name is Adam. He is a lad Alison knows," she replies, smiling at me.

I glare over in Allison's direction. "Oh, please tell me there are no more strippers tonight," I enquire.

"No more strippers, unless you want us to get the bar staff to strip." Michele laughs, running her fingers through her hair.

"No thank you," I reply, laughing it off, as I look at the bar staff. Nah, none of them are cute, or I would request their shirts off.

I leave Michele laughing with some of the girls and head outside for a few minutes of air. *It's too hot inside.* It is so wonderful how much the girls love me and how they wanted to make tonight special for me. Megan is the best friend a girl could ask for, and I love her to bits. I can't wait for her hen do; I will get revenge for tonight. I just hope Mark is the *one*. He is everything she wants and needs in life. Megan has mentioned for a while that she wants to move away, be as far away from her ex-boyfriend John as she can get. I just hope she does for her own sake, not for Mark's.

Megan appears beside me with a cock balloon attached to her wrist and two glasses.

"I can't believe you lied to me, telling me you had gone away when you hadn't, Megan," I state.

"I know, but I wanted to surprise you. Rich knew all about it," she replies.

"Good job I love ya, isn't it?" I question.

"I know you do. By the way, your cookies are ready. I will drop them off tomorrow," she states with a huge smile.

"I forgive you. There better be *lots* of cookies for what you did to me. Thank you for everything, Megan. You mean the world to me," I say, giving her a big hug.

Chapter Five
29 Days to Go

Oh, my head is banging. Last night was amazing, though. I have never laughed so much in my life. I am happy I took off work today. I would have been a zombie if I had gone in. After Adam, the stripper, finished his strip tease, we had some time to relax. He came out and joined us. At first, talking to him made me feel so uncomfortable, but as our conversation continued, I realised he was only stripping to make extra money for his children, who have complicated diseases. He is saving to take them away on holiday, just to escape the stresses of their real life for a little while. He really is a sweet man. It was nice to find out about the real man underneath the act he puts on for women.

He spent quite a while sitting outside with us in the garden area, asking about Rich, or as he called him, "The Lucky Man."

I still remember the first time I met Rich, just like it was yesterday.

I had gone to my auntie's for the week, visiting with family. I had kindly offered to go to the shops for her to collect the necessary things for the barbecue later that day. My sister had come with me. She was busy playing on her mobile when a football flew towards me, followed by a young man whose eyes connected to mine immediately.

"I'm so sorry, Miss. Are you okay?" the young man questioned.

"Yes, fine," I said, looking down at the ground.

"You don't look it. Sit down, please," he said, pointing to the curb. I sat down with his help.

"Thank you."

"No, I am sorry. I shouldn't have let the ball come over here."

"It's okay. Accidents happen." I smiled, looking up at him.

I sat there staring into his eyes, the most beautiful colour I had ever seen. I couldn't fully work out their colour because the sun was so bright. He bent down so he was kneeling in front of me. I could feel my heart fluttering. He was perfect.

"Miss, are you sure you're okay?" he asked again, placing his hand on my knee.

"Yes, call me Jenny," I said, smiling again.

"Jenny, it's lovely to meet you. I'm Rich."

We were inseparable from that day forward.

Those were the days when we had no real worries. It's amazing how we have grown as a couple, and our feelings have matured. I know I love him more than ever, and I worry about him all the time. My only problem is the wedding. With everything that happened with Chad, I don't want him there, and I know Rich says nothing happened, but that is not the point. Rich has been acting weird around me. Our sex used to be wild, unplanned, fun, and earth-shattering. We always made each other orgasm before finishing together. Now it's quick and emotionless. It's like he doesn't want me; he doesn't want us.

I plan to get all housework done today then curl up with a film or two. The house is empty, which is good. I need something for this hangover. *Oh, why did I drink so much?*

I slowly climb out of bed and place my pink fluffy dressing gown over my underwear. *I really was drunk last night to have woken up almost naked.* I head to the kitchen to collect a glass of water and headache tablets before lying on my new sofa.

This sofa was a gift from Rich's mum. It's beautiful, a brown cotton with a white spiral pattern on it. It fits in with the front room perfectly. It has a matching circle footstool. His mum also bought the matching love chair, a circle chair with sides that I love to curl up on. It even has a little bit to add a music player.

I reach out for my mobile.

Oh Megan, my head kills. Xx

Haha, Jenny, you went onto shots with Michele. What did you expect? Xx

Oh no, How is she? Xx

Throwing up for the 6th time in 40 minutes. So rough. Xx

Haha, unlucky. I'm never drinking again. Xx

I have heard that before. Xx

Well this time I am serious. I'm going to lie on the sofa all day. I'll txt you later. Xx

Have fun. If you need anything, text me. Xx

"Jennifer?" I hear, slowly opening my eyes. "Jennifer?"

I slowly sit up and glance over at the clock. It's ten in the morning. Oh no.

"Jenniferrrrrrrrrrr."

I walk to the front door and unlock it.

"Oh, you're alive then."

I glance up.

"Yes, I'm alive, Uncle Dave," I say, moving to the side. Uncle Dave is a tall, slim man with no hair. He started losing his hair before he turned thirty. His eyes are a hazel colour, not like any other family member's eye colour.

"So, you're hungover?" he questions before sitting down on the sofa.

"I was," I state.

Uncle Dave makes himself at home as usual. He is my mum's brother. He has always been a father figure in my life. At one time, my dad was really close to me, adored me, talked to me, and just spent time with me. When we lost Martin, he became different. I spoke with Mum a while back over who to give me away at the wedding. She spoke with Dad, and he said he would be happier if his brother did it. *Nothing better than knowing your own dad blames you for his only son's death.* I guess I'm getting used to it.

I asked Uncle Dave the other day if he would give me away. He said yes, and we agreed to discuss the details later. But, why today? Luckily, he did not come around too early. I don't think I'm in the mood to talk too much.

Chapter Six
28 Days to Go

Today is my final dress fitting before the big day. I had the dress sent here by courier from the bridal shop in London. I did not bring it up myself; otherwise, Rich would have seen it before the wedding. I had it delivered directly to the shop that carries the bridesmaid dresses I chose. We spent hours dress shopping around here, but never found the dress that was the *one*. Even though I had no particular dress in mind, I just did not want anything straight up and down. I wanted a little bit of sparkle and something to enhance my chest, but not a dress so large that I could not walk through the doors, or one that made me look like a toilet roll cover. *I have to keep Rich happy.* Megan found a little boutique in London on the Internet, so we checked it out. It was the best decision I made.

I remember walking into that little boutique wedding shop down a little alleyway and seeing the most beautiful dress hanging on a manikin in the middle of the store.

There was an array of dresses hanging around the room on rails, but this one stood out above all the others. I walked straight up to the dress and touched it. It was absolutely perfect.

"Megan," I said, turning to face her.

"That's the dress. That's your dress," she said with a big smile.

"Good morning. Welcome to Hope Boutique. My name is Caroline," a tall, older lady with long grey hair said while walking over to greet us.

"Hi, any chance my friend can try on this dress?" Megan questioned.

"Of course," Caroline answered with a smile.

The rest of the day is a bit of a blur to me. I followed Caroline into the fitting room, and she assisted me into the dress. I remember slipping it over my head with Caroline fastening it at the back before pulling it out at the bottom so it flowed just right. The dress was a perfect fit, no alterations needed. This can't be right? Most dresses don't fit like this the first time. I took a deep breath before walking out of the fitting room and into the main room where Megan stood. Her mouth instantly dropped.

"You look like a princess," she stated with a wobble in her voice.

"Really?" I questioned.

Megan nodded her head, unable to speak. I saw tears rolling down her cheeks. That was the moment I knew for sure this was the dress. The one.

The purpose of today's dress fitting is to make sure everything is right. I am so eager to try it on one last time before the wedding. It's going to be the first time since Lucy was born that Megan will be in her dress. She has worked hard to get her figure back quickly. She has lived off a "rabbit food diet" as she calls it. She never drank at my hen do either, but I think that might have something to do with Lucy. I get to see them both in just under an hour. I fling my hair into a loose bun and add a necklace that's the same length as my wedding one. I grab my keys and jacket as I walk to the door to leave. I am so excited I feel like a child at Christmas.

*****

I stand by my car. It is only a two-minute walk from the shop, and I am twenty minutes early to meet Megan. Everything is done by appointment times in the shop, so I have to wait here for her. I check my mobile.

Hi Jen, I'll be there in 5. Xx

Hi Hun, can't wait. Xx

I have a little time to wait. There is a shop beside the wedding boutique that sells iced fruit drinks. I decide to take up some time and get one for Megan and me. Megan loves them. They are the best thing to keep her in a good mood. Lucy is too young for them, but I bet she will be like her mum and love them when she gets older. I walk to the counter and wait for the attendant.

"Good morning, Miss. What can I get you?" the tall brunette haired man asks, displaying a full smile across his face.

160

"Two diced red fruitiest, please," I reply.

"To take out or sit in?" he questions with a voice so sweet and brown eyes so intriguing they are giving me butterflies.

"To take out, please." I pull out the money from my new purse and pass it to him. Our fingers touch, and the hairs on the back of my neck alight. He drops the change into the palm of my hand. I move over to the side while he makes the drinks.

I can't help myself from watching him work. He bends down to the fridge, then stretches high to the cupboard. *Oh, wow!* He is so cute and looks in fantastic shape from the back. He is wearing a black shirt, not the normal uniform that everyone else in the shop wears. The staff normally wears a baby blue T-shirt displaying the company's logo. I wonder if he is new. I'll definitely be coming here more often if he is.

I shake my head. *Get out of it, Jenny. You are marrying Rich.*

A man wearing the company shirt walks past me and straight over to the man.

"Mr. James, what are you doing here?" he questions him.

"I just popped in to drop off those folders," he replies, pointing to some black folders on the side. "You were really busy, so I thought I would help out for a bit, Mat."

"Thank you, Mr. James," the man says, looking worried.

He finally has a name. Mr. James walks over to me, carrying one drink in each hand and placing the two clear plastic holders onto the table.

I gaze up at him. "I'll just get you a holder for them, Miss," he states, turning around and bending to get one. *Oh, wow! What a close-up view!* He is wearing a pair of black jeans that shows off his amazing arse.

"Here you go," he says, placing the drinks into the holder and fastening it. "What colour straws would you like?"

"Any." I don't care about the colour of anything right now.

"Pink it is. All females like pink, or so I have been told." He places the straws alongside the drinks and winks at me.

"Thank you," I state, taking hold of the carrier.

He is very attentive to me. I normally never get this kind of treatment. The attendants usually order the drink, then pass it to someone else to make. Today, the shop is really busy, but Mr. James pays attention to me longer than usual. I walk through the crowd of people, taking a sneaky glance back to see that Mr. James is still looking in my direction.

Pushing the door open, I notice Megan standing against the wall with Lucy in her pram.

"Hey, Meg, how are you?" I ask while walking towards her.

"Hi, I thought you would be in there. I'm good," she says, giving me a hug.

"Here you go," I state, giving her one of the drinks.

"Are you ready?" she asks.

"Of course." We stand outside sipping our iced drinks while we wait for my appointment time. Out of the corner of my eye, I see Mr. James walking down the little alleyway to where the cars are parked. I turn slightly to watch him. He walks straight over to the posh black car that's parked beside me and climbs into it. I shake my head and turn to Megan.

"Let's go."

We walk over to the bridal shop and open the door.

"Good morning, Miss," the lady says. "I'm Olivia. You must be Jenny."

"Yes, I'm Jenny, and this is my maid of honour, Megan," I say, pointing to her.

"Shall we get on? Who's first?" she asks.

"Megan goes first. I'm dying to see her in her dress."

Megan heads off with Olivia while I take a seat on the white circle sofa in the middle of the room with Lucy in my arms. The circle sofa is unique with an open middle section enhanced with different accessories on it. Megan told me earlier that Lucy has been a little fussy today and has spent most of the past twenty-four hours crying. She wonders if Lucy has started teething.

This shop is stunning. Its walls are painted a light red colour and feature full-length mirrors all around the fitting area. There is a thick, cream coloured curtain behind the front of the shop so people cannot see inside. Two side walls showcase the selection of dresses the shop boasts.

*****

"Wow! Megan you look fantastic!"

"Thank you, it fits," she says with a huge smile covering her face.

The dress is a dark pink colour with a sweetheart neck and floor-length bottom. It is not made out of anything clingy, so it floats. On the right side of the dress, just above the hip area, is a little flower in the same colour with a hand-stitched diamond inside. It looks absolutely stunning on her. The other bridesmaids' dresses are the same colour, but differ with a halter neck and flower located on the other side. Megan's dress needs to stand out, but not be too different from the others.

Chapter Seven
20 Days to Go

I have spent the past several days running ragged at work. Today is the first day in over a week that I have gotten to do anything for the wedding. The last two days for me have been spent in bed with a viral infection, the first one that has knocked me down for a while. That is part of the joys of being a nurse, I guess. I am so excited that it is nearly time for me to say "I do". I will admit that I am worried something will go wrong. Rich is still distant with me. He has spent so much more time away from home, going for longer runs after work, eating and then heading straight to bed. He has continued his morning routine, but now he changes in the bathroom, away from me. His behavior grew more indifferent when he came back from his stag do, which consisted of paintball with the lads. That was the first time he had been anywhere near Chad since he opened up over kissing Megan. I still play the conversation in my head.

"Why did you kiss Megan?" I shouted as I jumped into the car.

"I don't want to talk about it, Jenny," Rich replied, looking down at his legs.

"You have to tell me! We are getting married soon." I paused. "Or did you forget that and think you can kiss anyone you want whenever?"

I sat there, looking at him as he placed his hand over his face.

"Just tell me why!" I snarled.

"I was scared," Rich said. I heard the worry in his voice.

"Of what?" I paused. "Please tell me, Rich," I pleaded and placed my hand on his back.

Rich shrugged.

"Do you not love me anymore?" I asked while my eyes began filling with tears.

"I do, I think I do, I was just confused," Rich replied, turning around to face me.

"Go on."

"I kissed Megan to see if I had feelings for another woman."

"Why? Why Megan?" I questioned. Tears began rolling down my face.

"I love her."

"What?" I asked, unclipping my seatbelt.

"I loved her, or I thought I did. I did not feel anything when I kissed her." He paused. *"I am so confused."*

"Why?"

"I have feelings for a man." He paused. *"I think I do."*

I opened the car door to get out. Rich took hold of my arm, stopping me from leaving.

"Let go!" I yelled.

"No, Jenny, we can sort this."

"Not if you're a flipping gay boy!" I yelled as more tears streamed down my face.

"Jenny, I was drunk. I have never been around him since."

"Who?"

"Chad," he replied as he kept a tight hold of me.

"He is straight. Right?"

"Yes, but we got drunk and close. I felt something." Rich pulled me close and forced a kiss on me. I used all my strength to push him off me. I didn't want him anywhere near me. Rich kept tight hold of my wrist. *"I love you. The feelings I have for you are more than I have for him. I love you more than anyone, than life. You are my world, Jenny."* He paused. *"Please forgive me. I said nothing happened. It was just a feeling, a feeling I never acted upon. I never will act on it. I can't be without you. Please, Jenny."*

I took a deep breath. *"Take me home."* I needed to get home. I needed time to think. I didn't know what to do.

Later that night, we sat and talked through everything. Rich recounted the entire story. He had been at Chad's twenty-sixth birthday party. They had been drinking all night at a strip club, and I knew that was where they were. I trusted Rich enough to know he was not going to do anything stupid. Well, I thought I did. He told me that someone started a fight with them, and Chad pulled him close out of the way so he wouldn't get hurt. They ended up really close.

He said, "It just felt right. It felt like we should be close. At the time, it was like the world stopped, leaving just the two of us." He paused and turned towards me. He placed his hand on my knee and said, "I'm sorry."

"Sorry?" I questioned.

"Yes," he answered, tilting his head down to the floor. "I know I shouldn't have done it, but you know as much as I do, when something feels right, you act on it. That's how we became an item. That moment with Chad...it felt right. I felt like I was doing the right thing. I wanted him to kiss me. I wanted everyone to disappear."

I spent the rest of the night wanting to be away from Rich, but he was not going to have that. I agreed to sexy time with him, so he would stop worrying so much. I did not want it, and definitely did not want to be near him, have him touch me or anything dealing with him. Once he fell asleep, I took a long shower and washed everything off me. That night I slept on the sofa alone.

After a few days break, Rich came back to the flat we shared at the time. He had seen Chad and talked everything out with him. He was definitely over it all. He spent the next few days helping me with wedding plans and going back to the normal Rich, the man I fell in love with, the man I wanted to spend the rest of my life with. My Rich.

I think I will always worry a little bit that something did happen. I think I would rather not know, though. I chose not to tell Megan; I cannot have her worrying over this. Yes, she is my best friend and like a sister to me. I know she wants to do what is best for me and protect me, like I do with her. I just hope Rich and me are sorted now, that Chad is history in the love life side. I know they are still friends. I never asked him about Chad when he came back from the stag do. I do know they all got drunk, like men always do, and Chad was in some of the pictures, but never mentioned.

Today, I'm going to write all the name place cards and match them to the seating plans. I love being able to write in calligraphy. It is such an easy thing to learn and looks so nice and pretty. It saves a lot of time and money being able to do the little bits myself. I switch on the stereo and get everything set up to begin writing.

Finishing touches are the best.

Chapter Eight

Today seems to be going by quickly, and I don't have enough time to accomplish everything on my list. Rich finished work ten minutes ago and should be home soon from his twenty-minute run, only to leave for a thirty-minute run later. He only worked until lunchtime, so I thought it would be nice if we could just relax and have fun like we used to do.

"Jennifer?" Rich yells as he comes through the door, slamming it behind him.

"Yes, I'm in the front room," I reply. Rich never uses my full name. He hates it and feels that it is old-fashioned. He has never used it during the entire time we have been together.

"What are you doing?" he asks.

"Name place cards, seating plan, and other stuff," I state, turning to face him.

"More fucking wedding stuff?" He storms out of the room. Something must be wrong. I have never seen his eyes so cold before.

I get up from the floor and follow him up the stairs. I walk into our bedroom to find Rich sitting on his side of our bed. The window is wide open, and his mobile and keys lay to the side of him on the bed. His head is tilted towards the floor.

"What's wrong?" I enquire as I walk towards the bed.

"Go away," he says in a calm manner with his head still pointing down.

"No, what's wrong?" I climb onto the bed behind him and crawl to him.

"Nothing," he says in a sharp tone.

"Yes, there is," I state, remaining calm.

"Everything," he replies, lifting his head up and staring out the window.

"Talk to me," I demand.

"The wedding, work, Chad, Luke, *everything!*" He is shouting now.

I take a deep breath. *Why did he have to say his name?* "Let's start at the top. The wedding."

"It's taking over our lives." He turns on the bed to face me.

"I know, but it will be worth it. It will be over soon," I say.

Rich sighs.

"Do you still want to get married, Rich?" I feel the stinging in my eyes.

"Yes. Well, I think I do," he answers.

"You need to know for sure, Rich." I look down at my legs. I definitely don't want this to be happening right now.

"I love you," he adds, placing his hand on my back.

"Are you sure? Or do you want Chad?" I ask, moving slightly away from him.

"No, I want you!" he yells.

"Okay, what's wrong with work?" I quickly change the subject to the second item at hand.

"Just a bad day," he states with anger in his voice.

"Okay, Luke?" I question. Luke is another one of Rich's friends. He is such a sweet man. I have never connected with someone as easily as I did with him. I met him a month after Rich and I got together when he was just himself, not the big actor he is today. To me, he is still the same sweet man. He is always there if Rich and I ever need him. I know he loves to act; I just hope he can find his personal happily ever after like the characters he plays in his films.

"He wants me to go away with him for a few days. To get away from the wedding stress," he replies, smiling.

It is nice to see him smiling for a change. "Then go," I state, thinking maybe the time away will help him.

Rich turns and faces me. "Are you sure?"

"Yes, where are you going?" I ask.

"Vegas, for three days," he says with excitement in his voice.

"Have fun." I give Rich a kiss on the cheek.

He jumps up from the bed and rushes to his wardrobe. Very quickly, he pulls out his suitcase and begins packing his things. I decide not to ask if he wants any help. I will have to repack the suitcase anyway so it is neat and everything fits properly. I lie back on the pillows and watch him pull out things from drawers and throw them into the suitcase. He's taking all his favourite clothes. I let my mind race as I sit there observing his strange behaviour. Everything is off with us. When we have sex, he just rushes it as quickly as he can. Rich does not cuddle up with me or anything. He will not allow me to touch him, scrape my fingernails down his back, play with his hair, or suck him. *None of the things he has loved before now.* He will not even let me go on top. It's all the normal way, me on my back with him over me. He will not even let me wrap my legs around him. I think he needs time away. Maybe that will fix our sex life as well as everything else. I want him here with me. I grab my mobile.

Megan, can I come stay at yours tonight? Rich is going away. Xx

Of course you can, Jen. Xx

I'm feeling all low and sad, and I really don't want to be alone tonight. I just want to cry. I need to come clean, so I plan to tell Megan everything tonight. I just don't know what to do anymore. I have to work tomorrow, so I will have something to keep my mind busy. Also, it is Alison's leaving do after work, and I need to choose something to take with me.

It only takes Rich fifteen minutes to get ready.

"That's me off," he states as he fastens his case. "Bye," he says, walking out the door. No kiss or anything.

I quickly grab my clothes and fold everything neatly into my purple overnight bag to prevent creases. I'm ready to head over to Megan's.

Chapter Nine

"Megan," I say as I walk through the door.

"In the kitchen, honey," she replies.

I place my bag on the hallway floor, close the front door quietly so as not to wake Lucy, and head straight into the kitchen. Tears pool in my eyes to the point I'm unable to see anything. I lower myself to the floor against one of her cupboards.

"Jenny, what's wrong?" I hear her say, as her footsteps get closer.

I sit there with my head resting on my knees and tears now rolling down my face. I'm unable to speak, then I feel Megan's arm wrap around me.

"Shhh, it will be okay," she whispers into my ear.

"Jenny, come into the front room." She pauses. "We can talk in there."

I don't move. Questions begin plaguing my thoughts. *How can I tell her? Is she going to be mad at me? Have I ended our friendship over some secrets? Will she ever trust me again? Is she going to be mad at Rich?* I shouldn't be here; I should have stayed home where I can't hurt anyone else or lose people from my life. I feel safe around Megan, though. I don't understand how she makes me feel safe. *She just does.* She will do anything for me.

I hear Lucy crying in the background. "Shhh, Jenny." She pauses. "I'll be two minutes." I hear her footsteps move towards the stairs. Over the baby monitor, I hear her with Lucy.

"Shhh, Lucy, what's all this noise about?" She pauses. "Shall we go find Auntie Jenny? Give her some special cuddles?" *Please don't bring Lucy with you.* I take a deep breath; I can't look like a mess, not around Lucy. I don't want her thinking the world is all bad.

"Hey, Jen," she says in a soft delicate manner.

I stand up slowly and turn to Megan. "Hey, beautiful Lucy," I say, fighting back tears and rubbing under my eyes.

"Come sit down," she states.

I go ahead of them, taking a seat on Megan's black fabric corner sofa. She always said she was going to get a corner sofa. She never had plans for this one, but it's easier to clean with a new baby in the house.

"What happened?" Megan asks.

"Rich," I state.

"*What happened?*" she repeats.

"He's changed." I look down at my lap and fidget with my fingers. I need the distraction if I am really going to go through with telling her.

After placing Lucy in her baby bouncer, Megan sits on the sofa and looks at me, waiting for details.

"He just rushes sex, no cuddles, no kisses, no anything," I blurt out.

"Do you think it could be wedding nerves?" she questions, placing her hand on top of mine.

"No idea. He kissed you," I state while looking directly at her.

"Please don't remind me." Megan pulls a face of disgust. "He needs to stop doing that. He knows what I think." Urgh...men.

"It was all over the fact he thought he might have feelings for Chad."

"Chad!" she yells.

"Yes, Chad." I nod.

"What?" She covers her mouth in shock.

"There was a fight, and they got close," I add.

"Oh my." She shakes her head.

"I just don't know what's going on, Meg," I state.

"Do you love him?" she asks.

"I think I do. I just don't want to get hurt." I tilt my head back down to my knees.

"Place the wedding off then," she firmly states.

"*What?* And waste all the money?"

"It's only money," she kindly points out.

"True." I agree because she is right. Money is only money. I don't need the money from the wedding.

"You don't want to be standing there on your wedding day with Rich deciding he doesn't want to go through with it," she adds.

"Megan, I just don't know." A tear rolls down my cheek.

She places her arms around me, giving me a big hug. "I love you, sis."

A little later, she settles Lucy in bed while I take a nice warm shower. It's much needed time alone with my thoughts. I turn on the water while looking through Megan's collection of toiletries. This woman has it all. I choose a two-in-one shampoo and conditioner and some strawberry body wash. I love the smell of strawberries. I slowly stand in the shower, letting the water wash away my tears as they fall.

Chapter Ten
19 Days to Go

I slowly wake up the next morning in Megan's bed. I could not stand the thought of being alone last night, so I crashed in here. Megan is with Lucy. I can hear her over the monitor. Megan is such an amazing mum. I feel jealous sometimes. It's been just over seventeen months since I had a miscarriage. I remember it all like it was yesterday. Rich and I were in a car accident when I was thirteen weeks pregnant. I was crushed against the dash while Rich was thrown from the car. I lost the baby. *Our* baby. It was like my entire world fell apart that day. It took us a while to regain the spark in our relationship. We did try to have another baby, but after no luck and some routine tests, we received the news we didn't want to hear. Rich was infertile due to the pelvic injuries he sustained during the wreck.

I sit up in bed and shake my head. *Stop thinking about it, Jenny.* I have four hours till I'm needed at work. I need to get on with my day, so I slide out of the cotton sheets and sit on the side of the bed.

"Morning, honey," Megan says in a cheerful manner as she walks into the room with Lucy.

"Morning," I reply.

"I was just going to grab some clothes to get dressed," Megan states. "Now that you're awake, let's have breakfast in our jammies."

"Deal."

Megan passes me a baby pink cotton dressing gown from behind her bedroom door. I stand up and slide it over my purple winter pyjamas. I didn't think when I packed last night. These were the first ones I found, and it's really too warm for them. As I tie the dressing gown, I look down. On the right side of the lapel, there is a small purple embroidered butterfly. I can't help but smile. Megan heads downstairs to get sorted while I do what I need to do. I head to the bathroom to pee and brush my hair and teeth. Hopefully, I will begin to feel more like a human now. I take a deep breath before descending down the stairs.

Megan's house is very big with plenty of space. It's the house she wanted from day one of house hunting. I love walking down her stairs. On one side, you can see what's below; on the other side, she has pictures. There are a couple of us, some of Lucy, and my favourite one— the picture of Megan and Mark when Lucy was born. Anyone can see how much he loves them in that picture. He is looking down at Lucy with a twinkle in his eyes. At the bottom step, the first drawing Mark did of Megan is hanging on the wall. Megan had a fight on her hands to get that off him. It has only been hanging a couple of weeks, but looks like it's been there forever.

"What's for breakfast?" I question as I walk into the kitchen, yet another big, spacious room complete with one large window on both sides. She had this dream kitchen designed for her. She always wanted to have a breakfast bar. As I walk towards the bar, I see Lucy sitting in her pink high chair.

"Whatever you would like," Megan states.

"Fried egg sandwich, please," I reply.

"I should have guessed. Do you just eat them at mine?" She laughs, walking over to the fridge.

"Of course, or I would burn myself like I did last time." I take a seat at the breakfast bar with Lucy.

"Hey, Lucy Doo, who's a cutie?" I ask.

I stand up and take Lucy out of her high chair, and then sit back down with her on my knee. I take hold of the pink baby rattle and give it to her. I love watching Lucy. I'm always offering to babysit for Megan so she can have some time to do as she wishes. The problem is, she has only taken me up on the offer once, when she attended the funeral of a work colleague who died in a terrible car accident. Ally was only twenty-six years old. Megan and she had been working together for six years, so her death shocked Megan. I worked with Ally, but was not as close to her as Megan. Mark stood by Megan's side the entire time. He would not leave her for anything. Ally was due to get married the day of her funeral. It stunned everyone. That day is the only time I have gotten to babysit Lucy. Even with sadness all around, I enjoyed my time with her.

"One fried egg sandwich," Megan says, placing it onto the breakfast bar, followed by a cup of coffee, and some fresh orange juice. She looks after me well. I love her to bits.

"Thanks, hun," I say, pulling the plate closer. "Your mummy's so clever, Lucy. She makes Auntie Jenny happy."

The next five minutes are heaven. I love fried egg sandwiches. Oh my. It's like the world stopped. Megan is sitting on the other side of the bar eating cereal. She is still on a health kick to ensure she fits into her maid of honour dress. She does not need to lose anything at all. She is perfect as she is, but she will not listen to anyone.

"What are you two going to do today?" I question.

"Nothing much. Go to town, get a couple of things, and then wait for Mark and Mia to come."

"Oh, I forgot they were coming today."

"Remember, Mark is going to come to the venue tomorrow," Megan says.

"Yes, I remember now. I hope Mia does, too. Is she going to come to the wedding?" I met Mia in passing once before today. Megan gets on well with Mia, and I would love to get to know her some more. I might have to suggest that Mark babysits and we girlies go out one night.

"I don't know. I haven't asked her."

"Ask her, will ya?"

"Okay, okay." She laughs.

"Time for Auntie Jenny to get dressed, Lucy Doo," I state.

"Time for Lucy to get dressed, too," Megan says while shaking Lucy's rattle in front of her.

"Can I get her ready?" I ask.

"You can if you want." Megan smiles.

"Of course, I want to. I want lots of time with Lucy."

"Go on then." Megan waves us off using the back of her hand. I stand up and walk to the door with Lucy on my hip.

"What is she wearing today?" I ask because some mums are fussy about what clothes their children wear.

"Whatever you want her to." Megan smiles and collects the pots off the bar.

I run up the stairs with Lucy. "Lucy Doo, you need to get changed. I bet we can find a pretty little dress for you to wear."

*****

"There you two are," Megan says, standing in Lucy's bedroom doorway. She's wearing black leggings and a white strappy top that seems longer than the ones she normally wears. It has a little purple three-dimensional flower on the chest. As usual, her feet are bare.

"Yes, sorry. We were having a girlie chat," I state, sitting in the rocking chair in Lucy's room with her lying in the crook of my arm.

"It's okay." She pauses. "I'm off downstairs to do some housework. Are you okay?"

"I don't know. I keep thinking about Rich and what to do, but I can't do anything with him away with Luke."

"You will figure it out."

"I know, hun." I nod.

"What time are you at work?"

I look down at the watch Megan bought me. "I need to leave in an hour. I also need to run home for some nail polish because I forgot it with all the rushing I did."

"I have loads, so use some of mine."

"Thank you." I look down at Lucy. "What colour shall I paint them, Lucy?"

"What are you wearing for the leaving do?" Megan asks.

"A red halter neck dress that comes just above my knees." I point to show her the length. "It doesn't cling too badly, and I have some black heels to go with it."

"So, red it is. I have a beautiful shade of red." She smiles. "All of my polishes are in the normal place. Shall I leave you girlies to it?"

"You can if you want, then I can teach my goddaughter how to paint nails."

"Sounds like a plan. Oh, that reminds me. I need to ring about the venue later."

Megan leaves Lucy and me, and we head into her room to find a nice red nail polish for my toes. She definitely won't mind me borrowing it. I can't polish my fingers till later. I'm not at all sure I want to go out tonight, but I *really* need a drink.

Chapter Eleven

I'm so happy that my shift is over. It was stressful, and I'm in dire need of a drink now more than ever. A big, stiff drink. I walk upstairs to the staff changing area and take my mobile out of my locker. I notice a text from Megan.

Have an amazing night out tonight, Jen. We love ya. Xx

Thank you, Megan. Love you too. Xx

I head off into the side rooms and give myself a little wash in the showers. I do not like public showers, but there is no way I am going out tonight smelling like the hospital. Just the thought of being watched in the shower by someone that I do not know makes me cringe, so I make it quick when I use public facilities. I do want to look good, though, since it's a night out with the staff. I slip on my dress, add heels, and brush through my hair, leaving it down the way it naturally falls. I take a seat in the green bucket chair near the window and grab the red polish to finish off my nails.

I glance at my mobile, seeing Megan has messaged me.

Go shake your bum. Xx

Haha, I will do. I need to de-stress. Xx

Any news from Rich? Xx

No, nothing, hun. Xx

Oh well, get a move on. Xx

With that response, I separate everything in my bag that I don't need for the night, keeping just the items I do need. Walking down to put my things into the car, I turn around to see Lori, one of the new girls at work. She seems very quiet, but I don't think she will be like that for a long time.

"Lori." I wave.

"Hi, Jenny, how are you?" she asks.

"I'm good. Are you going over to Alison's leaving do?" I question.

"Yeah, just for a couple," she replies.

"I'll walk over with you then," I add.

Lori, a newly qualified nurse, has beautiful long brown hair clipped back with a little flower hair clasp. She has mesmerizing blue eyes; she is like a dark angel. She is wearing a long pink top with a little tie around the middle over some cute jeans. Lori's topped off her outfit with black heels. She looks amazing.

"I hate walking into events alone," Lori states.

"Me, too," I agree.

As we approach the bar door, I take a deep breath. I do not really want to be here, but I promised Alison I would see her before she left for Australia. She plans to continue doing the same job, just in a place she really wants to live and work. She will be close to her best and oldest friend Kristy. I think she will be a lot happier once she gets settled in there.

"Jenny! Lori!" Alison yells as we walk into the room.

"Hi, hun," I say as I'm being dragged into Alison's arms with Lori right beside me.

"Oh my! I can't believe how drunk I am. Everyone keeps giving me wine," she says, holding up a glass of red wine.

"What would you like to drink, Alison?" I laugh.

"Water, and lots of it." She places her hand on her head.

"I'll get you water." I turn and face Lori. "What would you like to drink?"

"A small white wine would be great. Thanks," she replies.

Alison goes off to join everyone at the table while we get the drinks. I love this bar because it is quiet and only a ten-minutes' walk from my work door. The setup is such a clever idea; it is attached to a club. People just move within the same building to go from the bar to the club. I especially love the décor because it is all different colours throughout.

184

The bar staff are busy as always. They wear plain black T-shirts to set them apart from bar patrons. I stand there waiting for our drinks to arrive, watching everyone talk and eat nibbles. There is nothing better than seeing everyone relaxed.

"There you go, Miss," the bar man says.

"Thank you." I take hold of the drinks and walk over to sit at the table with Lori. The next hour or so is just full of drinking and laughing about the things we have done.

"Let's head into the club!" Alison yells.

Of course, some people jump at the chance to go, while others decline due to work tomorrow.

"Jenny, are you coming to the club?" Alison asks.

"Nah, I'm going to head home."

"Nooo! Come on, Jen. We need to party," she says, grabbing ahold of my wrist and pulling me into the club.

I love the club side; it is so much fun. There is only about an hour till it closes, so I guess it will be fun to dance the rest of the night away. Alison runs over to the DJ before appearing back on the dance floor where we are all dancing together. All the lads left, so it has turned into a true girls' night out. The lights are flashing, the music is pumping, everyone is dancing, and there is not a care in the world.

I need to pee, so I leave everyone and head over to the bathroom. Through the crowds of people, I see *him*. I'm unable to move. I never thought I would see *him* here.

I instantly feel sick to my stomach, my nerves shot. I quickly run into the bathroom, hoping he did not see me. I pee before standing in front of the mirror surrounded by loads of drunk women. I touch up my makeup, making sure I look good before I take a deep breath, push open the door, and step back out onto the dance floor.

I walk straight over to the bar to get a drink. "I'll have a water, please," I tell the bartender.

"I'll have a beer. Place hers on my tab." I turn around to see him, standing so close to me that there is not even an inch between us.

"I can buy my own drink. Thanks," I say.

"It's my treat."

Chapter Twelve

"Mr. James, you don't need to," I state.

"You remember my name from the other day." He smirks.

"I do, but only because one of your staff said it," I add, not wanting him to think anything.

"Yes, that's right. He did. But, please call me Warren," he says, leaning closer and grabbing the drinks from behind me.

"Nice to meet you, Warren." I can feel my heart beating fast.

Our fingers touch when I take the glass of water from his hands, causing the heat to rise to my cheeks. The club is so dark it is hard to see what he is wearing, other than a dark-coloured shirt and trousers.

"I best go and join the rest of them," I state, looking toward my group of girlies.

"Who are you with?" he questions.

"People from work. Alison is leaving, so we are having a party," I reply.

"Oh, that's nice." He pauses. "Stay here with me."

I shouldn't, but I want to. "Come join in. They are too drunk to care," I say, taking a deep breath.

"Perfect." He gently takes hold of the top of my arm and follows me through the crowd to the rest of my friends. They don't even seem to notice I'm back from the bar or that I brought a guy with me.

I keep a safe distance from Warren on the dance floor. I dance like I don't have a care in the world. I'm trying hard not to think about Rich, the wedding, or anything else. I just want to have fun. I want to be me.

The song changes to "S & M" by Rhianna, and I can't help but laugh. I stand there singing and dancing away, suddenly feeling someone's hands on my hips. I turn around to see Warren. I don't move away from him; instead, I keep dancing with his hands on my hips, my bum so close to his cock, my arms in the air. I'm suddenly brought to a standstill when I feel his lips on my neck. My heart stops beating momentarily. *Oh.* He kisses me again, slightly parting his lips this time for me to feel the wetness of his tongue. I turn and meet his eyes while his hand slides straight into my hair, pulling me closer to him, his lips finding mine. Slowly, his tongue invades my mouth. *Oh, this is heaven.*

"Jenny," Alison says, tapping me on the shoulder.

"Yes, Alison?" I step away from Warren. *Why did I just do that?*

"I'm off home," she states.

I give her a huge hug and watch her leave. I turn to Warren who is standing there with a look of desire on his face.

"Sorry, I shouldn't have done that," I say.

I bend down, grab my bag, and start to leave. He takes my wrist and pulls me close. "Please stay."

"Why?"

"Let's just talk," he suggests.

"Okay, fine," I agree. I don't want to go. This is the most alive I have felt in years.

Warren walks over towards the bar to order a couple of drinks as I find a little table in the corner of the club.

"Here you go. Another water," he states, placing it down in front of me.

"Thank you."

"So, do you come here often?" he asks.

"Oh, none of *those* lines, please." I laugh, taking a sip of my drink.

"I was just asking. I have never seen you here before. I own this place, that's all, so I'm here a lot." He points to the dance floor.

"Oh, wow. I come here sometimes, but normally just to the bar after work."

"What do you do?" he asks.

"I'm a nurse."

"Maybe you can be *my own* private nurse." He winks.

"Maybe."

The club closes and everyone disappears, leaving us sitting here talking. I cannot stop looking at him, watching his chest rise up and down. Now that the lights have come on, I can see his shirt is midnight blue and tight. The colour suits him very well.

"I should really go," I say, glancing at my watch.

"Let me take you home," he counters.

"I'm not sure that's a good idea. You have been drinking." I point at his barely touched glass.

"I've only had one." He smiles. "Please, it's no problem."

"If you insist." I slowly rise and walk towards the bar, placing the two glasses on the other side.

"Thank you," he murmurs. "You could work here, no problem."

I turn to face him, my back leaning on the bar, "Oh, could I?"

He places his hands on my hips and lifts me onto the bar counter.

L Chapman

Chapter Thirteen

I find myself squealing with shock. "Why did you do that?" I question.

"So I could do this." His hand slides slowly up my legs along my inner thigh. I lean back on the bar. "You're perfect," he whispers.

He lifts me a little, pushing my dress over my bum. I look directly into his eyes, mesmerized by his desire. His head moves towards me, his lips meeting mine, his tongue entering my mouth, and his hand softly tugging my hair.

"Mmm."

He releases me. "Mmm, indeed." He pauses. "You're so beautiful."

I move closer to him, placing my lips on his. *I want him. I need him. I really shouldn't. What about Rich? I can't help but want him, though.*

His hand goes around my back, pulling me even tighter to his rock hard body, while his other hand slides up and down my thigh. I am glad I am not wearing any tights. His lips leave mine, moving down the nape of my neck in slow, little intense butterfly kisses. I reach forward, slowly unbuttoning his shirt, feeling the structure of his body and anticipating the vision of what is underneath.

I slide his shirt off his shoulders, getting to see the man under the clothes—the bulging muscles of his arms, a toned six pack, and a hair-free chest. *Just wow.* I notice a tribal tattoo on the top of his right arm, and as I glance to the other side, I spot another tribal design that winds completely around his left arm. I want to explore this man and find any more tattoos he has. He looks straight at me. His eyes light up and a huge smile covers his face. He moves his hand through his hair before placing both at the bottom of my dress and pulling it down off of me.

"Wow, babe, you're going to kill me," he whispers into my ear, slowly tugging on the bottom of it.

191

I let my hands slide down his body to his belt, undoing it with one hand.

"Plenty of practice, I see," he whispers, unclipping my black lace bra with his hand.

I feel myself start to blush. I hope he doesn't think I am some kind of slut. His lips fall down my neck and onto my chest, his mouth wraps around my nipple, and his other hand caresses the curve of my back.

"Mmm." I have not felt like this in years.

He looks directly at me before leaning me farther back over the bar. Moving with me, he reaches behind my head, and I hear something I'm not sure of. "Ice, babe. It's getting hot in here," he says, placing the ice just below my breasts and letting it slide down my stomach. His tongue follows the trail the ice leaves behind.

He stops at my navel, slowly placing his hand under my bum, lifting it up and pushing down my thong. "Oh, wow." I feel the heat rise through me.

Taking the ice in his mouth, he follows down my stomach before placing it on my clit. The coldness is such a shock that I jump from the intense feeling it creates. *Oh, man.* I feel him slowly slide a finger inside me and withdraw it.

He lifts his head, taking the ice with him. "Are you okay?" he questions. I nod. He glides a finger inside me again, sliding it in and out, and then adding another finger, teasing me with each withdrawal. I moan. He rubs my clit with his thumb, and I begin to feel the intensity building inside me. He leans towards me, places his lips on mine, and kisses me deep and hard.

I feel the buildup of tension before the orgasm washes over me. He continues thrusting his fingers deep inside me. His lips slowly come off mine, and his eyes twinkle. "Oh, babe, I'm so happy right now," he whispers. I start to regain my senses and try to sit up on the bar as he removes his fingers from inside me.

"Oh no, you don't, babe. I'm not finished yet." He winks.

"I hope you're not, but I want to get my mouth on that cock of yours," I say.

"Oh, you can any day, babe. But, I want to get you in my bed where I can have you and not worry about anything."

I nod, "Okay then." This will be the first time I have slept with anyone other than Rich. He was my first. I never intended for this to happen, but I feel alive for the first time in years.

I reach for my bra. "No, you don't, babe. Pop this on, only." He passes me his shirt.

I do as he says and place it on, buttoning it up fully. I watch Warren collect my clothes and lay them on the bar beside me.

"Here, babe," he says, lowering me from the bar. I can't believe how strong he is. He grabs my clothes and bag and walks beside me to the door.

"I can't go outside dressed like this," I state, looking at him towering above me.

"You can, babe. My car is just to the side of the door." He points to the door. "I have a jacket in the car that you can add to your sexy outfit if you want."

I take a deep breath and walk out the door. It is all dark and quiet with no lights or sounds anywhere. There is a car to the left-hand side of the door. "That one?" I question.

"Yes, babe."

I walk over towards the passenger side. Warren unlocks the doors as he walks towards the car. I slide into it, admiring the leather seats. It must be a posh car. He throws my clothes onto the backseat, then starts the engine as some slow, romantic music starts playing.

"Oh, a romantic man, I see." I look over towards him.

"It's the radio, but I don't mind romance if it comes with spice."

"Oh, *really*?"

"Yes, really. *Your spice.*"

Chapter Fourteen

I cannot stop glancing over at him. I watch him swing the car out from the parking spot on the street, and his confidence pours. He keeps looking back at me and winking. I'm happy he has kept his top off; it is truly an amazing sight to see.

"Are you watching me, Mr. James?" I question.

"Of course, I am, Jen. I need to keep an eye on the most beautiful woman I have ever seen," he murmurs.

"Oh, are you flirting?"

"More than flirting, babe."

"I can't wait to get my mouth around that cock of yours. I can see it's eager to escape."

"Now, naughty babe."

"Are you going to stop me?" I ask.

"Hell no, you can suck him whenever you want." He winks again.

"How long till we are back at yours?" I ask.

"About ten minutes."

I lower my seat belt so I can move my hand over the gear stick onto his leg. I look up at Warren's face; his eyes remain on the road. I slide my hand over the bulge in his trousers.

"Mmm," he says.

I let my fingers find the button of his trousers and unclip it, sliding down the zipper, and revealing a big lump. I slide his boxers down over his cock, letting it spring free.

"Well, hello, little James."

"Hey, less of the little, please."

"Okay, we will see."

"You will soon be revoking that comment, babe."

"We will see about that." I let my hand slide up and down his cock. Okay, I will not admit it yet, but damn, he is big. I lean farther over, licking the tip of his hard cock with my tongue.

"Mmm," he moans again.

He tastes so good. I slowly slide my mouth down his cock, taking him all the way to the point that I almost gag. I slide it back out again. I continue sliding him in and out of my mouth, letting my hand grasp his balls, hearing him gasp with pleasure as I suck harder, gently pulling his shaft between my teeth.

"Oh, babe, I'm going to come. Please, babe," he says in between moans.

I take the full length of him in my mouth before feeling a wash of warmness in the back of my throat. The car engine stops, and I slowly sit up.

"Thankfully, we are here," he states as he tries to catch his breath.

"Oh, good timing then," I reply, looking directly into his brown eyes.

"Come on inside. Now!" he states, placing his cock back inside his trousers.

"Now?" I question.

"Yes, now. I want you in my bed. You are going to scream my name."

He climbs out of the car, shutting his door. I reach into the back and grab my bits. *A one-night stand can't harm me*, I reassure myself. The passenger side door opens, and there stands Warren with one hand on his hip, the other on the door holding it open. I slowly climb out of the car, trying to keep my legs as close together in order to remain lady-like. Well, as much of a lady as I can be in this kind of situation.

I stand up, walk around Warren, and feel him tap my arse. "Get a move on, babe, or I will pick you up and carry you myself."

I walk faster towards the apartment block. "I'm not waiting to find out if you're telling the truth with that one." I giggle.

Chapter Fifteen

As we reach the door to the block, Warren pushes me against the nearest wall. His lips meet mine, his chest pushes against my breasts, and I can feel his heat. His lips slip from mine, remaining in close proximity. "Stairs or lift?" he whispers. I turn my head and gasp as he pulls my earlobe gently between his teeth.

"Lift. I don't think I can go much farth—" His lips find mine again before I'm able to finish what I was trying to say.

I hear the "ping" of the lift as Warren takes hold of my hand and walks me into it.

I watch him press the *Up* button, then lean against the wall with one knee bent and his foot on the wall. "You're amazing to watch," he says.

"Me?" I question as I stand on the other side of the lift.

"Yes, *you*," he says. He walks towards me, pulling me in tight. My lips hit the base of his neck, leaving him with a small kiss. I let out a little squeak as he lifts me, forcing me to wrap my legs around him. I take the opportunity to move even closer to him, kissing his neck, and letting my hand slide up and down his back. Warren walks towards a black door before reaching into his trouser pockets and pulling out a card. I take the card from him and lean back to unlock the door. Warren winks before walking us into the room and through another. He flips on the light switch. I turn my head around to see a bed with black bedding.

"I hope you're ready," he murmurs as he gently lays me onto the bed. I climb backwards a bit before reaching forward and pushing down his trousers. His cock bounces, all ready to go. Warren climbs onto the bed, moving closer to me and stopping at my side as I sit upright near the pillows.

"This has to come off, babe," he says, unbuttoning his shirt and pushing it off my shoulders and down my arms.

My eyes remain locked on his as I lean back. I am naked except for my shoes on a stranger's bed, yet I feel desirable, wanted, and alive.

I want him so deep inside me. I want to ride the hell out of him. I don't want any worries, no strings, just fun.

"You're leaving those sexy shoes on," he orders as he begins placing little kisses on my stomach and continues upward to my breasts. His tongue thrashes around my nipples while his hand glides up and down my back. I place my hands in his hair, leaning my head back as he hits my weak spots.

His lips slide onto mine as I push him over onto his side and place my leg over his. *I will get what I want,* I think to myself. His hand goes to the back of my head pushing me in closer to him, deeper.

He rolls backwards, forcing me on top. I can feel his pulsating cock in between the lips of my pussy. I let my hand glide down his chest and stomach till I reach his cock. I rub it before letting it slide into me.

"Oh," I say with pleasure as I adjust to his size. He feels so good.

Warren lets go of my head, letting me sit upright before I lean slightly back and slowly start moving up and down. I watch his face explore my exposed breasts while his hands glide over my hips to help me move faster.

"Oh, babe," he moans. "Oh, you're killing me."

I can't remember the last time I felt like this. I lean forward placing my hands on his stomach. *Wow, what a body.* Warren's hands slide over my bum before giving it a little tap.

"Oh," I moan, my speed increasing.

I feel the tension start to build between us. The heat is incredible. He is so deep inside me. I can feel him throb. He does not let up; his hands squeeze my hips harder as he drives himself into me at the same time I push down.

"Oh, babe, I'm going to explode soon," he says between moans. I smile. I want him to come, and I'm so close it's unreal. "Arghhh, Jen!" he shouts.

"Warrennnnnn!" I scream as I collapse on him with my head falling on his bare chest.

"Oh, babe," he whispers as he moves my hair out of my face. I feel his lips gently caress my forehead.

I slowly climb off him, lying down by his side. He wraps his arm around me, pulling me closer. "I haven't finished with you yet, Jen," he whispers before placing a delicate kiss on my head as his spare hand rubs my breasts.

Chapter Sixteen

Today is the day we set aside to go to the venue one last time before the wedding. I have always wanted a traditional wedding, and when it came time to pick the venue, I said it had to be a church. I did not care which one, so Rich suggested the little church he was christened in since it is located in the town we just moved to. It's a quaint looking church. I didn't want to get married too early in the day, so we chose two in the afternoon, that way I have time to get ready. The reception will be posh because we are hosting it in a castle.

I slowly open my eyes. The sun is blaring straight through the window towards me, so I pull the cover up over my face.

"Oh, babe, are you not a morning person?" I hear him say.

Oh my, last night was not a dream. I look under the cover to discover I am naked, just as I suspected. I roll over to see Warren lying there with his shoulder bent to raise him a bit higher.

"Hi," I reply sheepishly.

He still looks amazing, but I should not be here. I should be at home waiting for Rich, the man I am marrying in a matter of days. Last night was the best night of my life. *Ever.* I cannot stop smiling. So naughty, but nice. *Is it bad that I want to do it again?* Warren was so wonderful, so gentle, yet so exciting at the same time. I never knew what he was going to do next, and it made the sex that much better.

I shake my head; I need to stop thinking about last night. I need to go home and tell Rich what I did. Tears start to roll down my face.

"Hush, babe. What's wrong?" Warren questions, placing his arm around me. I push back against him, freeing myself from his grip. I sit up on the side of the bed.

"Where is my stuff?" I ask while trying to hold back tears.

"Here," he says as he passes my clothes to me.

I sit there slipping on my underwear, then adding my heels.

"Jen, what's wrong?" he asks, appearing beside me, fully dressed.

"Nothing," I say, slipping my dress over my head.

"Tell me," he says, his normal calm voice now a firm tone.

I shake my head. Warren gently pushes me back onto the bed. "Tell me," he repeats in a pleading manner.

"I'm getting married in a few days. Last night should have never happened." I stare into his eyes, waiting for his reaction.

"Okay. I'll drop you back off wherever you need to be. No one ever has to know what happened between us." I can tell he is hurting because his eyes turn dull, and their usual sparkle is gone.

"Thank you," I reply, taking a deep breath. I do not know what to do. I really should just walk away.

I follow Warren topless, just in his boxers down from his bedroom along the hallway, past the cream walls with paintings hanging. We walk into the dining room and face a large table.

"Would you like some breakfast before you leave?" Warren asks with sorrow in his voice.

I shake my head to say no.

"You need something, even if it's just a drink, Jen," he pushes.

"Coffee, please," I state, placing my hand into my bag and pulling out my mobile.

"How do you take it?" he asks.

"Milk and one, please."

I lean against the dining room table watching him move around in the small kitchen. I glance down at my mobile to see a missed text from Megan.

Hi Hun, did you have a good night? We will meet you at the venue just before 2. Heading out to get a couple of things. Xx

Megan, I did something really wrong last night. Xx

"Here you go. Shall we sit in the front room?" Warren asks while passing me a blue cup of steaming hot coffee.

"Okay." I follow him into the room.

"So, you're getting married. When?" he asks, taking a seat on the dark blue corner sofa.

I sit down, ensuring some space between us. "In seventeen days."

"So, are you going to tell me about the lucky man?"

"You don't really want to know about him. You're just trying to find out something. What do you want to know?"

"Are you really happy?" he asks, placing his hand on my bare knee.

"I'm not talking about it." I drink my coffee as quickly as I can. I need to get away from Warren. My chest hurts, and I feel like I am breaking into a million pieces. I want last night to last forever, but I am with Rich. He is my prince now.

"Where is it that I am taking you to?" Warren asks as he grabs my empty cup.

"Just back to the club, please." I stand up and follow him into the kitchen. His apartment is perfect. The walls are painted cream with a feature wall covered in wallpaper and large windows to allow light to enter. It is a very stylish place, but it is lived in and easily recognised as a bachelor's apartment. He has a large television with a game console and a rack full of video games. It is odd that I do not see any family pictures on the wall.

"Are you sure? Where is your car?" he asks, grabbing his car keys from the side where he threw them when we came in last night.

"At work."

"I will just take you there."

"No, you don't have to do that."

"I'm taking you to your car," he says in a stern voice.

"Thank you." I look down at the floor, not knowing what else to say.

The journey to my car is quiet; we don't say anything to each other. I feel like I have broken Warren. *Why did I have to sleep with him?*

"Thank you, Mr. James," I say as we pull up beside my car.

"It's Warren, and you're welcome, Jen." He leans over to me, placing a little kiss on my cheek. Tears begin to well up in my eyes, and I take a deep breath before I open the car door.

"Jen." I turn to face him. "Here is my card. Please stay in touch." I take the card and nod as I exit the car. I walk over to my car and rummage through my bag to find my keys, sliding his card into my bag in the process. I jump into my car. As I start the engine, the tears begin flowing freely down my face. *Why? Why did I do it?* I love Rich, or I don't know anything about what I want anymore.

Chapter Seventeen

As I pull into the driveway of our house, I am elated to see no other car is parked there. I don't think I can cope talking to anyone today, but I know I need to. I jump out of my car and head inside, straight up the stairs and into the shower. I need the shower to wash away everything that I did. I place my hand in to check the temperature before climbing into the bath. We still have to get our separate shower sorted. We are planning that as a project after the wedding. I stand there letting the water hit me and allowing my mind to recall what Warren and I did in his shower last night. I had never had sexy time in the shower before, and it was mind blowing.

I shake my head. *Stop thinking about him, Jennifer.* I grab the shower gel and flannel and scrub myself over and over again. Before climbing out, I wrap a big pink towel around myself. I walk into my bedroom and open the wardrobe. I need something to wear. I pick out a black skirt with a little slit at the side. It only comes to my knees, but it looks smart. I pick out a plain white blouse to go with it and place them both on my bed so I can critique the outfit matched together. It will have to do. No one will care what I wear today anyway. I turn to the drawer and grab some underwear before getting dressed.

I leave my hair as it is, just throwing the brush through it. By the time I get sorted and to the venue, it should be dry. I choose some black peep-toe shoes and slip them on. I walk over to my wall-length mirror and stand there looking at myself. I rub down the creases in my clothes and turn to the side to make sure I look smart. I have a long black cardigan in the car that I can place over my blouse. I add the finishing touches of a little mascara and purple eye shadow. I am ready to go to the castle.

Before I leave, I stand there rubbing my finger where my engagement ring should be. I do not wear it at work, so it has been in my bag. It feels weird when it's not on my finger. I guess that's a sign that I'm used to it being there. I take it from my bag and slide it back on. It's simple, but beautiful. Rich knows me well.

I head back downstairs with everything I need in my bag. I have ten minutes to spare before I need to leave to make it to the venue on time. I head into the kitchen, grab a glass from the cupboard, and run the cold water tap. I test the water with my little finger before placing the glass underneath it. I then turn to the cupboard to get some headache tablets. They might ease the dull pain I have in my chest. I feel like such a bitch.

Climbing into the car, I turn on the radio as loud as I can. I quickly check my mobile.

Oh, Jenny, what did you do? Xx

I slept with someone. Xx

I place my mobile on the passenger seat, pull out of the driveway, and sing along to the radio all the way to the venue. I try hard to keep my mind from racing back to last night. Anything but think of what I have done.

As I pull into the car park of the castle, I see Megan standing there with Mia.

Taking a deep breath, I grab everything and head over to them.

"Hi," I say.

"Jenny, it's lovely to see you again," Mia says while giving me a welcoming embrace. Mia is such a bubbly person. She is a little bit younger than me if I remember correctly. She always wears girlie glamour clothes. Today, she has some black leggings under a floating dark, plump purple top that only just covers her bum. It clings to all the important parts. Her attire is complete with some lovely heels. Her straight hair is down. It is noticeable that she has money to waste since all of her stuff looks brand new.

"Hi, Jenny, I got your text. We need to talk," Megan states, giving me a hug.

"I know. Where is Lucy?" I question.

Megan points to the grassy area beside the castle. I see Mark sitting on the grass with Lucy leaning against his leg. We walk over towards them. Lucy is growing up too fast.

"Hi, Mark," I say, going down on my knees behind Lucy and tickling her. She lets out a cute little laugh.

"Hi, Jenny," he says. "Look who's here, Lucy. Auntie Jenny."

I smile at Mark. I feel safe here, and Megan will make sure I'm safe. "Can I have a cuddle with my gorgeous goddaughter?" I ask, looking at Mark.

"Of course, you can. My bum is getting numb, and I need to move anyway." I take Lucy from Mark, pull her in close, and give her a hug.

Chapter Eighteen

I turn around to see Luke walking towards us wearing a black suit that makes him look very smart.

"Hey, I thought you were away?" I state.

"I got back three days ago."

"Oh."

"*Oh?*" Luke repeats.

"Rich said you and he were off to Vegas."

"That's next month."

"Do you know where he is then?" I ask.

"I have only just got back to town. He said he was staying at mine while you sorted out some wedding stuff with Megan."

"Okay." That lying fucking bastard. I need to get to Luke's as soon as possible.

We walk into the castle.

"Hi, I'm Michael," a tall man wearing a grey suit says.

"We have a booking."

"Oh, yes, you do. You must be Jennifer," he says before I am able to give him all the information.

"Please call me Jenny or Jen."

"Of course, Jen."

This should not take long. I give him all the bits he needs and inform everyone else of the plans. It is so nice to be back in here; it is such a pretty castle. Michael leads us for a walk around the grounds, showing everyone the reasons why I fell in love with it.

As we hit the car park, the screech of a car breaking instantly stops us. *I know that car.* I continue walking but keep the car in my sight. I was right. It's Warren. I place my head down and rush inside before he sees me.

Megan and I head to the bathroom. I need to talk to her alone. I push the heavy doors open, and we walk inside.

"Oh, Megan, why did I do it?" I ask.

"No idea, hun."

"He's here now."

"Who?"

"The man that just followed us in from the car park."

"I have seen him before."

"Yeah, from the day of my wedding dress fitting."

"Yes, that's right."

"What happened?" she questions.

"We started talking, dancing, then it just happened."

"You were confused. You need to talk to Rich."

"Oh, I intend to. I cannot believe he lied to me."

"You will sort it."

"Megan, I did stuff with him I have *never* done before. Stuff I have always wanted to do but was too embarrassed. I felt so alive with Warren. He was a breath of fresh air at a time when I needed it."

"You do have a sparkle in your eyes for the first time in ages," Megan points out. I turn around and look in the mirror. She is right; I do have a gleam in my eyes.

"I feel like my heart is breaking."

"You have to do what is right for you."

"I need to see Rich."

"You go. I'll finish here," she states.

"Are you sure?"

"Yes, you go."

"Thank you. You're the best. Love you, babe," I say, giving her a huge hug.

I walk out of the bathroom and straight into the car park towards my car.

"Jen."

I turn to see Warren.

"Yes, Warren?" I stand still.

"You left this." He passes me my necklace.

"Thank you."

"You're welcome."

"How did you find me?"

"I just came to drop off something here and saw you. I stood waiting for you to come back out."

"Well, thank you."

"You're welcome again. You're getting married here?"

"No, reception."

"Oh, I see." I feel dampness collect between my legs. *I want him. I want to hold him. I want him to hold me.* I have to get away from him. I need to see Rich, my husband-to-be.

"I need to go," I state, turning around and walking to my car. Warren grabs my wrist and pulls me back, wrapping his arms around me tightly.

"I need this; I need to hold you. I know I will see you around, but you will be a married woman. Your fiancé does not need to know about this." He places a little kiss on my forehead. I wrap my arms around him.

I...I don't know what to do.

"I need to go and sort some stuff, Warren."

"Okay, babe, I'll let you go. Please don't be a stranger."

"Goodbye, Warren," I say as I walk away from him, tears streaming down my face.

Chapter Nineteen

It is a short drive to Luke's, which is good because I really need to see Rich. I want to know why he lied to me. The number of questions plaguing my mind right now is unimaginable. Luke's house is not posh; it is just a normal house on a street with lots of other houses. You would not think he is a celebrity. Well, he does act like a dick sometimes, but I have grown to like him. He is a giggle.

I park in the car park of the cul-de-sac where Luke lives. I do not notice any cars I know, not even Rich's. I walk up to the door. A while back, Luke gave me a key so I could house-sit for him while he was away filming. I push open the door a little bit and quietly walk inside. I hear a faint noise in the background. I gently close the door before walking along the hallway. The noise seems to get louder as I hit the bottom of the stairs.

"Ohh... ohh... ohh."

I slowly walk up the stairs.

"Ohh... ohh." I stand still on the top step listening to find the room the sound is coming from.

"Oh, I'm going to come." I hear Rich say. I storm to the door, open it slowly... I do not want to see what is going on inside the room.

I stand there in shock. *Rich.* Chad turns to face me, his cock buried inside my husband-to-be, while Rich's hand is stroking his own dick. The tears flood down my face.

"What the hell are you doing?" I scream.

"Jenny, what are you doing here?" Rich asks as he moves from Chad.

I slam the door and run down the stairs, unable to see with the tears falling from my face.

"Arghhhh!" I scream.

*****

I slowly open my eyes. *Where am I?*

"Jenny, you're awake," Megan says as she grabs ahold of my hand.

"Where am I?" I question.

"In the hospital, you tripped going down the stairs at Luke's," she informs me.

"Oh, I remember now."

"That's good. Bad news, you broke your ankle," she says.

"Oh, fuck."

"You will be okay. Rich and I will look after you." She smiles.

"I don't want Rich near me."

"Why?"

"He was having sex with Chad!"

"What?" A look of shock covers her face.

"Yes, Chad had his cock in Rich, so I ran."

"Oh my."

"Where is Rich?"

"He is with Luke getting some drinks."

214

"Please ask him to leave. Tell him I will move my stuff out of the house." I begin to cry.

"You can stay with me."

"Thank you."

"Knock, knock," a tall skinny man says as he walks through the hanging privacy curtain.

"Hi, Miss Wright. I'm Dr. Ding. How are you feeling?" he asks, moving up the bed towards me.

"I feel sick, and my head hurts," I say, placing my hand on my head.

"You cut it when you fell. You received twelve stitches, and you broke your ankle. No wonder you feel sick," he informs me.

"Can I go home, please?" I ask.

"Not yet. You need to stay for a few hours longer. Then I can release you if you have someone to look after you," he says as he picks up the clipboard.

"Megan will," I state. *Please, let me go, please. I do not want to see Rich.*

"Still need to wait a few more hours," he states before leaving us to talk.

I roll over on my side and cry. "Please, don't cry, Jenny. We will sort everything."

"Can you get rid of Rich for me, please?" I ask.

"I will."

Chapter Twenty

Once the doctor released me, I went straight to Megan's house. I have been here for about an hour now. I have had a wash and put on some of her pyjamas. That's one good thing about being the same size. Megan spoke to Rich for me, and he left the hospital without a fight. I never want to see him again. I am thankful that Megan's house is big with plenty of room for us all to sleep.

Mia offered to stay in a hotel, so I could stay here. Megan is planning a special tea for us all. I smell some type of food, but I can't make out what it is. I start to walk towards the landing when I hear Lucy crying.

"I'll get her, Megan," I bellow down the stairs.

"Shhh, Lucy what's wrong?" I pick her up from her basket and cradle her in my arms. "Shhh...shhh." I place a little kiss on her head.

"Shall we change that bum bum of yours?" I question before sorting her out.

"That's you all sorted, baby."

I turn around to see Mark standing there smiling.

"You're going to be an amazing mum sometime, Jenny," he says.

Tears start to fall from my face. "Thank you."

Mark walks over to me, giving me a hug with Lucy between us. I can see why Megan likes him so much. He is good at comforting.

"I came to see if you wanted a hand. Tea is ready," he whispers.

"Thank you. You can take Lucy. I should manage to get down the stairs okay." I turn off the baby monitor before following Mark along the landing.

"Would you like a dressing gown or anything? It is chilly downstairs." he asks.

"I don't know if there's a spare," I state.

"You head downstairs. I'll get you something," he says, heading off into Megan's room.

"Thank you." I smile.

I hope it gets easier moving up and down the stairs because it seems to take forever. Hopefully, I will work out how to do it without the worry of falling again. I had a hard time walking upstairs when I arrived here.

"There you are," Mia says as she stands in the doorway of the front room.

"Yes, I'm here."

"Come sit down," she says, pointing at the sofa.

I sit down on the sofa as Mia places a footstool under my feet.

"Thank you." I feel like an invalid. Everyone is trying to mother me. I just want to be alone. I need time to think; I need to work out what to do.

Mark comes around the door. "Here you go." He passes me a little jacket in the same material as a dressing gown.

Mark places Lucy into her baby bouncer before they all leave me. I reach for my mobile and check my messages. They are all from Rich.

Jenny, baby. I love you. Xx

I love you. I'm sorry. Xx

We need to get the rest of the wedding things sorted. Xx

Why will you not talk to me, Jenny? Xx

I delete them all because I refuse to read any more.   With shaking hands, I type him a text.

Rich, it's over. You're GAY. Accept it. No wedding, no nothing. I will collect my things. The house is yours. I will ring and cancel all the wedding things. I will place anything of yours at the house and leave the car there, too.

I hit *Send* and sit there crying. I'm losing everything by leaving. The car is Rich's because mine is broken. I have nothing. Because of my ankle injury, I cannot work for the next six weeks. I don't even have a place to live. There are too many people living at my parents' house, so that's not even an option. I need to face the fact that I am homeless.

"Hey, what's up?" Megan questions as she walks through the door with a tray of drinks.

"I have lost everything," I say between the tears.

"Not everything."

"What can I do?"

"Let's have tea, an early night, and we can sort out everything tomorrow," Megan suggests.

I nod. I need to sleep.

Chapter Twenty-One

I should be getting married in sixteen days, but instead, today I am cancelling everything. I slide up in the bed, lifting a pillow to place behind my back. I reach over for my mobile.

It's nine a.m. I check through my messages. I am happy to see there is nothing from Rich. I go back to find my daily to do alert.

16 days to go list:

Flowers

Wedding Favours

Thank you gifts

Thank you cards

Tears roll down my face. My dream day is gone. There is no way I can cope with all of this. It is just too hard. I have always wanted to be married, always wanted to have a day set aside just for my husband and me. Today is meant to be a girlie day for Megan, Lucy, Mia, and me. We are going shopping and having lunch away from the boys to sort out the list.

I need to return to my house to pick up all the contact numbers and ring or text everyone regarding the change of plans. My mind is racing all over the place. I want to be alone to sleep, but I also feel the need for someone to hold me. More importantly, I want everything finished so I can get on with my new life. Just me, myself and I.

I slide onto the side of the bed, taking it slow. Megan has given me some of her clothes, but I need my own. I inch down the bed and grab some black leggings and a white jumper. That will do. I could care less what I look like right now anyway. I take them over the landing to the bathroom. I apply some mascara and make my eyes smoky, so maybe people won't notice I have been crying. I step out of the bathroom and straight into Mark.

"Good morning, Jenny," he says in a cheerful manner.

"Can tell *you* got some last night, Mr. Cheerful," I comment before laughing. "Morning."

"Well, maybe I did, maybe I didn't. How did you sleep?" he asks.

"Really well, thank you. I crashed."

"Great. I'll see you downstairs for breakfast." He jumps down the stairs. I am surprised he does not hurt himself.

Breakfast goes really quickly. I don't want to eat, but do just to keep the peace.

"Change of plans, Jenny. You and I are off to sort out the stuff. Mark's going to collect your car and drop it off at Rich's," Megan states.

"Thank you."

"Let's get on. Sooner we start, the sooner it's over with," Megan says while grabbing her keys before walking over to Lucy and giving her a little kiss.

"I love you, baby." I stand there watching Megan with her. She was born to be a mum.

We head out to the car. "We are going in Mark's. More room for your things. The seats are already down and ready to roll," she says.

The journey to what used to be my house does not take long. I just sit there with my eyes closed, pretending to be asleep. I really don't want to be around people, but I need help with moving everything today.

"We are here, but so is Rich," Megan announces. I open my eyes and take a deep breath.

"Can you give me ten, just to talk to him, please, hun?" I ask.

"Of course."

I climb out of the car and knock on the door. About a minute later, Rich opens the door.

"Why didn't you use your keys?" he asks, standing at the door in his favourite red tracksuit.

"It's not my house," I state.

"Come on. It's ours." He moves to the side.

I walk in through the door looking at everything I did to make the house perfect. I spent months decorating this place making it like the dream home I had always wanted to raise our children in.

"Okay, it's over. You are with Chad. That's it," I state.

"B-but...Jenny," Rich stutters.

"But *what*?"

"I love you. I always have."

"You're fucking gay!" I scream at him.

"I'm bisexual."

"Finally admitting something," I say, placing my hands on my hips.

"I will still marry you, be with you."

"Do you *really* love me, Rich?" I question.

"No." He looks down at the floor.

"There you go. That answers everything. I will get my stuff and leave."

I turn around to head upstairs when Rich grabs ahold of my arm. "Why are you not shouting and screaming at me?"

"I have no energy. I'm tired, and I feel sick. My head hurts, my chest hurts. I just don't care anymore. I'm losing everything all at once. You have changed, Rich."

"I know. I'm sorry," he states, tilting his head down to his knees.

"No, you're not. You're happy. You get to be with Chad," I snap.

"Don't be like that," he says.

"How long?" I demand, staring directly at him. I now him too well. I knew something wasn't right.

"How long what?" he questions, lifting his head.

"How long have you been fucking him?" I fold my arms, staring him down.

"About eight months now."

"*What?*" I exclaim, my eyes widening.

"Just after my birthday party that you surprised me with."

"Why didn't you just tell me?" I feel myself start to well up.

"I was scared."

"Scared of what?"

"This." He makes a motion with his hands between the two of us.

"You're not losing anything. Your family will be fine with it all."

"I'm sorry," he states.

"Go get Megan, will you? I'm off to pack." I walk away using my crutches. Tears begin flooding my face as soon as I reach the top step.

"Jenny, are you all right?" Megan asks.

I nod. "Let's do this."

It does not take long for us to pack my clothes, pictures, jewelry, and other important items. Rich leaves us alone to do it. Megan places everything into the car while I see Rich for one last time.

"Here." I stand at the front room door.

Rich walks towards me. "Your house keys and ring. Mark will drop off the car key with the car when he brings it."

"Thank you."

"Goodbye, Rich."

I turn around and walk out of my house. My dream house. My life is gone. *Where do I go from here?*

Chapter Twenty-Two

When we pull up in Megan's driveway, I just sit there not knowing what to do. I want to cry, but I can't cry anymore because I have no tears left. I need to sort out the last remaining things linking me to Rich. Then, maybe I can finally move on with my life and look forward to my new life. Why can't everything be like a fairytale? Trouble free.

"Thank you, Megan," I say, turning to face her.

"You're welcome, hun. What are your plans for today?" she asks.

"I am going upstairs and cancelling everything wedding related, then I can move on," I state.

"If you need a hand, give me a shout," she says. "I will take all your stuff upstairs for you."

"You're the best," I say, climbing out of the car, grasping my wedding folder.

I settle myself on the bed, placing everything I need around me. I look down at my mobile to check my unread messages. There is one from Michele.

Jennifer, I am so sorry that my brother did that to you. I am here if you need me. XO

I cannot talk to her yet. I start at the top of my list ringing each one and holding back the tears as I say goodbye to my dream. Goodbye to my life.

I have one last call to make, but I need the number. I take my bag and pull out the card with the hotel's number on it. As I place the card on my knee, Warren's card falls out from behind it. I pick it up and stare at it. All the memories of that night with him flood my mind. Do I call him? I just don't know. I toss the card onto my pillow and ring the last number on my list.

"Hey," Megan says, standing at my room door.

"Hey, they are all done," I state.

"That's fab. Mark's dropped off the car. He is going to pick up some takeout on the way back," she says as she walks towards me.

"Michele texted," I say, showing her the message.

"Are you going to answer her?" she questions.

"Yeah, I'll do it now before I chicken out."

It's okay. He needs to be happy. Thanks for everything. XO

"Done. Right, that's everything done. I just have to collect some stuff from the hotel and the castle," I state.

"I can drive you," she says, taking a seat on the side of the bed.

"Thank you. Can we do it tomorrow? When do you go away?" I question. I have only just remembered that Megan is going away to Mark's for his mum's birthday.

"Yes, we can. I leave in two days' time. Will you be okay without me? I can stay. Mark will understand," she states.

"No, you go. Have fun."

"Come with us," she states.

"No, you go," I say. "Right, I need to burn all this."

"Wow, really?" she questions while collecting the bits together.

"Yes, really. Do you have any matches?" I question.

"Yes, I do."

"Let's do this." I slide off the bed and head downstairs into the garden with everything.

"Do you have anything we can burn it in?"

"No, I don't think so."

"What can we burn it in?" I question. "I have no idea what we can use that's safe."

"Me either."

"Shall we shred it instead?" I suggest.

"Come on then."

I sit there in the front room shredding everything, shredding my life away. This is it. My life is officially over. As I place the last remaining papers of my dream wedding into the shredder, my mobile signals an incoming text from Michele. Her words are encouraging at a time when I need them most.

Jenny, we are friends for life, sod my brother. You're still family to me. Is there anything I can do to help you? XO

I smile and send a quick reply. She always seems to know the right things to say.

Thanks, hun. No, everything is done. Megan's helped me. XO

Where are you staying? XO

Megan's. XO

Chapter Twenty-Three

I take a deep breath as we pull into the car park of the castle. This is the last place I saw Warren. I hope he is not here; I do not want to see him. I wonder if I can run in and get the stuff out as quickly as possible.

"Do you want me to come in with you?" Megan asks, turning off the engine.

"Will you?" I am so lucky to have an amazing friend like Megan. She is always here for me and will do anything for me. The thought of losing her kills me. I hope she does not move away from me. I don't think I could cope without her.

She nods, undoing her seat belt and sliding out of the car.

"Hey, Lucy Doo, time to go into the princess castle," she says as she takes her out of the backseat. She holds her on her hip and locks the car.

"Ready." I smile as I hobble along the gravel path towards the castle. *My castle*. The place my world was going to become perfect. We were going to spend our wedding night here, while everyone else stayed at the hotel. This place was my dream. I cannot believe how much money I wasted on this place, and I am not going to get anything in return. It leaves me penniless with nowhere to live. I feel tears start to stream down my face. I turn to face Megan as we walk through the door.

"There is no way I can go through with this," I say, placing my hands over my face.

"You can. Believe in yourself, and everything will be sorted in time," she assures me while moving Lucy onto her other hip before placing her hand on my lower back.

"Thank you, Megan."

"Jenny, so lovely to see you again," Michael says as he hurries towards me.

229

"Hi, Michael, we are here to collect the things I dropped off last time."

"Oh, yes, I'll go and grab them for you." He turns around and heads off to one of the side rooms.

"Is it me, or is he really happy today?" Megan enquires.

"Really happy." I laugh. "Someone got some last night."

"Here is everything." Michael walks over to us.

"Thank you. Nice to see you again," I state.

"You, too. Just be happy you found out before the day," he says.

As we walk out of the castle, I feel a huge weight lift off my chest. I can do this. I just need to listen to what Megan said. *Believe in myself.* I climb back into the car and take my mobile out of my jeans pocket.

We need to talk.

"Rich has texted, saying we need to talk," I tell Megan.

"Are you going to?" she questions.

"I'll find out where he is."

Where are you?

At OUR house.

"Megan, can you drop me off at Rich's?" I ask.

"Of course."

The drive there seems long this time. I am so scared of what he wants from me. Why does he think we need to talk? I do need a few more items from the house, so I am willing to go back to pick them up and leave. I just can't think of anything I want to say to him.

"I'll wait here," Megan says as she turns off the engine.

"Are you sure?" I ask.

"Yes."

I stand at the front door of what was mine and knock.

"Finally," Rich says. "Come in."

"Hi to you, too," I say as I walk into the house.

"We need to talk."

"About?"

"I have a sexually transmitted infection."

"*You what?!*" I scream at him.

"I have an STI."

"Yes, I heard that. How? Why? Who? When?" I question.

"I found out this morning. You have to get checked out."

"You fucking dirty bastard!"

"I'm sorry."

"Who gave it to you? Chad?" I question.

He stands there motionless.

"I asked you a question, Rich."

"Yes, Chad."

"You didn't even get Luke to cover for you very well. Did you?"

"I know. Luke will not talk to me now."

"Doesn't surprise me." I pause. "Do you have information about what you have?" I ask.

He walks over to the other side of the front room and picks up some leaflets before handing them to me.

"You have fucked up my life."

"I know. I'm sorry."

"*Sorry?*" I question.

"Yes."

"I'm out of here. I'm not staying near you any longer."

I turn around and storm out of the house as fast as I can, trying to make a point. I climb into the car quietly, seeing Lucy asleep in the back.

"And..." Megan says.

"He has an STI."

"What?" Megan asks, placing her hand over her mouth.

"Yes, exactly."

Chapter Twenty-Four

I did not sleep much last night because all I could think about was what disease I might have. What a messed up life I have. I spent most of it crying. Megan's going away today, even though she does not want to. She stayed most of the night in here with me, holding me as I cried.

"Morning, sunshine," Mia says as she knocks on the slightly opened door.

"Morning, Mia."

"Right, get your arse out of bed so I can paint your toe nails before I leave, like I promised," Mia demands.

I laugh and slide around in bed. "I'll get dressed then be down soon, Mia," I inform her.

"No. PJ party, come on."

I nod and follow her down the stairs. I do not want to be around people right now. I keep looking at the clock. It is another hour till the doctor's office will be open for me to ring to sort out everything.

"Morning," Mark says as he walks past me into the kitchen holding an empty cup.

"Morning, mine's a coffee," I say cheekily.

"Oh, really." He smiles.

I can see why Megan fell for him. He is so sweet. "What colour are we going for?" Mia asks as she sits herself down on the front room carpet.

"Sexy red, of course," I state.

Alison always told us to wear red nail polish because men love that look on women. I am going to take her word now that I am single and need to look good. I sit down on the sofa.

"Morning, hun," Megan says as she yawns.

"Morning, I'm sorry," I state.

"Don't worry. Mark's driving." She tilts her head towards him.

"Coffee all around," he says as he passes cups out to us all. "What would you like for breakfast? Please do not all shout at once."

We sit there looking at each other then all shout, "Bacon Butties!"

"Okay, I get the picture," he says, giving Megan a little kiss on the cheek before leaving us to it.

The hour seems to fly with breakfast and nail painting keeping me busy. I head up the stairs back to my room and grab my mobile. I take a deep breath and call the doctor.

"That was a quick call," Megan says as she walks into my room.

"Yes, I have to go to the hospital drop-in. It will be quicker, and I will get the results back in five days instead of seven."

"That definitely sounds better for you." She pauses. "Do you want me to take you down before we leave?"

"No, go. I will work it out," I state.

I quickly throw on some black leggings and a long, tight purple top with a round neck. Perfect. That will do. The sun is shining today. It is going to be a nice, warm day. Hopefully, I can get in and out of the hospital quickly.

"Jenny." Megan pauses. "You do realise you need to get in touch with the man you slept with," she adds.

"What if I'm all clear? Then I don't."

"But if you're not, he could get ill or pass it on," she points out.

"Okay, I'll ring him." I shrug my shoulders. I had not even thought about notifying Warren.

"Right, we are going now," Megan says, coming towards me, giving me a big hug.

It takes at least another ten minutes and a lot more hugs before Megan finally leaves. Before saying her final goodbye, she makes sure I know where everything is and informs me that if I say I need her she will come straight back. What a lovely friend she is. I head back over to the bed, sit down on the edge, and lift the pillow to find Warren's card.

Quick. Do it. The faster you do it, the less it will hurt. I try to calm myself down as I dial the number. One ring. Two rings. Three rings.

"Hi, it's Jenny from the other night," I state. "Can we meet up? We need to talk." I pause to listen to him. "Yes, that's fine. See you then."

I gather my things and head downstairs. Warren's meeting me at work in half an hour. I am about fifteen minutes away and without a car, so I will have to call a taxi. I look through my mobile to find a taxi to book quickly. Right, that's everything done. I just need to get this over with. The taxi is only going to be five minutes, so I make a swift check to ensure I have everything, lock up, and head outside to wait.

"Hi, can you take me to Saint Georges Street?" I ask the taxi man as I climb in the backseat.

There are only five buildings on the street, so I will walk down to work. I reach into my bag and pull out my mobile. I see a message from Rich.

Chad has it too.

I shake my head, holding back tears. I do not want to know about that man. If it takes so long for the results to come back, he knew before I caught him in bed with Chad that he might have it. Why did he do this to me?

Oh great.

I scroll down my mobile to see if I have any more messages. I smile when I see one from Megan.

Hun, miss you already. Please let me know how you get on. Mia has left some turquoise nail polish on the fireplace for you. She thinks you will look amazing with it on. Xx

Thank her for me, please. I'll give it a go. It might work well with that turquoise dress I bought the other week. Miss you too. XX

I am happy for these distractions to take my mind off possibly hurting Warren even more with the news I need to tell him. I want a stiff drink. Shame I cannot have one for a while yet. I might pick up a nice bottle of red wine before I head back to Megan's tonight anyway and drown my sorrows while looking for somewhere else to live.

"Here you are, Miss," the taxi man says. I smile, pay, and climb out. I had been in my own little world and had not even noticed we had reached my destination.

I walk along the path to the building where I work, taking a seat on the small wooden bench that has *Forever and Always* engraved on the back slate.

Chapter Twenty-Five

I look up to see Warren slowly walking towards me. He is early. He is wearing dark blue jeans and a tight white T-shirt, a very relaxed look compared to what I have seen him wear before.

"Hey, babe," he mumbles as he sits on the bench next to me.

"Hey." I pause. "Sorry for what I am about to say."

"Go on."

I take a deep breath. "My now ex-fiancé has an STI. He has been sleeping with someone else. You need to get checked out."

"Oh my. Are you okay? Have you been checked out?" he questions.

"I'll be fine. I am off to get checked after I talk to you," I state.

"Right, is it at the hospital?"

"Yes, that's right."

"I just noticed you have a pot on your foot," he says, pointing down at my foot. "Why?"

"You are full of questions, aren't you? I fell down the stairs," I tell him.

"You can't drive then," he adds in a concerned voice.

"Correct."

"Let me take you to the hospital. We can talk, and you can explain the full story."

"But..."

"No buts." He pauses. "Come on."

I stand up and hobble towards his car. Warren holds open the door as I climb in, then closes it behind me before jumping into the driver's seat.

"Now, please tell me all that has happened. It's been two days since I left you. You seem so different now."

"Different?" I question.

"Yes, not bubbly."

"Too much is going on. I'll be back to myself soon, I hope," I state.

The journey to the hospital is not far. I sit and answer every question. Warren has to hear the entire story about my ankle and Rich. He sits there, silent in shock, as I try to hold back the tears.

As we pull up into the hospital car park, I suddenly begin to feel sick.

"Let me out!" I yell.

Warren stops the car. "What?"

I jump out and walk as fast as I can to the grassy area to throw up. *Oh my*. I have never thrown up this bad. *Ever*. Well, not that I can recall. After reading through the leaflets Rich gave me, vomiting was listed as one of the possible symptoms. I slide myself down onto the roadside, place my head into my hands, and sit there crying. Crying like I have never cried before. I feel Warren's arms wrap around me, pulling me close. I am so close that I can smell his cologne, a sweet smell, one I have never smelled before. In his comfort, I manage to slow down my breathing as the tears gradually begin to fade.

"You need to get this over with, go home, and rest," he whispers into my ear.

"Being sick is one of the symptoms," I inform him.

"You never know, babe." He places a little butterfly kiss on my cheek.

"I am so scared. I have lost everything. I just hope I don't have a disease on top of it." I pause. "I don't want to."

"Want to what?" he enquires.

"Oh, forget it," I say, shaking my head.

"Tell me," he says, taking hold of my hand and rubbing little circles to calm me.

"I don't want to lose something that might change my life for the better."

"I hope you don't either, babe." He pauses. "Shall we do this?"

I nod, standing up. I wobble and Warren catches me. "Don't be falling on me, babe." He giggles.

"I hope I don't fall. I'm still hurting from the last one," I state, rubbing the dust from my bum.

"I will protect you as much as you will let me, Jen," Warren says, turning to face me. "Let's do this."

We walk into the hospital side-by-side, straight into the lift, and up to the right ward. Warren takes care of everything. He talks to the receptionist, who then gives us an identification number and a form to fill out. I hobble over to the waiting area to fill out the form.

"It will soon be over," Warren whispers into my ear. I think he noticed my hand shaking as I was writing.

I face him and give him a delicate smile. "I know. Thank you."

Leaving me in the waiting area, Warren takes the filled-out forms to the reception desk. I admire his bum as I watch him lean over the desk. *What a view*. Those jeans are nice and tight. I giggle to myself. *Stop it, Jennifer. Behave yourself.*

He turns to face me and places his hand up with all five fingers showing before heading off with one of the nurses. I sit there shaking even more than I had before. I cannot believe I am alone, again.

"ID Number 0504, please go to the reception desk," the tall lady at the desk calls out. That's me. I stand and walk over to the desk.

"Hi, just follow me," she says. On the way down to the room, she explains the procedure is a simple blood test with nothing to be worried about. I am happy I can cope with needles.

She was right. In and out in two minutes. I hobble back to the waiting room. Looking around, I don't see Warren anywhere. I feel tears starting to collect in my eyes. *He left me*. I shake my head, take a deep breath, and walk out of the waiting room to the lift and down to the front desk on the first floor.

I do not need him. He never said he would be back or what I should do once I finished the procedure. I will call for a taxi to take me back to Megan's.

Chapter Twenty-Six

"Jenny." I turn around to see John, Megan's ex.

"John, hi," I say in a shocked manner.

"How are you?" he asks.

"I am good, thanks. How are you?" I kindly repeat the gesture.

"I'm good. My nana passed away three weeks ago. I just came to drop off a thank you card," he says, pointing down the corridor to one of the wards.

"Oh, I'm so sorry for your loss," I state, rubbing his arm. I really do not like this man. He is the type of man people just hate, not even love to hate. Just hate. He hurt Megan. I will never forgive him for that. I am happy she has Lucy from it all. She is an angel, such a blessing.

"I hear congratulations are in order," he states.

"Huh, what do you mean?" I ask.

"I saw Megan pushing a pram the other day in town. Congratulations, you finally got the baby you have dreamed of," he says, coming towards me with open arms.

I step back. "No, she is not mine. She belongs to Megan and *you*. If you had cared enough not to cheat and lie, you would have known about her. Oh, I forgot. You love to lie, *and* you changed your number and moved away."

"What? I have a child?" His mouth drops open.

"Yes."

"Why didn't she tell me?" he asks.

"Did you not listen to me?" I pause. "You changed your fucking number, moved away, and changed jobs. Now, how the hell was she supposed to tell you anything? You were so ashamed of what you did you fucked off and left her. It was the best fucking thing you ever did for her. If you loved her at all, you will fuck off and leave her to bring up your daughter alone." I stand there with my hands on my hips. I am not taking any crap from him. *Ever.*

"Okay, I'm sorry. If she is my child, I'm having contact with her."

"Why? So you can fuck up her life, too?" I ask, prepared not to back down.

"No, she is my child. I have rights over her. I will be able to gain full custody with no problem since I'm already a father," he states harshly.

"What the hell?" I yell.

"She is my daughter, and I *will* have her," he says before storming off.

I stand there with tears falling from my eyes. *What? Why? Oh my.* I need to call Megan and explain the situation to her. I suddenly feel someone's hand on the base of my back. The feeling startles me, and I jump.

"Jen, why are you crying?" he asks.

"Warren." Relief washes over me. "Megan, that I mentioned earlier, has a daughter. I just spoke to her dad. He is on about having full custody over her."

"What?"

"Exactly." I pause. "I'm sorry. I need to go. I need to call Megan."

"I'll take you to Megan's," he states, returning his hand to my lower back and walking me to his car.

"Thank you."

Warren continues to be a gentleman and opens the door for me. Once inside his car, I pull out my mobile and immediately send a text to Megan.

Megan, can you talk? It's an emergency. XX

Moments later, my mobile rings. "It's Megan," I inform Warren.

I explain everything to her. She flips out, just like I did. I have not heard her swear this much in ages. I just do not know what we can do. I have a lawyer's number, as it looks like Megan is going to need one. I always said John was trouble. From the first moment I saw him, there was something about him that troubled me. I never thought he wanted a child, definitely after his reaction when Megan miscarried previously.

"Megan's going to ring back later. She is going to see what she can find out on the Internet," I state.

"If she needs anything, let me know. I have contacts," he informs me.

"What, a hit man?" I ask, laughing.

"Well, no, not really, but I am sure I could find one." Warren smiles.

"It is just over there," I say as I point to Megan's house.

Once we make it to the driveway, he pulls up as close to the door as he can and turns off the engine.

"Thank you, Warren." I smile.

"Any day. Now, can you promise me one thing?" he asks. "Will you contact me if you need anything, and I mean *anything*? Someone to talk to, somewhere to go. *Anything*."

"Okay, I will. Thank you."

"I mean it, Jen."

"I know you do."

I slowly get out of the car and hobble to the front door. Warren kindly walks with me.

"Thank you, again. I would invite you in, but this is not my place. Sorry." Megan would not tell me off for it, but it would feel wrong to me. I would not like a stranger in my house without me being there. It is just wrong.

"Can I have a little kiss bye?" he asks sheepishly.

I nod, moving my lips closer to his and dropping a little kiss directly onto them.

"Perfect, a little sweet memory."

I feel the heat start to rise in my now bright red cheeks. I am happy he cannot see the other effects he has on me like the dampness pooling between my legs and the hardening of my nipples. There is no way he can be the man I desire, not this quickly.

"I will come and collect you to get the results. Text or call me if plans change," he says while taking hold of my hands.

"Okay, I will. Thank you," I state.

I stand and watch Warren walk away. Could he be *the one*?

Chapter Twenty-Seven

Five days have finally passed, and today is the day I get my test results. I cannot wait to find out what they say. I am slowly feeling normal again and beginning to move around better. I roll out of bed and reach for my mobile.

Morning, babe. I'll come and collect you at 11ish, then we can go for lunch after. X

I am surprised he remembered me today.

HI, that's fine by me. Thank you.

I will be happy to finally see someone. It is a huge bonus *that* someone just happens to be Warren. I keep thinking about him. I cannot get our night of passion out of my mind. Every time I am in the shower, I get all hot again. He took my shower sex virginity. He did things to me I have only ever dreamed of. I just don't know what to do, though. I need to place myself first.

At five this afternoon, I am off to visit a studio flat five minutes away from where I work, and hopefully, I will like it and can get the contract signed in the next few days. Then, I can get out of Megan's hair. I am sure she does not want me hanging around all the time.

Megan is due back today. She stayed away longer to sort out stuff in order to protect Lucy. Unfortunately, she does not have many available options in which to choose. I just want her to marry Mark and be happy. That way the problem with Lucy would be fixed. Well, I think it might be, but I have not looked into it as much as Megan has.

I do not think Megan is the big wedding type like me, though. After all this with Rich, I am definitely never getting married. I grab my favourite pink silk top and little vest and slip them on. I add a pair of jeans and some dolly shoes. I decide to put my hair up in a loose bun. It will be the first time Warren has seen it up. I smile at the thought as I hear my mobile go off.

Jenny, let me know if you have it. Will you?

Ok, I will, Rich, even though it's none of your FUCKING business anymore.

I am so annoyed with Rich. We have spoken about the house and other important items a couple of times. He is keeping the house, and Chad moved in with him two days ago. I told him I want my name removed from the mortgage, and I plan to cancel the direct debits that are paying for items linking to the house. I emailed him all the codes he needs and contacted all the suppliers. He refuses to give me anything else from the house, not even a photo album that contains pictures of Lucy. I'm heartbroken over it. It's sentimental to me, not him.

My neighbor, Lori, went past yesterday and said there was a skip outside the house. She told me what she saw inside it. He has thrown out all the little things I bought and asked him to return to me. I wish he had just given them back. That is *my* money he is throwing away. It is a joke and not a funny one at that.

I stand there getting angrier the more I think about my belongings inside the skip when my mobile signals a text.

I'm here. Sorry I'm early. I'll wait in the car till you're ready. W

I smile, grab my bag and jacket, and head out of the house. It is the quickest I have moved in days. I lock the door and head to the car just as the heavens start to open. Warren gets out of the car to open the door for me. I wonder how long he keeps that up.

I watch him run around the car to the driver's side. He has such a fit body. He is wearing a black shirt and those same jeans again, very smart and casual. I like it. *I like it a lot.*

"Hi, babe. Trust the rain to start now."

"Hi, I was always told to love the rain." I laugh.

Warren pulls out of the driveway, swings the car around, and starts heading towards the hospital.

"Everything will be fine today," he states.

"I hope so," I add.

The journey does not seem to take as long this time. He is eager to get it all over and done with just like me. I am sure he has been driving over the speed limit. *Naughty Warren*. When we arrive at the hospital, we park in the same space as last time.

"Now, no throwing up this time." He laughs.

"I will try not to," I say.

We head straight up to the ward, standing side-by-side the entire way. We stand in line at the reception desk waiting for our envelopes.

"Please take this down to Room 4," the bald man says to me, giving me the envelope. I head down the only corridor and take a deep breath as I knock on the door.

"Hello," the tall lady says. "I'm Olive."

"Nice to meet you," I state, trying to seem polite.

"Let's open this, shall we?" she asks.

"Yes, please," I reply.

She opens it and reads it to herself, then nods.

"And..." I add, impatient.

"You have the all clear. You have nothing at all," she informs me.

I jump from my seat and head over to her, giving her a massive hug. "Thank you so much."

"You're very welcome. Now, please take a seat." I sit down. Here we go. *The safe sex talk.*

"We need to do a small blood test. Some of your levels are not right. It will take about five minutes, and we will have the results back straight away."

I nod, unable to speak. Olive is very quick and gets on, not making me hang around.

"Miss Wright." She pauses. "I have some news for you."

"What?" I ask, shaking like a leaf. I suddenly feel sick to my stomach.

"You're pregnant."

"What?" I pause. "That can't be right."

Olive gets up and shows me the test. She's right. I sit there crying uncontrollably. *Why? Why now? Why me? Oh, my life is screwed.*

I calm myself and head out to find Warren.

"All clear," he says as he walks towards me.

"Me, too," I reply.

"Let's go to lunch."

"I don't know. I have an appointment at five to view a studio flat."

"We can do lunch, and then I will go with you to view it." He pauses. "You are *not* staying in some grotty run-down shit hole."

I laugh. "Thank you."

Chapter Twenty-Eight

We drive to an old village pub near the place where Warren grew up. I love spending time with him; I keep finding out all these little things about him that make me smile. I have never been here before, but I have heard the place serves amazing chicken dinners. I think that is what I am having for sure.

"Here we are," he says as we pull up into a car park beside an old barn.

"Is this the pub?" I ask.

"Yes."

"It's beautiful." I look towards the pub, a very old-fashioned barn. It has a rustic feel outside and looks exactly like a barn for animals. I climb out of the car and walk towards the building, placing the pregnancy news at the back of my mind for the time being. I do not want to think about it because you never know what might happen. I feel really hungry today like I have not eaten for days. I skipped breakfast so that I would not be sick, and now I am starving.

"Welcome, how many for the table?" the short male waiter asks.

"Two, please," Warren replies.

The man takes us to the far side of the pub near an open fireplace that I am happy to see is not lit. It is too warm for it. I take a seat on the opposite side of the table facing Warren. The waiter explains everything to us before leaving us with the menus.

"What do you fancy?" Warren asks.

"I don't know," I state.

I continue looking down the menu pretending I am reading when I already know I want to order the chicken dinner.

"I am going to have the chicken dinner," Warren states, placing his menu back in the wooden table stand. I jump as I feel his foot slide up the side of my leg. Oh my. I place my menu with the others.

"I think I will to," I add.

"Perfect. I'll go and order."

The food arrives to our table within minutes of Warren placing the order. *Wow, it is amazing.* The chicken dinner features loads of chicken, a big Yorkshire pudding, and three different types of potatoes. It also comes with a shared plate of different seasonal vegetables. As I start to eat, I find little sausages and bacon rolls in it, too. *Oh, I'm in heaven.* As soon as I have a car, I will be coming here for lunch, even if I am by myself.

"Is your dinner okay?" Warren enquires.

"It is, thank you. Yours?" I ask.

"Beautiful. What an amazing day! Eating this and spending time with the most gorgeous woman in the world," he states.

I turn around and pretend to look for who he is on about.

"I was on about you," he adds.

"Yes, I got that. I was just checking. Thank you, but I don't feel gorgeous." I know my face is turning a shade of red the more I talk.

"What else do you need to do today, hobbly?" Warren asks.

"Hobbly?" I question, placing my cutlery down onto the empty plate.

"Yes."

"Just to see the flat. Get it over with, then I can get a contract and everything else signed tomorrow," I inform him.

"Have you seen it before?"

"No, I have read the information. I just need to be out from under Megan's feet. I want to be independent."

"I understand that, but please do not rush into a place that is not safe," he adds.

"I won't. I promise." I take a sip of my water.

"Pudding?"

"I think I am too full to eat any more."

"Okay then, we can take it out to eat. Their hot chocolate fudge cake is to die for."

"I'd like that." I smile because that is my favourite pudding.

"I will go and get them to box it up. We can pick up some ice cream or cream later. Oh, what fun we could have with that." His eyes light up. No doubt about it. We both desire each other. Is it just sex for him, though? I do not want to be someone's sex toy. I am not saying I want a relationship, but I could cope being friends with benefits. *That is, if I were the only friend that got those benefits.*

"Right, let's go. Can you move your appointment to see the flat?" he asks.

"I can view from two, just go when we want."

"Let's go then. Give me the address," he demands.

Chapter Twenty-Nine

The drive to the flat takes a while and slowly gets my mind off the worries haunting me. We pass lots of fields with a variety of different things happening in each one. I would love to live in a cottage in the countryside. I think it would be amazing. It would be nice to have a place for my horse Topaz and to be able to spend more time with her. I do wonder what it would be like to be a full-time country girl and live off the land. I do not think I could do it, though. However, no one ever really knows what life will bring.

I wonder if I can ride Topaz now that I am expecting. I cannot get the fact I am pregnant to sink in my mind. I have decided not to tell anyone till after my doctor's appointment to ensure things are all right. I do not even know who the dad is. How bad is that? Am I one of *those* sluts now? I feel my eyes sting.

"What are you thinking about, babe?" Warren enquires as he continues to drive.

"Nothing," I answer.

"Has to be something. Your eyes are starting to fill up." He is so attentive.

I shake my head and look down to my knees.

"Tell me."

"I will in time," I state.

"Something happened at the hospital, didn't it?" he asks.

"Yes, I'm okay, though," I say, turning away from him. I do not want him to see me weak.

"Babe, please tell me," he says, pulling over into a parking spot.

"I'm pregnant." I turn to face him, gathering strength to tell him everything.

"Oh, wow. Congratulations."

"I don't even know who the dad is. You or Rich..." I pause to gauge his reaction.

"It does not matter. *Does it?*"

"No, but I feel bad."

"I will support you no matter what, babe," he says, placing his hand on my knee.

"Thank you. Now, let me go and get this flat so I have somewhere to raise the baby."

"Okay," he says, restarting the car to drive to the house.

"Please don't tell anyone I'm pregnant yet."

"Sure." He smiles with a little twinkle in his eye.

"What are you smiling about?" I ask.

"Pregnant women have a good sex drive, or so I have been told."

I can't help but laugh. "One track mind."

"How couldn't I with you? The other night was amazing."

I feel myself start to blush. "Maybe we can repeat it sometime, take my mind off everything," I add. *I really want a repeat*. The thought of him doing those things to me again makes me wet. *Oh, please, please make me scream.*

"Here is the street. Now to look for the number," Warren says.

"It is that one there," I say pointing to the *For Sale* sign in front of the building.

Warren parks close to the flat. I jump out of the car and head to the building. I am eager to start my new life. I stand at the front of the three-story building with only a few little steps to walk up the door. I slowly climb them. There is no garden with this place, but it is somewhere to stay for now. Two of the flats are for sale, but the third one, which I am considering, is to let. That works for me. We walk through the entrance hall, only to be greeted by the horrible smell of urine and muck covering the grey walls.

"I do not care what you think, Jen, but I am not letting you live here. I dread to see what the flat looks like."

"But..."

"But nothing. Come stay with me. We can sort out something."

"As friends?" I question.

"Jen, you are going to have to get used to this. I am never leaving you. There is something about you. A spark I cannot explain, but I felt it the first time I saw you. I do not care who the dad of your baby is. I will still be there for you. You are not moving into this shit hole. You are moving in with me. I want to look after you, love you, and be with you. If it is not what you want, then I understand. I think I might love you, Jen."

I stand there crying. I am an emotional wreck. *I love this man.* I have never felt like this before. I want all he wants. I can do this. I can be happy. Can I really trust him? I need to believe that he will be different, but I just don't know anymore.

Do You Believe?

A Believe Series Christmas Special

L Chapman

Cover designed by Sprinkles on top design

Edited by - Paige Maroney Smith

Proofread by – Wendy Schaefer Samuels

Formatted by – Angel Steel

Dedication

To all those who believe in the magic of Christmas.

Merry Christmas.

Grandad – Thank you for everything you have ever done for me and the hours you have spent teaching me those little things that I will never forget.

I love you.

You will lead a rich and successful life.

Table of Contents

Our First Time

Mark is sitting on the sofa while working on his laptop. I have seen him do this so often in the months we have shared together, yet each time he does, I am taken aback by how sexy he can make mere work look. His eyes mesmerize me. The saying, "the eyes are the windows to the soul," must have known Mark's eyes. I don't believe I can stay away from my feelings of desire anymore. All I can think about is touching him, and in turn, him touching me. I can almost feel his lips trailing kisses and covering my body as we fall into each other. He says he is patient, but the patience is wearing very thin for me. I want him more than I have ever wanted anyone in my life. Tonight, I will place Lucy in her own room to sleep. I want alone time with Mark. I *need* alone time with Mark.

"I am just off to place Lucy to bed," I state, letting out that little smile. I hope he knows what I want.

"Okay, night, night, Lucy Doo. Sleep tight."

As Mark places a little kiss on Lucy's head, he looks into her sleepy little eyes, and my heart melts. I love seeing how he is with her. He would be such a great dad. I wish he were Lucy's father.

"Then, I am just going to do the dishes when I get back."

"I'll do them, baby," Mark states, letting out a little smile.

I quickly head upstairs, placing Lucy down to sleep, watching her eyes slowly close as she goes off to the land of nod.

Mark walks into the kitchen and wraps his arms around my waist, pulling me close. I flick some water at him as an attempt to be playful. All I am thinking about is how I want to play the seductive role.

"Did you really just do that?"

"I did, Mr. Reed." I spatter more water at him.

"Oh, that's it, Miss Madden."

Mark spins me around so we are facing each other and then flicks a bit of water at me.

"Are you starting now?"

"I am indeed."

He places his hands at either side of my hips, lifting me onto the kitchen counter. His lips lock with mine as his tongue teasingly seeks entry into my mouth.

He pulls back from our kiss and looks at me with the expression of complete love. "You're so beautiful, Megan."

I moan. Mark places his lips onto my neck and passionately blazes kisses down my nape, ending on my chest at the top of my breasts. I cannot help but exhale deeply.

Looking directly into my eyes, he commands, "Upstairs now, Miss Madden."

I smile knowingly at Mark. As I move forward, he slowly slides me down the front of his body. His taut abdomen is firm against my core, and his growing erection has caught my breath and caused wetness to form between my thighs. As he lets my feet hit the floor, he takes my hand, but I take the lead up the stairs in front of him. His hand taps my bum, and I squeal, picking up my pace.

"Behave, Mr. Reed."

I run ahead, straight into the master bedroom.

"As if you'd run away from me."

Mark grabs me and pulls me straight into his arms with my back against his chest.

"You are mine now," Mark states in his powerful man voice.

He spins me around, placing his hands at the bottom of my top and sliding it over my head. I do the same to him, and I can't believe how good he looks.

His lips go straight to my neck, kissing it fervently, going from one side to the other. He travels down to my black lacy bra. Sliding one hand around my back, he unfastens it and then lets both hands drift to my matching panties. I stand still as he moves effortlessly to slide them down my legs.

"Oh, I am going to devour you, baby," he says as he kneels in front of me.

Moving his thumb to my clit, he rubs while placing little kisses on it. He slides his finger inside me really slowly, sending me over the edge in ecstasy.

"You're wet, so wet," he moans. "I want you, need you." He withdraws his finger and stands up to slide off his jeans. His tight boxers strain around his throbbing erection. I gracefully move and slide them down, freeing his cock.

Wow, I can't help but look at how big he is. I giggle to myself. Mark lays me down onto the bed, kissing my neck and then sliding his lips down my chest.

"Baby, are you sure?" he asks in a caring voice.

I nod, and he automatically slides on protection and then smiles at me. At least I don't have to worry.

He slowly slides himself in me, and I take a deep breath. Oh, baby. He places his hands above my head, and I bend my knees to wrap my legs around him. I put my hands into his hair and gently pull, causing him to groan in pleasure. As he begins to gain speed, he lowers his head and his tongue invades my mouth, kissing me passionately. The intensity is so strong that I arch my back to meet him thrust for thrust.

"Baby, you're so perfect," he says as he takes one hand and starts squeezing my nipple and caresses my face with the other.

"Oh my," I say. I don't think I can hang on much longer.

"Megan, I love you," he declares as he continues to pump harder and faster, never losing his rhythm.

I can't manage to form words; I just moan. I knew our first time would be easy and special.

"ARGH!" Mark lets out a massive growl not long after and falls down onto the bed beside me. He places his hand on my bum, rolling me onto my side and pulling me in close.

"You're wonderful," he whispers as he strokes my hair.

"No, you are."

Chapter One

I'm so excited for this Christmas. I have always dreamt of the Christmas season where I would have my little baby with me, someone for me to spoil and spread Christmas magic. This is Lucy's first Christmas, and I'm trying to make sure everything is perfect. I'm lucky that Mark and Jenny have decided to spend Christmas with us. After the past few months, Jenny doesn't like the thought of spending Christmas around her family and listening to them talk about Rich. Her family hasn't gotten over it yet. They keep having a go at her and telling her she should have done what was right for the family. He still agreed to marry her, and they think she should have been willing to just do it. Her mum says, "Marriage is not just love; it's friendship. It doesn't matter if you love the person."

Jenny's Christmases have always been the opposite of mine. All the family, including cousins, go over to one house on Christmas Eve and stay there until the day after Boxing Day. Enjoying the full family thing, the men assemble the self-build gifts and children's toys while the women and young girls cook. They are taught from a young age how to prepare the food. At our house, it's just close family for Christmas, and everyone goes to Nan's on New Year's Day. She cooks the family meal, and we sit, play games and have fun.

I am doing things my way this year. Today is Christmas Eve. The tree is up, and it looks beautiful. I wanted to make the extra effort with this being Lucy's first Christmas. After years of having it drummed into me that you can't put up your tree early, only for the twelve days of Christmas, I stuck to it. I didn't want bad luck. Mark wanted it up earlier, but I made him wait, and it took a lot to keep saying no. I did let him have a few things his way, though. We bought a new seven-foot tree and decorations, too. For outside, we bought some icicle lights to hang at the front of the house. I love them, but I won't admit that to Mark.

Mark has only placed a little tree up at his house. He wanted Christmas with me, so he didn't go crazy decorating his place, even though he has had it up since the first of December. He has been driving me mad by playing his special Christmas CD in the car since November, and if I hear one more Christmas song, I will scream. It is a good thing that I love him.

Mark is curled up beside me as I quietly crawl out of bed and creep along the landing into Lucy's room. I gently push open the white door a little bit more to see her lying still on her cot. I walk slowly into the room, as I don't want to wake her. I just need to check on her, so I place my hand on the beech wood cot and look down to see Lucy with her eyes wide open, followed by her little giggle.

"Oh, good morning, princess," I say as I tickle her tummy. She giggles even louder.

I slowly peel back her pink cover with a white rabbit embroidered on it and pick her up. "Come here, baba," I say as I lift her. I walk on the cream carpet towards her large bedroom window, looking at the frost that has fallen over night.

"It looks cold out there, little miss." I place a small kiss on the top of her head. "Shall we get dressed for our busy day?" I question before turning around and walking over to her wardrobe and drawers. I open the drawers first, choosing a clean baby grow, before grabbing a white top with a picture of a reindeer and some red and white striped leggings from her wardrobe. Annabella got her some cute little Christmas-related outfits. I plan for her to wear them all over the next few days. She looks too cute in them. Annabella isn't joining us for Christmas; she plans to spend the time with Mark's family.

I turn around to see Mark standing there in just his black underpants. "Good morning, sexy," he says as he leans on the doorframe with his arm. He's running his fingers through his hair.

"Morning," I reply, feeling myself start to redden. This man still manages to make me blush.

He walks into the room, coming over to us, as I lay Lucy down onto the changing table. He places his lips on my neck. "Mmm."

"Mmm, indeed," he whispers. "Hello, Lucy Doo," he says, moving around me and placing a kiss on her head.

"She is just getting dressed. Then, we are going to have breakfast. Aren't we, princess?" I say, tickling her. I love her giggle.

"Sounds like a good idea. I'm just going to take a shower. I believe Connor is up. He could keep an eye on Lucy while you get dressed," he replies.

"Do you think he would mind? I don't want him thinking I'm going to use him while he's here."

"He will not think that. I will go and ask him. You finish getting Lucy Doo dressed, and I will inform him," he says, tapping my bum as he leaves.

"Thank you," I reply before finishing dressing Lucy.

"Morning, Megan." I turn around to see Connor standing there in blue jeans and a white T-shirt with a logo I have never seen before. I have never seen him dressed like this before. It is unreal how relaxed he looks. I love this natural appearance.

"I'm here to take Lucy off your hands while you get dressed. Take as much time as you want. You know I love spending time with Lucy," he says.

"Thanks, Connor."

"While you're busy, I will give her some breakfast. Is that okay?" he questions.

"Yes, that's fine, if you want."

"I do. I have it ready on the side, baby food and milk. I'm well-trained. Annabella made sure I knew everything when I was expecting Kate. Now, go and get dressed."

Chapter Two

I walk into my room to find Mark standing there with his clothes hung up on the outside of the wardrobe all ready to go.

"Now, there you are." He points out.

"I'm here. I was going to have a shower, but you haven't finished with it yet." I smile.

"That was the plan." Mark winks.

"Oh, was it now, Mr. Reed?" I question.

"Yes, Miss Madden, you know I love taking showers with you. I can get you all dirty and clean in one go," he replies before grabbing my hand and leading me into the bathroom.

"Now, behave. I need to shower and get ready, Mark," I say, trying not to laugh.

"I'll behave, but I will make you scream *and* get you clean somehow." He bends over the bathtub and turns on the shower. I stand there in my nightwear. After fully closing the door, I lean over the sink to the glass cabinet and take out a bottle of shampoo and Mark's favourite strawberry body wash. He loves the smell of strawberries, but not the taste. He uses strawberry syrup for special occasions. He keeps it in the fridge, so it's extra cold when he drips it down my body. The thought of it makes me smile.

I feel his wet hand tap my bum. "Oi!" I say, turning around.

"The shower is ready."

I place the gel on the side, so I can grab it from the shower. I slowly take off my black lacy baby doll nightgown, letting it fall to the floor. I stand there, watching Mark's eyes seductively wander over my naked body. I look up at him.

"By standing here, I'm not getting clean. Am I?"

"No, but I just want to watch you. Your body is amazing. I want to place my lips around those sweet nipples of yours."

"Then, do it."

"Oh, I'm going to. Now, get that sweet arse of yours into the shower." Smiling, I turn around and wiggle my bum at him before climbing into the shower.

"That arse." I giggle. "Get in here, or I'm going to do it myself."

I have never seen Mark move so fast in my life. He jumps into the shower. The water falls all over his naked chest, running down him, and touching every part of it. He places his hand around my back, pulling me close to him and letting the water pour down my body. His lips find my nipples. The coldness of them on my now warm nipples makes me gasp.

Mark moves back, grasping the bath puff and rinsing it under the water. As I turn to get the shower gel, he leans over me and takes it from my hand. He then covers my back in gel, rubbing small circles with the puff. His lips kiss my neck as the water flows around us.

He spins me around on the bath mat, pulling me so close to him that I can feel the heat from his mouth on my bare skin.

"I'm never letting you go," he whispers as he places his lips on my neck, kissing me down past my breasts and letting his fingertips walk up and down my spine.

I take the puff from him and start rubbing it tenderly over his chest. His eyes never leave mine. He reaches up and takes down the shower head, placing it between my legs. I stand there, rubbing the puff up and down his arm. Slowly, I take a step towards the wall. I don't know how long I can cope with this. The water is warm, making everything tingle. He gently takes the puff from me. Lifting one of my legs, he places it on the side of the bath. Mark turns the dial on the showers, and I find myself leaning farther onto the wall. As he slides his fingers into me, the water turns colder and I gasp. Oh, this is so cold. Mark looks straight into my eyes as I lose control, using the wall to steady myself.

"Come on, baby," he says, climbing out of the shower. He places his hand out for me to hold as I step out of it. I'm shaking like jelly, so I let him wrap a towel around me. Pulling me close to him, he places his lips near my ear and blows just a little.

"Bed now," he says suggestively.

We creep along the landing, making sure no one hears us. I need Mark. I need to feel him inside me. I close the door quietly, leaving the shower running to muffle any noise we make. I will have to be quiet, though.

"Now, let's get you all dry," he says as I sit down on the bed.

"Well, get over here then." Mark walks towards me, pushing me back down onto the bed. Leaning over me, he begins to kiss me like his life depends on it. He stops looking at me and slowly pushes the towel off my shoulders.

"Did I ever tell you that you're so beautiful it's unreal?"

I just cover my face. I can sense myself burning up. I feel the bed move and uncover my face to see Mark lying on his side and looking at me alluringly.

"You look so sexy when you blush," he says, sliding his hand through my wet hair.

I roll onto him, straddling his lap. It's my turn to be in charge. Mark's eyes look up and down my body as I slowly lift myself and slide down onto his bulging cock. His hands slide to my bum, lifting me up and down. My hands rub up and down his chest, and I lean forward a bit to run them through his hair. As I move up and down, I watch his hands caress my breasts and his fingers rub my nipples while he delicately tugs them. Sitting back up, I place my hands behind me on his legs. I lean back, keeping my pace and not wanting to break the friction. Mark's hand slides to my clit, and he starts rubbing it. The heat builds up. I can't hold on much longer.

"Come with me, baby," he whispers.

We come together in silence. I lie next to him, feeling his legs intertwine with mine and his hand grazing through my hair.

He smiles. "You're mine forever and always."

I smile in return. "We need to get dressed. We don't want to be found like this."

We slowly get dressed. My legs are still a little unsteady, so I will not be doing anything in a rush yet. Mark keeps running his fingers over my neck, making me shake. I reach out for my body lotion, leisurely rubbing it up and down my legs.

"Oh, baby, I so want to do that for you."

"Here."

I hand him the bottle and move my hair from my back so he can rub the cold lotion into my skin. He slides his hand over the top of my shoulders, massaging it into my breasts as he goes. I tip my head back onto his chest, looking up him.

"Don't you give me that look, Miss Madden, or I will have to take you right here and now."

I can't help but giggle.

Chapter Three

Kate came down the other day, and we spent the day writing our Christmas lists to send off. It was so exciting to see a little girl write her wishes. For a five-year-old, she is so generous, not at all what I expected to see. She wrote what she wanted for Grandma Betty and Daddy first before writing what she wanted for herself, which was just a pram for her dolly.

"Aw, Kate, is that all you want?" I question as I look down onto her pink note paper.

"Yes," she replies, drawing love hearts on the page. She enjoys spending her time drawing and is turning into a right artist. She has been busy covering my fridge with pictures, and I love all of them.

"What would you like from us for Christmas?" I ask as I take a seat next to her.

"Nothing. Maybe you could get my daddy a new tie," she adds.

"I can do that. What colour?"

"Daddy's favourite colour is blue."

"Does Dolly need anything?" I question.

"No, she will be fine. If I get the new pram, I can look after her then. I can wash her clothes before bed."

Listening to her say this hurts me. She is so young, and she shouldn't be like this. Kate has lived with her Grandma Betty, her mum's mum, since she was three months old. Her mum passed away after a terrible car accident that involved Kate and Connor. Kathy was thrown from the car and died instantly. Both Connor and Kate escaped uninjured. Connor has never gotten over the accident. He feels like he is the one to blame. Kathy was driving with Kate in the passenger seat behind her, and a drunk driver hit their side of the car. A lorry hit the back of the car, launching Kathy from the vehicle. Kate was restrained in her car seat and saved. In Kathy's will, there was a clause stating what was to become of Kate if anything happened to her. She was to go to Kathy's mum Betty, and Connor was to have no contact. No one knows why, but Betty has developed dementia and has begun forgetting to look after Kate. With Mark's help, Connor has managed to have more contact with her, and they are in the middle of getting permanent custody granted to him. I'm not sure about the full ins and outs of everything, but I do know that Kate is the most introverted, unselfish child I have ever met. I know Connor will be a great full-time dad for her. I just hope they manage to get it sorted.

"Kate, what do you want? You can have something just for you," I state.

"I want Grandma Betty back," she says as tears stream down her face.

"Aw, Kate, what do you mean? She is at her house."

"No, she isn't my grandma. She's changed."

"She is poorly. She will always be different now. That's why you're staying with your daddy," I inform her.

"Does Daddy love me?" she questions.

"Oh, Kate, yes, he loves you. He doesn't want to ever let you out of his sight. You're his princess," I say. "How about you and me go shopping? We can get Daddy his tie and anything else you want."

"Please, can Daddy come, too?" she asks.

"Of course," I reply as she runs ahead into the front room. I follow her in to see her picking up a book, sitting herself down and starting to read to Lucy. We bought a Christmas book the other day, and after our long talk, she seems more settled. She is starting to come out of her shell a little bit and becoming more talkative. I love seeing her happy. I hope we can get her to fully open up in time.

Chapter Four

We spent last night at home, waiting for Jenny to come and join us before we sent the Christmas letters up the chimney. It's a little tradition that Mark did as a child on Christmas Eve, so I thought it would be nice to do it with Kate. Maybe that little bit of magic will help her. I would love for her to believe in Christmas magic. This Christmas needs to be special for all of us, including the children.

"Hi, everyone," Jenny says as she walks into the room with her boyfriend, Warren, standing beside her and holding her hand.

A smile spreads across my face. The old Jenny, the one who was carefree and fun has been brought back. I am so happy that she is here and not alone. She has a spark now because of Warren. The pregnancy glow is unmistakable as well. I'm looking forward to next year with two little ones here for Christmas. It will be doubly special. I want everything to work out for her, because with only just over three months left, anything can happen, so we are on our toes. She finally went for a scan last week to check everything. The doctors are keeping a close eye on her this time, so she has more scheduled regular appointments to ensure nothing goes wrong. I think that is on everyone's mind at the moment. We want both Jenny and the baby safe and healthy. I'm scared that something will go wrong. I love Jenny, and I don't want her to go through the pain of losing another child. She is lucky to have Warren; he tries to go to every appointment with her. If he can't, he gets me to go and rings five minutes after the visit. At her twenty-week scan, they couldn't determine the baby's sex.

Finally, the little monkey let them find out, and I'm so excited Jenny shared her secret with me. I remember the day she told me.

"Megan?" Jenny bellowed as she ran into my kitchen.

"Yes?" I paused. "What's up?"

"It's a boy. I'm having a boy!" she squealed.

"Oh, I am so happy for you."

We spent days messaging each other boy's names we like. She has chosen to keep the baby's surname as Wright, the same as hers. She doesn't want to know who the father is. She is scared it will be Rich's baby. He refused to have anything to do with her or the baby when she told him. By keeping the baby's name as Wright, she saves her job. The only thing she's decided for sure is the baby's middle name is going to be her baby brother's name. Jenny knows her mum will be okay with it, but she is worried about what her dad will say, if he says anything at all. He had a go at her when she first told the family about her pregnancy. He called her a slut, so she hasn't spoken to him since. She hasn't told her family what she is having. She wants to keep it a surprise, but she can't keep everything from me. She never has been able to.

"How are you and bump?" I enquire as Jenny takes a seat on the sofa behind me.

"We are both good." She pauses. "How are you all?"

"Good. We have been waiting for you to come, so we can send these letters up," I reply.

"Oh, I can't wait."

"Kate, are you ready to send your letter to Santa?" Jenny asks.

Kate sits there and nods. She doesn't talk to strangers. She hasn't spent enough time around Jenny yet. Kate runs off into the kitchen and comes back with all the letters she made us write— hers, Lucy's, Connor's, Mark's, and mine.

Kate comes over to me, whispering into my ear, "Does Jenny have a letter for him?" she questions.

"I think she does. Why don't you ask her?" I ask.

"I'm scared." She grabs ahold of my top.

"I'll come with you." I turn around to face Jenny. "Kate has a question for you."

"Do you have a letter for him?"

"I do and so does Warren. Are you going to send them all up?" Jenny asks, taking the letters from her bag and passing them to Kate.

Mark takes Kate's hand. Leading her to the fireplace, he helps her send the letters up before running out of the house to watch them float into the sky. I sit there watching her giggle. It is so amazing; I love it.

"Jenny, I'm going to make mince pies tomorrow with Kate," I inform her, with a nice little smile.

"I can't wait. You know I love them, and I love watching you make things," Jenny points out, watching her face light up. I know her too well. Mince pies are one of her favorite seasonal foods.

"I know you do. I thought Kate could help."

"That's a good idea. I hope she relaxes soon. She seems so scared of me," Jenny states.

"Hopefully, she will settle soon. Since you'll be around for the next few days, she will get to know you some more. I'm just hoping she likes her present," I say as I glance over to the tree that has only a few presents under it.

We have left the rest of the presents upstairs in my attic room behind the bookcases so that no one can see them, even if they go up there. I don't trust the boys from shaking the packages to find out what's inside. Annabella warned me that she found both Connor and Mark doing it last year only hours after finding Mark's siblings doing it. Mia had unwrapped the presents and re-taped them so no one could tell that she had opened them. I remember doing that when I was younger, not that I would ever admit it. I hate surprises, but love them at the same time. I'm excited to see Kate's face, because I know Lucy will understand Christmas more and be able to open her presents next year. This year is more for me, and I have been good.

"I love the new hairdo, Megan," Jen says, running her hand over it.

"Thanks, I decided to treat myself. I love the blonde tips, and I think it's a nice change. I just might keep it like this," I state, shaking my head from side to side, letting my hair fall naturally.

"I love it. It suits you, and you seem happy with it," Jenny replies.

"I do love it. I enjoyed a full-on pampering session. I even had a manicure and a pedicure; my toenails are now an icy blue. Mark took Lucy for me, so Kate and I could have some girlie time. Her grandma cuts her hair. I thought it would be a nice treat for her to have her hair cut by a professional."

"It looks good. She has such long, wavy, blonde hair, and she will either love it or hate it when she is older," Jenny points out.

"Don't we know it?"

Chapter Five

What are we doing with the rest of today?" Connor enquires as he takes a seat on the edge of the sofa.

"Well, I had planned to do some baking. I want to make some mince pies for tomorrow. If you want to help me, Kate, you can."

"Yes!" Kate bellows as she runs into my arms.

"Then, baking it is," I reply.

"Oh, not yet," Mark says. "I have plans for us all first."

"What? What? What?" Kate replies, bouncing up and down.

"Well, get your coat on, and I will show you," he answers, pointing to the coats hanging on the coat rack.

I slowly stand up, taking hold of Mark's hand as I do, to steady myself. I smile at him as I slide my arms around his body, pulling him closer. Taking a deep breath, I'm able to take in his scent and his lovely cologne. I now have a thing for it. I love it. I can even smell it when I'm in bed alone, while he is away working. I miss him like crazy. I'm so happy that he decided to spend this time with us.

"Megan," Kate says as she walks into the room, pulling my cream coat. "Here."

"Thanks, Kate," I say as I take it from her and slip it over my arms and onto my shoulders.

"Come on," she replies.

"I need to get Lucy a jacket first. Then, I'll be ready," I reply, turning around to see her asleep in her purple baby bouncer with the cream teddy bear that Mark got her. She's so peaceful and innocent.

"Okay, come on!" she says, grabbing ahold of my hand.

"Why don't you come upstairs with me, and we will find a snowsuit for her?" I say, heading towards the stairs.

"Yeah," Kate says, running up the stairs in front of me.

I follow Kate up the stairs and walk straight into Lucy's room to find Kate sitting on the floor in front of the drawers waiting for me. I walk over to the wardrobe and pull out two different snowsuits, a white one and a pink one.

"Which one, Kate?" I ask as I hold one in each hand.

"Pink," she says, pointing to the pink one.

"Okay, let's go," I say as I follow her down the stairs. At the bottom of the stairs, Mark stands wearing his black coat and holding Lucy in his arms.

"Hey, princess," I say, passing the snowsuit to Mark. I don't have any worries when he's holding her. He knows what to do, and Lucy looks up to him. It's so amazing to watch. I hope Warren is the same way with Jenny's little one when he makes his arrival.

"Right, are we all ready?" Connor asks as he stands in the doorway, holding the car keys.

"Yes!" Kate yells, jumping up and down.

"Let's go then, okay," he says as he bends down, scooping up his daughter in his arms and pulling her close.

I let everyone leave the house in front of me and watch them climb into the car before I lock up. I pull out my phone and see a message from Jenny.

We are waiting for you at the surprise. I can't wait to see Kate's face. XX

We will be there in 10. Kate is so excited now, and I just can't wait. She has forced us all out of the house. XX

Aw, that's totally sweet. I have my camera with me. It's the first time I have gotten to use it. XX

No, and I mean, NO, pictures of me. Lol XX

Of course, loads of pictures of you. XX

Jenny knows how much I hate having my picture taken. When I was younger, I went through a stage where I liked to smile, but as I matured, my teeth didn't grow straight and everyone laughed at pictures of me. Now, I avoid all cameras and the embarrassment.

Chapter Six

As we pull up into the car park of one of the local parks, I look over my shoulder into the back of the car to see Kate looking through the windows to find out the surprise.

"Are we there?" she questions.

"Yes," Connor replies.

Kate looks at him, all confused and lost.

"Let's go," Mark says as he jumps out of the car. He walks to the boot and pulls out Lucy's pram before walking around to Connor and taking Lucy from him. Kate runs around, taking tight hold of my hand.

"Are we really there?" she questions again.

"Yes, we need to find Jenny and Warren. Then, we can go to the surprise."

"Oh."

"Come on. It's worth it," I say, smiling at her. "They are over by the swings in the park. Why don't you and Daddy go ahead and find them?"

"Come on, Daddy. We need to find them," Kate responds as she runs over to Connor, grabbing his hand and pulling him over towards the fenced off park.

I stand back and watch them run ahead of us. I turn around to see Mark pushing Lucy in her pram towards me.

"Thank you, baby," I say as I stand on my tippy toes and place my lips on his.

"Anything for my angel. Did I ever tell you that I fucking love you?" he asks, lightly running his fingers through my hair.

"Oh, I don't know if you have," I say, laughing.

"You're such a tease, Miss Madden."

"Oh, don't you know it, Mr. Reed. Let's go and join everyone."

I walk alongside Mark with my arm hooked through his while he pushes Lucy. I feel so safe in his arms. I didn't know I would feel like this, ever. The air has a little chill behind it, but it's not unbearably cold. It does feel cold enough for snow, though. I wish it would; I want Lucy to see it. Within the garden of the house, there is plenty of room for us to build multiple snowmen and snow families and so much more. I'm so happy.

"We found them," Kate calls over to us, waving.

I wave back, walking over to them.

"Hey, hun, you got here," Jenny says, pulling me away from Mark and giving me a massive hug.

"Hi, Warren," I say. I can see why Jenny likes him. He looks like a sex god. I have heard all about his tattoos. Now, who doesn't like a man with a great set of abs and tattoos? All I need to know is if he rides a motorbike. Then, I'll know she has gotten herself a perfect sex god and bad boy in one package.

"Let's go," Connor says, leading ahead. Kate is holding his hand and looking up at him every so often.

We walk past the rides in the park and the trees shading the big field. I feel something hit my nose. Rubbing it, I look up to see large snowflakes falling from the sky.

"Yeah! A white Christmas Eve," Jenny says, spinning around in the falling snow.

We all laugh and continue walking past the football goals. I have never seen snow fall so fast. It's gorgeous. Kate is skipping along, singing Christmas songs as loudly as she can, and Jenny has her hand in Warren's. Mark stops me from walking.

"Hey, pop this on," he says, passing me my grey wool hat with matching scarf and gloves.

"Thank you," I say as I watch him put on his black hat to cover his ears. He wants to go au naturel for Christmas, the one time he feels that he doesn't have to be clean-shaven. I'm not fully sure that I like the facial hair, but if he wants to go without shaving, then it's fine with me. I want him to be happy.

"ARGH!" I hear Kate scream.

I turn around to see her lying on the grass, crying. I rush over to see what has happened, leaving Lucy with Mark.

"What happened?" I ask Connor.

"I have no idea. She fell over," he answers as he stands her up.

Kate's arms wrap around Connor's as he pulls her tight. "Shh, you will be okay," he tells her.

I kick the ground to uncover a large rock under the freshly fallen snow. I shake my head. That's what she fell over.

"My knee," she says, turning to face me.

"Let's have a look," I say as I roll up her leggings and find her knee grazed.

Connor reaches into his pocket and pulls out a tissue. Getting back down onto his knees, he cleans her scrape, comforting her as he does it. He then pulls out a pink plaster from his other pocket. I wonder what else he is going to pull from his magic pockets.

"Come on, Kate. I need to go and see the surprise," I say, trying to distract her.

"Come on, Daddy," she says as she gives him a kiss on his cheek before grabbing his hand.

I stand up and shake the loose snow from my knees. As we take a few more steps, we are all able to see the surprise.

Chapter Seven

"Megan, is that what I think it is?" Jenny asks.

"Yes, it is," I reply.

"I'm guessing this is down to you, Mark," Warren says.

"Yes, I wanted her to have a magical Christmas. What is more magical than meeting a reindeer?" he questions.

"Hats off to you, mate. I never thought it would be that," Warren replies.

I turn and look at Warren. Really, did he just say that? I watch Kate jump up and down as Jenny takes out her camera to capture the moment in pictures. Kate is full of questions for the reindeer's handler, Andre. I know all the details from when Mark and I went to meet him the other day to finalize the plans. Andre has been a wild animal handler for over twenty years. He is originally from Australia, but he decided to travel the world. He has his own farm with different animals located a little over twenty miles from us. The reindeer's name is Rider. I stand there listening to Andre tell Kate all about him.

"Rider is one of the spare reindeer. He steps in when needed, and he's a very special rare one. He loves carrots and people feeding him. He helps out the other reindeer by going and meeting people so the other crew members are able to have a rest before the big night," Andre says.

We spend over an hour with them, taking pictures and walking around the field as the snow continues to fall. I have not seen Kate smile as much as I have today.

"Rider has a little present for you," Andre says as he passes her a red bag with white snowflakes decorating it.

Kate slowly takes it from him and turns around to face Connor. "Can I open it, Daddy?" she asks enthusiastically.

"Go on. Don't tell, though," he replies.

A huge smile covers her face as she opens the bag and pulls out a brown teddy bear with a sparkly purple bow in its hair. A little note is attached to the bear.

My name is Lexi. Please, look after me. I'm yours forever, and I will always be there when you need me.

"Look what I got, Daddy," she says, waving the teddy at him. He kneels on the cold snow and reads the note to her.

"Megan, I have a new teddy," she says, running up to me. "Can she sleep at your house with me?"

I pretend to talk to the teddy. "Of course, she can. Nice to meet you, Lexi."

Kate runs around, showing everyone else her teddy before climbing into her dad's arms and slowly going quiet. We stand there listening to Andre tell Warren about his past and the animals he has cared for on his farm. I look over at Kate to see she has fallen asleep.

When Mark called me to arrange everything, we had to choose a name for the reindeer for Kate. Deciding on a name was so hard, because to my knowledge, they are all males and Kate doesn't respond well to men. She is going through a stage in which she doesn't like their names.

"Connor, Kate's asleep," I whisper into his ear.

"Thanks, I might take her home," he says.

"Good idea."

Mark goes over to Connor and chats before coming over to me. "Connor is going to take Lucy and Kate home. You're staying with me," he says sheepishly.

"How are we getting home then?" I ask.

"Oh, my other car is in the car park," he answers with a smirk on his face.

"Such a show-off. Is Connor sure?" I ask.

"Yes," he says. "You're mine for the next hour."

I smile. "Okay then."

Jenny and Warren say their goodbyes. They are planning to place some flowers on Martin's grave before heading back to Warren's. I'm left standing in the cold in at least two inches of snow. Mark stands there talking to Andre before he departs.

"It's just you and me. Now, what are we going to do?" I ask.

"Nothing. I just wanted to spend some special time with you, alone."

Chapter Eight

He slides his hand in mine before looking down at me and smiling. He starts to walk farther along the park near the river. I don't know how many times this river has flooded, but I still like it. It's such a quiet place to sit. A few years ago there were benches lined around the edges of the park, all dedicated to special people, but some kids threw them into the river. No one has ever replaced them. We make our way over to a wobbly, wooden bridge. It has a little bit of wood missing and is very scary to cross, but worth it. There is an amazing flower garden on the other side with so many flowers that it feels like you're walking through a field of dreams. It is adorned with colours I have never seen before, a few scattered benches, and wildlife. It's truly magnificent. I love coming here to be alone with my thoughts, because it is so tranquil and exquisite. You can see the flowers from the other side and rabbits jumping around. It's a great place to be one with nature. In the summer months, there are ducks that swim in the water, and in the winter, it turns to a playground of ice. I would love to bring Annabella here someday.

"Carson River." He pauses. "I know how much you like it here. I thought we could just spend a little us time."

"Sounds like a good idea."

"The only problem is, I forgot to bring a blanket."

"That's fine."

"We can just use my coat," he says, undoing his jacket.

"No, you're just wearing a thin T-shirt."

I undo the zipper of my coat and slide it down my arms as I pass it to Mark. He bends down and places it on the grass to the side of us. I sit down on part of the coat, letting Mark sit down beside me. I didn't realize how cold it is until now. As I sit on the ground with only my black leggings and grey jumper, I realize this may not have been a good idea after all. The snow is fresh and just fallen, and I can feel the coldness through my clothes.

"Baby, I did think of doing a picnic, but I changed my mind. I got you this instead," he says, pulling out a milk chocolate bar from his coat pocket. I can't help but laugh. He's a man after my own heart. I love chocolate; it's my thing.

"Aw, thank you. Share?" I ask, offering him the bar.

"Only if you want, baby," he says.

I open the bar, breaking it into the individual squares.

I place the open packet on Mark's knee before taking a square. Now, I'm in heaven. Mark wraps his arm around me before pulling me closer to him. I feel so safe, so loved, and so wanted. Mark knows me well, and just being close to him is enough for me. I don't need flashy, expensive treats; I just need him. Well, the chocolate helps, too. We both sit there in each other's arms, quietly watching the world go by. I feel his chest rise and fall and his warm breath blow on my neck, causing a tickling sensation and making my hairs stand on end. If it weren't for the cold air, I could get up to some real naughty fun. I still could, but icicles in some places…Eww…no thank you.

"What are you thinking?" Mark whispers into my ear.

"Nothing," I say, looking down at my knee.

"Tell me the truth."

"About how much naughty fun we could have if it weren't so cold."

"Oh, Miss Madden, I love your naughty side. The car is warm, though," he replies with a wink.

I turn around to look at him. "It is indeed. Is that the plan, Mr. Reed?"

"Only if you want."

"Come on then, Mr. Reed, or I'll throw snowballs at you." I quickly spring to my feet and run a little bit away from him.

"Oh, that's it, Miss Madden," he says, jumping up and grabbing my coat before chasing behind me. He slows down as he gets closer to me and bends down to pick up some snow, forming it into a snowball.

"Mark, don't you dare," I say as I start walking backwards.

I slowly lie down on the snow and begin making snow angels. Mark stands to the side of me and laughs as he watches me kick my legs and move my arms up and down.

"Don't you laugh at me," I say.

"Baby, you look so sexy. I could just jump on you."

"Oh, please do."

Mark falls to his knees and places his lips on my cheek and neck, while his hand slides down my stomach.

"You're my angel." His voice is barely above a whisper.

I place my hand under his T-shirt and slowly trail it down his stomach, ending my seduction by rubbing over his trousers.

"That's it, baby. Car now," he says.

I smile, standing up in front of him. "How fast can you move?" I ask.

Mark takes hold of my hand and walks as fast as he can towards the car. "I can't believe you have gotten me all hot, again. Twice in one day. You're naughty."

"But nice," I say as we reach the car park. "Where is the car?"

"Over there," he says, pointing towards the wooden cabin, which contains the dog warden's office. As we walk towards the car, I see people in the office and hear children as they run towards the park with their parents.

"Oh, crap, where are we going to go?" I ask.

"I know where we are going, baby. I'm not letting you go until I have made you smile in that special way. I want you to go back into the house with that special twinkle in your eye. I love it," he says while opening my car door.

I slide into the car and fasten my seatbelt. Mark closes the door before running around the car and jumping inside. He starts the ignition as soon as he shuts the door. I'm glad it's not slippery outside, or Mark would have fallen because he was moving so quickly. There is no question at all how much he wants me. I have never felt so desired, and not just in a sexual manner. That is an added bonus. He has such good stamina. I could never be unhappy with him. I feel like a teenager right now with trying to find somewhere to hide and have fun, so no one will see us. How bad is that?

I sit with my eyes on the road as Mark drives through the busy town traffic. Everyone is rushing around getting their last minute gifts and traveling to their relatives for the Christmas holiday. So many cars have silly flags on them. It makes me smile to see everyone's Christmas spirit come out. My hand slides over to Mark's leg, and I start rubbing it up and down slowly. I then move it around a little bit so it's more on his inner thigh.

"Oh, you're going to kill me doing that, baby," he murmurs.

I don't answer; instead, I continue rubbing. His breathing becomes heavier as he gets closer to quiet country lanes. I wish he would hurry. I don't know how much longer I can wait before I jump him.

"We are here," he says as he turns off the engine and moves his seat farther back.

I undo my seatbelt and turn to face him. Smiling, he moves my seat back as he moves over towards me. He kisses me, and his hands fly through my hair. "Oh baby," he whispers as he slips his fingers down my spine, making me moan.

"Bad day to wear leggings," he says as he lifts my bum at one side, pulling them down and then repeating with the other side.

"Don't I know it?" I say as I help him as much as I can. I'm thankful we are in his 4x4, because there's more room.

I slide my hand over his trousers, undoing his button with one hand. That really impresses him, and he is forever telling me that I'm super talented for being able to do that.

"Oh, not yet, baby," he says as he gently pushes me back. He smiles at me before he pushes up my jumper a bit and places a kiss on my navel. He follows down with little kisses, all the way to my entrance.

He slowly slides one finger into me, immediately making me gasp. He slides it out and then adds another, followed by another. He pushes them in and out slowly as he brings his head closer and blows on my clit. "Oh my," I moan.

His fingers start to speed up. As he moves closer to my clit, he lets his tongue slowly lick over it before he gently tugs on it with his teeth. I feel myself about to lose control, and I arch my back. He starts blowing on my clit again, knowing what it does to me. I finally lose control. He tips me over the edge.

Unable to move, I lie there with my legs wobbling like jelly. "I love how you look post orgasm, baby. You look so pretty."

I cover my face. I can't believe he said that.

"Don't you do that," he says, pulling down my arms.

"It's your turn now," I say as I sit up.

"Oh, is it?" he questions.

"Yes."

"Only if it's with you." He lifts me over onto his lap, facing him. "This is what I want."

"Oh, well, I'm sure I can do that." I wink. Mark's hands attach to my hips, lifting me up and lowering me onto him. I don't even remember him moving his trousers down. I lean back, placing my hands on either side of the steering wheel before moving up and down on him. I look straight into his loving eyes.

"You're giving me that look. You're going to kill me," he says as he moans.

I continue rising and falling on him, speeding up slowly, because I know how to tease him. He places his arm around my back, forcing me forward onto him while his breath blows on my neck and his hands slide through my hair.

Chapter Nine

"I love you, Megan," he says as he pulls me back in for another kiss.

"I love you, too," I say as I wiggle my leggings back up.

"You're amazing, sexy, and perfect. So carefree when it comes down to it."

"I know, but we need to get back. I have things to do," I state as I put my seat back to normal.

"I know," he says as he sorts his chair and then turns on the engine. "The windows are a bit steamed up."

"They are indeed."

Mark turns on the air-conditioner to clear the windows and starts to drive. I reach for my phone.

Megan, I can't believe what happened. Someone has written all over Martin's grave with paint. XX

WHAT? XX

Yes, all over his gravestone. It says "Burn in hell like your son." XX

Oh my, where are you? XX

Just about to hit your house. You? XX

About 10 mins away. Have you called your mum? XX

No, she will flip. I don't know what to do. XX

What about ringing Uncle Dave? XX

I'll do that. See you in 10. XX

I turn to face Mark. He's smiling from ear to ear, looking all relaxed and calm. I love him in this work-free mood. I inform him of what Jenny has just told me.

"What sick bastards," he says.

"Exactly. Do you know what would take it off?" I enquire.

"No, I don't. Message Connor. He will find out. I'll go with him and get it cleaned off. I'm sure we can do it. I don't want this on Jen's mind over Christmas," he informs me.

"Thank you, Mark."

"Anything for you, baby."

Hi, Connor. Do you know what cleans paint off gravestones?

Hi, Megan. Yes, I do. Why do you ask?

Someone has painted on Jenny's brother's grave. Mark wants to go and get it cleaned today.

Okay, I'll give him a hand. Local supermarkets will sell it. Kate is waiting for you.

Thank you. Tell her I will be with her shortly. Get the kettle on. I need a brew. I'm freezing. Lol

"He knows. He will give you a hand," I tell Mark.

"Good."

Who would do this to a child's grave? I hope I never find out, or I will blow and I mean *really* blow. I know Jenny is going to be seriously upset. She blames herself for it as it is, so I need to calm down before I see her. It will not help her if she knows that it has gotten to me. We hit the street where I live, and I start taking deep breaths, counting to ten, and telling myself that I can do this. Jenny needs me. As we turn onto the driveway at the front of the house, I see Warren's car parked to the side. Kate is standing in the front window, waving at me.

I step out of the car and wave back. "I love you, Mark," I say as he takes hold of my hand and walks towards the front door.

"Megan!" Kate yells as I walk inside. She runs straight into my arms, and I begin to look forward to baking with her.

"Hey, Kate, I hear you have been waiting for me."

"I have. I have. Can we bake now?" she questions.

"Of course, just let me get changed and then I'll be down. I don't want to get my new jumper mucky," I state.

"Should I get changed, Daddy?" she asks, turning to face Connor.

"You can if you want, Kate."

"Come on, Megan," she says as she runs up the stairs.

"I'll be up in a minute." I turn to face Connor. "Where is Lucy?"

"She is asleep in her cot. She's been an angel."

"Thank you."

"Come on!" Kate shouts from the top of the stairs.

"I'll be right back," I say as I run up to her. "Right, what are you going to wear?"

"This," she says, pulling out a red top with holes in it. It looks like it's never been washed. Ever. It's so unclean.

"Why?" I ask.

"Grandma Betty gave it to me," she answers.

She quickly changes her top before running downstairs to put on her apron, or so she says. It's one of mine, so it will be too big for her. I believe there is one under the tree for her, though. I peer into Lucy's room, checking to make sure she is okay. She is flat out asleep. Bless her. Before toddling into my room, I grab fresh underwear, a grey T-shirt and some clean leggings from the drawer. I change quickly, throwing my clothes into the washing basket before running downstairs to find Kate.

Chapter Ten

I walk into the front room to see Warren, Mark, and Connor all standing near the back window in deep conversation. They're whispering, so we can't hear them. What are they up to?

I turn to look at the sofa. Jenny is sitting there, talking with Kate.

"Megan is my best friend," Kate says, placing her hands on her hips.

"Oh, is she?" Jenny questions.

"Yeah, that's why we are baking together."

"I'm baking, too."

"Oh, well, you can be my friend, too," Kate says.

I can't help but smile. Kate has finally let Jenny in. "Who wants a brew?" I ask everyone in the room.

"Me," Jenny says.

"No, thank you, baby. We are going to sort that problem," Mark says as all three men walk out of the house.

"No hurting anyone," I tell them before Mark closes the door.

"Right, let's bake." I pause, "Come on, Jenny." We walk into the kitchen. Kate runs straight over to the chairs at the table and kneels on one of them. I'm glad I measured everything yesterday. I even did the pastry, and I didn't think Kate would enjoy it as much as she did. She can play with the leftover pastry. I remember playing with it as a child. It kept me entertained. My nan would keep it in the fridge in cling film until I came around for the afternoon, and I would spend hours making different things. I had so much fun.

"Right," I say as I place everything onto the table. "Jenny, can you roll out the pastry? Kate, when she has done that, can you use this to cut out circles?" I point to the circle cutter.

"Let's do this, Kate," Jenny says as she starts rolling it out. I walk over to get the rest of the equipment from the side and laugh. Last night as I made the pastry, Mark came to "help" or so he said. He threw flour at me, and I ended up in one big mess. He grabbed me by my waist and sat me on the kitchen counter to clean the flour from my face. I had been very naughty, wearing a float dress with no underwear, which he soon discovered as he trailed his hand up the inside of my dress. Let's just say, the kitchen got christened big time. Even if I did bang the back of my head on the kitchen cupboard, it was worth it.

"Now, what do we do?" Kate yells.

"Right, we grease these tins with butter. Like this." I take a bit of parchment paper and rub the butter onto the tin and then pass it to Kate for her to finish.

Jenny pulls me down to her level as she sits on the chair by Kate. She whispers, "What do you think the guys are up to?"

"I have no idea. Hopefully, they're just cleaning, like they said."

"I hope so. Mum hasn't rung me back yet."

"She will," I say, rubbing her back.

"Done!" Kate yells.

"Okay, now you need to take one of these circles and push it into the pastry, like this," I say as I show her how to cut out the circles.

"I can do that," she replies, straightening her back and wiggling.

"Go on then." I walk over to the side, grabbing another small spoon and the jar of mince.

"We're ready for the next bit. Place a spoon of this onto each piece," I tell her. She does it straight away, dropping a little bit in between, but that makes them more special. Jenny whisks up the egg before setting a little of it around the tops of the pies. Kate finishes them by placing on the tops.

"Perfect," I state. "Let's get them into the oven."

"Yeah, I can't wait to show Daddy."

"He has to wait until tomorrow before he can eat them," I inform her.

"Can we leave one out tonight with some milk?" she asks.

"Of course."

"What about a carrot?"

"I have some," I say, pointing over at the vegetable rack.

Kate runs over to the rack and digs until she finds the biggest one. "They can share this one."

I hope they eat all these mince pies tomorrow, because I really don't like them. Even the smell of them makes me feel sick. I clean the table and put away the dirty items to be washed. I sprinkle a little flour onto the table and place the leftover pastry and some cutters on top. That will give Kate something to play with for a while. I can still remember the time Mark told me his cousin, Suzanne, likes to eat leftover pastry. I hope he means when it's cooked; otherwise, she is weird. I still haven't met her yet. I decide to get all the vegetables prepared for tomorrow. The more I get done today, the more time I can spend with my loved ones.

"Hun, can I go and have a lie down?" Jenny asks.

"Of course, you don't have to ask. Are you feeling okay?"

"Yeah, my back's hurting a little. I'll just rest on the sofa, if that's okay."

"Go on."

I stand there watching Kate play with the pastry. She is so lively, just having fun playing with something simple. I hope tomorrow will be the same for her. I want her to be happy. I hate seeing her sad. She cried herself to sleep last night in Connor's arms. All she kept saying was Grandma Betty doesn't want me anymore. No matter what he said, she wouldn't listen. I hope she will not do the same tonight, because it really hurt Connor seeing her in that state.

"What else can we make, Megan?" Kate asks.

"There's nothing else to make, unless you want to do cookies?"

"Yes...yes...yes," Kate and Jenny say, jumping up and down.

"Okay, now who is the child out of you two?" I question.

"Kate," Jenny says, laughing.

"Right, you wash down the table, Kate, while I get everything together." I glance towards Jenny. "I thought you were having a lie down?"

"I came for some water. Indigestion."

"Oh, I see. Can you just keep an eye on Kate while I run and check that Lucy is okay?"

"Anything for you, hun."

I leave the two of them in the kitchen, chatting away about how much chocolate to add into the cookies. At this rate, there will be more chocolate than cookie. I walk into Lucy's room and hear her giggling. She is such a sweetie.

"Are you going to come downstairs?" I ask as I lift her out of her cot. I quickly change her nappy before heading downstairs.

Chapter Eleven

I take out the last lot of cookies from the oven and place them onto the cooling rack. The vegetables have been prepared, and the treats have been made. That means everything is done. There is nothing else to do until later. I walk into the front room to find both Jenny and Kate curled up together on the sofa, asleep. Jenny's arm is wrapped around Kate. I grab my phone and take a picture before covering them with the pink blanket from the back of the sofa. I don't want them to get cold.

I sit on the floor next to Lucy in her baby bouncer. She loves it and will cry the house down if you don't let her sit in it. I bought different attachments to go on it, so she has things to play with, as she loves to be around her toys. With her jumping up and down in it, she's strengthening her legs. She has made attempts to crawl, but she hasn't taken off. I hope she will soon, because she is nearly nine months old. I look at the clock. The fellas have been gone over two hours, and I don't understand what could be taking them so long.

Before texting Mark, I forward Connor the picture of Kate and Jenny asleep.

What is taking you so long, Mark? X

Sorry, we got sidetracked. X

Doing what? X

A Christmas surprise. X

Tell me. X

No, baby girl, you will find out soon enough. X

That's not fair. Did you get the grave sorted? X

Yes, we did. X

Thank you. X

Be home in 5. X

I turn on the television and scroll through the Christmas movies, deciding on a famous one to watch. I sit there calm and relaxed in my own world. I glance over to the tree and smile at the box that is full of all the little decorations Kate and I have made over the past few days. We are going to place them today.

As I hear the front door open, a gust of cold air hits me. I wrap my arms around myself and hope the door closes soon. Warren pops his head around the corner before slowly creeping into the room.

"What are you up to?" I ask.

"Nothing. Do you have anything that will cover this?" he asks, turning his head and showing me a large cut on his face.

"What the hell did you do?" I ask.

"Got into a fight. Come on. Do you have something?"

"Yes, I do," I say as I get up from the floor. "Who was the fight with?"

"Come here, and we will fill you in. I don't want Jenny to know."

"Jenny to know what?" Jenny enquires as she looks up at him.

"Nothing," Warren says, moving quickly out of the room.

Connor walks into the lounge, and I head upstairs and find Warren standing behind the little wall.

"She needs to know," I say as I point him into my room. I could have easily fixed him downstairs, but I need to know what happened, and I don't want to alarm Kate.

I reach for my handbag, pulling out a little first aid kit. It's a must-have for scraped knees and cut fingers when you have children around, as you never know when you will need it. Luckily, I haven't used it with Lucy, but with Kate around, I placed it inside my bag for emergencies. Yes, I'm an organised freak sometimes, and even though she isn't my child, I need to make sure she is safe while in my care. It took Connor a lot to get her here for the holidays. She doesn't go back until the beginning of next year.

Sitting on my bed, I open the kit and then pat the bed, indicating for Warren to sit. He complies.

"Right, sit still. This is going to sting," I state as I pull out an antiseptic wipe.

"Ouch, that does sting."

"Well, if you were not such an idiot for getting into a fight, you wouldn't be having this done."

"Yes, I know."

"Well, are you going to tell me what happened?"

"No," Warren says, pulling a mad face.

"You need a couple of stitches."

"No, I'll be fine. A plaster or makeup will do."

"What's the point in hiding it, Warren? Jenny knows."

I see Jenny standing in the doorway, listening to our conversation. She does not say anything. She knows that I can get information out of people when needed.

"Cream and a plaster. Makeup will make it worse," I state.

I rub on the cream, and Warren jumps high. I shake my head. What a wimp.

"Pink plaster?" I question.

"I don't think so. I'm a man."

"Blue?" I ask, giggling.

"You're such a funny lady. Brown, please."

I place on the plaster. "Right, now tell me."

"No, I don't want to."

"Warren, tell me. I need to protect Jenny, like you do."

"You aren't going to drop it. Are you?" he asks, looking down at the floor.

"I need to know," I say as I put my hand on his knee.

Warren sighs before looking up at me, "This is going to hurt Jenny." He pauses.

"When we got to the grave, a man was there. We stood back and watched him, thinking he was paying his respects. It wasn't until about five minutes later that I noticed he had spray cans and other stuff. I told the lads, and we went over."

"And..." I say, waiting for him to continue.

"Well, his name is Joshua. He is the one that caused the wreck that killed Kate's mum. His wife is sleeping with Jenny's dad."

"*What*?" Jenny screams from the door.

Warren suddenly turns around, facing Jenny. "How long have you been standing there?"

"Long enough. Now, tell me," she says as she walks towards the other side of the bed and sits on it.

"His wife, Sonja, is sleeping with your dad."

"Oh no, I need to ring Mum," she says.

Jenny runs out of the room with Warren not far behind. I sit there, shell-shocked. Why would Jenny's dad do this? Why would anyone defy someone's grave? How the hell did Joshua know about it? I have so many unanswered questions. I wish I could talk to both of them. Well, maybe I shouldn't talk to Jenny's dad because I would want to hurt him. I can't believe he has done this to his family. I understand a little why Warren would want to protect Jenny and not tell her, but she needed to know. That's the reason why I had him tell me everything while she was listening.

I hear a tap on the door as Mark walks in and sits on the bed beside me. He pulls me close, draping his arms around me and giving me a little kiss on the head.

"Will you tell me everything that happened, Mark?" I ask.

"I will never keep anything from you," he says before taking a deep breath and explaining everything.

Joshua had written on Martin's grave to get back at Jenny's dad. He hadn't just been sleeping with Joshua's wife; he got her pregnant. She is four months along and has not slept with Joshua in over six months, so he knows Jenny's dad is the father. Once Joshua had finished telling them everything, he said that he needed to destroy something that belonged to Jenny's dad so he would hurt, too. That is when the fight started. They all have cuts and bruises. Joshua threw the first punch, so I can relax a little bit, knowing there shouldn't be any repercussions.

Chapter Twelve

I find myself leaning on Mark on the sofa downstairs, not fully aware of how I ended up here. I sit, watching Kate and Connor sort out the leftover handmade decorations. He places them where she says. Connor has learnt what a woman says goes, even when it's a young girl. Kate is so chatty. "Daddy, shall we place this over here? Then, people can see it outside."

"No, it's too small. They will not see it." Ignoring him, she places it where she suggested. You can tell she is going to wear the trousers in her future relationships. I can't help but smile.

"Where is Lucy?" I turn and face Mark.

"You're awake. She is asleep, bathed, and in bed." He places a little kiss on my forehead.

"Thank you."

"Would you like something to eat?"

"No, have you heard from Jenny?"

"No, Warren rang, though. They will be back later tonight. All is sorted."

"Megan," Kate says, running towards me. "You're awake. Can we place our stockings up yet?"

"Of course, we can. Get Mark to go and get them for us, and we can hang them up while Daddy finishes what he's doing." I sit up, letting Mark move.

Mark smiles and goes running upstairs to get them. When Kate first saw them, they were just plain red stockings, but I couldn't leave them like that. I added everyone's first initial in their favourite colour to the front of each one.

"There you go, Kate," Mark says, giving her the bag with the stockings inside.

I sit there, watching her as she pulls them out and starts to scream and jump up and down. I slide to the end of the sofa before standing up and listening to Kate recite the order for them to be hung. I suddenly feel a draft and turn to see Warren and Jenny standing there. Both of them are wearing their big coats, covered with snow. Warren is holding onto Jenny's hand. They are such a perfect sight to see.

Jenny smiles at me and then looks around. "Hey, everyone."

"Jenny, you're back. Look at the magic stockings. There is one for everyone, including Warren." She runs over to him and gives him a hug. I don't know why, but she really has clicked with him. They spend lots of time playing together, and he is always picking her up and throwing her above his head and having tickle fights with her. She seems to gel well with the men.

"How are you?" Jenny asks me.

"I'm fine. And you?"

"Yeah, I'm fine. All is true. Mum left him. She is off to stay with a friend. Dad has that cow in the house."

"I'm sorry, hun."

"It's okay. Mum's happy and free from Dad."

I smile as I watch Warren place a present under the tree.

"What's next?" Kate enquires.

"Supper." I pause. "Go and get the apples."

I follow her into the kitchen. Grabbing the chopping board and six small plates, I cut the apples into small, thin strips. Kate takes a bottle of pop into the front room with some plastic cups.

"You pour it," Kate demands before running back in to me.

"Sugar," I say.

Kate smiles as I place a small amount of sugar to the side of everyone's apple slices before I give her two plates to carry through as I carry the rest.

"Yippee, I love Christmas Eve apples," Jenny says.

Everyone else looks questioningly at us, and I explain that it is a naughty treat you can only have today. It is a tradition from my childhood. After everyone eats, Warren gets up and grabs ahold of Kate, giving her a special reindeer decoration for the tree. It has Martin's name written on it.

Jenny smiles. "Thank you, Warren."

"Anything for you."

"What now?" Kate says.

"Bed, young lady," Warren says.

"Oh, but..."

"No buts, Kate," Connor interrupts.

"Come with me, Kate. We have something to do first, but...shh...because it's a secret." Warren takes hold of her hand and walks out of the room.

We remain in the room, just leaving the two troubles to it. Jenny and Mark fight over the television remote. I chuckle a little because I like my man and best friend getting on, but I'm on Jenny's side. No way am I watching the crap quiz show Mark wants to watch.

"Megan, help me," Jenny says.

I stand up and walk over to the sofa, grinning at Mark.

"Nah, you're not getting it, baby," he says, sliding the remote down the back of his shirt.

"Oh, you know I am." I sit on him with one leg on either side of his. Grabbing his hands, I pull him towards me.

"Quick, get it, Jenny," I mouth as Mark struggles to loosen my grip.

Jenny hastily grabs it as Mark frees his hands, placing them behind me and pulling me close. "You will pay for this, baby," he says as he lowers his lips onto my neck. I can't help but blush.

"Right, what are we going to do?" I say, struggling to free myself from his grasp.

"How about we play a game until *someone* is asleep?" Jenny hints.

"Kate?" I question. It doesn't matter as much if Lucy is still awake. She will not remember anything.

"Yeah, then we can get everything else out."

"Perfect," I say.

"Well, once Warren has finished with her, I'm going to take her for a bath and story, then bed."

"That's fine," Jenny replies.

Mark holds me tight and smiles. "I don't know what you're up to, Mr. Reed," I say.

"How about we watch the end of this film and then finish those orange things?" Jenny proposes.

"Daddy, we have everything out for him. It's in the kitchen. We have placed food outside for the reindeer, too," Kate says, jumping up and down in front of the tree.

Chapter Thirteen

The oranges are done, and the film is finished. Kate is bathed and in bed, but she is still awake counting stars. Counting stars when she can't sleep is something she learned from Grandma Betty. After checking on Lucy, I stand at the top of the landing to listen.

"Twenty-twelve stars, twenty-fifteen stars, twenty-one stars." I smile sweetly. One of her gifts will help her with numbers. I walk into the front room to inform everyone that she's still awake.

"Well, you can watch *that*, but there's no way in hell that I am watching it," Jenny says as she lies down on the sofa, placing her head on Warren's knee.

"That's fine then," Mark replies, sticking his tongue out at her.

"Megan, whose side are you on?" Jenny says as she grabs the blanket from the back of the sofa.

"Over what?" I question.

"The Queen's speech. Mark wants to watch it."

"He can, and we'll just eat all the chocolate. No way am I watching that; I'll fall asleep," I state.

"That's my girl," Jenny says, giving me a high five as I walk past.

"Sorry, Mark, it's repeated so much that I will find out what was said." I sit next to Mark.

"It's okay, baby. It's been forced on me all my life. Then, having to sit and talk about it." Placing my head onto his shoulder, I lift my feet onto the sofa beside me. Now, I'm comfortable.

"Poor you." I reach my hand up to him, giggling. Mark shakes his head and kisses the palm of my hand.

"Just like me, mate. We always watched it, too, but we used to go and sit in the doorway and play with our toys and just listen for the silly questions like 'what do you think of the colour she is wearing?' It's not my cup of tea."

"Let's do something fun," Jenny says.

"Like what?" Connor questions.

"Truth or Dare," Jenny suggests.

"Count me in," Warren says, and we all concur.

Oh, why did I just agree to this? Suddenly, I have reservations about this idea. No way am I doing a dare; I'm not that silly.

"Truth or Dare, Connor?" Jenny asks.

"Truth."

"When was the last time you had sex with another person?" As she asks, I can't help but cover my face.

"Nearly five years." He pauses. "Truth or Dare, Warren?"

"Dare," Warren answers confidently.

"I dare you to go outside and draw a cock on someone's car." Warren smiles mischievously, gets up once Jenny sits up, and runs outside with Connor. I just sit there, thinking why it doesn't surprise me. Not even a minute later, Warren comes back in through the door, showing us the picture on his phone as proof. Yes, he drew it, including all the little details.

"Truth or Dare, Megan?" Warren asks.

"Truth." I'm not sure I want to play anymore.

"Is Mark the best lover you've ever had?" I laugh and cover my face.

"Yes." I pause. "Jenny, Truth or Dare?"

"Truth." Jenny winks at me. "Ohhh, now this needs to be hard." I sit there, pretending to be thinking. I know the question has to play with our long- standing joke.

"Have you ever had a crush on a woman?" I ask, knowing the answer, but it's the only thing that comes to my mind.

"Oh hell, yes! You know what my answer is. Oh, babe, you know I have always wanted to nibble on rugs." Jenny bursts out laughing, then gets serious. "Hell no. Ewww...It's just so not my thing."

I sit there, laughing at Warren's face. I think he thought his luck had finally changed. Aw, bless him.

"Mark, Truth or Dare?" Jenny asks as she tries to stop laughing.

"Dare. It might be safer." He smiles at me while sounding very unsure.

"Take Megan out of the room and do a strip tease for her. You only have five minutes."

"Easy," Mark says.

"What? No!" I protest.

Mark stands up, lifts me from the sofa and places me over his shoulder. "NO! Don't do that, please!" I scream. He repeatedly taps my bum and carries me out of the room.

"I like this dare."

"I don't," I say, covering my face as he carries me up the stairs. Oh my, I feel sick. This is not a good look.

"I'm timing you!" Jenny yells up the stairs. Mark lays me down on the side of the bed, and I cover my face with my hands again in embarrassment.

"*Please*, baby, don't do this."

"A dare is a dare," he says. "Relax, baby. No one will see."

Mark stands there undoing a few buttons before pulling his T-shirt fully over his head from the back in one swift move.

"That's not the point." I really don't want him to go through with this, and if he does, I definitely don't want to upset him if I laugh. I know I will probably just want to throw him down onto the bed and have my way with him. I sit there with my eyes glued to his chest. I love his torso; he does not have an overworked six pack, just a shapely, grooved V down to his cock. He stands there thrusting back and forth trying to be sexy, and all I can do is laugh. He kicks off his shoes, and they hit the bottom of the metal bed frame as they fly. He bends down, rubbing his legs as he does and grabs the tip of his sock, pulling it off and dropping it to the floor. He takes off his other sock the same way. Turning around, he places his hands flat onto the wardrobe and shakes his bum slowly from side to side. I can't stop watching him because he looks so sexy.

"You can leave them on," I say, pointing towards his trousers.

"Never, baby," he replies as he slides down his trousers and boxers at the same time. I can't help but cover my face with my hand, only to sneak a little peek through my fingers.

"See. I did the dare." He pauses. "Come on. Let's go back down, or you never know what will happen." He slides his clothes back on. I stand up and rub my hand across his abs as I walk past him. He grabs my wrist and pulls me back, tipping me backwards, and placing one hand on my back and the other on my bum. As he slides his tongue into my mouth, my arms wrap around him, making the space between us almost invisible.

Mark slowly lets me stand up straight. "I'm sure our five minutes are over," I whisper.

"I know. I have something to finish before bed," he says, opening the door and letting me go out first. I walk over the landing towards Lucy's room. Opening the door, I see her snug and asleep in her cot. Mark stands behind me with his arms firmly wrapped around me, pulling me back, and my head leaning on his shoulder. I feel so safe.

"We should check on Kate, and then we can finish getting everything ready," I say. Mark takes hold of my hand, turns me around, and pulls me into his grasp.

"I'm so happy to be with you for Christmas. This will be the best Christmas ever." He places a kiss on my forehead. I lift my head and look into his sparkling eyes; I love how his eyes talk. I grab his hand and walk over to the room where Kate is sleeping. I slowly push open the door and hear her snoring soundly. Smiling, I close the door and turn around.

"Shall we get the bags down?" I suggest.

"Yes, come on." He walks ahead of me, up the stairs and into the loft. "Stay there, baby. They are heavy, so I'll bring them down."

I stand there beaming. I love that man, and I especially love the view of his tight ass walking up the stairs. I can't believe how lucky I am. I can't wait for tomorrow. Mark starts walking down the stairs, holding several bags in both arms and smiling at me. I didn't realize how many bags were up there. We didn't place anything under the tree, because we thought it might be safer with Lucy around and we didn't want her pulling presents from under the tree and opening them.

"Are you going to give me some to carry?" I ask. He shakes his head and continues down the stairs. I follow behind him and walk into the front room.

"Finally, I thought you must have been shagging him," Jenny blurts out.

"No! We checked on the kids and got the presents. Kate's asleep now," I state, winking at her.

Mark places the bags down onto the floor near the tree. "I will let you empty them. I need to pop out. I'll be back in about thirty minutes. Quicker if I can," he says.

"Okay." Both Warren and Connor stand up and walk out with him. I hear the car doors close and the engine rev as they disappear down the street.

"That's weird. Where are they going?" Jenny asks.

"No idea."

Chapter Fourteen

I sit in front of the tree, opening each bag and placing the presents underneath in no particular order at all. I don't want an organised Christmas tree. Some people do that, but I want it to be all fun, all higgledy-piggley. I love the array of the different sizes, shapes and colors of the gifts. Jenny is sitting on the sofa, passing me bits from the other bags. I don't want her sitting on the floor, because I imagine her getting stuck down there. She turned off the film a while ago. "Why is every music channel playing Christmas songs?" she asks.

"I don't know, but it's really annoying. I wish they wouldn't. Mark did say that 77 isn't playing Christmas ones."

Jenny quickly reaches for the silver remote and changes the channel to 77. "Yeah," she says. "Normal music." We sit there laughing as she begins singing along, doing a silly little chair dance. Oh, I love our crazy time. I jump up from the floor and move the empty bags into a pile on the sofa. Then, I push the small, glass coffee table out of the way for a makeshift dance floor.

"Come on, girl. Here is the dance floor," I say, pointing to the floor.

Jenny jumps up off the sofa, placing the music on a little louder before grabbing my hands and starting to dance. Thankfully, no one can see us. We must look like right idiots. I suddenly stop. "Jenny, do you hear that?" I ask.

"What?"

"Bells," I say, walking over to the window and opening the burgundy-lined curtains. I lift the blind to see outside.

"Oh my! Jenny, come here now."

Jenny rushes over and looks through the blind with me. "I bet this has something to do with the boys."

There in front of the house is a sleigh with reindeer and everything, just like you see in the books. I can't believe my eyes. Snow begins to fall from the sky as we stand there looking at it in amazement.

"I'll go get Kate," I say.

Running up the stairs, I head straight into Kate's room, bend down at the side of the bed and shake her. "Kate."

She groggily opens her eyes. "Come with me. I have something to show you." I pick her up and place her on my hip. I dash over the landing and pick up Lucy who has just started to stir. I place her on my other hip and wander down the stairs.

"Shall we open the door?" Jenny asks.

"Yes," I say, setting Kate on the floor and slowly opening the door. "Stay there, Kate."

"ARGH!" Kate screams as she jumps up and down. "It's him. He's really here."

Jenny takes Lucy from me and wraps the blanket around her tighter. I reach over, picking up Kate's red cardigan. "Place this on," I state, helping her before lifting her and taking a step out of the house. I can't help but smile. I walk along the freshly fallen snow towards the sleigh. I'm glad it's not slippery, because I'm wearing my pink fluffy slippers.

"Hi," I say. *What do you say to him?*

"Hello, Kate, Lucy, Jenny and Megan," he responds in a big animated voice. It's a voice I don't recognize. Who is it?

"Come here," he says to Kate. I pass Kate over to him as he sits in his sleigh.

"What would you like for Christmas, little one?" he asks pleasantly.

"A teddy," she says as she looks at him with pure astonishment. "Is this real?" she asks as her eyes shift to his beard, and she begins rubbing her hand along the bottom of it.

"Yes, it's real, my child." He pauses. "Turn around." He points to his side.

"A teddy!" she shouts, picking it up and enfolding it into a close hug.

"Merry Christmas, Kate," he says as he gives her back to me.

"This is for little Lucy." He hands me a smaller teddy, identical to the brown one that Kate received with the exception of a different coloured bow. It has one pink and one purple bow. Kate's teddy has only a purple bow. She has told me that purple is her favorite colour since the first time I met her.

"For you, Jenny." He grins, passing her two little bags. She thanks him before opening them. One has a pearl necklace inside, and the other contains a blue bib that reads "Created in 2013- Born in 2014."

"Now for you, Megan, the special lady," he says as I walk over to him, but he never looks up at me. He just passes a bag to me. I open it to find a bracelet with a little pink diamond in the middle encased in two interlocked hearts. It looks so pretty.

"Thank you," I say.

"You best get in and go to sleep, so I can drop off the rest of your presents. Goodnight, girls," he says matter-of-factly.

We walk back into the house and close the door behind us. We quickly run up the stairs into Kate's room. I tuck her into bed with her teddy in her arms.

"Read to me, Megan," she says sleepily.

I sit on the edge of the bed near Kate, and Jenny sits on the other side with Lucy in the crook of her arm. I pass the book to Kate because I remember it from my childhood and know all the words by heart. It's such a fascinating, memorable story. I sit there reciting it as they follow along with the book and look at the pictures.

"The end," I say. Jenny creeps out of the room, taking Lucy to her cot. I place a little kiss on Kate's head and turn on the little nightlight and leave her sleeping. I knew she would fall asleep before the end of the story.

Chapter Fifteen

I stand in my bedroom, looking out the window as the snow falls heavily to the ground. There are no tracks from the sleigh. Nothing. I do wonder which of the boys it was. But, whoever it was, it was a special moment that no one will ever forget. Jenny got lots of photos on her phone to commemorate the event.

It's been over an hour since the boys left. I suddenly see car headlights pulling into the driveway. It's Mark's car. Hurriedly, I close my purple curtains, slip off my jumper, and put on my black lacy nightwear. It's not an extremely revealing one, as I can guarantee that we will be awakened early. I wonder who will be up first. I always had to be gotten out of bed because I never woke up early on my own. Before they boys come inside, I reach down and pull out a long, black box and place it on Mark's side of the bed.

"Hey, baby. Sorry we were so long," he says, kissing my cheek.

"Oh, I saw you were busy. We enjoyed the visitor."

"What visitor?" he questions. I sit on the end of the bed and tell him everything. He doesn't give away any signs with his facial expressions, so I don't know if he knew about it or not.

"Right, I need to go and lock up," I say, walking around him and heading down the stairs. I go into the front room to turn off the Christmas tree lights and notice even more presents cascading the floor. The food and drink are gone. Shaking my head, I turn off everything and lock up before walking back upstairs. I check on Lucy and then head into my room.

"Hey," Mark says as he sits up in the bed with his bare chest on display.

"Where did you guys go?" I question as I close the door.

"To see Joshua."

"What?" I yell in disbelief.

"We needed to talk to him. Find out everything. He asked us to meet him. He showed us the pictures and all the evidence he had on them. There is no doubt, baby."

"I don't know what to say."

"Say nothing, baby. We will help Jenny through it all. She'll be fine. I have everything in my car. We will get Jenny's mum free, and the divorce will go through without a problem. She will get everything she wants." We need to get her into somewhere safe and away from everything on a more perminte base.

"She will not want anything. I know her."

"I know."

"Thank you," I say.

"Is this for me?" he asks, pointing towards the black box.

"Yes," I say as I walk around the bed and climb in next to him.

He opens it to see black tissue paper. Pulling it back, he reveals a red lacy baby doll with a matching thong. "Baby, you're going to kill me," he says as he kisses me excitedly.

"For you. For a different day." I smile.

I don't remember the last time Mark and I spent so much time being physical together. I can't keep my hands off him. We go to bed as normal. I lay on my side as he wraps his arms around me, pulling me as close as we can be. Pushing my hair out of the way, he kisses me along the back of my neck.

"I love you," he whispers.

His thumb rubs over my lips, and I can't help but kiss it. He has the gentlest touch. I roll over slightly onto my back and turn to face him. He smiles, placing his hand at the bottom of my black, silk lacy nightdress. His smooth fingers outline my skin. I lift my arms, craving more of his touch that sends piercing shivers down my spine. He drops the nightdress onto the floor. As he places his lips on mine and lets his fingers trace around my nipples, our eyes lock. Without a word being said, I move to slide off his boxers. He rolls on top of me, and I wrap my legs around him, letting him slowly slide into me and taking my breath. I just lie there, feeling him thrust sharply in and out with his bare body rubbing against me, intensifying the heat between us.

I don't know where the time goes. Our heat builds up, and it's not long before we are both panting after the most intense orgasm either of us has ever had.

"I love you, too," I whisper.

Chapter Sixteen

"It's Christmas, baby," Mark whispers into my ear. I slowly open my eyes and turn my face to him. His warm breath blows on my neck as he kisses my bare shoulder. I feel so safe.

"Baby, we should maybe put something on before the kids or Jenny wakes up. I don't think we want to be found with so little clothing on, even though I just want to keep my hands on your body and let my lips follow them."

There's a knock on the door. I close my eyes, pretending I'm asleep.

"Hey, Connor," Mark says.

"Hi, can I have a quick word?" he asks, walking towards the bed and sitting on the edge of Mark's side.

"Of course, what's wrong?"

"Kate." He pauses. "She was awake all night telling me about her teddy. How her teddy is away from her mummy, how she misses her own mum and wants Megan to be her mum."

"What?" Mark asks with concern in his voice.

"She wants Megan to be her mum."

"That's not going to happen." He stops to think. "Is Kate christened?"

"No, we never had it done. What are you thinking?"

"If you want and everyone agrees, why not have her christened and get Megan to be one of the godparents? Then, Kate will have the bond with her that she kind of wants. Does that make sense?"

"That's a great idea. Would Megan agree to it?" he asks.

"I think she would. We can ask her later."

"Will you be Megan's godfather?"

"Of course."

"I'll have a talk with Megan later. I would love for her to help me out. She could make it special, maybe help organise the little things with Kate so she has that bond. I think she really wants a mother figure around."

"Good idea," Mark says.

"Right, I'm going to wake up Kate. I want to see her face as she opens her presents."

As Connor leaves the room, I roll over to see Mark but I don't say a word. Mark hugs me close. "I'm sorry," he says barely above a whisper.

"For what?" I question, pulling back so I can see his face.

"Suggesting the christening thing."

"No, it's okay. It's a good idea. I was just shocked that Kate would want me as her mum," I reply, taking a deep breath.

"Let's get dressed, baby. He's gone to wake her."

"Okay, jammies time." I wink at him. I sit on the side of the bed and reach underneath, pulling out some pink pyjamas with little hearts scattered on them. Since I don't plan to change clothes until after breakfast, these are child friendly for me to wear in front of everyone. I slip on the bottoms and stand up. As I begin to pull them up, I feel Mark's hand tap my bum. I turn around, eyeing him accusingly.

"Behave yourself." I bend down and kiss him, making sure that my breasts are on show. Mark takes hold of one of them and sucks the nipple. I stand there, looking down at him.

"Now, get dressed, or I will have you lock the door."

"I'm getting dressed. You can have me later." I smirk, slipping on my top and slowly buttoning it. Out of the corner of my eye, I watch Mark glance over at me, following my hands.

"Megan," Kate calls as she comes running into the room.

"Good morning, baby," I say as I bend down and pick her up and sit her on my hip.

"Mark, come here," Kate says.

Mark does as he is told, while wearing only his black boxers. He comes and stands in front of me.

"Yes, little miss?"

"Merry Christmas," she says, jumping from my arms into his.

"Merry Christmas, Kate. Shall we go and see what is downstairs?" he asks with a hint in his voice.

Connor stands in the doorway, watching from afar. "Merry Christmas, Connor."

"Merry Christmas, Megan."

"Right, I'm going to get Lucy," I say, walking towards the door.

"I'll come, too," Kate says, running along and taking my hand. I look down at her to see her gazing up at me and smiling in admiration.

Connor moves to the side as we leave the room. I hear him talking to Mark, but I can't quite make out what they are saying. I walk into Lucy's room to find her awake. I love Lucy; she is my world. I love the way she wakes up but doesn't wake me up. She just lies there giggling.

"Morning, princess," I say, taking her out of the cot.

"Lucy," Kate says. "Merry Christmas." She reaches into the cot and gets Lucy's new teddy out.

"Let's get you sorted and then go downstairs." I walk over to the drawers and pull out a clean nappy and Christmas baby grow. She has so many different ones. This one is from Jenny. It has "My First Christmas 2013" with candy canes around it.

"I'll help," Kate says.

"Can you get me a bag from over there?" I ask, pointing to the drawers.

I quickly get Lucy cleaned up and changed into her new outfit. Kate stands on the chair, watching everything I do while singing Christmas songs to Lucy.

"Right, let's go downstairs and give Lucy some milk. Would you like some milk?" I ask.

"I love milk, but I'm only allowed it as a treat," she says.

"You can have it anytime you want while you're here."

Holding on to both teddies, Kate runs down the stairs and into the kitchen. She places them on their sides and gets me one of the bottles out of the cupboard.

"Aw, thank you, Kate."

I get milk for both of them and hear everyone chatting next door. Jenny has already gotten down before me. I can't wait for the fun to start.

Chapter Seventeen

I quickly check the turkey. All looks good. I set an alarm to wake me so that I could get it into the oven early. I have set another one to go off when it's close to being done. I want it to be perfect. I have made sure that I'm super organised with all the meats sorted. I cooked a bit of beef late last night for Kate. She has never eaten turkey, but she loves beef.

Kate runs ahead of me into the lounge and suddenly stops. She stands there in awe looking at the tree and everything around it.

I walk in behind her and take a seat on the floor.

"Look at all of them," Kate says.

"Shall we start opening them?" Connor asks, taking a seat beside her on the floor. He explains to her that we need to read each gift's label to see who it's for. She sits there, listening to him.

I reach over to try to grab my pink nursing pillow. Warren passes it to me, as it's a little too far away and Lucy is sitting on my knee, making it harder to stretch.

"Thank you," I say as I take it from him.

I place it onto the floor, creating a comfortable spot for Lucy to sit.

"This is for Lucy," Kate says. She comes over, laying a present in front of Lucy. I open it to find a baby walker with her name on it from Jenny and Warren.

"Thank you," I say.

I feel Warren tap his fingers on my shoulder, so I turn to face him. "Cuppa for you," he says, handing me a mug with a picture of Lucy from when she was in my tummy. I have never seen his before.

"Oh my! Thank you so much," I say, looking closely at it.

"You're welcome. Happy Christmas," he says.

"No, it's Merry Christmas, not Happy Christmas. It sounds silly as Happy Christmas," I state.

"She is right, Warren," Jenny adds.

"Not this conversation again," Connor says as he passes out more presents.

"Yes, again," I say.

Kate is sitting there, all happy with a bin bag full of wrapping paper. She enjoys tidying up for me. She is truly such a sweet child. "What did you get, Kate?" I ask her.

"Some clothes for my doll, Dolly, lots of clothes. A wardrobe for her with things to hang them on. She got some shoes, too. Look," she says, holding up some baby pink shoes that have a little strap across them.

"That will keep you busy. You will have to sort out all her clothes now."

"Daddy got a new tie," she says, covering her face and giggling.

"I did. It's a very pretty tie. Do you know anything about it?" he asks.

She shakes her head and covers her face with one of her doll's dresses.

"Oh, yes, you do, little miss," He says, tickling her. She sits there wriggling and giggling away.

"I asked for it," Kate responds.

"Thank you, princess," Connor says, kissing her on the forehead.

The presents seem to be never-ending. Warren has spoilt the kids with a play kitchen, teddies, clothes, and chocolates. There is so much stuff that I can't keep up with it all. He definitely loves Jenny. She received a chocolate hamper and a big box full of chocolate. Who wouldn't like that? I'm super jealous of that present. He also bought her a new baby kit full of little cream outfits.

Jenny opens some chocolate, offering it around to everyone. "Why bother placing stickers to reseal chocolate? I just don't get it. Some people have no idea," Jenny says as she places another square of chocolate into her mouth.

"You're meant to save some. That's why," Warren states.

"Okay, you name one woman that can do that?"

Warren sits there quiet for a minute. "All right, I get your point, my chocolate queen."

"One last thing, baby," Warren says, passing her a box.

She opens it. "A pearl bracelet. It matches my necklace."

She shakes her head and laughs. Now, was it him last night?

Warren sits next to her, pulling her close. "I have something for you," she whispers into his ear. She passes him the envelope she has been sitting on.

He slowly opens it and smiles, biting his lip as he pushes the paper back into the envelope.

"What was that?" I ask.

"Not for your eyes," he says with a big smile, and I can't help but laugh.

"Must be the sex vouchers then." Warren's jaw drops.

"What is the next present?"

"ARGH!" Kate yells, ripping silver wrapping paper off a large box.

"What is it?" Connor asks.

"Dolly's new pram." She pauses. "What I asked for. He didn't forget."

"Of course, he wouldn't forget. You have been a good girl."

"I need to get Dolly."

"Why don't we finish all of this first, and then I'll build it and you can get her?"

"Okay, Daddy." She takes the box, moving it out of the way and hugging it closely.

"Megan, I love your nail polish. Your toes look Christmassy." She laughs.

"It's called ice blue because it looks like snow," I say. As I wiggle my toes to show off the colour, my phone chirps. I reach for it and read the text.

Merry Christmas, Megan and everyone else around here. Love, Mia

Merry Christmas, hun. Hope you got everything you wanted.

I did and more. Check your email.

"Hey, how does Mia have my email?" I enquire.

"She asked for it, so I sent it to her," Mark answers.

"Oh."

Signing into my emails, I find one from her.

Megan,

I admit that I didn't know what to get you for Christmas because I think you have everything you want in life. So, here are your presents from me.

1 - Spa day in 2014— you, Jenny, and me. (Once Jenny's baby is here.)

2 - A day course for Jenny and you to learn how to paint French manicures. I have seen Jenny's attempts, and I think it would be useful. (Saves a fortune in money, too.)

3 - I'm babysitting for you for a full 24 hours, so you can do whatever you want.

I hope this is all good. Oh, I also have a stunning dress for you, but Mark forgot to bring it with him. MEN!!

Thank you for being so amazing. You are such a good mum.

Mia

Xxx

While sitting there, I read the email to Jenny, and all she does is scream. Mia's gifts include two things that we have both talked about doing for a while. They are truly perfect gifts.

Chapter Eighteen

I potter back from checking the turkey to see even more opened gifts. Kate kept running and showing me what she had gotten. She received lots of drawing supplies and craft items. I see so much potential in her. I told them all to carry on without me, so I don't know what everyone else has opened. There were many things that I had bought that had yet to be opened. I walk into the lounge, change over the bin bag and leave an empty one.

"Thank you, baby," Mark says as I sit back down with Lucy. He sits on the other side of her. "This gardening kit is amazing for beginners. It has lots of little herbs."

"I want you to teach Lucy. I want her to have the same passion about gardening that you and Annabella have."

"Of course, I will."

"I thought we could section off part of the garden and add some raised plant beds for you two to play with."

"That would be great." He kisses me on the cheek.

"Mark, this is yours," Kate says, giving him another box. Opening it, he finds lots of strawberry smellies and some adult strawberry gel.

"Oh, Miss Madden," he says.

"This is for you as well," I reply, reaching under the sofa and bringing out a box.

He slowly unwraps the black paper embellished with silver writing. Removing the tissue paper, he finds a plaque with his grandad's details on it, including his name, date of birth and death. It is all enclosed in a wooden frame.

"Thank you, baby," he says with a tear falling down his face.

"There is a cherry blossom tree in the back for you to plant wherever you wish and place the plaque in front of it as a memorial to your grandad."

Mark pulls me in close. His eyes are covered by my shoulders, and I can feel him crying. "I don't want to upset you."

"You didn't. It's just such a special gift." He snorts back more tears. "Thank you."

Mark told me weeks ago about his grandad and him always going to this cherry blossom tree where no one could see them to have their talks. It was their special time. The tree was cut down days after his grandad passed away. He was heartbroken over the tree because it was the last tangible piece that he had linked to his grandad.

He takes a deep breath. "For you," he says, passing me a box that he had hidden behind Lucy. He must have done that while I was out of the room. I'm so impressed with how Lucy is acting, sitting there trying to open her presents by pulling the paper and playing with the stuff, not crawling around.

I open it to find some little charms. "To add to the rest of them," Mark responds.

There is a silver heart locket. I open it to find a picture of Lucy that Mark took the day she was born. He's also placed a pair of little feet with Lucy's name and date of birth on them. The last one confuses me. It is a ring charm with an engraving on the inside, "You will be the future Mrs. Reed."

"I don't want to ask you today. It will not be as special. I will, though, and very soon. I don't want to be without you," he says.

I feel myself getting choked up. All I can do is nod in response to him. I'm totally speechless. "You will get the rest of your presents throughout the day. I hid them because I didn't want them getting damaged."

"Thank you."

I sit there watching everyone open their presents, but the excitement is gone, and people are starting to get bored.

"Okay, why don't we leave the rest until this afternoon?" I ask.

Everyone agrees. Kate is eager to get Dolly's pram sorted. She pulls Connor off to do that.

"I'm just off to get dressed," I say.

Leaving the rest of them sitting with presents all over the place, I quickly run upstairs and fling on black lacy underwear, leggings, and a cream jumper. As I grab my bag, I glance at the clock. I need to go.

I find Jenny changing in her room.

"Jenny, can you keep an eye on everything for fifteen? I need to pop out and get something," I tell her.

"Yes, of course, go."

Chapter Nineteen

The twinkling lights on the front of my house are so pretty and can be seen from a distance as I pull back into the driveway. I turn off the engine, grab the big white box, and head back into the house.

"Megan!" Kate yells.

"Hi, Kate." I pause. "Where is Mark?"

"Upstairs with Lucy."

I walk up the stairs, hugging the box close to my chest. I find Mark sitting on my bed with Lucy lying next to him. He's singing to her. I stand there watching before tapping on the door.

"Can I come in?" I ask.

"It's your house, silly. Get your fine arse over here." I walk over to him, placing the box onto the bed.

"For you."

Mark takes the lid off the box. "Woof, woof."

"A puppy."

"Just for you," I say.

"You're so cute," he says, lifting out the black ball of fluff.

"She is a six-week-old girl with no name and all yours, baby."

"I love you, Megan." He kisses me. "Now, we need to think of a name for you," he says as he playfully pets the puppy.

"That's your task for today."

Mark takes the puppy downstairs to show everyone. I hear a lot of coos and awes as he passes her around. Everyone must love her like I do. I change into my real Christmas outfit, a black dress with a bit of sparkle on the top half and a fluffy bottom that comes down to my knees. I add the bracelet Mark gave me. I shake out my hair and quickly re-apply my lip-gloss and mascara. Perfect. I change Lucy into a red dress with white frilly lace at the bottom.

"Now, who looks pretty?" I ask, looking at my daughter in pure amazement. I still can't believe that she is mine. I made her. She is a part of John and me. I'm still scared John will try to hurt her in years to come. I would do anything to protect her.

"Megan," Kate says, running through the door. "You look very pretty."

"Thank you, Kate."

"Are you coming downstairs?" she asks.

"Of course, I am. I need to finish the rest of the cooking."

Kate runs off ahead of me, holding Dolly close to her chest. I pick up Lucy and begin walking down the stairs. Turning into the lounge, I decide to leave Lucy in there because it will be safer than having her in the kitchen with me. There are plenty of people around to keep an eye on her also.

"Look at Dolly's pram," Kate says, pushing a traditional classic-style pram with a black storage basket underneath. It has a black base with a pink cover and hood and comes with a matching changing bag.

"It's stunning," I say as I place Lucy down onto the floor and watch her crawl into the room. She's gotten the knack of it now.

"I'll be back in a minute."

"Wow!" Mark say. I turn back around to face him.

"What?"

"You look stunning."

"Thank you," I say, blushing. "I'll be right back."

I walk out of the front door and to the car. Opening the boot of the car, I pull out another big box and return inside the house.

"For you, Mark," I say, passing him the box.

"What's this?" he questions. "You have already spoilt me."

"What do you think it is?"

"I have no idea," he says, opening the box. "Things for puppy?" he asks, smiling like a little kid in a candy shop.

I giggle to myself, thinking about Jenny's reaction when I told her I was contemplating buying Mark a puppy.

"You're crazy, Megan. What if he doesn't like it? What if you split? Who gets the dog?" Jenny asked me, waving her hands around.

"Calm down, Jenny. Mark loves dogs; he even bought Annabella one. I think it's the perfect gift. He has so much money, and whatever I buy, he could buy himself. If we split, we split. The dog is Mark's. Come with me. I'm off to see some dogs now."

"Okay, fine," she said.

The place was only five minutes away from my house. We walked up the path to a large house that no one would think there were dogs around. It was all posh, at least three stories high with an attic. It looked like one of those houses that could be seen on an American program. I took a deep breath and knocked on the door.

"Hi, you must be Megan. Come on in," this tall, blonde lady said.

We followed her inside and through a hallway into a large room. "Here they are. These are four-week-old Yorkshire Terriers."

I knelt down beside the playpen, looking at them.

"Do it," Jenny whispered into my ear.

The lady stood there and told me all about them, even introducing me to their parents. I couldn't keep my eyes off them, but the black girl really caught my eye. The rest of them were all black and white.

It's the black girl that I chose for Mark. Seeing her with him now makes me happy. "Yes, I can't just give you a puppy with no dishes and stuff. Her food is in the bottom cupboard near the fridge."

"Check you out," he says, pulling out dishes and a mat for them to sit on. I did spoil the little pup with some toys, yes, but I fell in love with her the moment I saw her. I just hope Mark does, too.

"What's this?" he says, pulling out a small box. I stand there, smiling. "A collar for her? It's perfect." I found a ruby red one that I thought would work well with her fur, and ruby was also his grandad's birthstone.

Mark continues looking through the box, finding a lead blanket and even more toys, her medical records and insurance code, everything the puppy would ever need.

"Her bed is in the boot of my car. I couldn't carry it with everything else," I sate.

"I'll go and get it," he replies, walking towards me. "Thank you." He places his lips on mine.

"Does she have a name?" I ask.

"No, not yet," he says, walking out the door after taking the car keys from my hand.

"I think she should be called Ella," Kate says.

"No, Max," Warren adds.

"It's a girl, Warren," Jenny points out. "I think she should be called Bella."

"Max can be short for Maxine," Warren says, picking up Lucy from the floor and lifting her above his head and making her laugh. "Airplane Lucy coming in for landing," he says as he takes her down to the floor, making plane noises as he goes.

"Well, I think Elle," Connor adds.

"Ella, Elle, Bella or Max?" Jenny asks Mark as he walks back into the room.

"None of them. I think I know what her name is," he says.

"Tell me," Kate says, jumping up and down.

"Daisy."

"It's perfect," I add.

As Mark gives out a big smile, I think I can happily say that he does love this gift. He sets down the small dog bed onto the floor near the Christmas tree and pulls out a few toys from the box and places them onto the floor near the bed.

"I can help," Kate says.

"Let's go and set up her food in the kitchen," he says. "Is that okay?" he asks me.

"Yes, go," I say.

"What type of puppy is Daisy?" Kate asks.

"A Yorkshire Terrier," Mark says, placing his hand onto the back of her head and guiding her out of the room first.

Reaching under the tree, I pull out a box and pass it to Jenny.

"What's this?"

"If I tell you, it takes away the surprise."

Jenny opens the box slowly while Warren sits on the floor, playing with Lucy. I love how he is with her. It helps me know that he will be okay when Jenny has her baby.

"OMG! I love it!" she squeals, pulling out a camera from the box.

"I knew you would."

Jenny runs up to me and gives me a massive hug. "Thank you, I mean it. You knew how much I wanted one."

"I know. Let's go and sort out these bags, then we can get the rest of the pans on," I say.

"Oh, yes, I can't wait to see them all done," she says, wiggling around. "Going to have to pee first."

"Warren and Connor, you need to pop something else on over your shirts. We are off outside, and I don't want you getting cold." I head into the hallway, grabbing Mark's and Kate's jackets.

"Pop these on, you two," I say, setting them onto the kitchen bar.

I leave the bags on the side and place my jacket on and then grab Lucy's. I turn to see Warren holding her.

"Let's get your jacket on," I state.

"Can I do it?" Warren asks. "I want to get some experience before the baby comes. I have never done anything like this. Will you show me?" I nod.

"Thank you, Megan."

Chapter Twenty

I see Jenny standing out in the garden next to the fence with a large smile spread across her face. Taking a deep breath, I slowly open the bags and pass out six balloons, three ice blue ones and three yellow ones. The last bag contains a big silver star. Jenny takes hold of them all.

"Right, you wonder what we are all up to. These are special balloons to remember the ones we have lost and can't be here with us today. Megan has done it every year, and this year we are all doing it."

"Are those people's names on the star?" Connor asks.

"Yes." Jenny pauses. "The ones we have lost."

"That's a great idea," Warren says.

"Kate, would you like the special star?" I ask.

"Yes." She takes the star from Jenny and holds it tightly.

We hand out the rest of the balloons, giving the blue ones to the men and the yellow ones to the girls, including Lucy.

"Shall we let go on three?" Mark asks.

"Yes." I pause. "Are you ready? Do you want to count for us, Kate?"

"One...two...three," she says as she releases the star, and the rest of us follow.

Jenny steps back to take more photos with her new flashy silver camera. She had taken a couple while we were passing out the balloons. Kate informs us when the balloons go out of sight, and she makes sure that she mentions that the silver star takes the longest.

"Let's go back in before we get cold," Connor says.

"I guess you're cold," I say as we head inside.

"I'm freezing. I've always been a cold-natured person," he says, gesturing for me to head into the house before him.

"Thank you." I slip off my coat and hang it up. I leave Warren with Lucy because I know he can manage her and wants to learn how to take care of her.

"I love you, Miss Madden," Mark says, placing a kiss on my neck.

"Aw...thank you, baby. I love you, too."

"Come sit with us."

"I need to finish cooking first. Then, I will come and sit on your knee."

"Oh, will you, sexy?" he asks, tapping my bum.

"You're a monkey."

I finish moving everything around and getting ready. Well, things are nearly ready.

"Megan, can we talk?" Connor enquires, standing in the doorway and looking down to the floor.

"Of course, is everything okay?" I ask because I can tell that something isn't right.

"Please don't feel like you have to say yes." He looks down and pauses. "Will you be Kate's godmother?"

"Yes, I will. I would be honored to be her godmother. I'll admit that you had me worried a little," I state.

I turn around and open a packet and fling the contents into a glass bowl. "Add kettle water to that. Will you, Connor? Mix with this. Thank you."

"Of course, anything to help." He does what I ask. The concentration on his face is amazing. "Would you be able to help me organise it?"

"The christening?" I question.

"Yes, Kate sees you as a mother figure, and I want her to have someone she can turn to. I thought that if you two planned some bits together, it might help her learn everything about it."

"Great idea, I would be honored to."

"You do know that you're dress shopping. Right?"

"Yes, I wouldn't trust you to do it." I laugh. "Do you wanna make them into balls?" I point to the mixture in the bowl.

"Balls?"

"Yes, stuffing balls."

"Oh, that's what this is," he says.

Finally, everything is done, and I don't think I have ever used so many pots and pans. I have dishes in all kinds of different pots. For the dining room, I bought a cream tablecloth and added a purple table runner with snowflakes all over it. I add the crackers alongside all the dishes.

"Dinner's ready!" I shout.

Chapter Twenty-One

"Wow! Megan, it smells wonderful," Warren says as he walks into the dining room with Lucy on his hip.

"You're getting the hang of this," I say, raising my eyebrows at him.

"Thank you. There are still bits that I need to learn, though. I have never done a nappy before," he admits.

"I'll teach you. Let's eat first. Do you want to pop Lucy in her high chair?"

I watch as Warren lowers her into her chair. He really has gotten the hang of it.

"What a surprise! I love the name place cards," Jenny says, lifting up her card.

They are white with a silver border and a little silver star to the bottom right-hand corner. I made them all myself. Each card has a Christmas joke written on the inside. I found them online the other night. Yes, they are the traditional bad Christmas jokes. You can't have a Christmas without bad jokes and silly paper hats. Everyone starts pulling their candy-striped crackers and getting an array of different coloured hats. Warren has a lime green one, Connor takes an orange one, Jenny grabs a yellow one, Mark puts on a blue one, and mine is purple.

"What colour is your hat, Kate?" Warren asks.

"Pink." She smiles brightly.

She finally places it on her head and then turns for everyone to see. We all dive in, doing the full family thing and passing the dishes to the next person. Both Warren and Connor help Kate, who decides she only wants mashed potatoes, pigs in blankets, and turkey with gravy. I cut up a few bites and place them onto Lucy's plastic Christmas plate. Jenny found it the other day; it's a white plate with red border that matches the rest of the collection, but Lucy's also has a green tree in the middle of it. It came with a matching bib, plastic cup, and cutlery. Warren placed her bib on her when he put her into her chair.

I sit there and watch everyone eat. Some go for seconds, thirds, and Kate even has four helpings. I feel so lucky. I'm sure that I'm going to be happy for life because I have such supportive friends and family members. I love everyone.

"Megan, you take the kids and get a film on, and we will clear up," Warren says.

"No, Jenny can. I'll help you out."

"No!" he says, shaking his finger.

"Okay, can you place the spare vegetables into a box? The meat goes into silver foil in the fridge and a few things go into the oven."

"Yes, Megan, show me the bits that go into the oven and then piss off."

"As if you just told me to piss off," I say, pushing Warren.

Opening the freezer, I take out all the bags of sausage rolls, mini sausages, and vol au vent cases and give him the rest of the instructions before exiting.

"I hope they can manage," I say to Jenny as I take a seat on the sofa.

"They will be fine."

"Shall we pop a film on?" I ask.

"Yes, you pick."

Lucy is sitting on the floor with Kate, playing with her dolly. I love watching them together, and they interact so well. Kate is trying to teach Lucy things. They are helping each other develop so much. I remember reading an article about that, but I never knew it was true. Scanning through the television guide, I find lots of Christmas films. I love the true ones.

"Jenny, have you ever noticed that in *every* Christmas film there is a man named Nick?"

"No, I haven't, but come to think of it, yes, I see what you're talking about. Why is that?"

"I have no idea, but it could have something to do with Saint Nicholas," I say, trying not to laugh.

"Oh, yes," Jenny says, shaking her hair.

"That was a full-on blonde moment there, hun."

"When can we open more presents?" Kate asks.

"You can open one now and the rest when your daddy has finished washing the dishes," I state. I'm sure he will be fine with missing one.

"This one," she says, pulling out a big box that's covered in sparkly princess paper.

"Go on," I say, watching her rip open the paper.

"ARGH!" she says animatedly.

"What is it?"

"A cot."

"Shall I build it up for you?" I ask.

"Yes! Yes! Yes!" she agrees, pushing the box over to me.

I quickly build up the cot. It's a simple pink travel cot for Dolly that matches her pram. Kate always tells me that you can only have girl dollies, not boy ones. I pull out the rest of the box, showing her a cover for Dolly and a mobile with different animals to hang over the top.

"I'll take that," Warren says, coming into the room and taking away the empty box.

"Thank you."

Kate puts down Dolly for her nap. "Night, night, Dolly."

Chapter Twenty-Two

"Here's one for Lucy," Warren says, handing me yet another present as I sit on the floor with my back leaning against the sofa and Mark's legs on either side of me.

"Lucy, what's this?" I ask as she crawls towards me.

I lift up the label. "To my Lucy, Merry Christmas! Love, Daddy."

"What?" I pause. "This is from John. How the hell did it get here?"

"A man gave it to me yesterday and said it was for Lucy, but he was in a rush," Warren says.

"Why? What's wrong?" Jenny asks.

"It's from John," Mark says as he takes it from me.

"I'm sorry," Warren says.

"It's not your fault," I reply.

"Are you going to open it?" Jenny enquires.

"I don't know. I think I need to, just to see what it is."

I take it back from Mark and open it. It's a pink teddy with a zip back. I unzip it and notice a letter inside that reads "For Lucy's eyes only" on the outside.

"I don't think so," I say, opening the letter. I immediately start reading it to myself.

To Lucy,

Hi, I'm your dad, John. Your mum chose for us not to be together. If I had known you were mine, I would have married your mum and given you everything you wanted and needed in life. I hope your mum has done that. Just be careful. She chose for me not to have any access to you. She placed things in the way that means I can't even talk to you. She is a very nasty woman. Contact me, please. I will look after you. We can be a family.

Love, Dad

XXX

"What?" I sit there crying.

"What does it say?" Jenny asks.

I drop the paper to the floor, pick up my daughter from my side, and pull her close. "I'm never letting you go," I whisper into her ear.

"Kate, can you pass me that paper?" Mark asks.

Kate runs over and passes it to him. He reads it aloud to everyone.

"You're a great mummy," Kate says, giving me an enormous hug.

"I'm going to fucking kill him," Jenny says.

"Watch the language," I state as I try to calm down.

"Sorry."

"Kate, are you going to help me make a snowman?" Warren asks.

"Yeah! You come, too," she says, pulling at my arm.

"I'll be out soon. You go and get started. Make sure you wrap up well." I smile, letting Lucy down onto the floor.

"What should I do?" I question, letting Mark's arms wrap around me.

"Nothing," Mark says. "Don't rise to him."

I reach under the sofa and pull out my phone to quickly text my mum; instead, I find a message from John.

Merry Christmas, Lucy! I hope you got everything you wanted. When we are finally together, I will give you everything and more. Love, your ONLY daddy XXX

"What the hell is he playing at?" I am so mad and confused.

"Baby, don't worry. I will sort it out. I'm not letting him do anything to you," Mark says assertively.

"Mate, shall we pay him a visit tomorrow?" Warren asks.

"Yeah, sounds like a fucking idea," Connor says.

"No, leave it," I say, running out of the room with tears streaming down my face. Mark is not far behind me.

"Baby, I can't just leave it."

"I don't want him to take my baby girl from me, though," I reply.

"He won't, hun. It's Lucy, you, and I forever." He grabs my hand. "She has had a great Christmas," Mark says to comfort me.

"Right," I say, regaining my composure. "Let's go make snowmen."

I grab my coat and gloves before heading outside to see Kate and Warren busy making large snowmen with lots of small ones all over the grass. Connor follows after them with a bag of carrots.

"I have noses for them," he says as he runs over the grass to join them.

"You're silly, Daddy. They are carrots," Kate exclaims.

"There's my scarf," I tell her, pointing at Kate's neck.

"It's mine for now," Kate says, giggling and holding it tightly.

I stand there watching them add the facial details to the last snowman. They use gravels for the eyes, and mouths and carrots for the noses.

"What are their names?" I ask.

"Crystal, Michele, Jennifer, Suzanne, Ella, Elle, and Johnathan," she says, pointing at each one in turn.

"Who's Johnathan?"

"A boy at school."

"Oh, do you like him?"

"Yes," she says, covering her face.

Chapter Twenty-Three

We run inside and throw off our coats as the snow begins to fall again. As I'm checking on everything in the oven, there is a knock on the door. I place my new Christmas oven gloves onto the bar before walking to the door.

"Hi, Luke," I say as I open the door, finding him standing there in black jeans and a black fitted jacket with a black scarf wrapped tightly around his neck. He reminds me of an Army man.

"Hey, babe."

"Come on in," I say, pushing open the door farther.

"What's with all the bags?"

"It's Christmas. Did you think I forgot about my sexy babe?"

"I'm not your babe," I state. That still annoys the crap out of me.

"I know, but you are a babe, Megan. You're a right little hottie. May I add that you look fantastic today, and I can see why Mark wants to fuck your brains out."

"Luke!" I shake my head in disbelief that he just said that.

I contacted him a few weeks ago to give me a hand with part of a gift Warren is getting. He was the first person I thought of.

"Hi, everyone," Luke says. "I have a few things to drop off."

"Oh, do you?" Jenny says. I can see the worry in her face. I bet she is worried that Rich has something to do with the reason why Luke is here.

"Yes, I do, babe. Megan contacted me."

"Oh," Jenny says, leaning her head towards me.

"For you, Warren," I say, passing him the bag that Luke brought with everything I needed.

"Oh my." He looks inside the blue bag. "It's guitar books on how to do everything, even some of those guitar pluckers. Oh wow! They have my name on. Thank you, how did you know?"

"Jenny told me. Look inside the envelope."

Warren pulls out a black envelope with his name written on it in silver block letters. Opening it, he pulls out the cream paper.

"Oh, thank you so much! It's for guitar lessons. I have always wanted to learn."

"You're welcome. If you're ever stuck and need extra help, I'm sure Luke will give you a hand," I state.

"Thank you," he says, slipping everything back into the bag.

"One last thing. Look behind the sofa," Jenny says, pointing behind him.

Warren stands up and looks behind it. He pulls out an oversized brown box and quickly opens it. "A guitar," he says with a smile.

"Yes, for you, baby. Just want you wanted," Jenny says.

"I have more presents," Luke says, passing out bags to people. Jenny receives perfume, Mark opens a drawing set, Kate gets another dolly, Lucy receives an activity pad, and Connor gets some aftershave. It's great seeing them open all the gifts and stand in excitement at what they received.

"Megan, babe, this is for you," he says, passing me a pink bag.

"There was no need, Luke," I say as I pull out a box. Opening it, I find a picture of Lucy from when she was about three months old burnt onto wood.

"I love it," I say, wiping away the tears that have collected under my eyes.

"Glad you do." He pauses. "Now, I'm going to get on. I have people to see."

"Do you wanna take some Christmas cake with you?" I ask.

"Oh, yes, that would be great," he says before sitting on the sofa next to Warren and teaching him a few cords.

I stand in the doorway with a tin in my hands. "This is for you, Luke."

"Thanks, babe."

"I hope you like it," I say.

"I bet I will. It's a shame that Brenda passed away last year, or she would have done it."

Luke told me all about Brenda, his manager's mum. She always kept an eye on them, making sure they had home-cooked meals and anything else they needed. She had become a second mum to him. She had a sudden heart attack and died. She used to make him a Christmas cake every year, so I made him one to enjoy this Christmas. I just hope it's good enough.

Chapter Twenty-Four

"Let's play Twister," Mark says, pulling an unopened gift from under the tree and passing it to Connor.

"Let me guess what's in here." He unwraps it. "Oh, it's Twister."

"Well, I'm going to sort out the rest of the food, and then I'll be back," I say, standing up.

"I'll give you a hand," Warren says, following me.

"Do you wanna take Daisy with you?" Mark bellows.

"Okay," I say, bending down and picking her up. I pull her close to my chest.

"Shall I show you where the toilet is, Daisy?" I sit on the floor of the kitchen and place her on top of a puppy-training pad.

"The Christmas pudding is ready," I state, looking at Warren.

"Oh, is it? I love the stuff," Warren says. "Do I have to tell anyone else that it's ready?"

"Yes, you do, but they don't have to eat it. Tell Jenny that I have a chocolate one for us if she wants some."

"Mummy!" Kate screams she runs through the door and throws herself onto my knee. She is crying almost hysterically.

"What's wrong?"

"My finger," she says, lifting it up for me to see.

"Aw, do you need a plaster?"

She nods.

"Is she okay?" Warren mouths.

"She is fine. Can you get me a princess plaster out of that drawer next to you?" I ask him, pointing to the drawer.

"Princess Kate, this is for you," he says, bending down and wrapping it around her finger.

Kate jumps up and runs back into the room.

"What happened there?"

"No idea. I think she cut it on the spinner." He pauses. "Kate wants a mince pie, Connor. Mark and I will have Christmas pudding. Oh, and Jenny wants a blueberry muffin."

"What a weird craving. She always hated blueberries," I say, getting up from the floor. "I have homemade blueberry muffins, and I did some chocolate ones, too. It was my first time to make them, so she can try them and tell me if they're good."

I stand there, placing everything onto plates and sending them out with Warren. I quickly finish off the cooking and cover the sandwiches. I walk into the room with a bowl of chocolate pudding and ice cream. I'm so going to regret eating this much food. I just hope I don't gain any weight. I know Mark says he loves me for me, but as I have gotten smaller, back to the real me, the more he has started to physically touch me.

"Megan, these muffins are *amazing*. Please, tell me you have more," Jenny says while rubbing her bump.

"I do. They are in a tin next door."

Mark walks into the room, holding two small canvases, facing him so no one can see what's painted on them. "These are for you, baby."

He spins them around, revealing the first picture he ever drew of me on one of them and the drawing he did of Lucy when she was first born on the other. "They are perfect," I say, trying to hold back the tears. He is so talented. They look so good that you would think they were black and white pictures of the events.

"I hope you're good at DIY, Mark," Warren says.

"Yes, you will be hanging them tomorrow." I wink.

Chapter Twenty-Five

"Come with me, Lucy," I say, bending down and swiping her off her feet. I walk into the hallway and run up the stairs to find Warren sitting on the ottoman at the side of the stairs, looking down at his phone.

"What's wrong?" I question.

"Nothing," he replies.

"Tell me the truth," I say, taking a seat next to him.

"My ex lost a baby on Christmas Eve last year, so today has been very hard on me. I really don't know if she was pregnant or not. She told me she was, and then the next minute she left me. She just said the baby was dead, and it was all my fault. But, she was sleeping with an ex-college mate of mine named Branden. He's everything a girl wants—money, brains, and a six-pack. He's a total show-off. I have the so-called scan picture of the baby, but I'm not sure that it's real. Someone told me she had done it before to another guy. She was supposed to be on the pill, but I just don't know." He looks up at me. "It's a blessing, though, because I have Jenny now. She's a woman that I have such amazing feelings for, but I still wonder. I wanna know the truth. I do want to know if the baby was mine, and I also want to know if Jenny's baby is mine."

"Have you ever asked your ex?"

"Yes, loads of times. She will not give me a straight answer; she just says, 'if I did, it's your fault anyway.'"

"Honestly, I would think of happy times because you may never know the truth," I say, wrapping my arm around him.

"Thank you, Megan."

"You're welcome. Now, I'm going to change this little miss."

"Can you show me how to change her?" Warren asks.

I stand up, making Lucy take steps along the floor and holding her hands while walking behind her. "Of course, sorry about the view."

Warren laughs. "I hadn't really noticed it, but now I have. Have you got on underwear?"

"Oi! Cheeky twat, yes, I do."

"Sorry, I had to ask." He pauses. "What do I need?"

"Nappy from over there and the wipes are below the changing table. Do you want to pick out a Christmas baby grow from that drawer? We're going to get her changed, and then she can just get messy again," I state, lifting Lucy into the air and making her giggle.

I stand there watching Warren, telling him every little bit. He soon gets the hang of what he is meant to be doing. I leave him to change her clothes with no worries; he knows what he is doing. I can trust him. I still don't know what to do about John. I can't have him after my daughter, and I definitely can't have him saying nasty things to her in the future. Yes, she is our child, but why can't he be an adult? He did the damage himself. I feel a tear begin to roll down my cheek.

"Will you be okay here?" I ask.

"Yes, then we can go and get those stockings opened," he says, tickling her tummy.

"Thank you, Warren. I'm going to take a five-minute walk. I need some time to myself," I inform him.

I creep downstairs and grab my coat. I walk straight out of the back door. I slip my phone into my pocket and just walk. There are so many lights on; some people have decorated their entire house, while others just adorned the simple tree. Snowmen of all different shapes and sizes are dressed up in varied designs. They line the streets like soldiers, protecting the houses. I can't help but smile.

I reach into my pocket and pull out my phone.

"Hi, Mark."

I'm okay. I needed five minutes to myself."

"What? It's been an hour already?"

"I'm on my way."

I can't believe I have been gone an hour. I don't even remember how I got here. I look up to see miles and miles of fields with animals in them. I turn around and start walking. It takes a while before I notice anything familiar. I hear my phone chirp, alerting me of an incoming text.

Baby, I'm getting worried. X

Mark, I'll be home soon. I had walked farther than I thought. Can you get the food out on the table for me? Then, everyone can start eating. X

I turn onto the path that goes down to my house and see Mark standing there. He's been waiting for me. Running to me, he grabs me firmly around the waist. "I thought you were gone," he says, pulling me closer.

"No, I needed time to think. I just don't know what to do with this John thing."

"Forget him. He can't touch you or Lucy. We will cross the rest of the bridges when we get there as a family."

Chapter Twenty-Six

It's so nice to be back inside the house. I didn't realize how cold it was outside. I finish helping Mark place the food onto the table, re-arranging everything to make space. I set out the plates and send Mark to get everyone. The best thing about Christmas Day tea is you just have what you want, where you want it. I just want onions. Yes, I'm weird, but onions and cheeses on a cocktail stick are the best, or as I always call them, "things on sticks." Some have pineapple on a stick as well, but I don't like them. I place the tins of mince pies and muffins on the side. I even open the Christmas cake and cut a couple of slices.

"That cake looks amazing," Mark says.

"Thank you."

"You're amazing, baby." He pauses. "Warren, she handmade it with no machines at all."

"That's how you get the love into it," I say, lifting my shoulder.

Sitting on the sofa in the lounge, I look around at everyone as they eat and chat. They are laughing and looking relaxed. Kate is feeding her dolly in her high chair. Lucy is trying to throw food from her high chair; she is turning into a right monkey. I'm very impressed that she hasn't needed a nap today. I can feel the love in the room. I don't need anyone else.

I lean over to Mark. "Kate called me Mummy earlier," I whisper.

"Aw, bless her."

"Have you managed to sort the custody stuff for Connor?" I ask.

"The paperwork should be here in the next few days."

"Thank you," I say.

"Don't thank me." He kisses me on the forehead.

"Read to me," Kate says, running to me with one of her new books. I shuffle back in the chair and start to read, getting Kate to help me by pointing at the pictures to fill in the blanks. Mark sneaks out to take

Daisy outside for a wee. Bless her. It's too cold to be out there. Warren stands up, taking Lucy from her chair and places her onto the floor. She uses her new toy from Luke to stand up and starts walking towards me with nothing in front of her.

I sit there watching her, not saying a word because I'm totally speechless. My baby did it. My baby is finally walking.

"Hello, Lucy," I say as she grasps ahold of my knees. "You did it."

I turn her around, and she walks again, but loses her balance and falls to her knees. She crawls to the toy, stands up, and does it again. Mark stands in the doorway, pulling out his phone to record her.

"Call Annabella," he says.

"Okay, I don't want to ruin her day."

"She will want to know." I do as he says and ring her.

"Hi, Annabella, Merry Christmas. Lucy just walked all on her own." I place her on the loud speaker so everyone can hear.

"Oh, wow! That's amazing."

"Isn't it just?"

"Congratulations, Lucy."

Mark sits and tells her all about the amazing day he has had and all the presents and games everyone has received.

I place the phone on loudspeaker. "Annabelle, you're on loudspeaker."

"Oh, great! Hi, everyone."

"Hi, Annabelle," Jenny says.

"How are you all doing?" Annabelle asks in an ecstatic tone.

"We are great. Bump is getting bigger," Jenny says. They met a few weeks ago and clicked right away. I knew they would, no question about it.

"That's wonderful. How is that sexy bar man of yours doing?"

"I'm doing well," Warren speaks up.

"Oh, crap! I didn't know you were there," she says, giggling.

"It's okay," he replies, amused.

"Did Kate like her present?"

"What present?" Kate says, jumping up and down.

"The one behind the door," I answer, pointing at the door. "I thought it would be more special for you to hear her reaction."

Kate grabs it and unwraps it very quickly. "A princess!" she shouts.

"Yes, open it," I say.

"Her face is a picture," Connor chimes in.

Inside the princess carrying case are loads of all different coloured paper, crayons, and everything else she needs to do drawings.

"What do you say?"

"Thank you!" she yells in a high-pitched voice.

"Have you had a good day?" Mark asks.

Annabelle tells us about her day. Even though she says it has been mostly uneventful and quiet, she has enjoyed lots of food.

Chapter Twenty-Seven

"Oh, you will so have to come to my place on New Year's Day. I plan to cook my favourite," Mark says.

"You what?" I ask surprised because this is the first I have heard of this.

"Mac and cheese with a twist," he says.

"Baby, any other day, yes, but not for a special day," I say.

"Ha-ha, mate, she has you wrapped around her finger," Warren says.

"Well, I'm not doing anything. Warren will be working, and I'm not partying," Jenny says.

"Join me. We can have a onesie party," I respond.

"That's pregnant friendly," she says, rubbing her bump.

"And kid friendly, too. Connor and Mark can go out," I add.

"Baby, I will be with you. It's our first New Year's together. I'm up for a onesie party, but do I actually have to wear one?" Mark says.

"Of course, you do, or you can't come," Jenny answers.

Jenny and I have always ended up together on New Year's. Even when we are out at a bar, we leave before midnight because neither of us really likes it. I think a party would be a good idea and something that Kate can be involved in. We could do some fun dressing up. I would love to see Mark as a lion because he seems to have a thing for them, or at least the roaring part.

"We will sort the full-on plans tomorrow," Warren says. "I don't want to be at work, but I will have to go in at one point, though."

I will be glad when I can crawl into bed tonight. I'm shattered. Today has been such an emotional day. I need to sort out my head. I love Mark, and I want to be with him. I have to think of my daughter, though. I don't want John taking her, and I definitely don't want him. I just don't know what to do. Why has this been such a complicated

Christmas? I just wanted a simple, magical one.

"Bed now," Connor says, picking up Kate from the floor. She fell asleep with her head on the pram cover hugging her dolly.

"It's been such a busy day for her," I state.

Lucy has been asleep for a couple of hours now; she will be up soon for a feeding and then out again until morning. I hope she grows out of getting up so often during the night.

"Megan, would you be upset if I went to bed, too?" Jenny asks.

"No, go," I say, standing and picking up our empty glasses. Well, I have been drinking Coke all day.

"Night, hun," Jenny says, "Thank you for an amazing day."

I finish collecting all the dishes and load them into the dishwasher. Yeah, I'm feeling lazy now. I don't like washing dishes, though, so the dishwasher was one of the first items I bought when I got the house. I don't use it as much as I should. I feel Mark's hands wrap around my waist, pulling me back and close to him.

"Baby, do you want me to do Lucy Doo's milk? That way you can get that sweet arse of yours to bed," he says as he kisses my neck.

"That would be great, but only if you want to, baby," I answer, spinning around to face him.

"Anything for my two special ladies."

"Thank you," I say, kissing his cheek.

Before walking upstairs, I turn off everything and move the presents to the side so that no one trips. I can hear Mark chatting to Lucy.

"Lucy, you're so cute. I can't wait to have a house full of more little ones. I hope you can see me as a dad. I would do anything for you. I'm never going to let your dad hurt you."

I walk into the room and place a kiss on my daughter's head. "Good night, Lucy." I walk back out, leaving him to it.

"Hey, baby, you're still awake." Mark points out as he creeps into the bedroom.

"Yeah, I was waiting to cuddle with you."

"Give me thirty seconds, and then I'm all yours," he says, pulling off all his clothes and leaving just his tight arse black boxers.

He climbs into the bed and pulls me close. I lay my head on his chest, and he wraps his hand around my back. I feel so safe.

"Thank you for sorting Lucy," I say.

"Anything for you."

I lift my head and place a kiss onto his lips.

"Megan, I'm sorry, but I need to ask you something. I just didn't know when the right time would be."

I sit up straight because this sounds bad. "Go on."

"Don't look so worried. I have been looking into starting a new office in this end of the world, and I need to fan things out a bit more. With you here, it makes more sense. I want to be with you all the time. Will you move in with me?"

"What?"

"Will you move in with me?" he enunciates each word slowly.

I sit there looking down. What do I do? Follow my heart, or follow my brain?

"Mark..."

Redeemed

Believe Series book 3

L. Chapman

Image Copyright Eti Swinford

Image from Dreamstime.com

Cover designed by Sarah at Sprinkle on top Studnzt

Edited by - Paige Maroney Smith

Proof-read by - Nicki DeStasi

Formatted by Angel Steel

Dedication

To all who have believed in me. You mean the world to me, and I couldn't have done this without you.

~ * ~

You will lead a rich and successful life.

Table of Contents

Prologue

It's simply amazing how your life can change in a short amount of time. Only a few months ago I was going out with John. He was everything to me. We spent hours together, but we never actually spent the entire night together. It was just sex and maybe a few hours out on a date. Everything was always planned days in advance, never anything unexpected, but at the time, it was what I wanted.

Now, look at me. I have a gorgeous daughter named Lucy and a new man in my life. Mark is perfect. By perfect, I really do mean *perfect*. Unlike John, he shows me the respect I deserve. We are not just sex buddies; we are a couple. I never knew I could scream and go to as many heights as I do when I'm with Mark. He truly makes me feel wanted. He never wants to leave me, and we can't go a day without being in some kind of contact.

After having Mark in my life, I can see everything that was wrong with John. There was nothing special with John, no spark and all sex. Now that I look back, I understand why John and I never spent the night together. He was married the whole time we were together. I'm glad I'm free of him. Unfortunately, he is the father of my daughter, and I realise there is nothing I can do to change that, but maybe in time Mark will want to adopt her.

Chapter One

I can't believe Lucy is nearly four months old already. Time is flying way too fast. So many people have told me to treasure the time I have with her because she will not be a baby for long. She is slowly coming out of her shell into a right little character. She is my precious little angel, and there is nothing better than curling up in the bed with her and tickling her tummy. She is such a cute little giggler.

I would be lost without her. I can never lose her. I'm worried John is going to try to gain custody of her like he threatened to Jenny. She is my world, and without her, I would just be Megan. Lucy gives purpose to my life. Since Jenny told me what happened, I haven't slept at all. Well, it feels like I haven't slept, but I must have slept a bit, and just not realised it. I'm so scared; I need to spend all the time that I can with Lucy. Luckily, I have two more days here in London before I have the long drive back home. I don't mind driving, which is the one good thing.

When I visit Mark in London, I normally go via train, but he wanted to drive, so here we are. He drove my car, and Mia drove his. It makes no sense at all to me, but it's a man's idea, and we all know how men can be. They know best. Well, they think they do; we just let them believe it.

I turn to look at the clock. It's only 3 a.m. Why can't I sleep? Mark is lying on his back, wearing only his boxers. The duvet barely covers his bottom. I love the way he lies with his arm resting above his head. It means I can curl up and cuddle with him. Every time I do, his arm wraps around me. I love it; I feel so close to him. My man.

I'm scared this feeling might be love, and that I'm falling in love again. I think I already have because I have never felt like this before, like it's the real thing and not what I shared with John. Mark is a totally different person than John. He thinks of others, not himself all the time.

I roll over in bed, moving closer to him and placing my head upon his toned chest, feeling his arm slowly coming down to wrap around me. He does it every time, like an involuntary reaction, suddenly making me feel safe and wanted. I slip my leg between his, moving myself over a little bit, ensuring my chest is slightly pressing against his. This is heaven.

Mark has been everything I have asked for and more since the entire ordeal with John. He has gotten a security system placed inside the house to protect Lucy and me, and Connor has been researching my legal options so that I know what to expect. If anything does happen, which I hope it doesn't since I don't think John has the balls to start something, then I will make sure his wife and whomever else he has been sleeping with knows everything. The thought of being just one of those girls makes me nauseous. I went through years of thinking I meant something to him; I didn't though, and this proves it. I was just a sex toy to him when we were together.

"Baby, are you still awake?" Mark mumbles.

"Yes, sorry. Did I wake you?" I question.

"No, but you need sleep, baby," he replies, pulling me tighter and rubbing his chin against the top of my head.

"I know," I admit. He is trying to look out for me. I probably should just sleep; I know there is enough security around us.

"You can't stay awake twenty-four-seven. You will crash when you're home without me," he points out, placing a little butterfly kiss on my head.

"Okay, baby."

"I'll go get you some hot chocolate," he states, letting go of me and shuffling to the edge of the bed.

"There's no need to," I protest.

"Yes, there is," he states, rising from the bed and wobbling out of the room.

That man never listens to me. I don't want him to leave me alone. I'm scared when I'm alone, even though I will not confess that to Mark. It is just the uncertainty of not knowing when John will contact me, or if he will at all.

Annabella taught Mark how to make hot chocolate when someone couldn't sleep. He used to make it for Mia when they were younger when she jumped out of her bed and into his. There is one problem with hot chocolate. I don't like it that much and only drink it if I fancy some. I will just drink a little bit of it to keep him happy. Hopefully, he will then leave me alone and fall back to sleep. I know he is doing his best to look after Lucy and me.

I climb out of bed and check on Lucy. She is just lying there unaware of the worries the world offers and all the harm that could come to her. She's so perfect. Hearing footsteps behind me, I turn to see Mark.

"Hey, she is fine, baby," Mark states, placing his arm around me and pulling me close.

"I know, but I needed to see her with my own eyes. She is my world, and I can't have anyone harm her," I say, feeling a lump develop in my throat.

"Come back to bed," he demands, laying his hand on the small of my back and guiding me to the bed. I pull back the covers and climb onto the bed. I jump a little because the bed has gone cold quickly. As I sit up with my back against the metal headboard, Mark climbs in on the other side, sitting identical to me. He pulls the duvet up the bed, covering our legs.

"Here," he says, slowly passing me the hot chocolate in a tall white cup that has a red heart on it. He bought this cup for me to use when I stay with him. He will not let anyone else use it. I'm gutted to see that he has not added any marshmallows to it. I even got him to buy some for me the other day, so I could eat them. I guess I can't get mad since I don't think you're allowed to eat them at three in the morning.

I take a small sip, checking the temperature of it. I should have known he would have cooled it down a little to make it drinkable. He is such a thoughtful man.

"Go back to sleep, Mark," I state, looking at him and acting like a nodding dog. He can't even keep his eyes open. He has had a really busy week, sorting out some business deals and working late. I didn't hear much from him for two days; he was that busy. I don't like it when he works too hard.

"I will when you do," he replies.

I place the half-drunk hot chocolate onto the handmade wooden bedside table and lie down in the bed as close to him as I can get, placing my leg back between his and feeling his arms wrap around me, pulling me close. I lie there still as I can be; I don't want to disturb him. I want him to get some decent sleep. With me not sleeping much, neither is he. It isn't healthy for either of us. With my head resting on his chest, I feel it slowly rise and fall and hear his heartbeat. I close my eyes and let the land of Nod take me away.

*****

I slowly open my eyes. Seeing that the room is still dark, I push myself up slightly, realising I'm still lying with my head on Mark's chest. I look up the wall at the foot of the bed to check the time on the clock. What a fancy clock he has. It's red and black in the shape of an expresso machine with an attached cup. The clock piece is fastened to the cup. It's very stylish, very Mark. It's 5 a.m., so I lay my head back down. Oh, my head hurts, and it's too early for me to function. I really should check on Lucy, but...

Chapter Two

I feel the bed dip a little beside me. "Hey, baby girl." I hear Mark say, placing a little kiss on my head.

"Mmm," I grumble, slowly opening my eyes and seeing the blinding sunlight peeking through the red curtains. Mark is sitting on the side of the bed.

"Oh, you're so cute when you're sleepy," he adds, laying his hand on the arch of my back.

"Mmm." I reach for the thick winter duvet, pulling it over my head.

"Oh, baby. I'm sorry, but you're going to have to get up," he states, gently pulling on the duvet.

"But why?" I ask.

"It's ten."

"It's what?" I pull back the cover, rolling onto my back and sitting up. *Oh, that was a bad idea.* Moving too quickly makes my head start to spin. I think just having those few hours of sleep have affected me in a bad way. I need a good amount of sleep.

"It's ten," he repeats, rubbing his hand across my cheek. I kiss the palm of his hand as it slides down.

"It can't be," I say, looking down the bed towards the clock. "How did I sleep that late?"

"You were shattered," he replies, smiling at me.

"Lucy?" I ask with a hint of panic in my voice. She best be okay. I haven't checked on her in a few hours, and I need to see her for myself.

"She is asleep in her car seat, all dressed and ready to go. She's had her morning milk. Don't worry, Megan. I have looked after her," he says, leaning over the bed and placing a soft kiss on my head.

"Thank you. You're amazing," I tell him. "I don't know what I would do without you sometimes."

"Baby, we need to get up. I promised Annabella we would come around for dinner today," he replies.

"All right, I'm getting up," I say, moving a little bit.

"Come on, or I'll place you over my shoulder and sort you out." He winks.

"Oh, will you?" I tease, remaining motionless.

"You're going to test it out, I see," he utters.

"Maybe." I bite my lower lip.

Mark bends down, grabs hold of me and pulls me out of the bed and over his shoulder. "Argh! Seriously, let go. I was joking!" I protest. Mark taps my bum suggestively. "Hey, don't you start being Mr. Kinky on me."

"I'll let you go once you're in the shower," he adds, walking out of the room and into the bathroom. He lowers me onto the side of the bath. "And, baby? I'll be Mr. Whoever You Want. Anything to make you happy," he says, winking at me.

"Piss off. I'm going to take a shower," I add, pushing him away with my feet and holding onto the side of the bath.

"Oh, baby. You're such a tease. You look very sexy in your outfit." He rubs his hand slowly up my leg. I'm only wearing a black silk nightie. So, of course, I look sexy. I need to look my best around Mark, even though he always says how cute and sexy I look in my pyjamas.

"You said we needed to get on. If you start this, then you know we will be late," I say, standing still because I want him.

"I know. Now, get that fine arse of yours in the shower, and I'll make you a brew." I love the fact he is picking up my northern words. He leans forward, giving me a deep, passionate-filled kiss before reaching behind me and turning on the faucet.

"Hey!" I shout as the water starts to hit me, running down my covered back.

"Now, get on," he says, pulling me up to my feet. He places his hands at the bottom of my top, pulling it over my head.

"Are you going to wash my back?" I ask.

"I would love to."

My eyes lock with his, and he pulls me tighter. His lips hit my neck, trailing little kisses down the nape. "Mmm." His hand slowly rubs down the side of my face as the steam from the hot water fills the room around us.

"Baby, I want every time with you to be special," he states.

"Isn't that meant to be the girl's line?"

"Yes, it is. But, Megan, I have never felt like this before." He places a slight kiss on my lips.

"Go get the kettle on. I'll be down soon," I declare.

I want him to join me now and take me in every way he can imagine.

I quickly shower and brush my teeth before grabbing a pair of black leggings and a grey jumper and throwing them on. I add some little black fluffy boots. Perfect. I turn to get my hairband from the side table, but notice that it's not there.

"Mark!" I yell down the stairs.

"Yes?" he answers in a questioning tone.

"Do you know where my hairband is?"

"No, it was on the side table next to your brush the last time I saw it."

"Thank you."

I check the floor around it. No, it's not there either. *Oh, crap.*

"Hurry up, Megan!" Mark bellows.

"Okay, okay," I reply. I can tell how impatient he is today. He doesn't like to be late for family. Well, he doesn't like to be late at all, but never for family. He would be there hours early if he had his way.

I need to tie my hair up. I can't have it down while it's wet. I'm sure there is a hairband in the car. I reach over and grab a clean, black lace thong and throw it in my hair, tying it up out of the way. A simple bun will do. It will give it a small wave once it has dried or until I find a hairband in the car.

Chapter Three

We pull up just outside of Annabella's house earlier than we need to be. We have about forty minutes until we are due here, but I know what he is like. Mark is so worried when it comes to seeing her. I find it sweet that he thinks so much of her, but I don't like to be rushed. I know why he does it, though; he never arrives too close to the time, or he is scared she will panic thinking something has happened to him.

"Hey," Annabella says, tapping on the window of Mark's side of the car. He drove as he always does. He never lets me drive when we are together. I think it's a man thing. I don't mind him driving today. Since my head is banging, I don't think it would have been advisable for me to get behind the wheel.

Mark sends down the automatic window. "Hey, have you been out gardening?" he questions.

"Yes, I have. I have been pruning back the rose bushes," she replies, pointing over the grass to some roses. I notice her hands are covered with her forest green gardening gloves. She always has them on when she is outside dealing with the roses. They have some type of thick padding under them, which protects her hands from being damaged by the thorns on the rose bushes.

"Hi, Annabella. It's so nice to see you again," I say, closing the car door gently and walking towards her.

"Megan, you look stunning," she responds, taking hold of my hand and looking me up and down. She always checks everyone out to see what they are wearing.

"Thank you." I pause. "You're looking well. Have you gotten over your cold?" I enquire. Annabella had been really unwell a couple of weeks ago. She ended up spending several days in bed because the cold went straight into her chest.

"Yes, thankfully. It was the worst one I have had in years. I'm sorry if I seemed rude while I was sick. I just didn't want you or Lucy to get it."

We were supposed to come over and see her, but she told us all to stay away, including Mark. She didn't want him getting it either.

"I totally understand what you mean," I reply because I thought it was very considerate of her.

"There she is," Annabella says, holding her arms out to take Lucy from Mark. I stand there smiling while watching Annabella and how she reacts with Lucy. I love seeing her with Lucy; it makes me think about what she must have been like with Mark. I'm so happy that he had someone strong and loving around him as he grew up. It's been a great thing for him. He has become such a lovely man. I can see him being a caring father too since he is a wonderful father figure to Lucy now.

"Right, shall we let Annabella get all ready to go out for lunch?" Mark asks, looking down at Lucy, who is sitting on her hip.

Annabella peers up at Mark. "I thought I would just cook. It will be easier," she says, smiling at him while giving him a fluttery eye look. Even I know that will not wash with Mark. When he has made plans, they are final. No way he is going to change his mind that easily.

"No, I said we were going out for something to eat. I want to treat three of my favourite ladies," he says, kissing her on the forehead.

"But…"

"No buts, please," Mark challenges, fluttering his eyes back at me. I can't help but laugh at him. I love it when he tries to mimic one of us. His eye fluttering isn't as good as Annabella's or mine.

"Megan, watch out for those fluttering eyes," she says, pointing at Mark.

"I will," I answer as I shake my head. "I know all about them. I think those eyes are dangerous."

"I will agree to going out for lunch if you will let me take these two to see something special in the garden," she states matter-of-factly, pointing at me with her head.

"Okay, deal. I'll go see my favourite little four-legged friend." He leans over and places a kiss on Annabella's cheek before walking into the house.

"See, I always win," she says, laughing. "Let's go. I have something special to show you."

"Have fun, ladies," Mark tells us.

"Oh, have you got your key, Mark? I have locked the door," Annabella states.

"Good, you should always have it locked. That way you are safe," Mark adds. "And, yes, I have my key." He pulls it out of his pocket and waves it at her.

I follow alongside Annabella to the side of the house where the shed that Mark had already pointed out to me sits. Lucy is cooing in Annabella's arms, and all I can do is smile. She is secure. I have no worries.

"Here we are," she says, opening the creaking door to the shed. I might have to get Mark to take a look at that for her. She will let him, but I don't think she will let me. She sees something like that as a man's job.

"Oh, wow!" I exclaim. It is a room full of different types of roses. They are all various colours and sizes, and their smell is amazing. It hits you in the face as soon as the door opens. "This is where Mark gets his passion for roses."

"Yes, it is. He knows the meaning of every one of them. When I first came over here, I only wanted rose bushes in my garden. With every pay check, I bought another bush, and here they all are," she says, pointing at all the bushes lined inside the shed. The shed is very deceiving. Although it looks like a shed, it is more of a greenhouse inside. It's full of different pots with little roses. Annabella explains that once they have matured to be transplanted, she will plant them outside. They are all still too young to go out yet. It's lovely listening to her tell me about something that means so much to her.

"They are amazing," I state. I'm truly overwhelmed with how many beautiful roses I see in here.

"This one down here is new," she says, pointing at a little bush that just looks like it's starting to grow. "It's actually called Lucy and dates around 1997. It grows medium-sized pink roses. They are not full doubles, but semi."

"Oh, wow."

"I bought it the day Lucy was born," she says, bringing Lucy up closer and placing a little kiss on her head.

"That was so sweet of you." A tear rolls down my cheek.

"That way Lucy can enjoy this space just like Mark did all those years ago." She smiles adoringly at Lucy before turning her attention back to me. "What's that in your hair?" she questions with a raise of her eyebrow.

"Oh, pooh," I exclaim, covering my face as I feel myself start to burn up with embarrassment.

"Megan?"

"I couldn't find a hairband this morning when I was in a full-on rush to get ready, so I grabbed the first thing in sight," I explain.

"It looks so pretty with the lace effect. It's like a hair net," she adds.

I slip it out of my hair, sliding it into my jacket pocket.

"What is it?"

"A thong. A clean one, I promise." I cover my face in shame.

Annabella stands there laughing. "That made my day."

As we walk back towards the house, I see Mark lying face down in the front yard. The puppy is running around him and barking loudly. I start to walk faster towards him, leaving Lucy in Annabella's arms. Is he just playing around?

"Mark?" I enquire as I approach him. "Mark!" I yell as I fall to my knees beside him.

Chapter Four

I shake him, but nothing happens. There is no movement or sound at all from him. I place my hand at the side of his head to straighten it, so he is able to breathe better. When I slowly lift my hand away from the back of his head, I instantly notice blood. Mark's blood is all over my hand.

"Annabella, call an ambulance!" I shout, trying not to wake Lucy, who had fallen asleep a little while ago in Annnabella's arms. It is normal for her to take a nap at this time. "Mark, you will be fine. I love you. Please stay with me."

I walk around him to see his face. I notice that his head isn't elevated enough, so I move him a little bit more, ensuring that he is definitely able to breathe. I then bend one of his knees, moving him slightly. I'm scared to touch him. I don't want to hurt him any more than he already is. I don't know if he has broken anything. I'm not a mind reader, but I wish I were because I need to know what happened. Right now, I need to make sure he is safe. I need him to be in some kind of recovery position since I don't know what's happened. All I do know is he is unconscious, and there is blood coming from his head.

I turn to see Annabella standing there with tears streaming from her eyes. "He is going to be okay," I state, attempting to reassure her. I don't know if he will be all right. I don't know what will happen to him, because I don't know what happened. I should have gotten him to come with me. Did he fall over? Is the puppy injured? Oh, my head is such a mess, but I can't let Annabella know that. She will worry more.

"I hope so," she responds in a shaky voice. "I haven't gone into the house."

"Why?" I exclaim harshly. "We need an ambulance. We need help for Mark."

"No, someone has broken into the house. The door has been smashed through, and I can see from here there are things on the floor in the hallway. Everything I can see is destroyed and all lying over the place," she states, visibly trembling.

"Oh, no. Use this," I say, passing her my mobile. "We need an ambulance for Mark."

I reach into Mark's pocket and grab his little monogrammed handkerchief, the one he always carries with him. I place it gently on his head where the blood appears to be coming from, applying enough pressure to try to stop the bleeding. I hope Mark will not be mad at me for using his granddad's hanky. He passed away when Mark was six, and it is one of the most treasured items he owns that belonged to his granddad. His name was William, but his dad used to call him Bill. The name stuck with him throughout his life, and everyone knew him as Bill.

I remember the night Mark told me about his grandad Bill. We were sitting on the sofa with my head on his lap. As I listened to the stories about his granddad, he held the handkerchief close to him.

Granddad Bill passed away suddenly of a heart attack at sixty-nine years old. He used to spend hours with Mark, teaching him about vegetables. He told him how to plant them and to look after them like a keen gardener should. He used to come and visit Annabella and help her with the garden. Mark told me all about the hours they spent chatting and shopping for the garden. I wish I had met him.

Tears roll down Annabella's cheeks as she leans over and passes my mobile back to me. "Annabella, is everything okay in the house?" I question.

"I didn't really notice what was damaged. I saw bits of things, but I'm not sure what," she replies.

"I'm going to ring Connor," I state.

I reach for my mobile that I had placed on the ground beside me.

"Connor?"

"Mark has...I don't know. We are at Annabella's, and he is lying in the driveway unconscious with blood pouring from his head. Can you come here and check the house, or get someone to? I'm scared to go inside." I pause. "The house has been trashed. From what we can see, things have been smashed, and I don't know if anyone is in it or not."

It's not like Mark to fall. He is the most coordinated person I know. I have never known him to be clumsy, even when he has been drinking. I don't know what is happening. I stay at Mark's side with one eye on the door of the house. I hope no one in in there.

"Shhh...He will be all right," I say, trying to comfort the puppy, who has been running around and barking. He has finally settled at Mark's side, whining.

I hear the sound of the ambulance coming up the driveway. I'm so happy to see some help. I sit there unable to move, listening to Annabella tell the responders about Mark. As one paramedic looks down at Mark and prepares to move him, another one runs to get the splint board. I move out of the way, letting them care for the man I love. He is so lifeless, and it pains me to stand here and do nothing.

"I'll go place this little one away in the house," I finally say, trying to regain my composure as I walk towards the house. "Come on," I call to Jessie, the puppy, while entering the house. I suddenly stop, looking to the side. For as far as I can see, there is broken glass everywhere. There is no way I can walk through there, and I can't leave Jess. I don't know if anyone is in there. I should have thought about that possibility.

"Stop!" I shout at Jessie. "Come on. You can come with us." I walk hastily over to Mark's car, placing her into the backseat. I don't like the thought of locking her away, so I will have to drop her off somewhere safe. With the unexpected heat, the car is unsafe.

"What's going on?" Annabella asks.

"The house feels weird," I inform her. I know that must sound silly, but it does. I felt like I was being watched while I was standing at the door. I really don't want to be near the house any longer than I am. I want to get away now.

"I need to go in," Annabella states, walking towards the house. I run in front of her. I can't let her go into the house, just in case someone is still inside. I need to protect everyone.

"No," I demand. "You need to go with Mark." I pause. "Lucy and I will follow in the car, and I'll go find Connor." I take Lucy from her arms and watch her climb into the back of the ambulance with the help of one of the paramedics.

I can feel the tears begin to fall down my cheeks.

Chapter Five

"Where is Mr. Mark Reed?" I ask the tall, slim man who looks like he has had a late night because his blonde hair is all messed up.

"Can I ask who you are?" he replies, looking up at me. He definitely had a late night.

"His girlfriend," I answer. I still find it awkward being called his girlfriend. The title is strange to me. John never called me his girlfriend nor did he ever use a title to introduce me apart from my name. I was just there for him. Things with Mark are different. Not quite a year has passed, and I already have a title. I mean something to him.

"I'm sorry. You can't go in at the moment. I will check with the doctor and see if he will let you in. You're not considered a close relative, so he might say no. Please keep that in mind," he answers condescendingly.

"Okay," I say quietly, too stunned to say anything else. I should have known they wouldn't allow me to go inside the room.

I dropped off Jessie at Mark's house where I knew she would be safe, and Connor rang me just as I arrived at the hospital. He searched the entire house. It had been destroyed.

I just don't get it. *Why is someone after Annabella or Mark? Who would want to hurt either of them?*

Tears begin rolling down my face again. I can't see anything through my wet lashes, but I can hear the shuffle of feet moving past me. I tip my head down, pulling Lucy closer to me and placing my chin on her head. "No one will ever hurt you," I whisper.

"Megan," I hear a familiar voice say, and I lift my head towards the sound.

"Annabella, is he okay?" I question, rubbing my eyes.

"Why are you out here?" she asks.

"They wouldn't let me in because I'm not considered family," I state with an aching heart.

"Oh, bullshit. Come on. Mark is asking for you," she says in a firm voice. I'm full-on stunned by her language. I have never heard her say anything like that before.

I stand up, lifting Lucy onto my hip and grabbing my bag and changing bag that Mark gave me. It is a pretty purple with "Lucy" embroidered on it in pink thread. I take the tissue from my jacket pocket and rub my puffy eyes. Inhaling a deep breath, I follow Annabella. The unit is full off little bays with different curtains separating the beds. There is medical staff dressed in various coloured uniforms everywhere I look, making it easy to distinguish their jobs. Annabella stops at the end of the ward at a private room that has walls and a window with closed white blinds.

"We need to wait here. The lead doctor, who has been treating Mark, is in the room with him. That's why the blinds are down. He went into the room as I came out to find you."

I nod, placing a little kiss on Lucy's head. "I love you, baby girl," I say barely above a whisper.

"The young lad, I think his name is Len, told me Mark's girlfriend was here. I had to come find you," she informs me.

"Thank you, Annabella. I was getting so worried not knowing what was happening."

"Hi, can I get you anything?" I turn to see a young lady with short ginger hair, wearing a dark blue top.

"This is Kim, the nurse that has been looking after Mark," Annabella boastly states. It's nice to know who to talk to if I need to know anything about Mark. Right now, I need to see him. I need to see him with my own eyes.

"Hello, I'm okay. Thank you," I reply.

"Can we get two cups of sugary tea, Kim? Megan, you need to keep strong for Mark," Annabella says, being forceful as usual. I should have known she was going to order something for me; she is always looking after others. I could use a drink, though, so I can take some painkillers since my head is killing me.

It seems like I have been standing here for ages. I turn around, trying to gaze into the room through the gaps in the blinds. As I watch a tall figure walk past the window and towards the door, I hear the door slowly open, creaking as it does. The doctor walks out of the room towards us. Although he's wearing a doctor's badge, I really don't notice anything else about him apart from his solemn face that remains deadpan.

"How is he?" Annabella asks.

"He is awake. There are no signs of any major damage. He has had a scan, and we are just waiting for the results. I will be admitting him overnight, though, so we will be able to keep an eye on him, no matter what the results say."

"Thank you, Dr. Bradybury," Annabella says, smiling.

"This must be little Lucy," he states as he walks over to her, placing his hand on her back.

"Yes, it is," I reply.

"Mark has been asking if she is okay." He really does care about Lucy. She interacts so well with him; it's amazing to watch. I sometimes worry that it is Lucy he wants and not me because I have read articles in magazines where men pick up pregnant women just for the child. I hope Mark isn't one of those men. "You can go inside and see him," Dr. Bradybury states before spinning on his heels and walking towards the desk labeled "Nurses' Station". There are so many different people over there wearing either green or blue uniforms. Kim is wearing a blue one, but that lad Len, I think Annabella called him, has on a green one.

I follow Annabella into the room, taking deep, calming breaths as I go. I don't know what to expect when I walk in. I know it's Mark, but I don't know the extent of the damage that was done to him. "You're both all right," Mark says as Annabella and I walk closer to him. I don't try to hold back my tears as they begin to fall freely from my eyes.

"You're alive," I respond, hastily closing the space between us and reaching his bed. I sit on the edge of it, making sure I don't sit on him or any of the wires attached to him. Even though the doctor assured us he's all right, there seems to be a lot of medical devices hooked up to him.

"Yes, I am." He smiles, rubbing my back. I'm supposed to be comforting him, but he is comforting me instead.

"Your head must hurt." I look deeply into his eyes and see the pain he is in that's only slightly displayed on the surface. He has a black eye, three large cuts on his head that required stitches, and a cut lip. Who would do this to him? I just don't understand.

"It's fine. Have you contacted Connor?" he questions.

"Yes, he is on his way here. Someone broke into Annabella's house," I inform him. He needs to know. I can't keep that piece of information from him since it might be able to help the police.

"Annabella, you're staying at mine until further notice, no arguing," he states in a commanding voice.

"Deal," she replies. "I'm going to find our teas."

"Who did this to you?" I enquire.

"I have no idea. He was tall with blonde hair. That's all I know."

"But why you, Mark?" I probe further.

"Hi, everyone," Connor says as he walks into the room with a massive smile spread across his face. I have never seen him look anything but happy.

"Connor, we need to find him *now*," Mark orders, waving his finger at him.

"But who is he?" he asks. "Did he say anything to you?"

"The only thing he said to me was 'she's mine.'"

I sit there listening to the two men talk back and forth, attempting to absorb everything that is being said. Connor tells Mark about the damage inside the house and how all the photographs containing Mark were smashed and his head was ripped off. Connor had left the police and one of the security guards there while they finished checking out the place. Mark recounts what he had seen and heard, which isn't much. The man came up behind him and when he turned around, Mark smacked him in the face with the back of his fist, which explains the cuts on his hand. Mark continues saying that he didn't even know the man. He will not tell me any more about the fight. I want to know how he ended up with such a bad injury to his head.

"Megan, come with me," Annabella says, poking her head around the door frame and holding a brown tray with two cups sitting on it. I need a drink, and I need to take some painkillers. I leave Lucy's bag with Mark and head out with Lucy asleep in my arms.

Chapter Six

I can't lose the man I'm in love with. I still remember our first time together and how it was everything I dreamed of and more.

Mark is sitting on the sofa while working on his laptop. I have seen him do this so often in the months we have shared together, yet each time he does, I am taken aback by how sexy he can make mere work look. His eyes mesmerize me. The saying, "The eyes are the windows to the soul," must have known Mark's eyes. I don't believe I can stay away from my feelings of desire anymore. All I can think about is touching him, and in turn, him touching me. I can almost feel his lips trailing kisses and covering my body as we fall into each other. He says he is patient, but the patience is wearing very thin for me. I want him more than I have ever wanted anyone in my life. Tonight, I will place Lucy in her own room to sleep. I want alone time with Mark. I need alone time with Mark.

"I am just off to place Lucy to bed."

"Okay, night night, Lucy Doo. Sleep tight."

As Mark places a little kiss on Lucy's head, he looks into her sleepy little eyes and my heart melts. I love seeing how he is with her. He would be such a great dad. I wish he were Lucy's father.

"Then, I am just going to do the dishes."

"I'll do them, baby."

Mark walks into the kitchen and wraps his arms around my waist, pulling me close. I flick some water at him as an attempt to be playful. All I am thinking about is how I want to play the seductive role.

"Did you really just do that?"

"I did, Mr. Reed." *I spatter more water at him.*

"Oh, that's it, Miss Madden."

Mark spins me around so we are facing each

other and then flicks a bit of water at me.

"Are you starting now?"

"I am indeed."

He places his hands at either side of my hips, lifting me onto the kitchen counter. His lips lock with mine as his tongue teasingly seeks entry into my mouth.

He pulls back from our kiss and looks at me with the expression of complete love. "You're so beautiful, Megan."

I moan. Mark places his lips onto my neck and passionately blazes kisses down my nape, ending on my chest at the tops of my breasts. I cannot help but exhale deeply.

Looking directly into my eyes, he commands, "Upstairs now, Miss Madden."

I smile knowingly at Mark. As I move forward, he slowly slides me down the front of his body. His taut abdomen is firm against my core, and his growing erection has caught my breath and caused wetness to form between my thighs. As he lets my feet hit the floor, he takes my hand, but I take the lead up the stairs in front of him. His hand taps my bum, and I squeal, picking up my pace.

"Behave, Mr. Reed."

I run ahead straight into the master bedroom.

"As if you'd run away from me."

Mark grabs me and pulls me straight back into his arms with my back against his chest.

"You are mine now." I giggle.

He spins me around, placing his hands at the bottom of my top and sliding it over my head. I do the same to him, and I can't believe how good he looks.

His lips go straight to my neck, kissing it fervently, going from one side to the other. He travels down to my black lacy bra. Sliding one hand around my back, he unfastens it and then lets both hands drift to my matching panties. I stand still as he moves effortlessly to slide them down my legs.

"Oh, I am going to devour you, baby," he says as he kneels in front of me.

Moving his thumb to my clit, he rubs it while placing little kisses on it. He slides his finger inside me really slowly, sending me over the edge in

ecstasy.

"You're wet, so wet," he moans. "I want you, need you." He withdraws his finger and stands up to slide off his jeans. His tight boxers strain around his throbbing erection. I gracefully move and slide them down, freeing his cock.

Wow, I can't help but look at how big he is. I giggle to myself. Mark lays me down onto the bed, kissing my neck and then sliding his lips down my chest.

"Baby, are you sure?" he asks in a caring voice.

I nod and he automatically slides on protection and then smiles at me. At least I don't have to worry.

He slowly slides himself in me, and I take a deep breath. Oh, baby. He places his hands above my head, and I bend my knees to wrap my legs around him. I put my hands into his hair and gently pull, causing him to groan in pleasure. As he begins to gain speed, he lowers his head and his tongue invades my mouth, kissing me passionately. The intensity is so strong that I arch my back to meet him thrust for thrust.

"Baby, you're so perfect," he says as he takes one hand and starts squeezing my nipple and caresses my face with the other.

"Oh my," I say. I don't think I can hang on much longer.

"Megan, I love you," he declares as he continues to pump harder and faster, never losing his rhythm.

I can't manage to form words; I just moan. I knew our first time would be easy and special.

"Argh!" Mark lets out a massive growl not long after me and falls down onto the bed beside me. He places his hand on my bum, rolling me onto my side and pulling me in close.

"You're wonderful," he whispers as he strokes my hair. "No, you are."

Chapter Seven

I shake my head. Okay, Megan, get your head back here. I will soon have Mark home, recreating new memories. Who knows what fun we can have? I continue to walk out of the hospital room following Annabella. Why does she want to speak to me?

"Yes, Annabella, what's wrong?" I ask as I sit on the little bench just outside of Mark's room. I see worry in her eyes. There is something she isn't telling me.

"I need to tell you something, but don't tell anyone, including Mark." She pauses. "Promise me." She looks down at the carry-out tray containing our drinks that is sitting on her knees. The cups are decorated with a single yellow star and the word "Believe" written under it. *Is this some kind of message?*

"I'll try," I reply. I can't keep it from Mark if it is something that could help with the investigation. She must understand that. I would only tell him if I need to.

"I got a letter the other day," she blurts out, keeping her head tilted down towards her lap.

"Saying?" I state the word as a question and place my hand on her arm.

"It had the words 'I'll destroy you all' written on it," she says, lifting her head up slightly to look at me.

"Why didn't you mention it?" I ask. I really don't have any idea what to say to her. She placed herself and everyone around her, including my daughter, in danger. If she had said something, this might not have happened. I know I shouldn't blame her, but I don't know what is happening,

"I thought it was a joke," she answers with a tear rolling down her cheek.

"Do you still have it?" I ask. I hope she does, then maybe we can use it. It might help.

I need to remain calm.

She places her hand inside her bag, pulling out a torn cream envelope. "Here." I turn it over and notice the word "open" written in a deep shade of red lipstick.

"You do know I need to tell Connor, right?"

"Yes, but I don't want to worry Mark." She doesn't want to worry Mark, but does she think Connor won't tell him? Of course, he is going to worry.

"Don't worry." I take a deep, cleansing breath while placing the letter into my jacket pocket. I walk back to the door of the room and smile at Annabella before pushing it open and rejoining Mark and Connor.

"Is everything okay?" Mark asks, looking directly into my eyes. I think he realizes something isn't right. He knows me too well.

"Yes, she is just worrying," I say, looking down at him in the hospital bed.

"Tell me the truth," he states, reaching out for my hand.

"What?" I exclaim, moving my hand away.

"I know you well enough to know when you're lying," Mark points out. I knew he would be able to see right through me.

"Oh, she had a letter dropped off the other day," I say, pulling out the envelope and passing it to Connor. "Stop worrying, Mark. I told her you wouldn't say anything to her about it."

"I won't."

I sit on the side of the bed, holding Mark's hand and listening to him tell Lucy stories until he falls asleep with her in the crook of his arm. I hear a tap on the door, followed by Kim walking into the room.

"Miss, I'm going to have to ask you to leave," she says quietly.

"Sure, what time can I return?" I ask. I knew I would have to leave at some point; I know what these hospitals are like.

She politely hands me a printed copy of the visiting hours and days. "Different times, different days."

"Thank you," I say. I turn to face Mark and pick up Lucy. "I love you." I place a little kiss on his forehead.

I leave him asleep and follow Connor out to his car. We find Annabella asleep in it. I did wonder where she had gone. Since Connor had spent the afternoon taking calls and walking in and out of the room, I thought he might have taken her to Mark's house.

"We need to find out who did this, Connor," I insist, leaning against his car. It must be a new one because I have never seen him in a red car before today. I have to admit; it's very smart.

"I know. I will," he replies, rubbing the outside of my arm. "You're cold." I don't care if I'm cold. I care about everyone's safety.

"No, we will." I pause. "If they come back, my daughter is at risk, too."

"We have a plan," he counters, informing me of an extra security plan. Someone will keep an eye on Lucy at all times. "Mark thinks of Lucy as his daughter. Don't forget that. He isn't going to let anyone harm her. She is precious to you both."

"Thank you. We best get these too sleepy heads home and fed," I state, looking down at Lucy. "Oh, crap. I need some dog food, too."

"How about takeout for tea?" Connor asks before informing me of a little street that has lots of different takeout restaurants on it and a supermarket for other items. It's a place where we can get everything we need in one stop. How did I not know about this?

"Thank God I have you. I don't know this part of town." I slide Lucy into her car seat that Connor has gotten for me out of Mark's car.

"I know. Get in," he says, opening the car door.

"What about my car?" I question.

"Scott will collect it later when he collects Mia. She is going to come and stay with you. She is upset."

"Who is Scott?" Now this is a name I definitely haven't heard before.

"He's Mia's security guard. Well, that's his official title," he says, shrugging his shoulders.

"*So*...he's more than that," I say, laughing. That doesn't surprise me, though. Mia is at the age where she sleeps with several men.

Chapter Eight

It seems like I have been at Mark's for hours now, just waiting for Mia to come and join us. I can't relax until I know she is safe, so I send her a text.

Mia, we have Chinese here. It's your favorite, or so Connor said. I will keep it warm unil you arrive. I can't wait to see you. I need a hug. Xx

Megan, I'm on my way now. I need to drop off my final designs. Hug is on its way. Get Connor to give you one for now. Xx

Erm, no. That's just weird. See you soon. Xx

I love the fact the Mia is finally buckling down and working her bum off trying to get her work done, but seriously, I am not giving Connor a hug. That's just weird. Annabella is being so helpful, like an angel. She has kindly taken Lucy for her nighttime bath, giving me some much needed time to sort out my head. I definitely need it. I send Connor out to walk Jessie because I have no energy to walk her tonight. I can't do with her wanting me all night, so hopefully, she will be tired and settle down. I know she is in a strange environment, but I still hope she sleeps since I don't think she has ever stayed here before.

It doesn't feel right being in this house without Mark or without knowing he will be here shortly. I have never spent a night in this house without him, and I'm not looking forward to it.

I reach for my mobile to contact Jenny. I need to check how everything went.

"Hi, Jenny. How did today go?" I ask.

"*What? You're pregnant?* That's wonderful." A smile lights up my face, and I begin dancing up and down in my seat. I'm so happy for her. She is finally getting what she has dreamed of. I just hope nothing goes wrong. She is great with Lucy and will be a wonderful mum.

"Oh my God. You need to tell me everything. How

did the test go?" I probe.

As expected, we spend a while talking about what happened with her. She had tried to ring me earlier in the day, but I couldn't talk to her. I couldn't talk to anyone. I only wanted to know that Mark was okay. I was a mess, and I still am.

"Jenny, someone attacked Mark today. They got into Annabella's house while we were in the garden. Mark had gone to walk Jessie, so I don't know what happened. No one really does. The doctors say that he is going to be okay, but we are still waiting on test results. He is a mess with cuts and bruises. It's horrible."

"No, stay there. You have bump to think of. I'm safe. I have Connor, and there is some other security around. I don't know, but I will be fine. Mia is coming too, so we will all be together. Well, except for Mark, since he is still in the hospital."

Mia walks straight into the lounge, looking down. I can tell she isn't happy. She has a face like a slapped arse. I know I will find out soon what's happened. Oh God.

"Jenny, I have to go. Mia just got here. I'll text

you later."

"I'm fucking sick of men!" Mia yells as she walks over towards me, turning around to see if anyone else is in the room. Luckily, it's just us. Annabella is still upstairs with Lucy, and Connor hasn't returned yet.

"What's happened?" I ask, even though I'm not at all sure I want to know. I'm not in the mood for Mia's 'all about me' attitude. She should be worried about her brother, not herself. He could have died today.

Connor rang her earlier and told her about what had happened. He has kept in touch with Scott all day, and she hasn't once contacted him to check on Mark. When Connor rang, Mark had just been admitted into the hospital. You would think she would care about him, as he has always taken care of her.

Mia sits down beside me on the sofa. "Am I ugly?" she asks, looking up at me.

"No, you're so pretty, hun. What happened?" I shake my head in disbelief. *Who would say something like that to her?*

"Scott said it. I asked him to kiss me, and he refused," she admits.

"He is here to protect you, Mia, nothing else. Your brother would have killed him for kissing you. You will find Mr. Right. It took me years to find my Mr. Right." Mia is going through some faze right now. She doesn't seem like the girl I first met. She seems so immature for her age, and she is only a couple of years younger than me. Thank goodness I never went through the 'throwing tantrums over boys' kind of stage.

"Thanks, Megan." She moves her hand dismissively. "You're right. Anyway, he is like forty. That's old. He does not have much life left in his cock."

"Mia! You can't say things like that. Age is just a number."

"If you say so." She pauses. "Are you ready to eat?"

"I guess," I say, letting her leave to get everything sorted for tea. Although she is young, she is very organised when it comes to work. However, when it comes to men, she is terrible. She thinks everyone wants to sleep with her. I hope she grows out of it soon, before she gets herself in trouble. You can tell that Annabella has rubbed off on her in some ways, but not the ones that matter the most.

I don't want to eat anything, but I know I need to in order to have energy to look after my daughter. What I really want is to sleep in Mark's arms. Yes, for once, I want to sleep.

Chapter Nine

Thankfully, last night went really quickly, especially after we finished eating. Well, I mostly played around with my food, but I did eat a little. I took a quick shower and crawled into bed. I couldn't sleep without Mark, so I got up and looked around for something of his. I found his favourite hoodie and hugged it in my arms. You don't see him wearing it much, only when he is having some down time. He looks so relaxed and cute in it. I miss him like mad. I'm so worried. Who would do this? Why?

After hearing a tapping on the door, I sit up in the bed. "Yes."

"Hey, Megan," Connor says, standing in the doorway. "I came to check on you."

"Yeah, I'm fine. I'm going to get up, check on Lucy, and then get ready for the day. What time can we see Mark?" I ask.

"Not until one, unless he is released earlier." He pauses. "I'm sorry." He must have been in touch with Mark. There was no mention of him being released when I left him last night. Once I'm dressed, I will ring the hospital and check on him. I don't know what they will tell me, so I may have to ask Mia to do it. I need to know that he is all right. One o'clock is too long to wait.

"It's not your fault. Do you have any leads?" I enquire. I want to know what is happening. I know the police were talking to Scott and Connor last night.

"None at all," he responds, sitting on the side of the bed. I'm glad I put on pyjamas last night. "The cameras at Annabella's did pick up the incident with Mark, but no faces are visible."

"Faces?" I question.

"Yes, two people," he informs me. "It looked like a man hit Mark, though."

"Oh no," I say, taking a deep breath to calm myself.

"Do you want me to sort Lucy for you? It will give you a little more time to get up," Connor states. "I know Mark normally gets her ready for the day to let you have some alone time."

"I don't want you to feel used, Connor," I tell him. I can do everything by myself. Mark helps me out of love. Connor would be doing it for the fact he is getting paid to do it.

"I'll do it. I actually want to get her up. I love having a baby around the house. It makes me think of my Kate when she was that small." He smiles. I love seeing the spark in his eye when he talks about his daughter. I can't wait to spend a longer amount of time with her and get to know her more. I wonder if she is going to be a mini Connor or be more like her mum. I have only seen a couple of pictures of her mum, and right now it's still hard to tell who she looks like more.

"Okay, go on then," I say, sliding out of the bed and opening the curtains.

There is no sun in sight. All I can see is the rain

bouncing from the path. It's not going to be a nice, clear day. The sky is so dull. Without even moving, I can tell it's going to be one of those days where I will probably be cold, no matter what I wear. Opening the drawer, I pull out black matching underwear and a black jumper with a few sparkling gems scattered around the front. I reach for some dark blue jeans and immediately smile. These will do. Mark loves those jeans, or should I say, he loves my arse in these jeans.

"Megan," Connor says, walking into the room. "Sorry, I didn't knock. Do you know where Lucy is?"

"In her cot next door," I reply, walking out of the room and feeling my heart begin to race.

"She isn't."

"What? Has anyone got Lucy?" I shout, running around in sheer panic.

Connor follows me, reaching for the other security guards. "Search the full building," he says in a steady voice.

"Who has my baby?" I yell.

"Calm down, Megan. The guys are going to look

418

for her. She's probably with one of the girls," he says, placing his hand on my back.

I pull away sharply. "Don't touch me." Sprinting towards Mia's room, I barge through the door. "Have you seen Lucy?"

"No, not since last night when you placed her to bed. Why?" she asks, standing there in a flower-patterned dress and no makeup. She could go without makeup; she looks better without it on.

"She is missing," I say with tears rolling down my face. I turn around and run into Annabella's room.

"Have you seen Lucy?"

"No, I haven't since I went to bed last night. What's going on?" she asks.

"She's gone," I cry, running out of the room and looking down at the floor. I'm unable to see anything through the tears pouring from my eyes. I suddenly feel my head crash into something soft followed by two strong arms wrapping around me, pulling me in close. I can't do anything but freeze.

"Megan, we will find her. Everyone is looking for her. Would you like a drink?" Connor suggests.

I stand there, crying harder. "No." *Why the hell would I want a drink? I need my daughter, not a drink.*

"You need to keep strong, Megan," Connor says.

"I'm getting dressed. I *will* find my daughter." I run around him into my room, taking my clothes off as I walk inside. I don't care what I look like now. I fling on the clothes I had laid out, grab my mobile, and walk onto the landing.

"What is going on?" Mark asks, storming into the front room of his house.

"Mark?" I ask, shocked that he's home.

"Sir, what are you doing here?" one of the security guards enquires as he walks quickly towards Mark. I don't even know the guard's name.

"Something isn't right. Megan isn't answering her mobile and neither is Connor. Now, tell me what's going on," Mark demands, placing his hands on his hips.

"Lucy is missing," Connor replies hastily.

"What?" Mark shouts.

"She was in her cot at three when Megan checked on her, and now she is gone. We can't find her anywhere," he explains.

I stand there at the top of the stairs, shaking as I try to fasten the buttons on my jacket. I need to search for her. I have to find my baby. I don't want anyone except Lucy right now.

Chapter Ten

"Megan?" Mark calls after me as he runs up the stairs. Pain is clearly shown in his eyes.

I turn around to answer him. "What are you doing here anyway?" I ask. "You were in hospital. Now, you're here. I don't understand it."

"Megan, I felt something wasn't right, so I called Connor. He *always* answers his mobile, and when he didn't, I rang you and you never answered either. I just knew something wasn't right."

"You should still be in hospital. You need to be looked after," I plead.

"No, I was discharged. Well, I was being discharged when someone came for me." He pauses. "I walked out and got a taxi. I did get my prescription before I left, though." He smiles sheepishly.

"You're silly," I state.

"But, you needed me," Mark says, pulling me close.

I pull away from him. "Where is she?" I ask as I sit on the top step, absolutely exhausted.

"Oh, baby. I will find her," he says, sitting down next to me and rubbing my head. His voice is such a nice sound to hear. I know he will do all he can to find Lucy.

"Who would want her? How has anyone gotten inside the house?" I ask, sitting up and looking directly into his eyes.

"I don't know, but I will find out," he says, placing a little butterfly kiss on my forehead as tears flow like a waterfall.

"I need to phone the police," I state. *Why didn't I think of that before?*

"Connor has already done it. I asked him to. The guys are searching everywhere," he responds.

I quickly stand up, cover my mouth, and run into the bathroom, slamming the door behind me. I bend down over the toilet and throw up. I don't know where that has come from. After cleaning myself up, I slide down the bath, bending my knees up towards my chest. I sit there, allowing the tears to freely fall down my face.

"Megan." I look up to see Mia in a pair of black jeans and a long, vertical striped blue and white top. Why is she wearing a different outfit? She looked better in the dress, but it isn't the right weather for the outfit she had on earlier. She has put on makeup, too. We don't have time to play dress up.

"Where is she?" I ask.

"I don't know. Come downstairs," she begs, reaching her hand out to me. I use her hand to stand up and flush the toilet as I walk past it.

"Baby, contact Jen. Let her know just in case she hears something," Mark commands as he opens a cupboard and looks inside.

I take a deep breath and dial her number, but I don't think I can talk to her. I don't want her stressing out. It's not healthy for her in her condition.

"Jen, she's gone. Lucy's gone. We can't find her. Someone has taken her," I say in one breath before passing the mobile to Mia.

Why is this happening to me? I slide down onto the sofa, slightly listening to Mia explain everything to Jenny. I see Mark walking up to her.

"Megan, do you want Jenny to come up?" Mia asks.

"No." I pause. "Tell her to stay home."

I sit there in a daze thinking, not hearing any of the noises around me. I see so many people running around and looking at things. I lower my head, peering at the floor. I need to leave and do something. As I raise my head to prepare to get up, I notice a male and female in police uniforms and Mark standing in front of me.

Chapter Eleven

"This is Police Constable Blair," Mark informs me, pointing towards the woman, "and PC Carter." He motions at the man. "They are from the local police station. I have worked with Steven Carter in the past," he comments as he pats his hand on Carter's shoulder. PC Carter then walks into the kitchen.

"Hi," is all I can utter. I just want my daughter back. I feel like I'm going to be sick again, so I place my hand over my mouth.

Mia stands there, smiling at me before walking away to the kitchen to join Annabella, who is talking with PC Carter.

"Hi, I'm Becky," PC Blair says, sitting on the sofa beside me and stroking down her uniform. "We need to know all about Lucy and when you last saw her. I plan to be as quick as I can." She takes out her notepad and pen.

"Sorry, Megan. Here is some water," Mia says, handing me the glass and a little packet of tissues. "I don't want you to get sick again."

"Thank you," I say, taking a little sip of the water before turning back to PC Blair. "Lucy is my only child." I inhale deeply, trying to hold back the tears. "I don't know anyone around here. I don't know who could have taken her. They got into the house. It makes no sense." I feel myself opening up to her. I have nothing to hide. I just want my daughter back.

"Megan, this is Natasha. She is a liaison officer, and she is going to spend some time with you. She will keep you up-to-date with everything that is happening. We will find your daughter," she says, motioning for Natasha to come and join us. I didn't see Natasha enter the house at all. Why didn't she come in with Becky? It would have made more sense.

Natasha is tall with skin like chocolate and brown hair that is tied neatly into a bun. As she comes to sit next to Becky, she lets out a beaming smile with pearly white straight teeth. "Hi, Miss Madden. I'm Natasha."

423

"Call me Megan," I state, looking down at the floor. I have never liked being referred to as Miss Madden or Ma'am. It makes me seem old. I have always been told you use those names for your elders, and I am definitely not an elder.

"Megan." She pauses. "I'm going to sit with you and help you with everything until we locate your daughter. If you want to know anything at all, just ask me. I will give you all the information you need and help you as much as I can."

"Thank you," I say, trying to remain calm. "Who has my daughter?"

"I don't know, Megan," Becky says. "Can we ask you a few more questions?"

I nod, feeling some movement behind me. I turn around to see Mark sitting on the arm of the sofa. He pulls me close to him. I need to be as close to him as I can get. I don't want him to let me go. I just want it to be Mark, Lucy, and me. It was supposed to be the three of us for a planned family day today. Mark even bought some films that were appropriate for Lucy. I was looking forward to it; it was just what I needed.

"Are you both Lucy's parents?" she asks, looking over at Mark who sits there shaking his head. I smile at him, turning back around to face Becky. A tear rolls down my face.

"No, a man named John is her dad. He lives in Yorkshire. He has never had any contact with her. In fact, he has no interest in her," I state. Tears are now streaming down my face. "He cheated on me or on his wife. I don't know who came first. He has other children."

I lose count of how many questions she asks me about my past and past lovers. I feel like everything about me has just been said. I don't understand how that information is going to help find Lucy. I don't even know how Mark coped listening to that stuff. I said things that I have never shared with him or anyone else.

Mia passes my mobile back to me. She winks at me before walking over to Carter. I can tell she's trying to flirt with him, and I'm not at all surprised. He is a male. I just hope she behaves herself. He isn't here to flirt; he is here to find my daughter.

"Will someone please find my daughter?" I yell.

Chapter Twelve

I have spent the past two hours pacing back and forth in Mark's home. Thank goodness he has not left my side.

"How do you know PC Carter?" I ask Mark. I need to know.

He moves himself away from me. "Steven and I used to work together," he says, turning his face away from me.

Why has he moved away from me? Is it something bad? What happened? There can't be any secrets between us now. "What, you used to be in the police or something? One of those community ones?" I continue pushing for answers.

"Megan, please. Leave it," he begs, tilting his head towards the floor.

"If you can't trust me with this, then how can I trust you to keep Lucy and me safe? Look what happened," I say, standing up and storming away from him. He is supposed to trust me. What the hell can be that bad? I head straight out the front door, slamming it behind me. I don't want him near me. If he can't trust me, then I can't trust him.

"Megan!" I hear Mark yell, just as I run off the path. The sound of his feet shuffling behind me lets me know he's running after me. I don't care; I just keep running. "Where are you going?"

I find myself sitting on the grass behind one of Mark's rose bushes that Annabella had planted a few years ago, and I believe she said it was a Red Knockout. At some point, it blooms red flowers. I remember her telling me about it. She said something about red roses being the most powerful roses around, because of their special meaning. I haven't seen any flowers on it yet. I hope that Annabella will pass on some of her gardening tips to Lucy. My granddad taught me how to care for plants when I was a child. I used to love spending hours with him, trying to water all the plants. He passed away when I was eleven, so I am grateful for the amazing memories I have. I miss him like crazy.

"Megan, come here!" Mark shouts. I hear heavy footsteps hurling towards me. I glance down to the ground, pulling my knees up to my chest and covering my arms over my head, forming a tight ball. I just want to be alone. *Please don't notice me, Mark.*

"There you are. What are you doing out here? You're going to catch pneumonia," he says, kneeling down beside me and throwing his black jacket around my shoulders. Why is he being so thoughtful? He doesn't trust me.

I lift my head just a little to see Connor standing at the top end of the garden watching me. He waves one of the security guards away with the back of his hand.

"Talk to me, Megan," Mark says, rubbing my shoulders to relax me.

"About what?" I ask, remaining stationary.

"What's wrong?"

"*What's wrong*? That's a stupid question!" I scream, raising my head and turning to face him.

"I know. Lucy will be home soon."

"Why are you hiding things about your past?" I ask calmly, looking up at him and directly into his eyes.

"I don't want you to get hurt," he says, barely audible.

"Hurt by what?" I ask. Nothing can be that bad. *Can it?*

He lets out a breath. "Steven and I met years ago when I was fourteen. We took a mini police course together at school. They taught us all sorts of beneficial things. They had us complete small tasks exactly like real police officers. It was amazing, a total eye opener to things none of us had thought about doing as a career. We had attended the same school for years; we were even in a couple of classes together, but we never spoke. We were partnered together during the course, and it brought us together as friends. Steven was the bad boy, and I was the really good 'do as you're told' boy. From then on, we were inseparable." He pauses.

"Go on," I state, giving him a crooked smile.

426

"Steven went off and became a policeman and lived the dream. We lost contact after a few years until..." He pauses again, taking a deep breath.

I place my hand on his shoulder. "Just tell me."

"Until I was dating a lady named Anna. She and I had been fine for months, ticking along. One day she was different with me. She was annoyed with everything I did. Later that night when I was asleep, she stabbed me. Steven was the man that was involved in my case."

"Oh, I'm so sorry." I wish I hadn't pushed for the answer now. I feel bad, but I needed to know.

"Her brother Damon was there, too. They had been planning to kill me and extort money from my family. They had done it in the past to someone else, but were never found because they had been using aliases."

"Oh, baby." I wrap my arms around him, giving him a hug.

"Miss Madden?" I hear a voice shout. I suddenly stand up.

"Yes." I start walking in the direction of the voice.

"Can you take a look at this? Is it Lucy's?" Natasha asks.

I run over to her with Mark not far behind me. She stands there holding her mobile in her hand. "Just let me know if Lucy has one. It might not be hers, but we need to know."

She shows me a picture of a pink cardigan with white spots all over it and a hood that's shaped like a cat's face. "That's Lucy's. Well, she has one like it. Hers has an 'L' written on the label."

"Did you bring it with you?" she enquires.

"I don't have a picture of the label, though, but I can get one if I need to."

"Yes, please."

I run past Natasha, straight to the house and up into Lucy's room. "It's gone," I say as Mark comes up behind me, placing his hand on my lower back. I had laid out the hoodie last night for Annabella to put on Lucy after her bath to keep her warm. I had left it beside the cot.

Chapter Thirteen

"Megan."

I slowly open my eyes to see Annabella on her knees beside the sofa. I slide up, sitting with my legs along the sofa.

"How did I get here?" I ask, not remembering being in here. The last thing I remember is standing by the French windows looking out into Mark's garden and hugging one of Lucy's favorite teddy bears.

"You collapsed. Mark laid you down on the sofa," Annabella says, passing me a glass of water. "It's cold," she adds.

"Thank you." I take a small sip and wince in pain. *Ouch! My shoulder hurts. Why?*

"Take it easy," she suggests.

"Megan, you're awake," Mark says as he lunges towards the chair next to the sofa.

"I am." I smile awkwardly.

"Dr. Kirk is on his way to check on you," Mark informs me.

"Why?"

"Because you went down with a bang. You hit your back and shoulder, and your shoulder is swollen now." He points to my shoulder as he speaks.

"I'm fine," I say, moving my right shoulder. The pain is excruciating. I can tell I have done something to it, but I don't know what.

"No, you'll do as your told," he states boldly, using his firm boss voice and waving his index finger at me.

"Lucy? Have they got her?" I ask without hesitation. Suddenly everything comes to light. How could I have forgotten what had happened? How bad of a mum am I?

"Not yet, hun," Mia says, walking over to sit on the edge of the sofa.

Tears well up in my eyes, and the ache in my heart returns. I want my daughter back. I need her back in my arms where she is safe.

"Jen rang," Mia declares. "She was checking on you."

I nod. I can't think anymore.

"She feels so helpless," Mia adds.

"I'll text her," I state.

"Here," Mark says, passing me my mobile from the coffee table. I look around, but I don't see any of the police or Natasha in the room with us. Are they all out looking for Lucy?

I quickly flick through my messages, reading one that sends chills down my body.

She is MY daughter, too. I CAN have her.

"What?" I exclaim in shock.

"What is it?" Mark asks.

"It's John. He sent me a text."

"Saying?" he grits through clenched teeth.

"'She is my daughter, too. I can have her.'" I pass my mobile to Mark. He rushes it over to Natasha, who is sitting in the dining room.

"Has he got my daughter?" I ask Mia.

"I don't know, Megan," she replies. "I wish I knew where she was."

"These are for you," Annabella says, passing me a bunch of flowers.

I'm not really into flowers, so I don't know what these are called. "Irises?" I question timidly.

"That's right. They stand for hope."

"Thank you, Annabella."

I take the flowers into the kitchen and run a little water into a glass before placing them inside. I don't care about these at all. I don't want flowers; I want my daughter.

"Miss Madden," Natasha says.

"Yes."

"I have some alarming news. John is in the area, and the police are going to see him."

"*What*?!"

"I will hopefully have some more news for you shortly."

"*Shortly*? I want news now! I want Lucy now!" I yell.

"I can understand that, but you need to stay calm. Your health is as important as Lucy is," Natasha responds, passing me a mug full of what looks like tea.

"I don't want it," I state, walking away from her. I reach the nearest window that looks onto the front of the house, sitting myself on the floor. I gaze into the outside world, watching cars pass. People are going on with their normal day-to-day business like no one cares that my daughter is missing. Someone came inside the house and took her. Who? Why? The two police cars remain in the car park with no sign of movement from them, but I know there are people inside them. Why are they not doing anything?

"Megan," Natasha says, placing her hand on my left shoulder.

"Why aren't those police officers doing anything?" I ask, pointing towards the cars.

"They are doing things. They are waiting for further instruction," she states, sitting down beside me. "I'm more concerned about you. You're looking unwell. You need something in your body, even if it's just a drink. You need to be fit and well for Lucy."

"Fine, I'll have some tea," I say because I know she is right. My head is pounding from the stress of the situation, and not having anything to drink is irritating it more. I want painkillers. My head and shoulder are driving me mad.

Chapter Fourteen

"Hey, baby," Mark says, sliding down beside me.

I let out a little smile. "Hi."

"Do you need anything?" he asks.

"A hug and some painkillers," I admit.

"I can do that," he states, pulling me close to him.

"Thank you." I feel secure in Mark's arms, like I belong.

"I'll get you those painkillers," he says, standing up. I don't want him to leave me to get them, but I need something for the pain. It's almost unbearable.

I glare back out the window, watching the police cars. There are four of them now, remaining idle and it's annoying me. I suddenly see an older gentleman with grey hair and bright green eyes walking up to the house. He's carrying a black briefcase.

I don't hear a knock on the door as Mark quickly appears in front of me with a box of painkillers.

"Megan, this is Dr. Kirk," Mark tells me.

I turn to him as he speaks. "Hi, Miss Madden."

"Call me Megan," I state. This is the man that I saw walking towards the door. He has taken off his black suit jacket since he walked inside the house, revealing a blue and white striped shirt paired with black trousers.

"I hear you had a little accident," he says.

"I'm fine. I collapsed, that's all. I haven't eaten all day. What do you expect?" I respond swiftly, shrugging my shoulders at him. I'm not trying to be rude, but really, I don't need a doctor. I just need to eat something. Why does everyone think they know what is best for me? If

Annabella or Natasha asks me one more time if I want a cup of tea, I will scream. I know they are trying to help, but I'm fine.

"Can I check your shoulder? Mark is concerned. Then, I will leave you alone, if that's what you wish," Dr. Kirk replies, trying to reason with me. If this will mean I will be left alone, then great.

"Fine," I say in a petulant voice.

"Do you want to take a seat over there?" he asks, pointing over to the wooden bar stools.

"Okay," I reply, taking a seat to comply. I was happier by the kitchen window where I could see everything, but I will do anything to shut him up. His voice is annoying me today. I must be tired because everything is getting on my nerves today.

He places his hand on my left shoulder, lifting the injured area and checking for movement before turning his attention to my right one. It hurts badly. I just hope it's nothing serious. As he assesses the damage, I can't help but wiggle around in the chair. I'm unable to follow his simple instructions because my shoulder hurts like hell.

"Megan, I need to have a look under your top," he says, slowly lifting my top at the hem. What the hell does he think he is doing? Did I say it was okay? Oh, man. I can't wait until he fucks off. "You have dislocated your shoulder."

"What is the treatment?" Mark chimes in, concerned.

"We need to reset it," Dr. Kirk states, moving around the stool so he is facing me.

"Okay, then do it." I clench my teeth.

"We can't do it here. I need to make sure that it aligns correctly. You need to go to the hospital," he says, taking a seat in front of me on another wooden stool and reaching into his briefcase. He pulls out a notepad and pen.

"Not until my daughter is back," I snap. There is no way in hell that I am leaving until I have Lucy back. Her safety is all that matters.

"Megan."

"Yes." I look up at him.

"It needs to be done safely. It's going to hurt."

"I know. Just do it," I beg. *I gave birth, so I'm sure I can cope with this.*

"I'll be back in a minute," he says, walking over to the other side of the room with Mark.

"Here is your tea." Natasha hands me a cup. *Here we go again. More tea that I don't want. Can't someone use their brain?*

"Thanks. Any news?" I enquire.

"Not yet. The police are with John. Once I know more I will tell you," Natasha states.

"Thank you," I reply.

I hear footsteps behind me. "Hi, Megan. I'm back," Dr. Kirk says.

"And..."

"I'll set it here, but there are some rules that Mark has agreed to," he confesses, looking at him.

I turn around abruptly. "What rules?" *It's my body and my choice. Why does Mark have to agree to Dr. Kirk's rules? Do I not exist?*

"One, you have to do this in my room. Two, you have to trust both of us. Three, you need to take plenty of painkillers after Dr. Kirk finishes. I will send Connor to get them for you. And, finally, once Lucy is home, you *have* to go to the hospital and have it x-rayed," Mark states in an authoritative voice.

"Fine."

Chapter Fifteen

"Right, I'm ready," I say, taking off my top and sitting on the side of the bed wearing just my bra. I couldn't care less what I look like right now. I just want my shoulder sorted and my daughter returned safely. I peer over to my shoulder; it's black and purple. No wonder it hurts like hell. I take the two painkillers from Mark's hand, swallowing them one at a time with the water.

"Megan, lie down and place your arm on here," Dr. Kirk instructs, pointing at a pillow. With my elbow situated on the pillow, he places more pillows behind my head. "Okay, Mark is going to place his hand under your shoulder, and I'm going to hold you here." He places one of his hands on my lower arm and one just above my elbow. "I'll pull."

"Please, just do it," I state, turning my head away because I don't want to watch. I have never had a dislocated shoulder before, so I really don't know what to expect. How can me just collapsing cause this?

"Deep breath," Dr. Kirk says. I heed his instruction, which is followed by severe pain that I have never felt before. My eyes start to water. I think I would rather give birth than this, but I can't show that it hurts to the lads because I need to appear strong.

"That feels right. Now, remember what I said, Megan."

"I will do and thank you." He places my arm in a sling before leaving me lying on my bed and walking off with Mark. I hear them talking about aftercare for my shoulder. I have to admit that it feels better. It's not hurting as much. I get up from the bed, grabbing my top to slip back on before walking past them to find Natasha for an update on Lucy.

"Any news?" I ask.

"Kind of," she says, taking a seat on one of the bar stools and pointing at the one next to her. "John knows where she is."

"And?" I add as I sit down.

"He doesn't want his daughter anywhere near Mark. He states that if you stay with Mark, you lose Lucy for life."

I sit there stunned. She is our daughter. He can't do this to me. "What do I do?" I question.

"Legally, if he is her father, he has rights to her, so you can't really do anything. Who is listed on her birth certificate?"

"Just me," I respond. John wasn't on the scene. Do people not listen to me? You need both parents' signatures when the certificate is made. If only one parent is present, the other one isn't listed on the certificate.

"Then, he has no rights legally without that," she informs me.

I listen as Mark shows Dr. Kirk out. I know what I have to do. It's going to kill the man I love, but I have to do it. I just hope he will understand.

Chapter Sixteen

I take a deep breath because I don't want to do this. I stand up, leaving Natasha sitting there. I run up the stairs to Mark's room and start packing my things. Well, the things I need. Mark has bought a lot of things to save me time from bringing my things here when I come over. He even bought some things I don't need.

Tears fall from my eyes like rivers. I feel my heart breaking. I'm losing both my child and the man I love in the same day, but I have to do what is right. If I leave Mark, John will give me my daughter back. I plan to make sure John will never come anywhere near her again.

I quickly type a text to Luke. He might be Rich's best friend, but since Jenny and Rich split, he has become a big part of everyone's life.

Hi, are you in London at the moment?

I finish packing my things, making sure I have everything I need. Hurrying over to Lucy's room, I throw her things into her bag. I can leave some of my things behind, but not Lucy's. She needs everything. I have been very lucky with Mark. He has treated Lucy as his own, even decorating a nursery for her in his house. The room is fully painted in cream with a pink strip in the middle and adorned in a teddy bear theme. He even had some things made for her room, including a toy box with her name engraved on it. Mark has completely spoiled her, making me question what it will be like when he has his own children. Will he spoil them like he has Lucy?

"What's going on?" Mark asks, standing in the doorway.

"I'm leaving you," I answer. My heart shatters into a million pieces once the words come out of my mouth. Words I had never planned to say.

"What?" he yells. I have never seen him so angry before. His eyes are bulging.

"I'm sorry. I love you," I state, rubbing his arm. Standing on my tiptoes, I place a little kiss on his cheek. I need to be close to him one last time. I feel like such a cow. I can't explain anything to him; hopefully, he will understand when I'm gone and not do anything stupid.

"Then, why are you leaving me?" he enquires, pushing me away with one hand.

"John."

"What about him?" he asks.

I grab my things and walk past him. If I tell him, it will make everything harder, and I don't need to further complicate the situation. I will just have to learn to live again without Mark because I can't see him ever taking me back again.

I look down at my mobile, seeing Luke answered me more than once.

Yes, babe. I'm in town. Xx

Jen just told me what happened. Anything I can do? Xx

Babe, I'm on my way to Mark's. Xx

I'm so happy to hear from Luke. He will let me stay with him. I can't see him leaving me alone. I just need to get away from Mark; I'm too scared to be alone. Hearing him yell at me and begging me to stay is killing me. Doesn't he understand this? Doesn't he know how much I love him? I just hope Natasha will tell him what John said and that he will catch on to what I am doing.

Chapter Seventeen

"Megan, stop!" Mark shouts as he follows me.

"What?"

"Explain, please. Why are you leaving me?" he pleads.

"If I stay with you, I lose my daughter and I don't know where she is, who has her or if she is safe. You need to understand this," I reply, grabbing hold of my dark purple jacket from the coat rack.

"I don't understand. The police will find her." I continue walking, straight out the door and along the gravel driveway. Tears pour from my eyes. I don't want to leave him.

"Hey, babe," Luke calls as he pulls up beside me.

"Hi, I've left Mark," I say.

"What?" he exclaims. "Get in the car!"

I do what he asks before telling him everything. I feel like I have nothing to hide with Luke. I have never had this kind of relationship with him before. It's like he has saved me. Saved me from more pain.

As the tears stream, I raise my hands, covering my eyes. I need to move forward in order to find my daughter.

"You're coming to mine. No arguing. I know what you're like, babe. I will contact the police and tell them," Luke states.

"Thank you."

Okay, I know Luke is loaded, but really? This car is so swish. It's a red, which I did expect, convertible with leather seats that have a red "LG" embroidered on each headrest. I look down at my feet to see his car mats. I'm not at all surprised to find they are black with a red outline and have his initials in the middle to match the headrests.

"Posh car or what?" I observe.

"Posh, do you like?" he asks, taking his eyes off the road for a second to smile at me.

"It's a car. A car is a car to me," I answer.

"What?" he interjects.

"I don't really know cars."

"Well, babe. I'm going to have to teach you."

I laugh. "Anyway, how come your initials aren't under my bum?"

"Special seats, babe. I'll get you all hot instead." He presses a button. "Heated seats."

"Oh, great." I wiggle my bum.

I have never been to Luke's house before. I don't know where it is or anything. I look up as we drive down the road, keeping an eye out since Lucy could be anywhere.

As we turn down the street, I see a beautiful three-story house. "Is that all glass?" I ask.

"Oh, you know it is, babe," he says, winking at me.

"So, that means everyone can see everything," I point out.

"Babe, it's posh glass. You can see out, but no one can see in." He smiles wickedly.

Luke pulls the car into the camouflaged automatic drive next to the house and straight into the garage. I slide out of the car, looking out of the glass. I can see everything.

"I'll get your bags, babe." Luke goes to retrieve my belongings. I stand there clueless as to how I get out of this garage. It must be double-sized plus more. It's full of wooden storage containers and boxes on the shelves. I can't help but think this is really tidy. He must have a helper here.

"This way, babe," he instructs, pulling a little handle on one of the cream walls.

"Wow."

Luke turns and smiles.

Chapter Eighteen

I reach for my mobile to text John.

I have left Mark. Now, where is Lucy?

He replies a few seconds later.

He knows where she is. He needs to pay.

Pay?

I want £ 20,000.

I don't have that kind of money.

Mark does. Get it for me, and I'll tell you where she is.

I fall to the floor crying, unable to hear or see anything. Why is he doing this? I feel Luke's hand on my shoulder, and I pass him my mobile. I can't talk to him; I can't do anything. I need Lucy.

"What? That's a joke." He takes a deep breath. "Come with me. I'll ring the bank and get you the money."

"What? You can't do that," I state as Luke pulls me up from the floor.

"I can and I will," he answers, pulling out a red retro-style chair. Of course, it's red. I have figured out that he likes red. "Sit." I never knew Luke would or could be so selfless.

"It will take the rest of my life to repay you," I say, feeling my world fall apart.

"I don't want it back. You getting Lucy back is all that matters."

"Thank you. I have to do something or give you something in return." I'm not letting this drop.

Luke pulls out a flat, handheld device from the wooden drawer. It is some kind of posh wireless Internet thing that I've never seen before. "You can design something for me."

"Deal." I can do that.

Luke pulls out his mobile, calling Natasha and telling her where I am as he clicks away on his online banking account. I'm impressed with his multitasking skills.

"Find out where John wants the money," he instructs me. I quickly send John another text.

John, where do you want the money?

Once you have it, I'll tell you where to come. Cash. I only want cash.

I read the message to Luke.

"Will you be okay here while I get the money?"

I nod, but I really don't know. Only time will tell. He gives me a brief tour of where everything is, telling me to treat it like my home. How can I? If I were home, Lucy would be with me.

I hear my mobile chime.

Megan, Mark is really going out of his mind here. Jen told me where you are. I'm on my way. Mia xoxo

I don't want to see her. I don't want to see anyone but my daughter. Why can't people leave things as they are? I can't have Mia here. If John finds out, I might lose Lucy forever.

Chapter Nineteen

"Megan." I hear Mia bellow as she walks into the house.

I stand up from the sofa, turning myself around to see where her voice is coming from. Who let her in? Luke has been gone about thirty minutes.

"Sorry. I let myself in," she says, hurling towards me.

"Oh."

"Why did you leave?" she asks, standing in front of me with her hands on her hips.

"John," I reply in disgust. Even his name makes me cringe.

"What about that wanker?" she enquires.

"He said I had to choose either Mark or Lucy. I can't lose my daughter. I don't want to lose Mark either, but I have no choice," I whisper.

"Why didn't you tell Mark?" she asks.

"I couldn't and it was killing me. I didn't want to leave. I want Mark. I can't imagine my life without him." I slip down on sofa, lowering my head as a tear rolls down my face.

"If you explain everything to him, I'm sure he would understand," Mia says in a comforting voice. I feel her hand rubbing my knee and look up to see her on her knees beside me.

"I can't lose Lucy though," I state.

"I understand. Isn't there something you two could work out? I mean, stay apart until you have Lucy and then get back together?" Mia suggests.

"I hope we can, but I can't get back with him until I know my daughter is safe, and the courts and everything else is over," I respond.

"You need to talk to him, Megan. He has been smashing things inside the house. He is heartbroken," she informs me in a pained voice.

I reach for my mobile from the glass coffee table. This doesn't fit in with the rest of the décor of the room. I do like the style; I bet he had some posh designer decorate the house because I can't imagine Luke doing this. The house is located in Yorkshire and is perfect for his style. It definitely suits the man I know.

I type a comforting text to Mark.

Mark, I love you. Don't smash things up. John said it was you or Lucy. You know that I can't pick you over my daughter. I don't want you out of my life. XX

"I have always wanted to have a look in this house. Luke is like super famous," Mia states, standing in front on the window and rubbing her hands up the curtains. They are black with red circles. I would hate to see the curtains closed; they would be really alarming.

"How did you know where Luke lived?" I ask with an inquisitive look.

"I know those kinds of things. Don't forget I love his movies. Oh, and his arse, too."

"Mia!"

"What?" She pauses. "I'm being honest."

I can't believe that. I know she loves the men. Well, she loves the attention men give her, but really? Luke is sort of a friend. I would never look at his arse.

"Anyway, why did you get changed? You were in a dress," I ask. I want to know because she spent time getting changed when I needed her as an extra set of eyes to help me look for Lucy.

"I didn't think it was suitable for the day. I looked out of the window and saw the dark clouds, then when you asked about Lucy, I knew I had to dress sensibly," she replies, shrugging her shoulders.

Why is time going by so slowly? It seems like hours since Luke left, but it's only been about fifty minutes. I can't stop looking at my mobile. Every little noise I hear makes me check it. I need to make sure I don't miss anything from John. I can't let him mess me around; he has hurt me too much today. He has destroyed by life. There is no way he will ever be able to fix this.

I'm pulled away from my thoughts at the sound of an incoming text from Luke.

Hey, babe. I got the money. On way back. XX

Thank you, Luke. I will owe you for life. XX

I walk over to my bags in the dining room. When I arrived, Luke placed my bags there out of the way. I quickly search through my bag, taking out my mobile charger. I can't have my mobile go dead. I need to contact John.

I have the money. Now what?

I go into the kitchen, finding the nearest outlet. I have some charge, but I'm not going to risk it. After placing my mobile on charge, I sit at the bar.

"Natasha is here," Mia bellows as she comes walking back into the room. I have no idea what she is doing or where she has been. I will find out when I have both the time and energy to care about her.

Chapter Twenty

I pace the kitchen back and forth. Why isn't John answering me? I'm surprised Mark hasn't answered me either. Everyone seems to be taken their own time. Luke should be back by now, and Connor should have my medication here. Why is everything taking so long? Natasha has a police officer with her in the dining room, trying to find out more information, but I still don't know where the money is to be dropped off. I don't care about anything apart from Lucy.

"Babe, I'm home," Luke calls as he runs through the door with a black and grey hold all bag.

"Thank you, Luke. I owe you everything." I pause. "I mean *everything*."

"You owe me nothing," he states, standing in front of me. He turns his head around the massive open room, seeing people he has never met before.

"I'm sorry. That's the liaison lady Natasha and a police dude I have never met. Over there is Mia."

"Oh, Mark's sister," he says, winking mischievously at her.

"Hey, no flirting. She already wants your arse."

"Oh, really?"

I stand there giggling and shaking my head. I suddenly hear the ping on my mobile and run to it.

The park down West Street near the river. NO POLICE.

Fine, what time?

15 minutes or Lucy is gone.

"Luke, I need to borrow a car," I say.

"You're not driving, hun. You can't because of your shoulder," he points out.

"I don't care about my shoulder anymore. Are you letting me have a car or what?" I snarl.

"No, I'm driving you." He bends down, grabs the bag, and flies out of the door towards the car. I run after him with my mobile in hand. Stopping at the front door, I turn around to face Mia.

"Mia, don't tell Mark anything. I will be back soon!" I yell.

I run into the garage, finding the car with Luke already inside. It's the same one he picked me up in earlier. I quickly jump in the passenger side. Before I'm even fastened in, he is already driving.

"Luke, you don't have to do this. I can do it on my own," I inform him.

"I know, but I need to keep you safe. I promised Jenny," he states.

I sit watching the roads. I feel so shaky because I don't know what to expect. I hope John just hands Lucy over to me and realizes what he has done.

"We are here," Luke says as we pull up into a car park on a hill. Turning off the engine, he gets out of the car. I unfasten my seat belt, slide out of the car, and inhale a deep breath. This park is enormous. Mark brought me here when Lucy was a month old. We had a lovely long walk and a picnic. I pull out my mobile and send John a text.

John, I'm here. Where are you?

By the river.

"He's by the river," I tell Luke.

We walk through the car park and down into the grassy area of the park. When we pass through a few trees, I see the river.

"You should stay here, please, just in case I need you. You can see him from here," I say as I point out where John is. Luke slowly passes me the hold all.

Chapter Twenty-One

"John, here is the money. Now, where is Lucy?" I enquire, standing in front of him, but with a little bit of distance between us. I'm scared he is going to hurt me. There is no way I'm giving him any of the money until I have Lucy back. I keep a tight grip on the hold all in my arms.

I have never seen John wear such an outfit. He's very untidy in blue jogging bottoms with holes in them and a brown short-sleeved top that shows off his arms. It's not at all what I'm used to seeing him in. His hair is messed up and mucky looking. As I look down his arms, I see cuts. What the hell is going on?

"Someone else has her." He pauses. "Come with me." He grabs hold of my wrist so tight that I'm unable to pull away. He leads me along the riverside, and I'm forced to willingly walk with him.

"Let go of me," I say in a solid voice. I don't want to make a scene since I don't know what will happen if people notice. I need to get to Lucy.

He lets go a little, but only a little bit, so some of the feeling returns in my hand. I wish he would just trust me; he knows I'm not going to run. I would lose Lucy if I did that. "Is Lucy safe?" I ask. I need to know she is safe. I knew he wouldn't have Lucy with her. But who could have her? Who would he trust with my child?

"I don't know nor do I care," he replies, pulling me in close to him and locking his arms around my back. I wiggle, trying to get free. "Stay close." He places his lips on mine, forcing me to kiss him. His hand clenches the back of my head, making it impossible for me to get free. As John tries to force his tongue down my throat, I edge my foot slowly forward into the gap between his feet. I quickly lift my knee, hitting him square in his groin.

"Don't you ever fucking do that to me again!" I shriek between gritted teeth as he bends down in pain.

"You fucking bitch! That hurt!" he yells, holding his cock and trying to catch his breath.

"Don't make a scene, John. Give me my daughter."

John stands up tall, rubbing his cock. "Walk now," he states with pure anger in his eyes. He grabs my wrist again, tighter than the first time.

"Why do you want all this money? You don't care about our daughter," I spit out. I need to know the truth.

"She wants Mark to pay."

"Who does?"

"You will find out soon. Cross over here," he says, pointing over to the main road. I do what he asks, walking straight over the calm road. I don't turn around to see if Luke is following us. I don't want John to know he is here. I need to keep him safe, so he can save me.

"John, I need answers."

"I'm not talking. Go into the third house on your left. It has a black door."

John lets go of my wrist, setting me free. I rub my wrist, trying to clear the red marks his fingers left behind. I rush ahead towards the houses, keeping the money close to me. I find the house and open the door. I walk inside, but I can't see anything. It's all pitch black. Why is it dark? Why would he let our daughter be in here?

"Lucy!" I yell.

"She is upstairs," John says, grabbing hold of my upper arms tightly and turning me around. "Walk. The stairs are there." I follow his instructions. I'm so scared. What is up there?

I am greeted by bright light. I turn around slowly, seeing a black figure. I take small, cautious steps towards it.

"Karen Walker, what the hell are you doing with my daughter?!"

452

Chapter Twenty-Two

"Hello, Megan," Karen says. "I bet you didn't think you would see me again." That's right. I haven't seen her in months, not since the first time I came down here. I haven't even heard Mark say anything about her.

I walk closer towards her, gradually taking one small step at a time. Looking down at the floor, all I can see is glass. What has happened here? Where is Lucy? I can't see her anyway; it's too dark. I can't see any signs of a baby.

"Karen, where is Lucy?" I ask, trying to keep my composure.

Karen seemed like a nice girl. What the hell is going on?

"Give John the money!" she yells.

I turn around slightly, grabbing hold of a wooden panel to steady myself. I reach out with the bag, giving it to John. He takes it, pulling it close to his chest.

"I'm done with you now, John. Go! Don't ever speak of this."

"What?" I shout, swiftly turning my head towards Karen. "Why is he going?" I ask. I need to keep calm, but I don't think I can. Where is Lucy? Why is Karen letting John go? I need answers, and I need them now.

"I don't want John. I want Mark," she says, seizing my wrist and dragging me into the room.

"Ouch!" I yelp.

"Oh, grow up, you silly fucking slut!" she yells, pushing me against the wall.

I stand there, not showing fear. "Where is Lucy?" I question boldly.

"Over there," she says, not moving.

"Can I have my daughter, please?" I ask.

"No, you will do what I want. You will get Mark to come here and then I will let both you and Lucy go!" she roars with the smell of garlic spouting from her mouth as she spits at me.

"Why do you want Mark?" I probe.

"He needs to be punished."

"Why?"

"Stop with the stupid questions, you fucking bitch."

"Okay." I reach down for my mobile, pulling it out. After I unlock it, I see unread messages, including one from Mark. I take a deep breath. I can't read it. As my hands tremble terribly, I find Mark's name in my contacts and press the *Call* button.

"Mark! Don't say anything. Just do as I ask, please." I pause. "Come alone to West Park and cross over the road towards the row of houses. They are the ones set back on the way to the lake. Go to the third one. It has a black door. Come inside and walk upstairs." I take another deep breath to control my nerves. "No one can come with you, and I mean no one."

I hang up before he has a chance to say anything else. I can't talk to him any longer.

"He is on his way," I state. "Can I see Lucy now?"

"Come," she states in a firm voice. I follow her across the large room that only has a couple of chairs in it and nothing else. The windows are covered in what looks to be black bin bags with slight openings in them, letting the light seep through them. I keep blinking, as the light is so bright that it's hurting my eyes. "There," she says, pointing down to the floor. "Sit." I do as she asks. Karen slowly opens the bin bags further, letting the light shine directly into the room. I look to my side where she stands to see that she is wearing a very short black dress, so short I can see that she isn't wearing any underwear. Her feet are bare with only the black dust from the floor covering them.

"Lucy?"

"Stay there. I will get her for you." She turns, walking along the window and then turns back around with a little box in front of her, kicking it towards me. "There."

I look inside the box to see Lucy still as anything could ever be with a newspaper covering her body. The box is so tiny; she is squished in it. Tears roll down my face. My baby. I slowly lift her out of the box. Her arms and legs are so floppy; she is completely limp.

"What have you done to my baby?!" I yell.

Chapter Twenty-Three

"I said what have you done to my baby?" I continue sitting there, yelling at Karen. She just stands there, motionless. The stupid cow has done something to my baby. I place Lucy on the floor, ensuring that she is breathing. There is only a slight movement in her chest, and the colour in her lips is a dull blue.

"What have you done?" I yell again, jumping up to my feet and leaving Lucy on the floor. I storm right up to Karen, squaring up eye-to-eye with her. "Are you fucking deaf?" I push her backwards against the wall. "What have you done?" I continue to shout. "Answer me, bitch!"

"It's just sleeping tablets and some Class A," she says, pushing me backwards with such force that I end up on my back on the floor.

"You know she could die because of what you did." I pause. "Can I leave with Lucy now?"

"No."

I turn over onto my knees and crawl to my daughter. I sit there, rubbing her chest. "Lucy, I love you. Mummy will get you out of here. You will be okay, baby girl." I begin singing to her. The sound of my voice should keep her going. I need to get us out of here. "Karen? Why do you want Mark?" I ask.

"He has to pay," she states, walking towards me.

"For what?" I question. *Why am I here?*

"Oh, he knows what."

"Will you tell me?" I ask. I really need to know and keeping her talking means she can't hurt Lucy or me anymore. I hope.

"Call him!" she yells.

"Okay." I quickly take out my mobile, finding Mark's contact information and pressing the picture of him holding Lucy under a tree during our first visit to West Park. He sat there for ages telling her different stories about fairies dancing around the magic tree. It was absolutely perfect. I felt so blessed, not only with an incredible baby girl, but also with an amazing man.

"Mark, where are you?" I ask. "Hurry, please." I turn to Karen. "He is in the park now," I inform her.

"Good." She walks over to the other side of the room, hitting the switch to turn off the lights.

I sit there in pure darkness. I quickly take off my jacket, placing it in my arm to wrap Lucy. I slowly pick her up, holding her in the crook of my arm and pulling my jacket around her. I restart rubbing her chest. I keep placing my hand over her mouth at a distance, feeling her inhale and exhale. "I love you, Lucy."

"Megan!" I hear Mark yell as he runs up the stairs, knocking against things as he makes his way closer to us. "Ouch!"

I watch Karen's shadow walk into the doorway. "You will pay, Mark!" she screams. Her shadow disappears, and I hear a large *thud*, like someone has fallen. There are no sounds from Mark. *Oh, no! What has she done?*

Karen's shadow then disappears.

Chapter Twenty-Four

I sit there with my back against the wall, motionless. I hear nothing, just silence. The type of silence that feels eerie, making me look around the room all the time. I feel like there is someone or something watching me. Where has she gone? What has she done with Mark? I need to get out of here and find him.

Taking a deep breath, I slowly stand up from the floor, leaning my back on the empty wall as I stand. I keep a tight hold on Lucy, pulling her even closer to my chest and wrapping my arms around her back to keep her supported. I'm hoping my jacket will keep her warm, because she feels cold to me. This can't be a good sign. I can't let anything else happen to her; it's my job as a mum to protect her in every way I can. I'm never going to let her out of my sight again. I can't.

I deftly take small steps towards the door, looking at the floor as I walk. I don't want to step on whatever is on the floor. Due to the darkness, I can't quite make out what everything on the floor is, but I can see some things that look like screws from a toolbox and little gaps in the hardwood. I just hope I don't hear any creaks in it. I don't want Karen to see me or hear me. I need to get out. Once I'm out, I can call for help. I take another small step and lean forward a little bit, seeing a shadow on the stairs. Who is it? What is it? I'm not even sure it looks like a person. Is it my mind playing tricks on me?

I carefully take another step towards the door, taking a deep breath as I close the distance. *I can do this. I have to do this*, I keep this mantra on replay in my mind. My daughter's life is in danger. I pull Lucy even closer to my chest. As I exhale, I place a little butterfly kiss on her forehead. "I will get you out of here, Lucy. You are my world. I love you."

I lift my head, straightening my back. I walk out of the room hastily, taking a sharp turn onto the landing where there is some light creeping through the windows. The shadow is gone.

"Megan!" Karen yells, but I don't respond. I can't. I don't want her to find me. **There is a long pause.** "Megan, I can see you," she says, pronouncing each word slowly while coming out from behind a corner and straight towards me.

"You have Mark. You don't need me," I state as I stand there holding my ground. I enclose my arms further over Lucy, trying to protect her from Karen as much as I can.

"I haven't finished with you yet," she says calmly as she walks towards me, placing her hands on my shoulders and directing me backwards back into the room.

I can't believe how unsafe I feel. I would walk back in myself, but I don't have a clue what is going on.

"Stay in here. I will be back," she says, pushing me backwards even more. I wobble a bit, taking a step back onto an unsteady floorboard that breaks, causing me to fall down. *Ouch! That really hurt.* I shake my shoulders. I'm extremely lucky that I managed to keep a grip on Lucy. I refuse to let any more harm come to her.

Karen storms out of the room, her feet banging against the floorboards as she exits. I can still hear her loud feet shuffling in the next room. What is she doing? I move Lucy from my chest, positioning her back in the crook of my arm. Her breathing doesn't seem to be getting any better at all, and her face is getting paler. I'm losing my daughter. My eyes well up with tears again, but I can't cry, though. I need to be strong for Lucy. I need to get us out of here.

I lower Lucy down onto the floor, leaving her lying on my jacket. I look over my shoulder in the faint light to see what looks like blood coming from it. *No wonder it was hurting so much.* I gradually move my hand down it, feeling sharp edges, almost like glass and the warmth of blood trickling down my fingers. That bitch has hurt me again.

"Megan!" Karen yells as she storms into the room, dragging something behind her along the floor.

I quickly pick up Lucy. "Yes."

"Put her in that box!" she bellows, kicking the box towards me.

"She has a name." I slowly move towards the same box that Lucy had been in when I found her.

460

"Put the fucking, stupid baby in the fucking box right now, you deaf fucking cow!"

I speed up, doing what she asked. She is seriously mad. I gently place Lucy into the box. "I love you, Lucy," I whisper into her ear.

"Get here now, you slut!" Karen shouts.

I sluggishly rise from the floor as agonizing pain shoots through my shoulder. I look down at the floor and see shards of glass with blood on them. *How did I not notice them before?*

Chapter Twenty-Five

"You stay there, you stupid bitch!" she howls as I sit there on my knees, listening. I'm so scared. What is going on? What has she done with Mark? I can't see what she has behind her. Is it a person? I'm lost in my thoughts when she begins to talk again. "Give me the box!" she yells.

"Why? Lucy is okay there," I state. I can't give her Lucy. I just can't.

"Give me the box, or I will kill her," she commands in a forceful voice.

"Don't hurt her. Kill me instead. She is an innocent baby. Just let her go, please," I beg, slowly standing up.

"The. Box. *Now.*"

I bend down, picking up the box and placing both of my arms underneath it. I don't want it to break, but it feels like it might. It's covered in rips, and the bottom of it feels damp on my bare arm. I'm glad I used my jacket around her. I just wish it was a bigger box. A tear rolls down my face as I stand in front of Karen.

"Place it down there," she says evenly, pointing to the floor at the other side of her.

Bending down, I'm able to see what it is that she has hidden behind her. It is a person, but it's too dark to see their face.

"Get over here now!" she yells.

I quickly move to where she wants me to go. I stand there, watching while she drags the body behind her. It is catapulting up and down over the many cracks in the floor. That has got to hurt. She walks past me and drops the body at my feet.

"Stay," she instructs before walking hastily out of the room.

I bend down, gently rolling the body onto its back. "Mark," I say, shaking his shoulders. "Come on, Mark." I whisper. I can't have her find me talking to him.

"Right, you help me get him on this chair," she calls, storming through the door and dragging a chair behind her. She reaches to close the door, causing the room to go dark again.

I stand there immobile. *Why? What is she going to do to him?* I really need to get us all out of here. I can't cope with losing Lucy or Mark. "Come on, you stupid bitch," she says, grabbing hold of Mark's wrist.

I lower myself, placing one arm under his and my other around his back. I don't want to hurt him, but I best do as she asks. I need help. I wonder if I can ring Luke, if he will try to get some help. I need her to leave the room again. I have a silly password on my mobile, so that's going to be a massive problem since I can't have her see the light from it as I put in the number.

"Lift on three?" I suggest.

"No, fucking drag him, you stupid cunt!" she shouts.

"One... Two... Three," I say, but luckily she doesn't move him on three. Instead, she pulls his arm up in the air, and I manage to get him into the chair as safely as I can, although it really hurts me doing it.

"Mark, wake up now," she states before slapping him across the face with such force that he flops off the chair. "Help me get him up," she adds.

I continue to do as she asks because I think it has now become the better option. If I work with her, hopefully, we will all get out alive.

I watch as Karen reaches over to a bag that I had noticed earlier. I can't see much of the bag to see the style or what's inside it, but I had managed to figure out it was a bag.

"Time to be tied up, Mark," she bellows as she walks behind the chair, pulling his arms behind him. I stand there in shock. I can't get the words out of my mouth. I just can't. "Right," she says before storming back over to the bag with her back towards me. I quickly pull out my mobile, entering the four-digit code and finding Luke's name. I press *Call* before sliding the mobile back into my pocket. I just hope this works.

"One last job for you, Megan. Then, you and your stupid baby can go free," she states, walking over to me. "Shoot him. I want the bastard dead."

Chapter Twenty-Six

"Oi, I told you to shoot him," she says, glaring at me and reaching behind her back to pull out a gun from the top of her trousers. She waves the handgun towards me.

"Why? What has he done?" I ask. I need to know why. I am not going to harm him; he is my baby. My world. I can't do it.

"He knows what he did," she says.

"Mark, what did you do?" I ask.

"Mmm..." Mark grunts.

"Mark, please wake up!" I yell with tears rolling down my face. I need him to wake up. Karen grabs hold of my wrist, turning my hand over and slamming the gun into my palm. I have never held a gun before or even seen one in person. I have seen them on television programs before, but this is different. This one is real. It can really hurt someone. I don't have a clue how to use it, and I don't want to know.

"Do it!" she yells, clearly annoyed.

"I can't. He hasn't done anything wrong in my eyes," I state.

"He has. My sister is in prison because of him. If he had just given her the money, everything would be fine," she says, trying to remain calm.

"We can sort this out like adults."

"*Adults*? I don't think so. Shoot him!" she screams. There is a slight pause before she speaks again. "Megan, shoot Mark, or I will shoot Lucy!"

Those last words numb me, and I suddenly feel something rising in my throat. I turn around quickly and throw up. I can't do this. I just can't. I won't. Tears pour from my eyes.

"Megan, get on with the job," she says, grabbing my hair and pulling it back.

"Do it, Megan." I hear Mark suddenly say. I spin myself fully around.

"Mark, I can't," I state.

"Do … it…I… love… you," he says, all broken up. What has she done to him? He seems out of it.

"Just fucking do it!" Karen yells.

"I have never held a gun before. I don't know how to shoot."

"Just point and pull that," she explains, attempting to show me the trigger. The light is too dim for me to see.

"I can't."

"This might help then." She storms over to the wall near Lucy, switching on the light. I close my eyes, rubbing them because the light is so bright. I slowly open them and instantly wish I hadn't. I place my hand over my mouth. I thought the smell in this room was bad enough, but seeing Mark makes everything suddenly worse.

"Now shoot!" she roars.

"No!" I shout back. "Look at the mess of him and the mess in the room. It's not right at all. If you want money, I will get you some. Just leave Mark alone."

I look over at Mark, noticing more cuts on his face. His shirt is covered in holes, and there is blood on his arms. *What happened to him?*

"Just shoot him!"

"Answer some questions for me first." I pause. "Why is there glass and stuff on the floor?"

"It's from the mirrors I smashed over Connor's head."

"Connor?" I question, not knowing the connection.

"Yes, Connor."

"Mark's Connor?"

"Yes!" she growls.

"Where is he?" I ask. *What the hell?* I don't get this woman at all. Why has she got Connor? Has he got something to do with it?

"Shoot Mark now."

"No!" I yell. "I'm not going to shoot him."

"Fine," she says really calmly, turning on her heel and walking over to Lucy.

"Leave her alone!" I shriek.

"No! Shoot him."

I stand there shaking, slowly managing to raise the gun. If I pretend to pull the trigger, she might leave Lucy alone. Or should I shoot her? I need her away from Lucy first. My hands are too shaky. I don't want to shoot either of the people I love.

"Just ... do ... it," Mark stutters.

I watch Karen bend down, grabbing hold of Lucy by her arm and pulling her from the box. My heart breaks. My baby girl looks so lifeless.

"Get off her!" I yell.

She pulls another gun from her pocket, pointing it at Lucy's head. "Do it."

I take a deep breath and pull the trigger.

BANG!

Chapter Twenty-Seven

As if everything is moving in slow motion, I watch Mark's chair fall over to the side. I can't believe I just did that. I love him.

"Now give me Lucy!" I shout, releasing my hold on the gun and placing it on the floor. I run over to Lucy, placing my arm around her and pulling her from that cow.

"Police! Place your hands where I can see them!" I hear a man yell as he runs into the room.

I collapse to the floor, pulling Lucy close to my chest. "I love you, Lucy. Auntie Jenny will look after you. Mummy is going away for a little while, but I will be back." Tears roll down my face. I push the gun away from me and pull Lucy closer to my lips. Tilting my head down, I place a little kiss on her head. I look up to see Karen with three police officers, screaming and fighting to get away from them.

"No, sir. You can't go in there!" I hear another man yell as Luke runs into the room straight to me, wrapping his arms around me.

"You're a very brave lady, Megan," he says, rubbing my back as tears run down my face.

"I killed him," I whisper.

"Don't worry about that, babe. Everything will be fine."

"Lucy needs help. Karen gave her something, and she's not acting right," I state, inhaling a large breath.

"Medic, over here, please!" Luke yells over my shoulder. "One is on her way now."

"Hi, Miss. What's happened here?" the young lady with red hair neatly tied up into a bun asks.

"Karen," I pause, pointing towards her, "drugged my baby."

"May I have a look?" she asks.

I nod, passing her Lucy.

"Miss, what is her name?" she enquires.

"Lucy," I state, forcing back more tears. I need to be strong for Lucy.

"Miss, I'm going to have to take her to the hospital. I need to get her to a doctor as soon as possible," she informs me as she waves over a police officer.

"Luke, I have lost everything," I say, lowering my head and covering my eyes.

"Sir, this young lady can go to the hospital with her daughter. We can get a statement there." I hear him say.

"What?" I exclaim. "I thought you would arrest me."

"Go and be with your daughter," he says.

"Come on, Megan," Luke says, slowly helping me up from the floor. I glance over towards Mark, seeing loads of people around him, but I can't directly see him.

"Connor!" I yell. "She said she had him. He is hurt."

"Okay, we will find him," the police officer says.

I follow the medic holding Lucy down the stairs and onto the street. Luke remains behind me with his hand softly placed on my back, rubbing it and trying to keep me calm. I keep sniffing back tears.

"Please get into the ambulance. We will be leaving immediately," the medic says.

I turn around, looking at Luke. "Will you stay with me?" I ask.

"I'm not leaving, babe."

Luke helps me into the ambulance, letting me use his hand to get up. I'm so lucky he is here with me. I don't think I could manage otherwise. I sit there, looking at Lucy. When did they place a breathing tube down her throat? I don't even remember anyone saying anything about it. I knew she wasn't right. I watch as the medic monitors the machines while rubbing her chest.

"Lucy, you can make it. Mummy loves you."

"We are here," the ambulance driver says as he jumps out of the cab. I never even realised we had started to move. I'm totally in my own world. The house couldn't have been far from the hospital then. But still, I seem to be losing time. I sit there as they take Lucy out of the ambulance, listening to them walk away as they say a load of things I can't make sense of.

Luke is great; he has been answering questions about Lucy for me. I can't talk. I'm in a complete daze.

"Come on. Let's go find Lucy," Luke says, standing with his hand waiting for me.

Chapter Twenty-Eight

I don't know what has happened in the past few minutes. The last thing I remember is watching them take away my daughter. I am now sitting on the side of a hospital bed with a man and woman around me. There is no sign of Luke. I look around the room, but the curtain is closed around me.

"Miss Madden?" the lady says, bending down in front of me.

I shake my head. "Yes," I say, but I don't hear anything. I don't hear my voice.

"Miss, can you talk to me?" she asks.

"Yes, I can," I say, but I still don't hear myself.

"Riley, can you go and get Dr. Black for me?" the lady asks.

What is going on? Not even a minute later, Riley reappears with a tall, dark-coloured man.

"Dr. Black, Miss Madden isn't talking. Even though she is trying, nothing is coming out," she informs him.

"Hi, Miss Madden. I'm Dr. Black, but call me Karl. I'm the head doctor on shift today. As my junior doctor said, we think you are in shock from the trauma of today's events. There isn't anything we can do to help your voice return. It should come back in time." He pauses. "If there is anything you need, please let one of my team or me know."

"How is Lucy?" I ask, rocking my arm back and forth.

Karl looks at Riley. "Keep an eye on her. Take observations every half hour. I will be back to check on her later. I will let you and Kathryn sort out her back and arm. Give me a shout if you need anything."

I feel so trapped. I can't get their attention. Why can't I speak? Seriously, is this from the trauma? I have a statement to make. I need to know that my daughter is okay. I need someone to help me.

"Hey, babe," Luke says as he walks around the curtain. I can't help but smile. Finally, someone I know.

"Sir, Miss Madden can't talk. Her body has reacted to the trauma by affecting her voice. It might be a short-term thing, but we don't know as of yet," Karl informs Luke.

"She doesn't like being called Miss Madden. It's Megan," he adds, slowly taking a seat beside me. "Trust me. I learned that a long time ago. Now, who is going to keep me under control with all these hot nurses running around?"

"First time I have been called 'hot' at work," Riley says, winking at him.

"Oh, man. I don't swing that way," Luke says, letting out a nervous laugh.

"How is Lucy?" I ask, rocking my arm back and forth again. Luke looks straight at my lips, trying to read them.

"Oh, Lucy?" Luke pauses. "She is being looked after. She is still asleep, babe. They are doing all they can."

Tears start rolling down my cheeks. I want to be with her. I need to see her. I promised her I wouldn't leave her alone. I can't break my promise.

"Megan, I'm just going to check your back and shoulder."

I just sit there, not moving. What's the point? No one is paying any attention to me. Luke keeps talking to me, trying to keep me calm. I don't care about my back or my shoulder. Yes, they hurt like hell, but I need to see Lucy while I can. Has everyone forgotten I'm a murderer?

"Megan, this will hurt. I'm going to take the shards of glass out of your back," Kathryn says, pulling them out slowly one by one.

"So, how long will this no voice thing last?" Luke questions.

"Well, it's different with each person, as it's a psychological issue. It depends on Megan."

"Okay, then," Luke says, giving me a funny look. "Oh, Jenny is on her way."

"What?" I yell, or at least, I think I yell.

476

"I can't understand you, babe. How about typing your response?" He passes me his mobile.

Using the keyboard, I type what I have been trying to tell him.

WHAT?

"I rang her. I thought you would need the support."

I type another response.

I need to see Lucy.

"Okay, hold on." He looks over to Kathryn. "Can Megan go and see her daughter?"

"Yes, that's not a problem. I will get the porter to go to Lucy's side room to get Megan when he is ready to take her for her shoulder x-ray," Kathryn states.

"Perfect," Luke says.

I can't help but smile at him. Finally, I'm getting somewhere.

"I'll get a chair," Riley says.

A chair? I type.

"Why does she need a chair?" Luke asks.

"Just to be on the safe side, sir. We don't want her hurting herself any further," Kathryn replies.

As Riley walks back into the little area, I stand up, getting myself straight into the chair. Come on. I want to see my baby girl.

Chapter Twenty-Nine

"Hey, this is Megan, Lucy's mum," Riley says as we walk into a large room through two revolving doors.

With Luke pushing me forward, we make our way towards Lucy, seeing all the empty space around her. In the middle of the room sits a hospital bed that is no different than any other one. I see Lucy, lying there on the bed. The tube is still in her mouth and attached to a machine. Luke pushes me further into the room, alongside the bed. She is so still, lifeless. My eyes start to well up and tears roll down my face. Why Lucy? I failed my baby girl. It's a mum's job to protect her child. *I failed her.*

"Hi, I'm Elizabeth, the doctor looking after Lucy today. She is on a machine that aids her breathing while we try to sort out everything. We need to find out what she has been given."

I nod. I want to know, too. I sit there, holding my daughter's freezing cold hand, slightly listening to Luke while he tries to find out all he can.

"John," I mouth incoherently, patting Luke. "John."

"What babe?" he asks. "Say it again, so I can read your lips."

"John."

"What about John?"

"Text him," I continue to mouth.

"Babe, I don't get it." He pauses. "Elizabeth, do you have some paper we could have?"

"Of course," she says, bringing over some paper for me to use.

Text John.

"Oh, why?" Luke questions.

He might know what she has had.

"Okay, will you be all right while I go and message him? I can't use my mobile in here with the machines," he states.

I shake my head yes and then turn back around to my baby. My baby girl. My world. I can't do anything for her but be here, holding her hand and watching her. I'm never letting her out of my sight again. I watch her chest rise and fall, hoping she will be breathing on her own again soon. Elizabeth explained that until whatever is in her system is dealt with appropriately, it will be too dangerous to see if she can breathe by herself.

"John knows," Luke announces as he walks back into the room.

"What?" Elizabeth exclaims.

"She was given sleeping tablets and cocaine," Luke adds.

"What?! Did he not think to let us know earlier?" Elizabeth asks, running over to the telephone attached to the wall on the far side of the room.

"Megan, he has owned up to everything, and he knows what Karen did. He is with the police at the moment. He doesn't have an issue with you being with Mark. Karen had his mobile, and she was using what she could find out against him," Luke states. "She was the one that kidnapped Lucy." What? What is going on? I can't deal with all of this. What is going to happen to my daughter? She has had Class A drugs, which can cause trouble later in life. *Oh, no.* I need Jenny. I need her here.

Elizabeth hurriedly walks back over to me. "Right, we are going to continue the current treatment with Lucy for now. We are just waiting on the rest of the toxicology screen to come back. Then, we can go from there."

I nod, keeping my watch on Lucy just lying there, so young. This isn't far.

"Megan." I turn around to see Riley. "Sorry, I need to take you for an x-ray."

Tears flow down my face as I grab the paper.

I don't want to go. I can't leave Lucy.

"Megan, you need to. I'm sure Luke will stay with her."

I look at Luke.

"I will stay. I'm not going anywhere," Luke says, placing a little kiss on my head.

I lean forward, placing a kiss on Lucy's petite hand before I'm wheeled away. As Riley pushes my wheelchair, I turn around and watch Lucy get further away from me.

Chapter Thirty

I face forward, looking past Riley. I don't want to leave my baby. I need to know she is going to be all right. I feel like such a bad mum.

"She is in safe hands, Megan," Riley says, rubbing my shoulder. He was definitely made for a job like this because he is very compassionate.

I give him a little smile. I know she is in good hands, but I should be with her. I lower my head to my knees. I don't want to see anyone. I should be locked up.

"Megan!" I hear a female's voice yell, and I'm sure I recognize it. "Megan!" The sound is getting closer, but I don't look up. I don't want to see her.

"Megan, there is a lady running after us. She wants you," Riley points out.

"Megan," she says, placing her hand on my shoulder.

I can't help but jump. That really hurts. I look up to see her. Mascara streaks line her face, and I can see the pain in her eyes and how angry she is.

"I did it. I killed Mark," I say.

"What?!" Mia exclaims.

"I. Killed. Mark."

"He's in surgery; he's not dead," Mia replies.

"What do you mean?" I cry out, turning around to gauge Riley's reaction to the news.

"Megan, I don't know anything about Mark," he states.

"I *need* to know Riley," I force out.

"I'll find out all I can once you have had the x-ray. Nice to finally hear your voice."

Oh, I didn't notice my voice had returned to normal. How did I not notice? Nothing makes sense today. My head hurts. Everything hurts. I just want answers. I need answers.

"Miss, I need to take Megan for an x-ray. Please, can you go with Olivia?" he asks, pointing at another nurse that I had seen floating around. "She will take you to the waiting room."

Riley pushes me into another room and right up to the wooden reception desk. "Miss Madden for her x-ray."

"Room Three, please."

"Here you go, Megan. You're back with Lucy. I stuck to my promise. You will need to be careful now. Your shoulder's been reset," Riley says, placing me beside Lucy's bed.

"Thank you."

"Wow, when you left, you couldn't speak. Now, you do?" Luke interjects.

"Yeah, I saw Mia. Mark isn't dead. He's in surgery."

"That's great," Luke says as a grin spreads across his face.

"I'm not sure yet. How is Lucy?" I ask Elizabeth.

"No change I'm afraid."

"Are the results back?" I enquire.

"Yes, I'm just waiting on the medication from the pharmacy." Elizabeth smiles, looking straight back down to her notes.

"Thank you, Elizabeth." I pause and turn towards Luke. "Luke, thank you. I don't know what I would have done without you."

"Hey, babe. I'm here anytime you need me."

I smile, turning my head back around to Lucy. Getting my baby girl better is my only priority right now.

"Babe."

"Yeah, Luke." I turn my head slightly to see him sitting in a chair behind me.

"Will you be okay if I just pop out for some air?"

"Yes, of course, don't be silly." I pause. "I need Lucy's stuff from yours."

"I'll get Jake to call and get it," he says, smiling at me.

Who is Jake? I have never met him before or even heard his name. I sit there, thinking. Did Luke ever work with a Jake?

Chapter Thirty-One

"Are you Miss Madden?" I hear a male voice ask. I turn myself around to see a tall, slim man with blonde hair dressed in a police uniform.

I feel my heart begin to sink. *Oh, no. I forgot that they would be coming.*

I take a deep breath. "I am."

"Ma'am, we need to talk to you in regards to today's incident." He pauses. "Can you come with me to the office?"

"I can't leave my daughter for too long," I state.

"We won't be too long, ma'am," he says, taking hold of the wheelchair handles.

"I love you, Lucy." I place a little kiss on her hand.

I don't see anyone as I'm pushed down the corridor and away from my daughter. It's too quiet. Where is everyone? We suddenly stop outside a white door with a glass panel and closed blinds. I raise my hand over my mouth. I feel sick. *Keep breathing, Megan. You can do this.*

"Hi, Miss Madden. I just want you to tell me in your own time what happened today," he says, taking a seat at the desk.

I turn to the side to see another male officer in uniform with his black notepad and pen, looking down.

"From the beginning when Lucy was taken or me killing Mark?"

"The beginning, please. Mr. Reed is in surgery."

I feel like I'm going around in circles. I have answered the same questions at least twenty times. Seriously, does this man ever listen?

"Miss Madden, that's all we need for now. Once we have spoken to Mr. Reed, we will go from there. Thank you for your time. I will take you back to your daughter now," he says.

I feel a wave of sickness flood over me. This is my fault. I can't cope with all of this. All I can think about is my baby girl alone in her own little world and not hearing anything from her. I can't wait to hear her giggle.

I don't understand how Mark is alive. I thought I killed him, or did I? Are the police lying to me? I can't handle these unanswered questions.

Chapter Thirty-Two

"Megan!" I hear Jenny's voice yell as I'm pushed into Lucy's room.

"Jenny," I reply, tears flowing from my eyes. I'm so happy to see her.

"Shhh...She'll be okay," she says, leaning down to give me a hug.

It is an immense relief to have Jenny here. I need someone. Someone I know really well. Someone I can trust. I know Luke, but not as well as I know Jenny. Even though he is still fairly new to me, I know I can trust him. It's going to take me the rest of my life, but I plan to repay him for everything he's done for me.

"Thank you, Luke," I say, taking deep breaths to compose myself.

"Anytime, babe." He pauses. "Jake will be here soon."

I smile. "Can I get out of this chair?" I ask Elizabeth.

"I can't see an issue with it, but then again, I'm not taking care of your treatment."

"I'll ask Riley," Luke says, walking out of the room.

I turn to thank him, but he's gone. "I really don't know what I would have done without Luke. He's been a huge help."

"That's great," Jenny says. "Lucy will be okay. You know that, don't you?"

"I hope you're right, Jenny." I let out a small fake smile as my thoughts drift to losing Lucy and the fact that I'm now a murderer.

"I heard what happened."

"I'm a murderer," I say, lowering my head.

"No, you're not. You did what you had to do. If you hadn't, Lucy would be dead. The police didn't arrest you. That's good."

"They say Mark is in surgery."

"Then you didn't kill him."

"I killed us, though. There is no chance of getting him back."

"Oh, Megan. You never know. You never know."

I hear a tap on the door. I turn my head around to see a tall man wearing a baggy white t-shirt and black baseball cap. Once he walks inside the room, I notice that his dark jeans are so tight I can see his manhood. As I wave him forward, I look at his bare arms covered with tribal tattoos.

"Hi, I'm looking for Luke," he says.

"He's just gone to find a nurse. Is there anything I can do for you?" I ask.

"He just asked me to collect some things from his car for Megan," he informs me. His voice is deep, rough, and sexy. He stands there, placing most of his weight on one side and holding my bag in his hand at the other side.

"I'm Megan."

"Nice to meet you, Megan," he says, walking over to me and holding out his hand. I take hold of it. What a strong grip he has. "So, this is yours."

"It is, thank you." I smile, taking the bag from him.

"Are you okay if I wait for Luke?"

"Of course, grab a seat." I release a half-smile. "I have never heard him mention your name before."

"Oh, is that a good thing?" he questions.

"I don't know."

He takes a seat in the corner, taking off his hat and placing it on his knee, revealing his bald head. He needs some hair; he doesn't look right without it.

"I'm one of Luke's assistants. Like a personal assistant. I do everything he needs me to do."

"I see," Jenny states as Luke returns to the room.

"Right, babe. I have some news for you." Luke pauses and then turns to Jake. "Hello, Jake."

"The news?" I enquire.

"You can get out of the chair. Your doctor, not that I can remember his name, will be over to see you soon."

"Thanks, Luke. I can't remember it either," I admit. I don't really remember anything that has happened since I have come to the hospital. Everything is a blur.

"And, he said you can eat," he states, smiling at me.

"Oh, great."

"Megan, you need to eat," Jenny says, placing her hands on her hips.

"I know," I confess.

"What do you fancy?" Luke asks.

"Why don't you and I go and get some food?" Jenny suggests to him.

"Good idea. Do you need Megan's wheelchair?" he jokes.

"Hey, I'm not an invalid," she teases back.

"I know, babe." He pauses before looking at Jake. "Can you stay with Megan, Jake?"

"Yes, of course."

"I don't need babysitting," I protest.

"I know, babe." He winks slyly while holding the door open for Jenny.

Chapter Thirty-Three

I slowly open my eyes and see nothing but darkness. As I lift my hands and rub my eyes, I shudder in pain. *Ouch! My shoulder really hurts.* I forgot about it. I gently sit up, using one hand to shuffle myself back. Taking a deep breath, I look around, but I can't seem to work out anything.

"Oh, you're awake, Megan." I hear a familiar voice in the background.

"Hi," I say, looking around to see where the voice is coming from.

Suddenly, a little light comes on beside me.

"Oh, hey, Jake." I pause. "What are you doing here?"

"Luke asked me to stay with you. Jenny is at his house with Warren. Luke is staying the night with Lucy in her room upstairs. She is in a private room and isn't going to let anyone harm her. He didn't want you to be alone."

"What time is it?"

"Just after five in the morning."

"What?" I exclaim.

"Hun, you fell asleep when they went to get some food. You have been out for the count since."

"Oh, how is Lucy?"

"She is settled. They have moved her to the baby unit to keep a closer eye on her."

I nod. "Thank you, Jake."

"I think they took the tube out of her. At least, Luke said they were going to."

"Oh, that's great," I say, smiling. "Do you think I can see her?"

493

"I'll go and ask the nurse."

I watch as Jake walks out of the room. I'm in a room now. When did this happen? I have walls, not curtains. I look around, seeing my bag on the floor on the other side. I swing my bare legs around. When did I get changed into one of these horrible backless hospital gowns? I dangle my legs off the bed, shuffle my bum forward, and reach my toes onto the floor. I lean forward, grabbing my bag and pulling it up.

"Hey, you be careful," Jake says as he walks back into the room.

"I will."

"They said you'll have to wait to see Lucy. The doctor needs to see you first."

"Oh, that's crap."

"I know. Can I get you anything?" he asks, standing beside the bed.

I shake my head. Going through my bag, I look for some underwear and clothes. I pull out a pair of leggings and a baggy green t-shirt. I can't find any underwear, though. They must be in my other bag. This is really not my day. I push the bag towards the end of the bed.

"Do you know where the toilet is?"

"Yes, just outside your room." He smiles, pointing at the door.

"Thank you." I place my feet onto the floor and slowly stand, holding onto the little bedside table for support. My legs feel like jelly, but I don't want to ask for help.

"Can I help you?" Jake asks, holding out his hand.

"Thank you." I take hold of his farthest hand, letting his other hand wrap around my body to pull me closer to him for support.

"Take your time."

"Hey, I have a kid. *Time?* You don't have time when you need a wee." I smile.

"So, I've heard, but I will get you there."

He does what he says, helping me right into the bathroom.

"I'm just outside, Megan," he says.

494

I quickly get dressed into the clothes I found. They will have to do. I swiftly brush my fingers through my hair. Trying to make myself look better, I reach over and grab a paper hand towel and wet it to give my face a quick wash.

"Is everything all right?" Jake asks.

"Yes, I'm nearly finished." I flush the chain, slowly standing up and holding onto the handicap rail behind me.

"Ouch!" I cry as I fall onto my bum beside the toilet.

"Megan, are you okay?" Jake opens the door. I quickly pick up the hospital gown, pulling it over my legs.

"I'm fine, Jake."

"You don't look it," he says, bending down beside me. "Do you need a hand?"

"Erm, no." I glance down. "I haven't covered my bits yet."

Jake lets out a little titter. "I'll turn around while you take care of everything. Then, I'll help you up."   Before I have a chance to say anything else, Jake is standing and facing the other way as he covers his face. I lift my bum and pull up my underwear.

"Thank you. I'm sorted."

"Let's get you up," Jake says, helping me to my feet and back into the room.

"So, I need to know something about you. You're here with me, and all I know is your name is Jake."

"Jacob William Evans, but I prefer to be called Jake. I have worked with Luke for four years now." He pauses. "I can't think of anything else."

"Anything at all? Favorite colour, car, anything. We have serious time to waste."

We seem to spend hours just chatting and passing the time until Jake falls asleep in the chair. It gives me some time to myself. Time to relax and finally think.

"Good morning, Miss Madden," a large man says as he walks into the room.

"Hi."

"I'm Doctor Hugh. I have just come to check on you and discharge you. All your tests have come back fine, but you need to follow up with your doctor and have him keep an eye on you."

Chapter Thirty-Four

"Megan," I hear Mia say as I walk along the hallway to the lift.

"Hi, Mia."

"Come and see Mark. He is asking for you."

I feel like a knife has just been stabbed into my heart.

"Do you think that's a good idea?" I question Mia.

"Yes." She pauses. "Come on."

Taking hold of my hand, she pulls me around to walk the other way down the hallway. I turn to face Jake, who gives me a little smile, and then follows me. I don't seem to have walked far before I'm faced with a door. It's a door that looks the same as the last time he was in hospital. I inhale deeply as Mia forces me into the room.

"Megan, it's so nice to see you," Annabella announces as I walk into the room.

I see Mark, lying there in bed while drips flow into him. He turns and faces towards me.

"Can you all leave Megan and me to talk?" He pauses. "Please?"

Everyone leaves the room apart from Jake. "You can wait outside, Jake. I should be fine," I tell him.

"I'll be outside the room, hun," he says, smiling at me and closing the door as he leaves.

"Remind me not to give you shooting lessons," Mark says, letting out a cheeky smile.

"I'm so sorry," I say as tears stream from my eyes.

"Hey, don't worry. I told you to do it." He pats the side of the bed. I slowly walk over, taking a seat beside him.

"You're a crap shot anyway. You hit my arm." He grins.

"I aimed for your chest."

"See, you're a bad shooter."

"I'm so sorry," I repeat, tilting my head down.

"Tell me why you left, Megan. I need to know," Mark says, placing his hand on my knee.

"John." I pause. "John told the police that I couldn't see my daughter ever again if I was with you."

"Why didn't you tell me?"

"I didn't want to hurt you. It killed me to leave you," I explain, lifting my head and looking into his eyes.

"I love you, Megan. That wasn't going to bother me. I would have understood it more."

"I heard you wrecked your house."

"Easily fixed, baby," he states, smiling at me.

"I best let you get some rest." I stand up, turning to leave.

"Megan, don't."

"Don't what?" I reply, walking towards the door.

"Leave."

"I need to check on Lucy."

"Come here." I do as he says and walk back towards him. "I understand why you left. I don't want to lose you."

"But, if I get back with you, he will go for Lucy," I tell him, openly stating my worry.

"I understand, baby, but can you see the police letting him anywhere near her now?"

"No, but until I have Lucy better and paperwork in place to stop John from getting her, I can't. I just can't." I quickly run out of the room. I can't be near him.

"Hun." I hear Jake bellow behind me. I stop at the lift, pressing the button. *Come on. Hurry up.* "Hey, Megan," he says as he wraps his arms around me.

"I can't do it," I say, tears falling from my eyes again. Jake pulls me tighter.

"Don't worry. Let's go and see Lucy."

I slowly walk into the baby unit. I don't know what to expect at all. What will be new with my baby girl? I hope she is better. I can't have her poorly.

"Megan," Elizabeth says firmly.

"Morning, Elizabeth."

"You're looking loads better today." She pauses. "I have good news. Lucy is fine. There are no signs of any permanent damage from the drugs."

"That's great. When can I take her home?" I question. I don't want to be here any longer.

"She can go home today, but she needs to come back in three days for repeat blood tests."

"Can I have it done at the doctor's office where we live?" I ask.

"I'd rather have her close, just in case something happens. No long journeys."

"Fine." I hurry over to see Lucy.

"Hey, gorgeous," I say as I see her climbing around her large cot, giggling as normal. "I love you, baby girl." I pick her up. Finally being able to hold my little girl is such a relief.

"You're staying at Luke's. It's already sorted," Jake says.

"Thank you."

Chapter Thirty-Five

I'm so happy to be out of the hospital. I do wish I was at my home, but Luke's will work. It's big enough for all of us. Well, it's big enough to fit all my family. I found out that it has eight bedrooms. *Eight, really?* I don't get why he would need that many. He did explain that it helps when his manager and team are here working. *That kind of makes some sense, but only a bit.*

"How can I repay you?" I ask Luke.

"Two things."

I take a deep breath. Oh, no. I'm really dreading what he wants. I just hope it's something I can do. I do wish I had the money. "What are they?"

"I need some tickets and stuff designed for my twenty-fifth birthday party," he says, running his fingers through his hair.

"I can do that. What is the theme?" I ask.

"Hollywood glam. Yes, I know. It's a bit predictable, but I have to play it safe." He smiles. "I did think about something more me, but as it's mainly a celebrity do, I need to think of my image."

"That's okay. I can do that. Just give me the information, and I'll make you some designs."

"Thanks, babe," he says, taking a seat on the sofa next to me and placing a cup in my hands. "Tea, babe."

"Thank you," I say, taking a little sip. He makes a good brew, but he always places sugar in it.

"I plan to do something more me with my friends and family. I want to go paintballing. I was going to see if Mark wanted in, too," he says, giving me a little smile.

Ouch, that really hurt. I don't want to hear his name. I want to be free of that man. I need to be free. I need to be with my baby girl.

"What's the second thing?" I ask. Now, I'm really worried since the first thing was easy.

"I'm getting a new tattoo, and I need, well, I want someone to come with me."

"Okay, do you want *me* to go with you?" I ask, double-checking.

"Yes."

"I'll get Jenny to babysit," I say, smiling.

Luke has made me feel so comfortable here already. Even though it's only been a few hours, I feel like I can do almost anything and not worry. He has made sure I have everything I need or what. He sent Jake out to get girlie things I need for the bath. Some of the stuff I had never seen before. Hey, it's the thought that counts. He even got Jake to get nappies for Lucy.

"Hey," Jake says, walking up behind me.

"Hi, Jake." I smile.

"How are you feeling?" he asks.

"I'm okay now, thank you. Shouldn't you be getting some sleep?"

"Nah, I'm good." He pauses. "I hope you don't mind, but I picked up something for Lucy."

"Oh, there was really no need. You have done plenty for us."

"Here." He passes me a little plastic bag. I take it, opening it up.

"Aww, that's cute," I say, pulling out a stuffed rabbit.

"It sings nursery rhymes. I thought it might help her at night, so you can get some sleep."

I stand, giving Jake a massive hug. "Thank you."

"Anything to keep you all happy and safe." He pulls me in closer.

Chapter Thirty-Six

I don't remember much about last night. I was so tired that I crashed pretty early. I didn't see Jenny because she went off with Warren. I still haven't met him. I do wonder why she is keeping him from me, but I will find out why.

Luke got the travel cot from Mark's for me. I slept with Lucy in the cot beside my bed. I kept waking up to check on her. She loves the rabbit that Jake got her. She went straight off to sleep, hugging it. It was the first time in a few days that I have been able to relax, knowing my daughter should be all right. Since we have left the hospital, she has gotten stronger and has been playing around all on her own. She is still not eating much, which worries me, but I'm sure in a few days' time that will settle, and she will be fine. I'm more worried about myself. I'm on so many painkillers for my shoulder. I need to stop taking them soon and return to being normal. I don't like it that they are making me drowsy and sick and more dependent upon others. I'm more of an independent person. Well, I was before Mark, and I'm going back to it now.

"Good morning, babe," Luke says, peeking his head around the corner.

"Morning, Luke."

"May I come in?"

"Of course." I nod.

"How did you sleep?" he asks, standing there in loose black trousers and no shirt. I have seen him shirtless hundreds of times in all his films, so it doesn't faze me at all.

"Okay, I went out like a light, but kept waking up to check on Lucy. She is in love with that rabbit, and she slept well, too."

"Come on down and get some breakfast. Jenny is waiting for you," he says, smiling at me. "And, my tattoo appointment is in an hour."

"Let me throw on some clothes, and then I'll be down."

"Deal, babe."

I jump out of bed, throwing a brush through my hair and grabbing some clean underwear from my bag. They don't match, but hey, it's not my house, and I don't know if I can do washing here. I'll have to ask because I haven't seen any machines. I need to get some more clothes for Lucy since she doesn't have enough. When she does eat, she spits it out, soiling her clothing.

I grab a black jumper and leggings. Right, that will do. I bend down, picking up my baby girl from her cot and quickly changing her into a pretty white dress with little pink flowers all over it. It's one that Mark got her; she looks so lovely in it, so tiny. I need to get rid of it, though. I can't have anything reminding me of Mark anymore.

I run down the stairs into the kitchen with Lucy bouncing up and down on my hip, giggling.

"Good morning," I state as I walk into the room.

Luke smiles as he turns around on one of the bar stools while Jenny stays on the opposite one. There's no sign of Jake. He will probably be sleeping for the next year after what he has done for me. I hear an unfamiliar voice behind me.

"Good morning, Megan. I'm Warren." I turn around to see him. *Wow.*

"You're from the coffee shop, right?" I ask.

"Yes, I am," he answers.

I turn to Jenny. I trust her.

"Right, I'm going to interfere here, Megan. You need to get your breakfast because we have a date," Luke demands.

"Date?"

"Well, a date that involves some ink." He winks.

"Okay," I reply as I grab a quick bite.

"Right, I'll be in the car waiting for you," Luke says, turning towards the door.

504

I make sure Jenny can babysit Lucy for me before I leave. I place a kiss on Lucy's forehead, grab my handbag, and head out the door.

"So, what tattoo are you getting, Luke?" I ask, getting into the car. It will help to know what I'm going to watch him have done.

"'Viva La Vie Boheme' in a fancy script with a mask above it," he says as he pulls out of the driveway.

"What does that mean?" I ask. "It sounds posh."

"It's not posh. It's from a stage show. I was in it when I first started acting. It means 'Long Live the Bohemian Life.'"

"Oh, wow." I smile. "Where are you getting it?"

"On my lower right side. The script will be just under my underwear band, though." He winks impishly.

"Oh, very sexy."

"Oh, babe, you know I do sexy," he says confidently, taking his eyes off the road and grinning at me.

"Now behave yourself," I say, pushing his arm gently. Luckily, Jenny was around and willing to look after Lucy for me, but I'm still worried. Both Jake and Warren are there with her, so they should be safe.

"Here we are, babe." I look out of the car window to see a parking lot with a few cars scattered around and different shops along one side. A car place, bookstore, and a tattoo parlor are all lined in a row.

I nod. "Let's do this."

"We are about ten minutes early." He points out as we step out of the car. He flops his black sunglasses down over his eyes. It's definitely not the weather for them. It's his celebrity side coming out.

"Luke!" a lady bellows as we walk into the shop.

"Stacey, it's so great to see you again," Luke says, walking towards her. "This is Megan."

"Hi," I say, smiling. She glares back at me with jealous green eyes. Her blonde hair cascades down around her face, and I can certainly tell she is a Luke fan.

"Alex is going to do your tattoo today," she informs him. "Your friend can sit in the waiting area while you have it done."

"Nope, she is with me."

I can't help but smile. I didn't think he wanted me just to sit and wait. Luke reaches out for my wrist, guiding me behind him through the wide-open spaces into a room.

"Hi, mate," a tall man says. He's wearing a short-sleeved t-shirt, and his arms are covered in tattoos.

"Hi, Alex. You know what I want, right?" Luke asks.

"I do. I have the stencil ready." He pulls it out, showing it to Luke.

I have never been in a place like this. I will admit; I have wanted a tattoo for years. I stand there looking through Alex's books with samples of tattoos he has done over the years. Looking up every so often, I check to see how Luke is holding up.

"Hey, chick. Are you thinking of getting one?" Alex asks.

"I have thought about it."

"Go for it, Megan. It's my treat."

I shake my head. "I'm not good with pain."

"Babe, you've had a child. A tattoo will be nothing."

"Go on," Alex pushes.

I continue flicking through the books, finding a large swirly heart with a little heart linked to the side. "I'll take this one on my wrist."

"Perfect, it will only take about ten minutes." Alex smiles as he puts the finishing touches on Luke's tattoo.

"Come sit down. I'll hold your hand." Luke smirks.

Feeling the needle hit my skin for the first time is scary, but not painful at all. I sit there watching him. It doesn't take long, and once he is finished, it's so beautiful.

"Thank you, Alex."

"Anytime, chick," he says, covering it with a bandage and telling me how to keep it clean and safe. I listen closely. I just can't wait to see it again.

As we prepare to leave the tattoo parlor, Luke stops me. "Hey, when we get back to mine, get ready. I have a surprise for you."

I wonder what he's got planned.

Chapter Thirty-Seven

I quickly place my hair up into a band. I don't know what Luke has planned, but a little fresh air will do me some good. All he said was, we are off, and Lucy is coming, too. I grab my handbag since I might be able to get a few things for Lucy while we're out.

"Are you ready, babe?" Luke asks as he stands at the bottom of the stairs dressed in a smart black and white suit, holding Lucy asleep in her car seat.

"Yeah, you look...well, smart."

"All will be revealed."

I follow him out of the house and into the car, letting him fasten Lucy in. I can't help but smile, but why does he want to take me out? I wanted to spend the day talking with Jenny because I need to find out the rest of the gossip. Earlier, she had followed me upstairs so we could talk about Warren, but she didn't tell me much about him. Well, everything has been really hectic over the last few days, and we haven't had much time together.

I did finally find out that she had slept with him before finding out about the baby. Warren does seem nice, but I don't know him that well yet. I plan to get to know him because I don't want him hurting her like Rich did. She is a large part of my life.

"Where are we?" I ask.

"A café," he says, pulling up into a small parking lot. No cars are in sight, only a few people. "Come on." He jumps out of the car before I have a chance to ask anything else. I climb out, holding the door as he gets Lucy out.

"Hi."

I freeze. Please tell me that's not who I think it is. Really, no, it can't be. What kind of game is Luke playing? I take a deep breath and slowly turn around.

"No, go away!" I bellow.

Chapter Thirty-Eight

"Megan, listen to me. We need to talk," Mark says, grabbing hold of my wrists so I can't move.

"Why? I need to leave you, be away from you, or I lose Lucy."

"We can work this out," he says, keeping a tight hold.

"No, we cant." I pull my wrists free. "Why?" I yell at Luke.

"Babe, I need you to be happy. Just talk at least."

"Why are you dressed up?" I ask.

"I have a meeting. Ring me if you need me," he says, trying to give me a hug.

"Don't you fucking touch me." I raise my hand, and without thinking, I slap him across the face. Tears instantly roll down my face.

Luke thinks nothing of it; instead, he grabs me tightly and wraps his arms around me. "I know you're mad at me, but you two need to talk. I'm not saying go and shag him. Just talk. I love ya. You know that. Just talk." He lets go of me and runs around the other side of the car and jumps in.

I take hold of Lucy's pram, seeing her lying there carefree, so unaware of what is happening and what people have done.

"Megan, can we talk?" Mark asks, placing his hand on my lower back.

"Fine."

"Shall we go into the café?" he suggests.

"What about that bench over there? I look a mess," I add.

"The bench is fine. You look amazing, baby, not a mess at all," he says, moving closer towards me.

"Don't," I say through grated teeth. I don't want him touching me. I start pushing Lucy to the bench with Mark following a few steps behind me.

"So, can we fix this?" he asks pleadingly.

"I shot you," I state.

"Yes, in my shoulder. I told you to do it," he states unemotionally.

"I aimed for your chest."

"I'll make sure never to give you a gun again." He titters. "You said that you left because of John."

"Yes, it was either you or Lucy."

"I understand that you picked Lucy, but I want us to be together."

"I can't be with you. He will take Lucy from me."

"No, we will get that sorted, even if it means court."

"I can't afford that. That's why we have to split up."

"Listen to me, Megan." He pauses. "We will do it. *Together*." I shake my head. I can't have this happen. I just can't. "Do you love me?" Mark asks.

I look him dead in the eyes, seeing the pain in them. "Yes, you know I do."

"Then, Megan, please."

"We can't be a couple to the world, though, not until everything is sorted," I admit.

"Baby, I love you so much. I can't be without you," he begs.

"We need to get out of the cold. I'm freezing, and I can't have Lucy getting ill again."

Chapter Thirty-Nine

I walk into the little café, not paying any attention to where Mark is. I don't want to spend time with him. I want to be alone. Alone so I can think and work out about mine and Lucy's future. I can't let him back in. I just can't.

"Megan, what would you like to drink?" Mark asks, gently placing his hand on my shoulder.

"Mark, I can get my own. You don't need to be here. I can look after myself," I say, not turning to face him at all. I can't because it hurts me to see him and hear him. Even smelling his aftershave makes me melt.

"Megan, don't do this. We need to talk."

"Fine," I state.

"Tea, hot chocolate, or what?" Mark asks, moving closer to me.

"Hot chocolate, please." I need a sugar hit.

For more room, I walk over to one of the round tables. It has three chairs and plenty of space to fit Lucy's pram in so that she is not in the way. I make sure there is no space for Mark to sit next to me. I can't have him that close. I'll just want him to hold me if he is. The table is by the window that overlooks the river. I glance up, seeing Mark with his back towards me. His bum looks so perfect. He suddenly turns around, and I quickly look out of the window. I hope he didn't catch me staring at him.

"Hey, here you go," he says, placing a tall cup onto the table with a little matching plate holding three pink marshmallows and two white ones. He always gives me marshmallows, even if he is making me hot chocolate at home.

"Thank you."

"You're welcome."

I place the marshmallows into my cup, watching them slowly melt into the drink.

"How is Lucy doing?" Mark asks.

"She's fine now. Hopefully, we can go back home soon."

"That would be good. I wish you would come to mine, though."

"Mark, don't do this. Please," I beg, tilting my head down.

"Megan, listen to me. You know how I feel about you."

"I know, and I feel the same, but we can't."

"Why?"

"We can't. Just drop it," I say, looking deep into his eyes.

I take the spoon from the plate and scoop out the melted marshmallows. I love the taste of them, but only when they are melted.

"I love how you eat them," Mark adds.

I keep sitting there, ignoring him. I need to work out how to get to Luke's since I don't fully know where I am. Thankfully, I have a couple of taxi numbers programmed into my mobile. I'll finish this cup, and then I need to get out of here. Taking a sip, I realise it is still too hot.

"Is Connor okay?" I enquire.

"Yeah, he's fine. He goes back to work next week."

I nod, taking another sip of my drink.

"Come outside with me," Mark says.

"No, I need to get Lucy home."

"Yes, Megan. Come on." He gets up from his seat, leaving his half-drunk cup of coffee. Taking hold of my wrists, he pleads, "Please."

I stand up slowly. Mark lets go of my wrists, taking hold of Lucy's pram and turning her around and heading out of the door.

Why is he doing this?

Chapter Forty

I follow Mark along the side of the café and down a small path by the river. The air has a chill along here. It always does whenever you are near water. *I don't understand it, but hey.* My arms are cold, causing me to worry that Lucy might be cold also.

"Stop, Mark," I say, standing still.

"Yes, baby," he says.

I walk over to Lucy, pulling her blanket up further. That's better. I worry more about Lucy now than I ever did. I have to protect her from everyone.

"See, you care about others more than yourself. That's why I love you, Megan."

I turn around to face him, and he gives me a half-smile that I return.

"Megan, I can't imagine my life without you. We have been through so much together as a couple. You're my world. I want to protect you, care for you, love you." He takes a small step back, bending his left knee. "Megan Madden, will you marry me?" He pulls out a black velvet box, slowly opening it to reveal a silver ring with a diamond in the centre. It's elegant and not too flashy.

"No." I grab Lucy's pram and quickly run back along the path towards the café.

What was he thinking, really? I can't be with him. Has he forgotten about the past few days?

"Megan, stop." He runs in front of the pram.

"What?"

"Why did you say no?" he asks.

"John."

"Megan, baby, we can't let John destroy our life. I love you."

"I love you, too. That's why I have to go." I try to move around him.

"No, we will sort this. Come on."

"We can't. I'll lose Lucy."

"Let me contact Connor."

I shake my head. "I'm not listening to you, Megan. I can see this is hurting you as much as it's hurting me."

Mark takes hold of the pram, pushing Lucy towards the café. I follow right behind him. I can't trust him with Lucy. I can't trust anyone with her. He takes out his mobile, but I can't fully hear what he is saying, so I just try to keep up. We walk straight past the café and up a small alley, stopping at a black car.

"Here we are. Get in," Mark demands.

"This isn't yours," I state since I know all his cars.

"I know. It's yours. I bought it for you." He throws the keys at me while securing Lucy in the backseat in her car seat.

"I can't take this."

"Just get in."

Oh, he is mad. I do as he asks, taking a seat in the driver's side of the car. I watch him get everything in the back. I have a quick look around. This is one hell of a posh car. It's not any car. It's a four-by-four, and they cost a fortune. There is plenty of room for Lucy as she grows up, and it appears to have all the modern conveniences in it.

Mark climbs into the car. "Do you like?"

"I do, but…"

"No buts, Megan. It's yours."

I can't help but smile. Mark turns on a screen and punches in a postcode. "Follow where it tells you."

I nod, starting the engine and then following my directions.

Chapter Forty-One

I have no clue where I am. I look around this large office with lots of white sofas and big glass windows. Mark went off as soon as he came inside, leaving me with a redheaded lady to keep an eye on me. He doesn't trust me not to run. The lady continues offering me drinks and following me to the bathroom. She's not been a step away from me since we arrived here.

"Hi, I'm Peter," a tall, skinny man with grey hair says.

"Hi."

"Mark has come to talk to me about your ex."

I nod. "Okay, but why?"

"I'm a lawyer. I want to explain your choices and what you can do. Mark says it's a big deal."

"Thank you. You do know you don't need to."

"I know, Megan, but I want to. You mean a lot to Mark. We have known each other for years, and I have never known him to be as persistent as he is right now," he says, letting out a little smile.

"Let's get this over with then," I add, looking into his mocha-coloured eyes. I don't know why, but they don't seem to suit his grey hair.

"Let's head down to my office. Mark will keep an eye on Lucy," Peter says.

"Can't Lucy come with me?" I ask. "I don't want to leave her after everything that has happened."

"I understand. Of course, she can."

I take hold of Lucy, cradling her in my arms. I don't need the pram, so I leave it with Mark. I follow behind Peter down a hallway, which continues the same theme of white walls and big windows. He opens a spacious glass door, holding it open for us. I take a deep breath as I walk into the room. A massive white desk is seated in front of me with some black chairs. I seriously think they need some colour since everything is so plain and sterile. Even a picture on the wall would make a big difference. It's making me feel like I'm in a mental hospital with all the glass around me.

"Please, take a seat," Peter says, pointing at the chairs opposite from the window. I walk over, sitting down as Pete walks around his desk and sits down at the other side. His eyes focus directly on me as he speaks, "Mark informed me what your ex did. John, is that his name?"

"Yes, John."

"We can get a restraining order against him, and I'm willing to make sure he won't touch Lucy."

"How though?" I question.

"I'm a very good lawyer. Trust me."

"I can't afford to pay you," I add. It's true. I have never been lucky in life; I have had to work my arse off to have anything. I was lucky to have saved up a fair bit growing up to be able to afford my house, but I need to get back to work because I'm going to be paying for all this stuff for the rest of my life.

"Don't worry. Mark is paying my fees. You know he will do anything for you. Just relax and fill out these forms. Miss Madden, I'm here to help you. I will make sure John can't touch you or Lucy."

I take a deep breath before agreeing to everything. I spend the next hour filling out the forms. Peter has his head straight. He seems to know what he needs to do and understands the law. I like him. I need to see Mark and thank him for everything. I just hope he is still waiting for me.

Chapter Forty-Two

The drive back to Mark's is almost silent; he doesn't say much at all. I have hurt the man I love. I need to keep my head straight. I just need to drop off Mark at home and then go back to Luke's, pack, and leave. I'll have Luke to return the car to Mark.

I don't get it. He wants me to marry him one minute and the next he doesn't want to talk to me. I feel so confused. Why is he being like this? Yes, I know I said no, but I need to protect my daughter. I slowly pull up outside his house and leave the engine running since there is no point in stopping it. I turn my head to face him.

"I'm sorry," I say with a strained voice.

"I love you, Megan."

"I love you, too."

"Why did you say no to my marriage proposal?" he asks.

"John," I say, sniffling back tears.

"We can sort that out," he replies, taking my hand.

"Don't do this." Tears run from my eyes. "I thought we could sort things in time."

"We can, Megan. I can't live without you." He unclips my seat belt and rubs my face, trying to wipe away the tears. "Don't cry."

"I can't help it."

"Come in. We can talk. I promise I will not ask you to marry me again. Well, I won't ask again today at least."

I nod, turning the engine off on the car. Talking is okay. Maybe we can get somewhere and move on. John will be out of my life by the end of the week. Peter is going to work his bum off to make sure of it. I just hope Mark does ask me to marry him again. I want to; I really do. I want to be with him for the rest of my life, and I want Lucy to be his daughter. I just hope we can fix everything.

I follow Mark into the house. Nothing has changed at all. It has been weeks since I have been in here. I take a seat on the sofa beside him, placing Lucy onto the floor with a couple of her toys. It's so nice to see my daughter happy and relaxed. None of this has damaged her. She is safe now.

"So…" Mark says.

"Can I just say I do love you, Mark, but we need to work this out. John can't know I'm with you until everything is sorted. That's the problem. Peter said it could stop things if John finds out we're together."

"Okay, I understand that," he says, taking my hand and holding it tight.

"What do we do?" I ask.

"We're going to be together, but we're just not going to tell anyone, including Jenny," he says.

"Jenny will know. She can read me like a book," I kindly point out.

"Good point."

"Can you forgive me for shooting you?" I ask.

"Well, I already have. I told you. You're a bad shot, baby." He giggles.

"Thanks." I glance over to check on Lucy.

"She is fine, Megan. She always will be. Nothing will ever happen to her." He places his hand on the side of my face, turning me back around to face him. "Can I kiss you?"

"Don't ask. Do it."

Within a second, his lips cover mine, gentle as always. As his tongue slides into my mouth, I realise how much I have missed this. He knows how to rock my world.

Chapter forty-Three

The last few weeks have been busy. I'm back home with Lucy. Luke stayed at mine for a few days to make sure I was all right. I liked having him around; it helped me stop worrying so much since the court stuff took a few weeks to sort.

Karen is spending her time in a mental hospital. She was determined too unstable to stand trial. John has been placed in jail for only six months for kidnapping. They didn't charge him with anything else, so he could be released early. I then have to fight for custody of Lucy. Peter says there won't be a fight since it came out in court that John just wanted money. His wife had left him, causing him to try to extort money to make ends meet.

Right now, I'm trying to look forward to my future. Mark has been nothing but supportive. He has been there for me all the time. He keeps his distance, not forcing himself on me. It's almost like we are newly daters. I even had to make the first move to get some adult time. He will not tell me he loves me anymore. I know I've hurt him.

"Hey, sexy." I turn around to see Mark standing there in his black suit.

"Hi, you're early."

"Traffic was better than I thought. Sorry I just let myself in. I knew it was Lucy's bedtime. "

"It's okay."

I had just come down from putting Lucy to bed. He knows how much I like keeping her in a routine. I was expecting him in a couple of hours. He planned to spend the weekend up here with us. I haven't been back to his house yet.

Jenny is watching Lucy tomorrow so I can have some time alone with Mark. Everyone knows we are together now, even John. I could not have him rule my life, and he was fine with it. I feel I deserve to be happy. Karen is the one who doesn't deserve happiness.

"I came straight from physical therapy, so I'm feeling all stiff now."

"I bet you are. I'm sorry."

I feel bad about everything. It's my fault his shoulder is messed up. Seeing him in pain hurts me.

"Stop it. Seriously, it is okay."

I watch as he takes a seat on the sofa beside me. He's sitting so close I can smell his aftershave, and it comforts me.

"For you," he says, pulling out a small bag from his pocket.

I take hold of the black bag, inhaling a deep breath. What could it be? I have started dreading gifts from him. I reach inside, pulling out a chicken teddy.

"What?"

"My baby loves to eat chicken. I thought it would keep you company when I am away."

I can't help but smile. "Thank you."

Chapter Forty-Four

"Well baby, you said you had never seen me in heels before." I lean my back against the door frame, wearing a black baby doll with a lace section over it and matching French knickers. Just what my Mark likes.

"Wow," Mark says, looking me up and down.

"What do you think of the heels?" I question, walking towards him seductively.

"They are sexy, baby. Just like you," Mark says, moving slightly further back in his lounge chair.

I instantly think of taking him in that chair. It's larger than a normal chair and has no arms. Perfect. I love having it here. It was a good investment. I stand at the end of the chair, looking at Mark and waiting.

"Oh, baby. Come here," he says, grabbing my wrists and pulling me onto the chair.

"Yes, Mr. Reed," I say, kneeling with my legs apart over his.

"Oh, you're such a tease. That tattoo is a massive turn on, too." He pulls my wrists closer to his lips and kissing each of them tenderly.

I do love the tattoo. It has been the best thing I have done for myself in a long time, and I owe it all to Luke.

"You're mine," Mark whispers.

"Oh, am I?" I question.

"What is the answer to my question then?" Mark pushes.

"Which question?"

"Will you marry me?" he asks, placing his arms around my back and pulling me close to him as he lands his lips on my chest.

"I told you the answer," I reply.

"Yes or no?"

"Yes."

"I love you, Mrs. Reed."

"I love you too, Mr. Reed."

About the author

L. Chapman was born in and continues to live in North Yorkshire, United Kingdom. She has spent most of her life helping others at one time, a DJ for a special needs club. Blending her love of helping others and her love of children, L dreams to one day own and operate a childcare nursery that will help mainstream special needs children with others.

In the rare times that L. is not working to help others or maniacally writing, she enjoys making a mess of things while creating beautifully detailed greeting cards. She spends time relaxing with family, friends, and good books. L. loves to travel and has been to many places in the United Kingdom; her favorite places all involve the ocean. She hopes to one day share a kiss with her happily-ever-after in the romantic shadow of the Eiffel Tower. Should she ever get over her fear of flying, those kisses may be shared in the shadows of the Egyptian Pyramids.

Ever the fussy eater, L. has never once tasted peanut butter, and she despises coffee. If you should feel the need to bribe her, it is suggested that you bring chocolate, as that is one of her known weaknesses.

Work by L Chapman

Trust #1 Believe series

Veiled #2 Believe Series

Redeemed #3 Believe Series

Do you believe #3.5 Believe Series

Healing

More from L Chapman Coming soon

Amazon fan picked debut romance author 2013

24191860R00315

Printed in Poland
by Amazon Fulfillment
Poland Sp. z o.o., Wrocław